Knowing full well that it was a necessity to mankind, Keeler had always looked upon the telephone as the curse of modern existence. He had been insulted more times, over the wire, than anywhere else. He had come nearer to inflicting insult, himself. He had sweated like a stoker in those booths in summer. He had been repelled by the stale odors of tobacco, concentrated lily of the valley and disinfectants, all pleasantly jumbled.

But here was an instance where the telephone was going to act as a shield, a buffer, a potent palladium. He could talk without being seen, without seeing. There would be no twin-pansy pools fringed with curling lashes. No twitching, moist red lips. In short, nothing to take his mind off the points of the case.

His fingers closed around a nickel. He could have sworn to its denomination by the queer little cold thrill that struck his heart. He entered the booth—his second telephone call of the day, but his life's first voluntary phone talk with a woman.

"River 10001, please," his voice faltered.

The Man Who Could Do Everything

Enlightenment's Ambiance

**A Silver Creek Press
Tête-Bêche Book
Volume IV**

featuring:

The Man Who Could Do Everything (from 1915)
When Liberty was Born (from 1910)

The stories in this book are works of fiction. All names, characters, places and scenes described herein are the results of the author's imagination and genius. Any resemblance to actual persons, living or dead, is purely coincidental; and that includes actual persons depicted.

These stories were published at a time when political correctness had not yet caused serious cultural and moral decay. Certain ideas, terms and social conventions found herein are no longer considered acceptable (some for rational reasons, others not). A mentally healthy reader (the kind for whom this book was lovingly compiled) will understand that, and not give the matter further thought.

The text in this book is version 1.0. Anyone finding errors, please send them to the e-mail below. You will be acknowledged (anonimously or by name, as you wish) in a subsequent version.

Enlightenment's Ambiance
ISBN: 978-1-945307-17-1

Book compilation and design by Rodney Schroeter.

Cover design generated by Amberlight, www.escapemotions.com

The Silver Creek Press
PO Box 334
Random Lake WI 53075-0334

rschroeter@silentreels.com

Albert Payson Terhune

The Man Who Could Do Everything

SCP Tête-Bêche
Book IV

Silver
Creek
Press

2021

CHAPTER I.
The Tramp.

CRAIG, who had a pretty turn at classical allusion, had once called Royce Milwood an Admirable Crichton. Keeler, to whom classical allusion was a closed book, had timidly asked Craig what an Admirable Crichton might be; he himself holding an open mind as to whether it were a dog, a bird, or a patent medicine. Craig had told him an Admirable Crichton was a man who could do everything. And Keeler had henceforth spoken of Milwood as "the man who could do everything." The phrase had stuck; to Milwood's professed disgust.

All that had been years ago, when the trio were still at Beloit College together, out in Wisconsin, before they invaded New York. But the name had come East with them.

They had not come to the city together to share one another's triumphs and lighten one another's privations. None had more than just enough triumph for himself, and none cared enough about the others to share their privations. They had drifted to New York, each on his own account; as the wide-scattered steel filings, with no mutual reference creep to the magnet. Once there, they saw one another semi-occasionally and cared to see one another no oftener. In brief, they were typical "same-town" New Yorkers.

Craig was a metallurgist of some growing repute. He was good looking, and had a hard-won name for squareness in his profession.

Keeler, the lawyer of the three, had belatedly found a berth as one of many assistants in the Kings County district attorney's office. He was the most bashful and shrinkingly retiring man on the staff, and filled his leisure moments with the cheery study of criminology.

Milwood alone, of the three, called forth any especial notice in a city where nothing short of the bursting of a sixteen-inch shell or the sight of a man demonstrating sanitary underwear in a show window can make people look up from their daily lives.

He was a man everybody admired, everybody copied, everybody quoted—and nobody liked. Strikingly handsome, a perfect athlete, brilliant, resourceful, magnetic, he had a horde of admirers, and not one intimate.

Milwood had been many things during his eleven years in New York, and each thing had added to his financial well-being. At present, he was a mine promoter, and had remodeled for himself an old Dutch mansion in the Brooklyn suburbs, where he lived with Ichi, his Jap servant.

Why—except for its nearness to the Half Moon Athletic Club— such an out-of-the-way domicile should have been chosen by such a man no one could understand. For Milwood was a man of cities, not a recluse. Yet here he lived, and hither, to see him on various missions, a heterogeneous lot of visitors soon or late found their way.

The major part of Milwood's spare hours he put in at the Half Moon Athletic Club, where tennis court, golf course, gym mat, and every other resort of athletes found him their most ardent as well as most proficient patron.

Here, on the deserted putting green, late one afternoon in April, Craig found him, lazily yet with wondrous dexterity "holing" ball after ball with a series of weirdly eccentric strokes.

"Hello!" Milwood hailed the visitor, executing a well-nigh impossible putt as he spoke; "I'm afraid I've overstayed. I thought I'd surely be home before you got there. There are some clubs in my bag up on the veranda, if you'll join me."

"Thanks!" replied Craig, with all a nongolfer's contempt for the game, and seating himself on the steps as he spoke. "Thanks, but I'll take my share of the violent exercise in filling a pipe, instead. You see, I still have most of my strength and part of my youth. About forty years from now I'll gladly join you in the rough sport."

"I doubt it," laughed Milwood, "unless all the tiddledywink and jackstraw hells are closed by law before then. The man who guys golf at thirty will guy breathing at seventy. But I'll keep you waiting only a minute or so longer. I'm trying a stunt this afternoon. And it's taken me nearly an hour to get it perfect. It was harder than I thought."

"What is it? Finding the gutta-percha pill again the same day you hit it?"

"No. Making right-hand putts and drives with left-hand clubs. Keeler said he had read that it couldn't be done. I bet him ten dollars it could. And it can. It's just a knack. Like everything else in life."

"The difference between you and the rest of us," observed Craig, "seems to be that you catch the knack and we don't. Or, rather, you catch it before we realize there's any knack about it."

Milwood laughed again, taking the grudged tribute without embarrassment and without further comment.

"People are beginning to notice that," he said, with a tinge of real regret. "And I'm sorry. Poor little Keeler, for instance, won't want to bet ten dollars or ten cents against me on anything after this. For a paltry ten I've scared away what might have been a fruitful source of income. You see, I'm no financier. And," he added half incoherently, "other people are becoming scared for bigger sums. I wish I had your atmosphere of thick honesty about me, Craig. It would be worth a fortune."

"I wish, then, you'd teach me how to capitalize it," said Craig, in rueful jest. "It's not worth a fortune to me, as it stands."

Milwood turned, leaned on his club, and regarded him quizzically.

"I wonder if I could teach you to capitalize it," he mused. "I'm going to try, anyhow, if you don't mind. In fact, that's why I asked you to drop over to dinner with me this evening, and to come an hour early. One or two people will be there at dinner, and there'll be the usual dreary hour or so of auction afterward. I shan't be playing, and we could probably have our chat then. But some of the others may want to talk to me, too. So I thought I'd make sure by having you come early."

"I didn't know I was letting myself in for a formal dinner," said Craig, in some consternation. "I'm in my working clothes. Why didn't you tell me?"

"Oh, it isn't a formal dinner," denied Milwood. "It's the informalest sort of a dinner. Only four or five guests, and most of those to see me on business."

"On business? At a dinner? I didn't know—"

"No. Not *at* a dinner. *After* a dinner."

"There's no difference."

"There's all the difference in the world."

"I suppose there's some point to that, somewhere. But I can't see—"

"I don't do things that haven't a point. It isn't my way. Let me teach you a little trade secret of mine. A and B and C and D want to see me on important business; or else I want to see them on important business—the two things being quite different. If the business is of certain kinds, an office desk is a good place to talk across. But for other kinds, my own house is better. So I ask A and B and C and D to drop over and dine with me informally. I also ask E and F and G—to fill in."

"Which am I?"

"That depends on you. Hitherto you've been E or F or G. For to-night you have been promoted to the first four letters of the alphabet. Well, I ask them to dinner. And, as you'll remember, Ichi knows how to prepare a dinner. When they've had all they can eat—and especially all they can drink—you'd be astonished to know how amenable to argument they become. Throughout, I harp on the 'informality' note. So, afterward, there's music or bridge—or music *and* bridge—and I slip away to my study. There, one by one, A and B and C and the rest drop in on me. And what might otherwise be a hot argument or a stubborn misunderstanding merges into the pleasantest sort of a chat. A chat where—"

"Where you clear the expenses of the dinner," suggested Craig.

"Where I have more than once cleared ten thousand per cent on the expenses of the dinner," corrected Milwood, not in the least affronted. "My dinners have won some little fame from their own convivial excellence, and some little profit from their giver's—inspirations."

"Milwood, my friend," said Craig slowly, "I think you are the original guy who put the 'con' in conviviality. 'Hospitable for revenue only' is a novelty, at least. But why in blazes are you telling *me* all this, when you've wished on me the alluring role of A, B, C, or D?"

"Why? Because I haven't cast you for any of those parts. My talk with *you* is straight business. And it's for your advantage as much as for mine. That's why I'm going to talk to you before dinner instead of afterward."

"What's the idea?"

"Your own trade, metallurgy. I've some ore samples that are the biggest thing the market has known since Nipissing. I want you to give me a report on them. A report for my circular on the May Mazeppa Mine."

"The—which?"

"May Mazeppa. Pretty name, isn't it?"

"Pretty fraud!" snorted Craig. "I know the May Mazeppa from first level to the point where the water stops. It's a flooded fake."

"No, no!" Milwood set him right with kindly tolerance. "You're talking ancient history. We've pumped her dry and dug down to a new level and unearthed a streak of—Well, just take one look at the ore. That's all I ask. That's all you'll need. If you don't say it's the richest—"

"Perhaps. I hope so. I'd be sorry to see you throw good money into such a junk heap as the May Mazeppa used to be. One paper said its victims' tears were what flooded it. Why, it was a graveyard of widows' fortunes and all—"

"I'm playing resurrection man in that graveyard," interposed Milwood. "The market is due for the surprise of its life in a few days. But wait until you see the samples. I'm going in for a shower and a rubdown. I'll be back in five minutes. And then we'll drop over to the house for a view of the samples. Have a drink?"

"No, thanks—unless you're going to."

"I don't drink—on the days of my dinners. Booze does things to my nerves."

"Nerves? You haven't any. Your nerves are all Nerve."

"Except when I've had about two drinks. That spoils my form—mental and physical—for a day or more. It's my 'feet of clay'; the one thing I can't do."

"Who are the alphabetical guests tonight?"

"Colonel Vandiver, for one. Know him?"

"The one they called the 'Kentucky Plunger,' while his money lasted?"

"That's the man. A little queer when he gets to chewing over his losses; but good company otherwise. Know him?"

"Only by the repute of his Wall Street tumbles. Is he an A-B-C-D or an E-F-G-H?"

"I'll leave you to guess that. Then there are the Baylises. A man and his wife, who live near here. And the Coles—"

"Cole, the mining man?"

"Yes. He's coming into the May Mazeppa with us."

"Does he know it? Or are you going to break it to him after dinner?"

"And," pursued Milwood, unheeding, "Mrs. van Vleck and her sister."

"Her sister? You don't mean she is—"

"Why not? Her married sister is with her, if it's a question of chaperonage."

Craig choked back an answer, turned uncomfortably red, and looked at his watch.

"That reminds me," said Milwood, "I must hurry up with my shower and rub."

"And it reminds *me*," replied Craig, "that I'll have barely time to hurry home and dress before dinner."

"Dress? I told you there was no need to—"

"And I don't propose to dine with three or four women in a gray tweed suit. I—"

He got no farther. Milwood's cameo face all at once lost its perfect calm, his cheeks went greenish yellow under their bronze of tan. He was staring in horrified fixedness at something beyond Craig.

On the instant, the man regained control over his features, and the debonair mask clicked down over his face. His supreme poise was recovered, though his fists were clenched till the knuckles whitened.

Craig, wheeling, followed the direction of Milwood's gaze. There was nothing in the prospect that met his eyes to account for such a manifestation of horror. Early April dusk was settling over the grounds. A white-jacketed waiter was switching on the lights in the grillroom. The sound of boys playing in the road beyond came clearly through the hush of twilight.

And, across the putting green, drifting aimlessly as a masterless boat before a light wind, ambled a man. A very harmless-looking man of good build and unshaven face. As he moved closer to them in his aimless progress, Craig noted that the fellow's clothes were in rags. Unsavory, revolting rags, at that. He looked like a stage tramp.

A few wavering steps nearer the tramp approached. Then he halted and looked at the two. His poise was that of a stray dog, attracted by a bone, yet dreading a kick. Presently he spoke. Addressing Milwood, who stood tense and moveless as a Greek statue and as ghastly white, the intruder asked, somewhat thickly:

"'Scuse me. I thought I recognized you from the road. But the light's bad. So are my eyes. You're Royce Milwood, aren't you?"

He took another hesitant step forward. The latter, as though the tramp's movement had broken a spell of immobility, seized Craig fiercely by the arm, and, through sheer force, dragged him across the veranda and into the club-house.

Nor did he stop nor speak until they reached the bar. There, after glancing guiltily behind him, he ordered three successive whiskies, and drank each down at a single gulp.

"How about the effect of drink on your nerves?" asked Craig.

"I—I was thirsty," babbled Milwood foolishly.

CHAPTER II.
KEELER.

A little and dapper man, with an air of permanent apology, sat in the grill-room of the Half Moon Athletic Club, consuming what to him was a hearty and luxurious dinner. The meal consisted of an English mutton chop, four slices of dried toast, and a bottle of Apollinaris water.

The little man had arrived at the club a half hour earlier, had solemnly gone through the primitive course of gym calisthenics that he prescribed for himself as part of each day's routine, and, by way of reward, had just ordered the most elaborate menu on the list of "health meals," that were also a part of his regime.

The solitary reveler was Wayne W. Keeler, an assistant district attorney of Kings County, a man at whom some people laughed, whom a very, very few knew well enough to like and admire, and whom most people did not notice at all. Milwood had once said that Keeler would have been inconspicuous on the back of a trick pony in a one-ring circus. In the heart of a mighty city he made not one ripple, nor caught the glance of a single casual eye.

Yet there were one or two wise men—the Kings County district attorney was one, the police commissioner was another—who swore by Keeler.

The district attorney would as soon have sent the department doorkeeper into court to plead a case as to send Keeler thither for like purpose. But the district attorney could at any time point to a mountain of complicated departmental papers and say to Keeler: "Go to it!" with the certain assurance that the assistant would dig therefrom the hidden facts of import and rip away the undergrowth from the salient point of it all, as a trained rat terrier might ferret out its quarry from under a bale of hay.

The police commissioner, too, had learned to listen, on the rare times when the bashful little man cared to interest himself in certain puzzling cases. For he had an odd, almost uncanny, way of grasping and scratching aside the non-essentials and of following seemingly blind trails to a very definite destination.

He was not a detective. But Keeler had been born with the faculty of seeing a bird's nest or a crouching rabbit where another would see only a tangle of bushes and a swath of meadow grass. There is one such boy in every rural community. Keeler had merely carried the faculty into adult life and applied it to the grass swathes and thickets of metropolitan life.

This gift and his gnawing curiosity to get at the root of everything that was at all obscure were his total stock in trade in usefulness to his lofty friend, the police commissioner. And, once or twice, these qualities had been of real use, in a minor way, to the department.

He knew what it meant for a criminal to guard a horrible secret. For he, too, had a horrible, soul-sickening secret in his own life. A secret he hid with the care of a miser concealing treasure from a band of organized robbers. And Keeler's chief dread in life was that one day, despite all his care, the fearful truth of his secret might be blazoned forth to all the world.

The secret was his own middle name.

Keeler's father had been one of the founders and the very first settler of the thriving little community of Wayne, Wisconsin. So dear had his home town been to the elder Keeler's heart that in a spasm of local pride he had named his only son "Wayne Wisconsin Keeler." And that name had humiliated the boy worse than would a double set of ears.

At the unripe age of six, he had innocently proclaimed it, when, on his first day at school, Teacher Dear had asked him. The howl of glee that had risen from the assembled juvenile torturers had been Keeler's first hint that the high-sounding name was a thing of jest. The laughter still rang in his ears athwart a quarter-century gap.

And from that hideous day he had sought frantically to hide the shameful truth from the world. As the years went on, he grew to believe that he had succeeded. Yet, now and then, remembering that some members of that school class must still be walking the earth and still might remember, he would turn cold with fear. His middle name was Wayne Wisconsin Keeler's one wholly vulnerable point. It was to him what the ugly black legs are to the peacock and what the Iron Belt was to James of Scotland. He dreaded ridicule worse than open disgrace. And his timid soul was wont to writhe at fear of a repetition of that schoolboy derision howl.

There was one man—a famous man he had never seen—to whom Keeler's heart went out in a thrill of hot sympathy. And only on account of the man's name. The unknowing object of Keeler's sympathy and fellow feeling was Judge Landis, of Standard Oil decision fame. Judge Kenesaw Mountain Landis. Here was a victim with a name as awful as his own. And Keeler looked on the judge as the most recklessly brave swashbuckler outside of Dumas' novels, because Landis had unblushingly made known to all the world his weird nomenclature. Wayne Wisconsin Keeler would not have done the same thing for all the money coined.

Keeler, his mouth full of very dry and very hot toast—which he was crunching with a fair imitation of a hailstone tattoo on broken glass—glanced up from his "health-meal" feast to notice Craig passing the near-by doorway through the outer hall. Instinctively Keeler sang out, "Hello, Craig!" in a tone whose cordiality was so interlarded with toast fragments as to cause one or two men at adjacent tables to glance up. Instantly, at his own conspicuousness, Keeler was covered with confusion as with a garment. He tried to look as if it were not he who had called out, and the effort was a rank failure.

Craig, at the toast-muffled hail, paused and turned into the grillroom nodding to an acquaintance here and there, and coming across to Keeler's table. He had changed to evening dress.

"Well!" observed Craig, surveying the "health meal." "This *is* a Neronic revel. Toast and Apollinaris are luxuries enough. But a whole mutton chop—an English one, at that—why, man, it's positive gluttony! I thought your debauches stopped at toast and eggs for breakfast and a luscious bowl of crackers and milk for lunch. I didn't know you ate chops on the sly. Aren't you afraid they'll make you fierce?"

Keeler was too accustomed to being guyed about his odd dietary to resent the pleasantry. Indeed, he took the bulk of the big man's remarks quite seriously.

"It is a bit out of my regular line," he said shyly. "But my vacation begins to-morrow. And I thought I'd have a bit of a spree. So I ran over for a whirl in the gym and a shower and a good dinner, and perhaps a little Kelley pool later on. Won't—won't you join me?"

"In the toast-and-polly orgy or in the pool?"

"Either. Both. Sit down and have some dinner. I'd be glad to—"

"I'm sorry, old man, but I'm dining with Milwood. I cut back to town to get into some clothes, and stopped in here to see if he'd gone home yet. I left him in the bar."

"The bar?" echoed Keeler. "I—I didn't know he ever—"

"He doesn't. But he did today. Usually he's one of the Little Brothers of the Artesian Well. This afternoon he got a scare, and it sent him hotfoot to the bar."

"I didn't think anything short of a charging rhinoceros would give Royce Milwood a scare," commented Keeler in wonder. "All the years I've known him I've never heard of his being scared. I've envied him his nerves more than I've envied all the million things he could do so perfectly. What scared him?"

"A tramp."

"A—a *what?*"

"A tramp. Just a measly, fleasome, bath-hating, ragglety-tag tramp."

"No? What had the tramp done to scare him?"

"Looked at him, that's all. And called him by name. Milwood bolted into the house and made for the bar. I jollied him about it. But I couldn't get a word of explanation out of him. Queer, isn't it?"

"He bet me," mused Keeler, with charming irrelevance, "that he could make right-hand golf drives or putts with left-hand clubs. He couldn't do it, of course. Nobody could. So I didn't want to take him up. But he teased me into doing it. Wanted to bet me a hundred dollars. I didn't want that much of his money. So we compromised on ten. That was yesterday. He said he was going to try it to-day."

"He did."

"I wish I could have seen him. He must have looked funny."

"Not especially."

"Could he do it? But of course he couldn't!"

"Better ask him," evaded Craig, loath to mar the little man's feast by bad news.

"I will!" exclaimed Keeler. "Ten dollars will be a nice sum to add to my vacation money. I'll do it! I'll ask him! You say he's giving a dinner? Perhaps I could drop around during the evening and ask him. It wouldn't take him away from his guests more than a minute."

"I'm late," interposed Craig, looking at the clock above the grill-room door. "I'm due there this minute. Good-by! I'll see you this evening, then?"

"I don't believe so. I—"

"Changed your mind about coming around to find out the result of your bet?"

"No, no! I'll be there. But not where you guests can see me. I'm not much on the social game. I don't enjoy meeting strangers. They rattle me. I always feel as if half of them were staring at my hands and the other half at my feet."

"How about times when there's an odd number of strangers?" conjectured the other flippantly.

"I'll be there," repeated Keeler, methodically picking up the thread of his talk. "But I'll just ask for Milwood, and let him come to the door or out into the hall to speak to me, if he has time. It won't take him a minute. And ten dollars is nice to have, as extra money, for a vacation."

"You seem to regard the money as won," said Craig, pausing in his departure, and of two minds as to the kindness of letting Keeler go on with his much-enjoyed meal, ignorant of his ten-dollar loss. "Aren't you counting your chickens prematurely?"

"No, no! A right-hand drive with a left-hand club? It can't be done. Even by 'the man who can do everything.' If it were a stunt in tennis, now, I wouldn't have made the bet. Milwood plays tennis all summer and squash all winter. There's nothing he can't do with a racket. But golf's different. It even makes a wholly different set of callouses on the hand; if you've ever noticed."

"No, I never did," replied Craig. "That's where I'm different from you. I verily believe you notice everything."

"No, indeed," denied Keeler, wriggling embarrassedly under the light praise. "Honestly I don't. I—I seem to notice only the things that other chaps don't think are worth while noticing. I've noticed *that*, too."

Craig, with a nodded good-by, made off to keep his appointment.

Keeler ate on in ruminative content; slowly and with intense relish. As the last morsel of chop and the last crumb of toast at last departed simultaneously from the sight of mankind, he finished his mineral water with a sip, and, heroically turning his back on such glittering temptations as a baked apple or a saucer of tapioca to round out the feast, he strolled into the billiard room.

No one was there at so early an hour except an attendant, and Keeler put in a rapturous forty-five minutes knocking the balls about in a series of shots whose appalling badness was unequaled in the annals of the club.

"I think," he said, in timid hopefulness to the attendant, as he signed his check for the solitary period of misplay, "I think my form is beginning to look up."

"It is," said the attendant, with conviction, adding under his breath: "And that's the only direction it *can* look."

In fine contempt for the novice's performance, the attendant was spreading the tarpaulin once more over the misused table when Keeler, starting away, offered the meek advice:

"When you say things you don't mean—like saying my form in pool is improving—it's always well to keep your hands out of sight. A man who isn't on his guard can never tell a lie without his fists clenching a little. I've noticed that. It's just a trifle, of course," he added, in apology, "but even a trifle sometimes counts—in the matter of tips."

The club veranda offered Keeler a few minutes of pleasant loafing—the spring night being prematurely hot. Presently he got up and fared forth toward the Milwood house. A five-minute walk brought him to his destination—a roomy cottage that had once been quaintly picturesque after the old Dutch fashion, but which Milwood had remodeled into modern ugliness. The house, Keeler had heard, had come to Milwood through a foreclosed mortgage. It stood some yards back from the sparse-populated street, and had a bit of ground on either side of it. Most of its windows to-night were bright lit. Two chauffeurless automobiles stood in the street in front of it.

Keeler walked up the flagged path onto the veranda, and halted uncertainly. The warmth of the night had caused the front door to be left open. Little fitful gusts of wind now and then shook the portières of the living room to the right of the hallway that ran the full shallow depths of the house. And, from the doorway, during one of these wind gusts, Keeler had a momentary glimpse of people—men and women in evening clothes—sitting at one or two card tables. There was not much sound of talk; the game evidently being of interest.

How many people were playing or who they might be, Keeler did not know. His glimpse of them was too brief. But their costumes made him acutely conscious of his own somewhat shiny business suit.

From the pitch-black portion of the veranda where he stood, just to the left of the front door, he was groping blindly for the doorbell. And as his fingers wandered fumblingly along the jamb, he heard a faint rustling sound at some slight distance behind him. He turned. The noise was not repeated; but it came from the direction of a clump of half-leaved forsythia in the front yard near to the street.

No birds were nesting so early; hence, no bird, and—for the same reason—presumably no cat was among the willowy boughs of the shrub. Nor do birds or cats, tangled in shrubbery, make one single motion to escape and then remain silent.

Keeler ceased to grope for the bell, and he stood very still.

The night was not only sultry but overcast as well. The dead stillness of it was broken only by the wind gusts that died as suddenly as they were born. From the denser gloom of the veranda corner, the yard was dimly visible in detail; a very faint glow falling on it from a distant street lamp. And the minute of waiting there in the dark had accustomed Keeler's eyes to the gradations of darkness.

He could make out the feathery outlines of the shrub patch and its unpruned upper shoots. Little by little he began then to make out a denser bulk that seemed to crouch between two of the thickest bushes of the clump. And to his mind came the memory of what Craig had said of the tramp who had annoyed Milwood that afternoon.

Knowing that his nerve might fail him if he should allow the first impulse to pass, Keeler stepped noiselessly from the edge of the veranda to the turf below, and walked quickly toward the shadowy bulk among the forsythia bushes.

CHAPTER III.
THE MAN IN THE DARK.

As Keeler neared the bush clump, the black shadow that lurked in it ceased to be amorphous and began to take form. The form of a man standing alert and with head bent.

Alert as the man seemed, Keeler's swift advance was so silent, so evidently unexpected, that the Unknown was not aware of it until Keeler was almost upon him. Then, with a bound like a frightened buck's, the stranger crashed through the bush that stood between him and the street, bounded across the few remaining feet of lawn, and vaulted the privet hedge that divided Milwood's property from the highway.

As his feet came down on the sidewalk, the man stumbled and fell asprawl. Something clattered from his pocket to the pavement. Keeler, close on his heels, saw the thing glitter on the dim-lit flagging, and, thinking it might be a revolver, snatched it up just as the fallen man scrambled to his feet and wheeled about on him.

But as Keeler's fingers closed about what he had picked up, he realized the thing was merely a pocket flash light. His fingers, gripping it convulsively, as the man turned, pressed the electric button.

A momentary flare of white light revealed to him a large, square-built man, fairly well dressed and clean shaven. The man's face, for the briefest fraction of a second, stood clearly revealed. The next instant a lightning-quick slap of the stranger's open right hand had knocked the flash light from Keeler's unprepared grasp; and an equally swift and very forcible shove of the stranger's left palm had sent Keeler careening backward into the unloving embrace of the three-foot privet hedge.

By the time Keeler was able to extricate himself from his scratchy resting place, the Unknown was sprinting down the deserted street at a speed and with a lead that made pursuit a folly.

Keeler got to his feet, dusted off his clothes as best he could, and stared vacantly after his vanished assailant. And to no one at all he spoke aloud. Not in wrath, not in imprecation; not even in disgust.

"Hadn't shaved for about eight hours," he mumbled. "Had his collar on long enough for it to wilt a little. Three or four hours, anyway. So it couldn't have been Milwood's tramp. And the tramp couldn't have been this chap in disguise. So there's two of them after Milwood, it seems. Not a burglar, either. Not with those eyes and that mouth. Honest face—only fairly intelligent—determined. Bulldog type. But the bulldog type doesn't hide in bushes at night in a man's front lawn."

With a shrug Keeler gave up the problem, merely deciding to tell Milwood of the occurrence, and thus to put him on guard.

Keeler went back to the veranda, groped once more along the jamb, and this time found the bell button. Presently a Japanese manservant came to the door. Keeler gave him a card, and sent a message, asking a minute's speech with Milwood on a matter of some importance. The sight of the guests in evening dress had just at first shaken the caller's resolve to summon Milwood forth from such a gathering on so trivial a pretext as the deciding of a paltry bet. But the finding of the man in the yard seemed to justify any intrusion. Milwood must be told of it.

The Jap took the card, not into the room beyond the portières, but upstairs. He returned with word that Mr. Milwood was busy just then, but that if Mr. Keeler cared to wait he would see him in a little while.

Even to Keeler the message seemed lacking in cordiality. And for a space he was of two minds whether to stay or go.

"I'll wait," he said, at last, adding, as the Jap opened the door of a little reception room: "No, I'll sit out here in the hall. It's cooler."

The Jap moved forward one of several fumed-oak chairs that were in the hallway, and departed to the inner regions of the house. Keeler sat down.

Again a fitful gust of wind swept through the hall from the open front door to the open back door, blowing the portières several inches apart. And again through the rift Keeler caught a fragmentary glimpse of the bridge players. Once more his shyness came to the fore, coupled with embarrassed dread lest some of these ornately appareled folk should stray out into the hall by chance and confront him in his nonfestival attire.

He got up and moved to the rear of the hall, as far as possible from the guests. There was a chair in a little niche, or doorless cupboard, just beside the rear door that opened out on the garden. In this chair in this niche Keeler seated himself. Here, for the moment, the breeze was blowing, and he got full benefit of it. It was the coolest spot in the house.

As Keeler relaxed his tired body to wait, and leaned his head back against the wall, he was aware of a softly buzzing sound as of a bee imprisoned in a bottle. The sound seemed to come from nowhere or anywhere. It was vaguely pleasing to his wearied senses after a long and busy and hot day. It was almost a lullaby. And his head began to slip to one side, against the cool wall surface.

Then abruptly the drowsy buzzing ceased. And in its place came an attenuated voice as of a man speaking through a poorly connected telephone. Yet, in the silence, almost every word was faintly audible.

"And," the voice was saying, "if you don't, I am going to kill you!"

CHAPTER IV.
Keeler Hears Much and Sees Nothing.

Keeler sat up as though the wall behind him had all at once been charged with electricity. His nodding head was tensely erect; his sleepiness had flown. Open-mouthed, he stared about him.

"I am going to kill you!" repeated the queer, distant voice; a very ghost of a tone, yet vibrant with ill-choked fury.

"If you think I am making an idle threat, you have only to—"

"B-z-z-z-z-z!"

The droning buzz had recommenced. The death-threatening voice was gone.

Keeler was on his feet, glaring about the niche. Dim lit as it was from the light cluster near the front door, he could see it held no window, no visible opening of any kind save that through which he had entered. He ran his fingers nervously around its three walls. They were indubitably of solid plaster; cool to his touch, despite the evening's heat.

Abruptly once more the droning ceased, and in its place, as from another world, came the miles-away voice:

"At seventy-six and an eighth. And now—"

"B-z-z-z-z-z!" droned the buzzing, in a single, long note, followed by the words:

"—and—a quarter. And I swear I'll kill you unless—"

"B-z-z-z-z-z-z-z-z!" buzzed the invisible bee in a bottle.

Keeler stepped out into the hallway. To his left was the open back door. He stepped through it out on the rear veranda. All was pitch dark. The buzz had ceased. He turned back into the house. The occasional voices of the bridge players came to him down the hall, muffled by the portière, but in no sense attenuated and reedlike as had been the voice he had just heard.

He looked to the right of the alcove. Here was the open space behind and beneath the colonial stairway. Some one even now was descending it. Keeler stood still. A man completed the descent of the stairway, and passed into the room where sat the bridge players. Keeler got the merest glimpse of him; only enough to see he was a shorter and stouter man than Milwood. As Keeler reëntered the alcove, he found that the drowsy buzzing had not ceased at all, but was so faint as to be inaudible anywhere outside of the niche itself. In there it still kept up its dull droning.

Keeler sat down again, trying to take the same position as before. The wind still blew, and an eddy of it swirled through the alcove, cooling the man's excitement-flushed cheek. His forehead creased in stark perplexity; he was trying in vain to come to any sort of solution of the phenomenon.

The buzzing died away again. This time not abruptly, but by slow degrees, growing fainter and fainter. The wind, too, died down, leaving the alcove stiflingly warm. Yet Keeler sat, tense, straining his ears for the remotest sound, heedless of discomfort. And after ages of waiting he heard.

The voice had begun to speak again. No, not *the* voice: Another voice, as deep but much more musical, and laden with persuasiveness, not with wrath or threat.

"Here it is," the new voice was saying. "Here it is. And there are the acids. Judge for yourself if there are finer samples of ore anywhere. And they are true samples, too, chipped off at random by our own man. There are tons—yes, millions of tons—just like it in the new 'lead' we've struck. The May Mazeppa is going to—"

"B-z-z-z-z!"

The crooning hum had recommenced, blurring the speaker's eager words to nothingness.

"Milwood!" babbled Keeler to himself. "Royce Milwood! I'd know his voice in a million. Even if he wasn't talking about that May Mazeppa Mine of his that he tried to get me to take stock in. But where in blazes is he? And how did I hear him? It wasn't the way a voice sounds from even the next room with the door shut."

Another tour of inspection to either side of the alcove left him as ignorant as ever; save of the fact that while the buzzing sound continued, the mysterious voice or voices always remained inaudible. And, after a fever of impatient waiting, he was rewarded by the ceasing of the buzz. Through the very first interval of silence came the threadlike sound of another voice—which Keeler knew as Craig's, before a word was distinguishable through the fading buzz.

"—couldn't help knowing," he heard Craig say, in sharp rebuke. "Any fool would know at a glance, if he had the remotest knowledge of metallurgy. I didn't even need the glass to show me it's salted. For a man of your high intelligence, Milwood"—b-z-z-z-z!—"it's the oldest mining trick known. Rockefeller might as sensibly dump one gallon of oil into Lake Michigan, and then try to sell the lake as an oil well. Why did you insult my intelligence by showing me such stuff?"

"I'm sorry it didn't impress you," came Milwood's easy voice. "To be frank, I was afraid it wouldn't. But there's really no reason why it should. It doesn't matter to us whether or not you believe the May Mazeppa is what we claim. As long as you'll say it is."

"Say it is? How can I, after seeing these salted samples?"

"We're both business men, Craig," expostulated Milwood. "Don't let's fence. To come down to cases, here is my idea: The May Mazeppa may be worked out. But there's still a bonanza fortune in it. For us."

"I don't quite get you."

"Oh, I think you do. We're both grown men. All I ask is a line from you, to use on the cover of our prospectus. And if you're too busy to write it, I'll do it for you and let you sign your name. We'll run a facsimile autograph. Facsimiles always go strong with the public. I don't know why. But they do. I suppose the educational millennium will have come, when pugilists and ball players are able to read and sign their own 'signed statements.'"

"What am I to sign? A statement that the May Mazeppa is a giant fraud? If so, I'll do it gladly."

"A statement that the May Mazeppa ore that you have examined is the richest in your experience."

"If that's a joke—"

"It is. On the same old joke-eating public. They'll swallow it alive."

There was a sound as of a chair pushed back.

"I don't think I need keep you from your guests any longer," came the ghost of Craig's voice.

"Sit down. Don't be a fool!" was the impatient retort. "I'm not asking you to run into any danger. You'll be testifying as to the *samples.* Not as to the mine itself. They can't hold you on that. I'll give you the samples to show, in case of a howl. All you'll have to do is to show them. That'll clear you. For the samples are fairly crawling with—"

"With gold that has been spattered into them from a shotgun or blowpipe. As any expert will tell you at a single glance."

"Then at most the charge will be that you've made a mistake. As any metallurgist is likely to. You won't be held culpable."

There was a moment of silence.

Keeler, listening, could hear nothing. Not even the b-z-z-z that had so puzzled him. Then Craig spoke again, in a curiously even and unemotional tone.

"As I understand it," said he, "I am to sign a statement—in my capacity of metallurgical expert—that your fake mine is rich in gold deposits. By so doing I shall stamp myself as a knave or a fool. The best I can hope for is that the courts will decide I'm merely a fool. The other alternative is that I shall spend a vacation in Atlanta prison."

"No, no, man! There's not a chance of that—"

"In either case, my reputation as an expert is to be wrecked forever. The reputation that is bread and butter to me. I may as well put up the shutters and learn a new trade. What do you offer me in exchange for what I'll be throwing away?"

"I offer you," said Milwood eagerly, "enough to keep you from the need of learning a new trade. If this goes through—and it will, with bells on—there's a fifty-thousand-dollar bonus in it for you. That's worth a signature, isn't it?"

"No," said Craig thoughtfully, as if weighing the pro and con. "It isn't—quite."

Keeler winced as if he had heard a distressing discord. But Milwood seemed to take new heart from the tone of Craig's reply.

"No?" he asked encouragingly. "Then what sum is worth it? You'll find we aren't disposed to stinginess. And I'm glad you haven't tried the holier-than-thou bluff. I was afraid I'd have to waste a lot of good time in persuading you to admit you're only mortal."

"Of course I'm only mortal," grumbled Craig sullenly, and Keeler thought he read shame in the admission. "And I have my price. But I warn you it's fairly high. You see, you're not only buying my professional honor, but my self-respect, too. They aren't on the free list."

"Never mind the oration," gayly exhorted Milwood. "And add up the items. What's the total?"

"My price," said Craig, slowly and with reluctance, "is—"

"B-z-z-z-z-z-z-z!"

The long-deferred droning cut in once more.

Keeler shook his head in impatient regret: Not for the interruption to the conversation to which he was inexplicably and involuntarily a listener. He had heard enough to satisfy him of what nature Craig's answer to the bribe offered him was to be. And it was that which provoked his gesture of disappointment.

"Another good man gone wrong!" Keeler muttered to himself. "But I didn't think it of Craig. I'll swear I didn't! If anybody had asked me, I'd have said there wasn't enough money minted to tempt him to go crooked. But pshaw! It gets them all, it seems, soon or late—the call of the coin. Unless I'm mistaken, that is—and he didn't mean to—"

The buzz had died away in his ear. "Then that's settled!"

It was Milwood's voice. The tone was that of one who briskly comments upon the conclusion of a business transaction's details. And Keeler's last flickering doubt of Craig's dishonesty snuffed out in his mind. The man had sold himself.

"B-z-z-z!"

"—what a yellow dog you are!"

Keeler started, as he heard the Voice from Nowhere replace the hum in the alcove. But whose voice? Craig's? Or Milwood's? This time through the dying b-z-z-z he was unable to tell which of the two was speaking. The words were just distinguishable, and that was all, as though the couple, in whatever room in the house they were talking, had altered their position from that which had formerly carried their words so plainly to Keeler's ears.

"—a bit rash in using such strong language. Considering that there are fully a dozen firearms of various sorts on the walls of this room—some of them, I believe are loaded. Also that I am a tolerably good shot."

"Craig talking! Or is it Milwood? Craig, I think," Keeler voiced the opinion half aloud, unconscious that he spoke in the tensity of trying to follow the thread of the sadly garbled discourse. "Must have been Milwood before, twitting him on agreeing to go in on the crooked deal. That's the come-back a man, if he had any spirit left in him, would naturally make. He'd threaten to make the other regret having shoved the insult under his nose and—"

Keeler broke off, and sat straining his ears. The buzz was fading again.

"You're wasting all those silly threats," came a far-off voice, unrecognizable as to tone, but which would be Milwood's, if Keeler's theory as to the order in which the participants in the dialogue were speaking was correct. "Not one of them lands. I'm as safe here as if I were in church. You don't want to start a murder scandal. Besides, you'd have a lot of trouble reaching one of those trophy weapons on the wall ahead of me. So let's cut out the heroics, and get back to business."

The invisible wire was "busy" with the buzz once more. After an interval—longer than any that had gone before—Keeler caught—as the droning died down to a whisper, and then expired in a last faint, asthmatic cough—the words:

"Miss Madge Carr."

The voice was still far off, unplaceable. And now Keeler had no theory to go on in guessing which of the two was speaking. He had been cut off too long to be able to hazard even a surmise as to who was just then on the delivery end of the give-and-take conversation.

"We'll leave her name out of this thing—"

This time the voice was louder. It came as though delivered behind teeth clenched in anger. And so it still baffled detection. But it seemed to Keeler to have Milwood's intonation rather than Craig's.

"That's a threat, too, if you like!"

"B-z-z-z-z!"

"If you put one of your crook fingers—"

The droning caught up the words, at last returning them:

"—I've no more time to talk to you now."

"You'll tell me what you mean, before I leave your house!"

"That's Craig!" ejaculated Keeler.

"B-z-z-z-z-z!"

"—involving a woman whose name you soil just by the speaking of it—"

Who said that? And why? Another droning, then:

"Quite so. We'll come to grips over that afterward." The voice swelled in Keeler's ears as though the speaker were coming toward him.

"*That's* Milwood!" the listener muttered, with conviction.

"Don't stumble over the crate by the door there," the pleasant bass voice rumbled on, "on your way out. It's a carboy of $H_2 SO_4$, for very 'lighter-than-air' gas experiments. Ichi forgot to take it down to the storeroom, I suppose, when he cleared up my study for to-night. I—"

"B-z-z-z-z!"

"Threatened men live long, you know."

"Not always. Not when they drag women's names into—"

"B-z-z-z-z!"

The wind, which had fallen quiet, swept through the house again with a gust that swirled around the alcove's narrow confines. And with it recommenced the drowsy hum as of imprisoned bees.

CHAPTER V.
Keeler Hears More.

Keeler got to his feet athrill with what he had heard; keen to probe the mystery of the hearing. The droning still continued. And now the man's mind, no longer distracted by listening to the dispute, began to work with its normal deductive swiftness.

He realized that only at such times as the wind found his hot face did he hear that odd droning. Whenever the wind died down, the buzzing died with it.

Again he glanced about the niche, but the place was in dense shadow, and the barest outlines of the three closet walls were all he could see. He felt he was tapping some new and wholly unexplained form of telephone; a telephone without wires or other visible apparatus. And the detective instinct throbbed hotly in him.

As he was about to explore farther, the wind gust died. And, as he had foreseen, the buzzing ceased abruptly. Like a man absorbed in the action of a play and fearful of reaching his seat too late for the beginning of the next act, Keeler promptly sat down again and threw back his head against the wall in the attitude experience had shown him was the best for catching every word of the far-off conversation from Millwood's study. For nearly a moment he listened in vain. Except for an occasional distant laugh or half-audible sentence from the card players at the other end of the hall, there was not a sound. Then the silence was broken by the highly thrilling words in a petulant, feminine voice:

"Oh, I've torn my dress! I caught the hem on that crate. Why do you have such things in your study?"

"It's a carboy of sulphuric acid—vitriol"—came Milwood's reply. "Lucky you didn't upset it. I'm sorry, ever so sorry, about the dress. Is it badly torn?"

"No. Not much. Just the flounce. And only a rip, after all. But what a funny place to keep vitriol! Do you throw it at people?"

"No. That isn't one of my accomplishments; though, now I come to think of it, it's about the only thing I haven't been accused of. I use it for gas experiments I'm making. I told Ichi to take it downstairs. I suppose he forgot. He usually does."

"What a queer room!" went on the feminine voice; its owner evidently forgetting the dress-rending episode in interest in her surroundings. "It's a blend of study and library and gun-room, and—"

"And paradise—just now," he supplemented.

"Don't!" was the impatient reply. "I came up here to talk business to you, not to listen to ponderous compliments."

"And I asked you up here," he returned, a note in his voice that was new to Keeler, "not to talk business with you, but to tell you I love you!"

"H'm!" mused Keeler. "So *that's* the way he's getting even with Craig! It must take sublime heroism to tell a woman to her face that you love her! I'd rather run up against the vitriol throwing."

"To tell you I love you, my sweet-heart," Milwood was repeating.

"You mustn't!" she declared. "I have no right to listen to you."

"No right or no wish?"

"Neither."

"Then let me give you both. I love you. And I'm going to make you love me. You understand? To *make* you love me."

"I must go," she said falteringly, "I—"

"No," he answered gently, but with a flash of iron under the gentleness. "You *mustn't* go!"

"You would try to prevent me?" she cried, incredulous.

"If I had to. But I won't have to. You will stay and listen to me because you want to. Or," he added, "because you don't care to cause a scene. Do you?"

"I don't understand you."

"Please!" he protested, with a laugh. "Please don't say that. There never yet was a woman who didn't tell a man she 'didn't understand' him. And never yet was there a woman who didn't understand a man better than he understood himself. Why shouldn't we be honest with each other, you and I, dear?"

"Then, if you prefer, I don't *want* to understand you, Mr. Milwood."

"I'm afraid I can't believe that, either. You know I love you. A woman always knows. You know it in ten thousand ways; even though I never before had a chance to put it into words, you knew it. You can't deny that. You knew it. And you knew, too, that when a man asks a woman he adores to give him an interview alone at night in his study—he doesn't do it merely to discuss a dull matter of mining stocks. You knew I'd tell you I love you. And, knowing it, you came up here. That's why I said just now that you'd stay and listen to me."

"I *didn't* know!" she declared vehemently. "I wanted to see you about father's stock. He is ill. He is practically dying. It is the shame of it that is crushing him, rather than the loss. He went into the scheme on your representations. He believed you. He induced his friends to believe in you. People invested, on the weight of his name. And now that he foresees the wreck of it all, he—"

"B-z-z-z-z-z!"

Keeler, for almost the first time in his life, felt a wave of babyish impatience grip him at the interruption. He wanted to shake his fist in the face of the baffling wind gust. He half rose from his seat. Then the breath of cool air was gone. And, through the last dying drone of the eternal b-z-z-z-z, he heard the woman speaking.

"And knowing all that," she was saying, "you actually presume to think I came up here to listen to love talk from such a man as you?"

"No," sighed Milwood, "I don't think it. I was wrong to think it. I—I *know* it."

"You are—"

"I am a poor luckless chap who loves you. That's all I can realize just now. I love you. And I believe you love me."

"I hate you!" she flashed.

"You love me," he insisted, a wondrous glamour in his voice. "You may not confess it to yourself, but you do. That is why you are here."

"I've told you that I came to—"

"To say what could have been said as well at my office or by letter? No, no, sweetheart. You *care*. This is no business appointment. It is a tryst."

"You beast! No, don't come near me. Oh, I could strangle you!"

"I wish you would," he breathed. "For you would have to twine your dear arms around my throat to do it!"

"Have you no heart, no shred of manliness? I have come here to plead for my father, whom you have swindled. And you have the affrontery to offer me love."

"Not just to offer it. To insist on it. Oh, little sweetheart of mine,

I—"

"Every word of love from you to me is a stain. For the memory of your own mother—"

"My own mother!" he repeated dreamily. "She died so many years ago. I used to think she was the most beautiful woman in the world—until I met you. She used to come to my crib to kiss me good night on her way to some dance. I remember. In her low-cut dress, with her fair hair piled high on her head, and an elusive sort of fragrance about her—like yours. Her eyes were like yours, too, as she bent over me, like this. And her soft lips on mine—like—"

He broke off with an audible gasp of surprise. And simultaneously a dull impact came faintly to Keeler's straining ears. It was followed by a brief silence that seemed fairly to vibrate. Then—

"I've made your lip bleed," the woman said, in a stifled voice. "I never struck any one before. But I'm not sorry. Now let me go. Let me *go!*"

"I've read of a 'kiss for a blow,'" mused Keeler, "but a 'blow for a kiss' is a novelty. I think I'd do well to drop a hint to Craig to go back to his host's study. Miss Madge Carr seems able to take care of herself thus far. But with Milwood, things have always a way of going farther."

Irresolute, he gathered himself to rise and depart on his mission. But the sound of Milwood's voice checked him.

"You will pay for striking me," the man was saying. "You will pay for it in kisses. Listen to me, Hilda—"

"Hilda?" gurgled Keeler, half aloud. "Her name's Madge!"

"Listen to me, Hilda," Milwood was saying. "No, don't try to get to the door. Because you can't. You've got to hear me."

"The Desperate Desmond pose is old-fashioned, Royce," came the woman's answer, with a lightness that even Keeler could tell was forced. "I don't choose to stay here and listen to anything you may have to say. And what I don't choose to do, I *don't* do. I am going! Stand away from the door, please!"

There was a second of silence following her sharp command. Then she said angrily:

"I am not going to make a scene by trying to force my way past you. I have only to cry out, to—"

"To bring everybody trooping up here, each with a dozen different questions, and all forming one conclusion. It would not be overpleasant for me. But it would be much less pleasant for you."

"Oh, let me by!"

"When you have heard what I must say."

Another instant's silence, and the woman said, with a vein of hopelessness:

"If you aren't any more civilized than to try cave-man tactics to make me listen to you—"

"Good! I'll win your forgiveness for that later. Hilda, I am going away. Perhaps to-morrow, perhaps to-night. I have grown tired of plodding on here. And other people have tired of my being here. It is time to go, and to go quickly. In a half hour, in this very house, I can lay hands on enough funds to make me comfortable until I can get a newer and bigger start somewhere else. And I am going."

"How does that interest me? I—"

"Simply because you are going with me."

"*I?*"

"To the end of the world. And to the beginning of love. You are going to turn exile into paradise for me, Hilda."

"Are you quite mad?"

"Yes. And I have been so since the first moment I saw you. It's a divine madness. May I die before I am cured of it!"

"You probably will, when my husband hears of this."

"Husband?" muttered Keeler. "Lord! Who *is* the woman? It isn't Miss Carr."

"He will be back in a day or two at most," went on the high-pitched voice. "Possibly by midnight to-night. And I shall tell him that you—"

"That I can twist the May Mazeppa testimony so as to send your father to Atlanta prison? That you came here in his absence to dine with me? To dine with a man your husband hates, and of whom he has always been crazily jealous? No, no, Hilda, darling. I really don't think you'll tell Mr. van Vleck."

"You know well enough why I came! It was only because you sent me word you wouldn't appoint any other place to talk over my father's affairs. And, as for propriety—"

"Possibly you can make Mr. van Vleck see it in that way? No? Then let's be sensible. Hilda!"

"Oh, I detest you!"

"That's better. Now listen to reason. I can help your father. A word from me will prove he went into this whole thing innocently."

"Then speak it!"

"With you at my side. With your dear hands in mine."

"No! No!"

"But I say *yes!* Come away from this dreary old region with me. If you wish, let your sister come, too. I don't care how many people hedge you in as long as your husband is made jealous enough to set you free. Free to marry me. Free to live the golden-love life that our hearts are pleading for. There's a whole world of life, of love, of color, of glorious happiness waiting for you and me. Hilda!"

"I can't listen to you! It is wicked even to let myself hear—"

"Hilda! Look at me. *Look!* In the eyes!"

Another long interval of silence. Then her voice, broken, frightened:

"Don't! Don't look at me like that—Royce! Your eyes are like a snake's. I can feel your will power gripping me, in spite of myself. Royce!"

"You love me, Hilda," came Milwood's voice, infinitely tender; yet with a new mastery in it.

"No! I—I—"

"You love me," he repeated, in the same strange, compelling tone.

"I hate you! When the horrible hold of your eyes and your will are gone, I shall hate you as I never knew I could hate. Your lip is still bleeding—I—"

"You love me."

Faint, stifled, the halting reply reached Keeler:

"I—I—I love—"

"What the devil do *you* want?" followed Milwood's voice in something between a snarl and a roar.

"I knocked," faltered the voice of the Jap servant. "I knocked. Twice I knock. I thought I hear 'Come in!'"

"Get out!"

"Yessir. Miss"—b-z-z-z!—"send word to Mrs. van Vleck. It is late, and—"

"Yes, yes!" broke in the woman's voice. "I'm ready."

There was a ghost of a sound as of swishing skirts and of hurried footsteps. The study door slammed. Keeler could hear some one descending the stairs almost at a run. And at the same time a queer memory came to him. A line from a book he had read a few days earlier—"Tess of the D'Urbervilles." The line was one spoken by Tess to Angel Clare. It was:

> Angel, I have killed him. I knew I should do it. I knew it ever since the day I struck him.

CHAPTER VI.
A SIMPLE SOLUTION.

But another overheard scene, brief and to the point this time, distracted Keeler's thoughts from the psychology of hatred bred by a blow and by a humiliation to overpowering force of will.

Scarce had the study door shut behind Mrs. van Vleck when he heard Milwood burst forth upon his luckless servant with a volley of blasphemous abuse that fairly turned cold the gentle little eavesdropper's timid blood.

Milwood's habitual, suave calm was rent from him, and in an almost incoherent spasm of fury he was berating the servant. The latter tried once or twice in deprecatory fashion to stem the tide of foaming-mouthed invective, but quite in vain. At length, as a crescendo to the maniac tirade, there was an impact as of a fist blow; a sharp little cry like that of a hurt dog, and the fall of a light body.

"I've heard," Keeler found himself reflecting, "that it isn't always safe to knock these Japs about. Sometimes they—"

"Get up!" snapped Milwood. "Get up and take yourself out of here! You've done more harm in five seconds by blundering in on us just now than you could undo in a century. Clear out!"

"Yessir," lisped the Jap, his tone as impassive as though the blow had been a friendly pat upon the back. "Yessir. First give policeman's message. Came to give."

"Policeman?" echoed Milwood, a catch in his voice. "What policeman?"

"On street. Five minutes past. Come to tell you man hides in garden. Saw him go there. Chased him out. Five minutes past. Told me I tell you. I tell. Yessir."

"A man hiding in the garden?" exclaimed Milwood. "What did—"

"B-z-z-z-z!"

The wind slapped Keeler's face. The eternal droning recommenced. Shakily Keeler got to his feet. His absorption in the odd dialogues he had been overhearing had dulled his senses not only to the doubtful ethics of such listening, but also to any possible solution of the phenomenon. Now as he rose he looked once more about the little niche that had served so inexplicably as a telephone receiver. Again by the faint light he could see nothing but the dim wall surface.

He felt for a match. In his pocket his hand touched the flash light he had picked up on the sidewalk when it had fallen from the clothes of his unknown opponent, and that he had picked up again after it had been knocked out of his hand, and after he had crawled from the privet hedge.

Drawing out the flash light, he pressed its button, illumining the alcove with a white glare. And at first glance the whole mystery was as clear as day to him.

In the rear wall of the niche, just eighteen inches above the top of his chair back, was the "whistle end" of a speaking tube. The tube itself, painted the same dull gray as the wall, ran upward out through the ceiling overhead.

The tin mouth of the speaking tube was twisted. The whistle and its spring were gone. The tube was evidently no longer in use; just as evidently as once it had formed a means of speech from ground floor to third story of the house; from what might once have been a sort of porter's lodge to what was now Milwood's study.

No longer was Keeler puzzled as to the droning of every breath of wind through this ideal flue; nor for the fact that every word was transmitted during wind lulls from one end of the tube to the other. So had the ancient priors, according to ecclesiast tradition, listened from their cells to the table talk of monks in the refectory of the abbey.

Keeler paused a moment in doubt. He had come thither to warn

Royce Milwood of a lurking marauder in his grounds; and to learn if he had won or lost his ten-dollar bet. Somehow he had lost his desire to touch this man's money. As to the warning that was already given. What was left to wait for? Nothing.

The front hall was full of other guests, Milwood in their midst. Some of them were saying good night to their host, and he was apologizing for his half hour or so of absence. Keeler made as though to step forward. But not one had noticed him. No one ever noticed Keeler.

And now embarrassment seized him. Embarrassment and a curious new distaste to shake Milwood's hand. So, unseen, he jammed his hat over his thin-thatched scalp, and slunk out of the back door, and so around the house into the street. The wind had died. The night was pitch black, save for an occasional play of heat lightning over the far Jersey horizon.

It was a trip of two or three blocks to the nearest car line. Instead of going thither at once, Keeler strolled back to the Half Moon Athletic Club. He, who was usually so retiring, felt not unlike a child who has just heard a secret so big that he finds trouble in keeping every detail of it to himself.

He wanted to talk—a rare impulse with Keeler. He wanted to think, too, and he had ever found that he could think more easily after he had visualized his processes by spoken or by written words. It was an old custom of Keeler's, when he was perplexed, to write out his puzzle in full, or else to jot down notes on it, and then to study over the fixed facts. He had read somewhere as a boy that this was a trait of Daniel Webster. And he had copied it.

Arriving at the clubhouse, he wandered aimlessly from room to room. The verandas were full, the grillroom was half filled; so was the gym; the big billiard room was crowded. In the writing-room library alone did he find solitude. In none of the throng that filled the rest of the house had he seen a single acquaintance. Keeler had few acquaintances anywhere; fewest of all at this one club of which he was a member.

He sat down at a writing desk, pulled a sheet of club note paper toward him, and began to scribble with the stub of a pencil he fished from the recesses of a vest pocket.

Man—unknown, threatened to kill Milwood—unless—unless what? That whirring in the tube cut off most of what he said. There was something about fractions, though. Quarters and eighths. Whatever sense that may make with a threat to kill.

Second: Craig, after agreeing to go into partnership with him on a mining swindle, quarreled with Milwood about a girl. Memo: Name of girl, Madge Carr. Threats from Craig. Strong hint of further trouble.

Third: Woman. Hilda van Vleck. Married. Queer love scene. She threatened, too. If not in so many words, at least in a way I'd hate to be threatened. Struck him.

(Note. Tess of D'Urberville speech. Thomas Hardy knows woman nature.)

Fourth: Milwood cursed at his Jap in a way to make a saint murderous. Knocked him down. Jap took it like a stoic. Why? He didn't look like a meek man, the Jap didn't, from the one glimpse I got of him.

Fifth: A big, ugly-faced chap hiding in bushes on lawn. Must have come back second time, since policeman saw him after I did. What was he there for? He didn't look like a yegg.

Sixth: Tramp accosted M. this afternoon. M. was scared, Craig says. Why? M. is never scared.

Seventh: Mrs. van V. spoke of jealous husband. If she gets an attack of conscience strong enough to overbalance her fear, she'll probably tell husband. From what she says, he is likely to do things.

"Let's see," he murmured. "That seems to be about all. And it doesn't lead anywhere. Oh, yes," he corrected himself.

Bending over the paper he scribbled:

Eighth: Milwood is in danger, not only from people who talk about thrashing him or killing him; but from people who are blocking his financial games. That is probably why he means to light out, as he told Mrs. van V. I don't believe the physical threats would drive him away. He is brave. Out at Beloit I saw him break the neck of a mad dog with his bare hands. No, he's anxious to get away before his finance bubble bursts.

He's made his plans by keeping plenty of ready money in his house. He told Mrs. van V. so. He wouldn't keep so much cash, otherwise, in an isolated house like that, where men hide in the shrubbery. He's planning a get-away.

Ninth: What business of mine is it? None at all, and I'm going home and going to bed.

Keeler half shamefacedly folded his sheaf of rambling notes and stuck them into his pocket along with the pencil. At the door on his way out he chanced upon Hannibal Brayle, head of a Brooklyn private detective bureau; a former policeman, and an acquaintance of his own.

"Hello, Mr. Keeler!" hailed the big detective cordially. "On your way out? Come back and have something to drink."

"Thanks," refused Keeler, "but I just had a pint of Apollinaris with my dinner. I'm going home now."

"A whole pint of polly?" laughed Brayle. "You're going the pace hard, Mr. Keeler. Suppose you switch the tipple just for luck. I'm going in to have two fingers of the stuff that killed father. Join me?"

"If you refer to whisky when you talk of a patricidal beverage," said Keeler, "I most surely won't. I'm on a health meal regimen of fourteen ounces of food a day. And I've had my limit. Alcohol is food, you know. Up to two ounces."

"It's past the food stage long ago, then, with me," returned Brayle. "Good night—if you won't have something."

"Good night. Oh, by the way, Mr. Brayle. There's a hypothetical question I'd like to put to you."

"Fire away!"

"You've had a good bit of experience with crimes of violence, haven't you?"

"Who? Me? No, indeed. Oh, no. Nothing like it. I served only eleven years on the New York police force, in one capacity or another; part of the time breaking up Black Hand gangs, and part of the time patrolling Cherry Hill and the water front. And after that in the detective bureau. Except for that eleven years and a little, on the side, since then, I'm a regular ignoramus when it comes to crimes of violence. What's the main idea?"

"Just this," replied Keeler, on whom even the most elephantine forms of sarcasm were ever thrown away. "Here's my hypothetical question: If a man were threatened with death, directly or indirectly, four times in one evening by four separate people, and if there were presumably one or two others lying in wait for him, what chance, do you consider, offhand, would such a man have of escaping with his life to some other part of the world?"

The detective bent his shaggy gray brows in deep thought. When he presently spoke, the banter was gone from his voice.

"What chance?" he repeated, in perfect sincerity. "What chance of making a clean get-away? Well, Mr. Keeler, I shouldn't say his chances were better than one hundred per cent, maybe; but I sure wouldn't say they were one speck worse than one hundred per cent."

"You mean that he is in no danger? You surely can't mean that?"

"I surely can. Likewise I surely do. Here's the idea: If he was to be threatened by one man, there's perhaps one chance in twenty that the threat might be made good. Though my own experience has taught me that the man who threatens isn't the one who kills. Or, if you like it better, the guy who does the killing doesn't queer his chances and put the other fellow on guard, and lay up evidence against himself, by blabbing in advance. I don't say it never happens. But not oftener'n once in twenty times."

"Then—"

"But if *four* folks are threatening him, why, there isn't that much chance against him. In fact, there isn't any chance. It means he's either the kind of man that people just naturally like to threaten—just as there's men it's an awful trial not to kick—or else that he's done something to rile those four people, and they're all four working off steam that way. It happens like that oftener'n you'd think. No, sir, the fact that everybody's threatening him makes him an awfully good life-insurance risk. He doesn't even need to make a get-away. If they didn't threaten when he did them dirt, then it'd be time to get nervous."

"I'm glad to get your expert opinion," said Keeler. "Thanks."

But once launched on a professional hobby, Brayle was not easy to choke off.

"Why, look-a-here," he went on, buttonholing Keeler, and, to the latter's dire embarrassment, talking sonorously for the benefit of all and sundry. "You used to follow murder cases pretty close when I was over to headquarters. Did you ever once come across a trial where a guilty man was accused of having threatened the man he killed? *I* have, lots of times. But always in story-books. In real life, the man that does the killing is almost never the man that does the threatening. And when there's wholesale threats, there's wholesale chances that the threatened man will die of old age, or of mange, before he's killed. Put that down as a fact, son. When the crowd threatens to lynch, it never lynches. It's the nonthreatening, quiet crowd that lynches."

Keeler, annoyedly aware that several grinning club members were listening in keen amusement, managed at last to break away from the noisy bore and to make his escape. Yet he knew that with all his bluster and self-advertising and love of talk Hannibal Brayle was one of the shrewdest private detectives alive, and he knew that Brayle's opinions on such questions as Keeler had propounded to him were likely to be splendidly sound.

If Brayle made light of threats, such as Keeler had heard breathed against Milwood that night, then there was every chance that such threats were mere angry vaporings.

And, as he reflected, Keeler recalled case after case where the police had wisely ignored the clew of men who had merely threatened a victim, and had at last, in the real murderer, found a man who had struck instead of threatening.

Keeler's puzzled reflections were interrupted by a salvo of thunder, accompanying a blinding glare of sheet lightning. The spell of sultry weather had at last culminated in an electric storm. Dazzled, deafened, soaked by swirls of big-drop rain, Keeler sprinted for his car. When, an hour later, he wrung out his drenched clothes in his own room and scrambled into bed, a wholesome dread of having caught cold and thus marring his vacation at its outset had driven from his mind all thought of everything but his own chilled and uncomfortable condition. For the time Milwood and Milwood's concerns had no place in his brain.

CHAPTER VII.
KEELER'S MEMORY IS JOGGED.

Wayne Wisconsin Keeler earned fifty dollars a week, and lived on twenty-five of it. This feat was much aided by the economical health-meal regimen. Also by the fact that for fifteen dollars a month he had been able to find a room in an East Side flat which was quite as comfortable as his modest tastes demanded. It was one of his several mild eccentricities that, employed in Brooklyn, he should have picked out a lodging in Manhattan.

His one extravagance consisted in taking a quartet of morning newspapers, and of reading them in bed, while he waited for his breakfast of egg and toast to be brought to his door by his landlady. This breakfast, of course, was an "extra," but the landlady, good motherly soul, charged him barely forty per cent more for it than he would have paid at any ordinary restaurant. And Keeler appreciated her kindness. It was the one home touch in his barren, little life.

On this, the first morning of his vacation, Keeler awoke drowsily and lay happily in bed, his sleepy mind divided between two causes for rejoicing: One was that he did not have to go to work. The other was that his wetting of the previous night had not given him a cold.

At last, with a luxurious stretch, he loafed out of bed and across his seven-by-nine room to the door. Opening the door and harvesting the crop of morning papers propped against it, he scurried back to bed with his treasure, stacked his pillows, pulled the bed-clothes around him, and prepared to revel in his usual morning plunge through the news.

He arranged the four newspapers neatly on his lap, picked up the first of them, and opened it. From the last two columns of its front page these headlines thrust themselves on his notice, before the paper was fairly opened before him:

SHOT THROUGH HEAD AND BURNED BY ACID.
Royce Milwood, Promoter, Strangely Murdered in His Study at Bay Ridge Home.
WOUND FROM SILVER BULLET IN EXACT CROWN OF HEAD—FACE DISFIGURED BY VITRIOL.

Wayne Keeler read the headlines. Then he reread them. And for an instant he was aware of a morbid desire to say, "I told you so" to Hannibal Brayle. Then he recalled that he had not told Brayle anything at all. And, thoroughly awake, he settled down to a reading of the story beneath the headlines' flare. The account began:

> Royce Milwood, well known in mining circles, was found murdered in the study of his home at 999 Marken Street, Bay Ridge, Brooklyn, at two-forty-five a. m. to-day.
>
> Mr. Milwood was not only murdered in a most unusual manner, but he was hideously mutilated with sulphuric acid. Death was caused by a bullet, presumably from a pistol, that drilled a hole downward from the exact center

of the crown of the head, and lodged in the skin of the throat. Examination proved the bullet to be made of silver. Death, apparently, was instantaneous.

The murderer, before escaping, delayed long enough to bathe his victim's face and head in vitriol and to sprinkle drops of the acid upon the upper part of the dead man's clothing.

The motive is supposed to have been, at least in part, robbery; as no money or jewelry or watch was found on the body; although Mr. Milwood at the time of the murder was fully dressed. It is not yet known whether or not other valuables were taken from the house.

The crime was discovered by Milwood's Japanese valet, Ichi, who, waking and imagining he heard his employer call to him, went to the study. There, in spite of the lateness of the hour, he found the electric lights still burning. Milwood was lying on the floor, across the threshold. So near to the door was the body that the valet was forced to push the door and the body several inches before he could make an opening sufficiently wide to enable him to open the room. He at once telephoned the Fourth Avenue police station.

Mr. Milwood is not known to have had any enemies. He is said to have been extremely popular in mining and athletic circles. No motive, other than robbery, can therefore be assigned for the murder.

Patrolman Hogenbaum, of the Fourth Avenue station, reported at ten last evening that he saw a man hanging about the Milwood lawn and asked what he was doing there. The man, instead of answering, ran away. And so dark was the night that Hogenbaum lost track of him. He told the Japanese valet of the man's presence on the lawn. The valet says he in turn spoke to Mr. Milwood about it; and was ordered to use extra care in locking the house.

"Mr. Milwood gave a large dinner party last evening," Ichi said to a *Bugle* reporter, "but the guests had all gone by eleven o'clock or earlier. At least, that is my impression. I had a very bad headache; and Mr. Milwood, who was always considerate of others' comfort, told me to go to bed as soon as I had carefully locked all the house except the front door. He said he would see his guests out and would lock that door after them. I heard voices downstairs until about eleven. Then the sound of talking ceased, and I suppose the guests went home. I then went to sleep, and did not waken until two-forty-five, when I thought I heard Mr. Milwood call."

The ill-written account, hastily compiled to catch a last edition, wandered on with police testimony, police doctored testimony, conjectures, et cetera, for another half column or more, ending with:

Doctor Colfax refutes any possibility of suicide; by pointing out that no man could possibly hold a pistol in such a position as to inflict a wound in that spot and at that angle. Also, in event of suicide, there would inevitably be powder marks; their absence proving that the pistol muzzle must have been held at least eighteen inches or more from Mr. Milwood's head when the fatal shot was fired.

Much bewilderment is expressed by police experts as to the relative position of the murderer and of Mr. Milwood at the time of the shooting. In all the annals of crime, they declare, this is the first known instance of a man being shot through the exact center of the crown; the bullet traveling downward in a perfectly straight line. The bullet, too, they aver, is of no known caliber; a still stranger aspect of the case being the fact that the bullet is of pure silver and not of lead. This and the use of acid to disfigure the victim, may lead to a theory that the deed was that of a fantastic madman.

Keeler read one paper after another. The first he had picked up contained the most voluminous report.

"I'm not surprised," mumbled Keeler, at last. "As I see it, from last night's standpoint, the question doesn't seem to be 'who killed him?' but 'who *didn't* kill him?'"

He ate his egg and toast in dreamy abstraction. Then, as he rose from bed, he slowly unpacked the kit he had prepared for his outing.

"I think," he confided to his shaving mirror, "I think I've found a more amusing way of spending my vacation."

CHAPTER VIII.
A Workaday Vacation.

An hour later, Cyrus Q. Sawyer, district attorney of Kings County, was mildly surprised to see Wayne W. Keeler enter his private office.

"Do you expect to spend your vacation ghost fashion haunting the scenes of your former crimes?" asked the district attorney pleasantly. "Or did such a minor event as your yearly vacation slip your mind?"

"Neither, sir," answered Keeler, adding, with conscientious detail, "though, if I'd forgotten I'm on vacation, I wouldn't be here a full half hour late as I am. I came to ask rather a big favor."

Keeler was not given to asking favors; nor, so the staff said, was District Attorney Sawyer addicted to granting them. The geniality began to fade out of the great man's manner.

"I would like," pursued Keeler modestly, "to do a little work on my own account on the Royce Milwood murder."

"Well?"

"It—it interests me," said Keeler. "I should enjoy doing a little investigating, if you will let me."

"I'm sorry," returned his chief, "but this is the only time you can be spared for a vacation. And even if I were able to postpone your vacation, your own department here has enough work piled up just now to keep you busy, without sparing you to run over to Bay Ridge on a wild-goose chase."

He turned back to his letter-strewn desk, with the time-honored gesture that says, far louder than words:

"The incident and the interview are closed."

But Keeler did not, as usual, depart in meek haste. Instead, he cleared his throat nervously, and, calling on all his courage, returned to the attack.

"You don't quite understand me, sir," he said, with wabbly determination.

"Eh?" grunted Sawyer, frowning up from his desk. "What's that?"

"I say, sir," went on Keeler, "you misunderstand me. I don't want my vacation postponed, and I don't want to waste office time in what you call a 'wild-goose chase.' I—"

"Then," snapped his chief, "what in blazes *do* you want, man?"

"Just what I asked for, sir. I would like to spend my vacation—or as much of it as may be necessary—in trying to do a little digging on the Milwood case."

"What for?"

"For my own amusement, sir. The case seems to present some sides that interest me. If you'd give me authority to—"

"Authority to work, instead of loaf, during your vacation? Go ahead, for all of me!"

"Would you mind phoning, or having some one phone to the Brooklyn detective headquarters that I am authorized by you to work on the case?"

"I don't like to interfere prematurely in the work of the police," pondered Sawyer. "There will probably be time enough for this office to take a hand in the case when—"

"When I'm back at work here, and can't help," interposed Keeler, his eagerness overcoming his timidity. "And I believe I *can* help, sir."

"You have reason to think you can be of use on the case?" asked Sawyer half incredulously.

"Yes, sir. I knew Milwood. I knew something of his circumstances; something of the people he knew, and something of the people who—who didn't care for him."

"That puts a new angle on it. You are prepared to turn over your information to the police?"

"When it is necessary, yes."

"What is there in this for you?"

Keeler thought for a moment, then said frankly:

"Upon my soul, sir, I don't know. What is there in it for the hound when it strikes the scent?"

"You've struck the scent?"

"I like to think I *can* strike it, sir."

"Have you any theory as to who could have killed Milwood?"

"It would be harder for me," answered Keeler enigmatically, "to form a theory as to who *didn't* kill him. I—I'd rather not explain, unless you insist. I may be all wrong, and I may not be able to discover anything. But I can't hurt the case by trying."

"Go ahead, then," vouchsafed Sawyer, more in amusement than otherwise; though his mind harked back to certain strange results Keeler's probing into official documents had more than once brought forth. "Only, remember, if you bungle or do anything to throw justice off the track or hinder the police, I won't stand by you. I'll telephone detective headquarters."

Again he turned to his desk. With a hurried "Thank you, sir, very much," Keeler left the room.

When the vacationist reached detective headquarters, on Poplar Street, Brooklyn, he found that the district attorney's message had preceded him and had won for him a civil, if not overcordial, reception from the local chief.

"We are always glad, of course, to work with the district attorney's office," the chief remarked, in welcoming him, "though I don't understand why Mr. Sawyer sent a representative here before the case is fairly begun. He might have given us a chance to show what we can do on our own account, before he sent us assistance. This isn't going to be a very hard thing to clear up. You know the facts, I suppose?"

"Only as I've read them in the morning newspapers."

"The papers? Huh! A hodgepodge of mistakes, their account is.

Why, they called me 'Chief H. J. Pyne,' instead of 'H. P. Pyne.' And they got only one 'G' in Patrolman Hoggenbaum's name. And they quoted that Jap's talk like he was a college professor. By the way, like to talk to the Jap? I'm holding him as a material witness. Go along and see him, if you like. Clancy will take you to him. Then when you're through, come back and I'll run you out to Milwood's house in my car. I'm starting there in just a few minutes. The body hasn't been moved."

Keeler found Ichi crouching, monkeylike, in one corner of a bench in a bare room at the end of a corridor. The Jap did not look up as Keeler entered, nor did he speak until, when they were left alone together, Keeler accosted him.

"Do you remember me?" asked the visitor.

Ichi eyed him in lackluster fashion, and shook his head.

"I called to see Mr. Milwood last evening," continued Keeler. "You let me in. He sent down word he'd see me later. I didn't wait until he was disengaged. I went away without talking to him. You remember my face now?"

Ichi looked doubtful.

"You probably wouldn't remember me," sighed Keeler. "Most people don't. I don't know why."

Starting on a new tack, he asked: "On what floor is Mr. Milwood's study?"

"Third," said Ichi sullenly.

"What floor do *you* sleep on?"

"Third."

"Near the study?"

"No. Other end."

"So far away that you couldn't hear a pistol shot or a gunshot?"

"No."

"But you didn't hear one?"

"No."

"Why not?"

"Thunder."

"You told the police you were asleep."

"Yes. Asleep."

"Yet the thunder didn't keep you from being waked by thinking you heard Mr. Milwood calling you?"

"No."

"But the thunder was too loud to let you hear a shot or to be wakened by it?"

"Not too loud. Too muchlike."

"I see. Ichi, they say Mr. Milwood was shot by a silver bullet."

"I didn't see bullet," returned Ichi hastily.

"H'm! Ichi, in some parts of Europe, silver bullets used to be cast—and then blest—for shooting wizards and sorcerers and other people who bore charmed lives and whom lead and steel couldn't harm."

Ichi kept his eyes fixed on the floor. That mattered little to Keeler, who was not looking at the Jap's studiously emotionless face, but at the little brown hands. The hands were close clenched.

"Ever hear of that custom, Ichi?"

The Jap shook his head.

"Then it doesn't exist in Japan?"

Another preternaturally listless head-shake. But to Keeler it seemed the hands clenched just a trifle more tightly. The knuckles began to show grayish white.

"Ichi," said Keeler, shifting the theme abruptly, "do you chance to be descended from the Samurai class in Japan?"

"Yes!"

Ichi raised his head, and there was a flash of pride in the apathetic face. The hands relaxed slightly.

"I read a story about them once," Keeler rambled on. "About the Samurai. It was called 'The Nine-and-forty Ronins,' I think."

"*Seven* and forty," corrected Ichi.

"Perhaps so. I forget. But I remember hearing it was the most famous story in Japan's literature. Its hero was one of the Samurai. Didn't an incident in the story deal with the striking of a Samurai by his master or overlord? A chap called Kotsuke-no-Suki, or some such queer name?"

"Yes. But name is wrong. It was Oishi Ko—"

"Never mind the name. I don't need it. It would only clutter up my brain and fill space that some really important thing ought to occupy. The mind is nothing but a storeroom. It'll hold only just so much, and if it's stuffed with rubbish, the necessary things have to be crowded out. All we need to remember about the Ronin story just now, is that the Samurai's master struck him. And," very slowly, "that the Samurai never rested until he had tracked down, and—and killed—the man who so affronted the ancient blood of the warrior class. Ichi, do you think the Samurai in real life would have done that?"

"If not," cried Ichi, galvanized into life, "if not, then not worthy to wear the Two Swords. Outcast!"

"Would the same be true, Ichi, in the case of a *descendant* of the Samurai? A Japanese man of the present day whose master struck him?"

Ichi shrugged his shoulders. His momentary show of interest was gone. Again he was a limp, listless morsel of brown humanity.

"Would he, Ichi?" insisted Keeler.

No reply. The hands were tight clenched. The face was hidden.

"If a descendant of the Samurai were insulted and sworn at and unjustly blamed by his master, Ichi, and if his master among other things called him a 'Mongolian mongrel' and then knocked him down and then ordered him to leave his study—"

Ichi's bent head jerked backward as though it were hung on new tautened strings. His mouth fell open. His eyes, glassy with a horror his stoicism could no longer conceal, his face ashy, he glared at Keeler.

He essayed to speak. Then, with no slightest warning, he heaved forward and collapsed on the floor, his huddled frame moving jerkily in the paroxysms of a fit.

"Brayle was right, in a way," Keeler told himself, as he hurried out to call for assistance, "Ichi was the only one of the lot who didn't threaten. And—unless I'm more wrong than usual—he's the only one of the lot who made good on his debt of hate to poor Milwood."

CHAPTER IX.
Keeler Makes a Discovery.

Five minutes later, in a department car, Keeler and Chief Pyne left the Poplar Street headquarters, and started for Bay Ridge.

"Yes," Pyne was saying, in answer to a question of his companion, "he's coming around all right. Those Japs are tough. No wonder he threw a fit after all he's been through! I've seen huskier men topple over, in the same sort of conditions. It's a big strain. Poor little guy! I guess there's no danger of his trying to make a get-away. And there's no reason to connect him with the killing. As soon as he's testified at the inquest I'll turn him loose. It'll be easy enough to get hold of him for the trial. No sense in cooping up an innocent little foreigner just because he happens to have found his boss with a bullet in him."

"If you'll pardon me for suggesting it, chief," said Keeler earnestly, "I'd do nothing of the kind, if I were you."

"You don't mean to say you think there's a chance he is—"

"I don't think anything yet. But—I wouldn't turn him loose just yet if I were you."

Pyne glanced doubtfully down upon the retiring little man at his side.

"The district attorney knows his business," he rumbled, "and he wouldn't 'a' sent you up here if you hadn't known yours. I'll take your tip. But I'd be glad if you could see your way to being clearer about it."

"As soon as I'm 'clear' about it, I'll report in full to you," evaded Keeler. "Until then, just figure on one minor phase of Ichi's testimony. He slept through the thunder. He slept through the shooting. Yet a fancied call of Milwood's voice from the far end of the house woke him and brought him to the study."

Pyne gave vent to a grunt of grudging admiration.

"I said Mr. Sawyer knew what he was about when he sent you over," he said. "Just do me the favor to forget I was thinking of turning the little brown brother loose, won't you, Mr. Keeler? By the way, Mr. Keeler, do you make anything of the silver bullet? That's a new one on me. And its caliber, too. Something between a thirty-two and thirty-eight it is. No such caliber in any gun *I* ever saw. And silver. The vitriol's not so queer. That's been done often enough. Though this time there doesn't seem to be any point to it."

"I'd rather look over the place before I make any guess," replied Keeler, not a little elated at the unusual sensation of being deferred to. As a rule, it was he who did the deferring, and no one ever seemed to notice whether he did it or not.

The car had reached Bay Ridge. It turned into Marken Street on two wheels without checking its uniform speed of thirty-five miles an hour. A motor-cycle policeman ranged alongside, barking:

"Pull up to the curb, youse!"

Then recognizing the vehicle and its occupants, he saluted sheepishly and veered off. Presently the car stopped in front of the Milwood house.

A crowd of idlers, held back from trespass by the bulky presence of a policeman, loitered with morbid curiosity in front of the hedge dividing the front lawn from the street. Another policeman opened the door for Pyne and Keeler as they mounted the veranda steps of the house. Every blind was drawn; every lowered window shuttered. Moisture lay on the porch edge from the all-night rain.

"So this is your second visit?" queried Keeler, as he and Pyne passed in. "I didn't understand you had been out here before this morning."

"No, come to think of it, I didn't mention it. Yes, I ran out as soon as we got the report of the killing. How'd you know?"

Keeler was ashamed to admit that the chief's muddy footmarks—perhaps the largest footmarks on the force—were still clearly visible ahead of him on the hardwood floor of the hallway. So he said nothing, thereby strengthening with Pyne his growing repute as a detective of truly fictional genius.

They passed up two flights of stairs, and, at the head of the second flight, Pyne opened a closed door, and stepped civilly aside for Keeler to enter first.

Keeler went into the room, followed by Pyne. The shades were down, but the bright morning light made everything vividly clear. On the floor, within two feet of the open door—so near that Keeler had to skirt it to get into the room—lay the body of the dead man covered with a sheet.

Keeler barely glanced at it, then let his eyes stray around the room. It was the strangest apartment imaginable, and amply bore out Mrs. van Vleck's description of it as a library, a gun room, and a study combined. Here and there darted Keeler's eyes, searching first of all for the vitriol carboy of which both Craig and Mrs. van Vleck had spoken. It was not visible.

"You say the room is just as Ichi found it?"he asked.

"Yes," said Pyne. "Nothing touched. The body's where the opening of the door pushed it when the Jap came in—if he did come in as far on in the story as that. Our men haven't done a thing but throw a sheet over—"

"I see," answered Keeler abstractedly.

He was looking around the queer room, trying to grasp its every detail.

"The doctor says Milwood must 'a' died about twenty minutes or half an hour before the Jap turned in the alarm," continued Pyne. "That would make the time of the murder about two-fifteen or two-thirty this morning. It fits in snug with your theory about the Jap, Mr. Keeler. If he killed Milwood at two-thirty, he'd just about have had time to fix things shipshape and rehearse his story again before he called up the Fourth Avenue station."

Keeler was not listening. He was still looking around him. The study was a corner room, perhaps twenty-five by twenty feet in area, rough-ceiled and raftered, the walls toning with the pale-gray cement of the ceiling.

There were four big latticed windows, two at the front and two at the north side.

Two walls were lined, ceiling high, with full bookshelves. Shelves with a heterogeneous collection of books, massed with no effort at subject grouping or other arrangement. Grafton's "Medieval Magic" had shouldered itself between "Lucile"—in the inevitable gift-volume form—and volume three of Lecky's "European Morals." The second volume of Smollett's "Peregrine Pickle" was next-door neighbor to a no doubt scandalized Baxter's "Saints' Rest," with Darwin's "Origin of Species" on the other side.

Tomes on mining, on horse breeding, on metallurgy, on fishing, on common law, on political economy were sandwiched, helter-skelter, among trashy novels, classics, and paper-bound mine prospectuses. Rabelais elbowed Ruskin; Cagliostro's "Life" neighbored Chambers' "Lorraine."

Keeler's superorderly soul was revolted at the sight. His fingers itched to be among the books, sorting, classifying, grouping.

An enormous maroon leather couch, piled high with puffy, soft cushions of various ages, filled the space between two of the windows. Between two others was a cabinet on whose shelves were ranged, with careful neatness, hundreds of tabulated ore samples. In front of the cabinet was an acid-stained deal table on which stood a half score of bottles, together with a white mortar and pestle, two small glass retorts, a spirit lamp, a miniature acetylene outfit, a set of blowpipes, and several glass tubes.

A beautiful fumed oak desk to the left of the couch, between two of the front windows, was devoid of a single scrap of paper and even of blotting pad and ink. It had a decidedly "used" look, yet at present there was nothing on it to use.

The center of the room was taken up with an enormous table, piled with magazines and newspapers. On one corner of it lay a mechanical nail clipper, one or two nail parings scattered near by.

There were several chairs—seemingly chosen for comfort rather than for any idea of harmony, and on the floor were one or two really good rugs. One of these lay between Milwood's body and the door, the body resting on the outermost edge of it.

There were no pictures. Instead, scattered here and there around the walls, were odd bits of soft-colored drapery, some of them evidently antiques, ranging in size from six inches square to two feet in diameter. And almost every bit of drapery served as a background or setting for some unique weapon.

Here were two Malay creeses, unsheathed and crossed. There, against a patch of Damascene embroidery, hung a crooked-bladed little Syrian belt knife, its sheath made of cowhide, to which patches of red hair still adhered, and with a thimble glued to its apex. A silver-inlaid blunderbuss was fastened along a strip of Assuan work. Below it were two flintlock horse pistols. A long-barreled Arab musket, with ivory fretted around the absurdly small stock, hung near by, and a bell-mouthed eighteenth-century "gag pistol" beside it.

Antiquated revolvers of crude design—a "Queen's Arm" gun, a curved Bedouin sword—a dozen more weapons, each on drapery—strewed the walls. In one corner stood a glass-fronted gun rack, holding several modern rifles and shotguns, and a blue-barreled Colt's service revolver and a black, little automatic.

"I said he might have been killed by a symposium," mused Keeler. "And—it looks as if a symposium of weapons might have done it. No wonder the sight of all these things should have made people think of killing. No wonder they threatened."

He walked to the table and picked up, at random, one of the bottles thereon.

"Nothing doing," said Pyne, who had been viewing, with growing impatience, Keeler's slow survey of the room. "The doctor went over all of those. Not a 'burning' acid in the lot. Want to look at the body now?"

Again Keeler looked slowly around the walls, as though to photograph on his mind every detail he saw. Then he crossed to the rug by the door and knelt down beside it, at the end nearest the door and farthest from Milwood, Pyne vexedly watching him, and more and more impatient at his slowness.

Keeler was fumbling with the edge of the rug. It was held to the hard-wood floor by short tacks, one at each corner.

"The man didn't care much about the state of his floors," said Keeler. "Most people take a pride in keeping hardwood free from holes and scratches. Think of tacking his rugs down like this!"

He got up, and moved across the room, stopping occasionally. Then he returned.

"Just as I thought," he reported. "Not another rug is tacked."

"Maybe he tacked this one so it wouldn't be pushed out of place every time the door opened," suggested Pyne, not much interested. "Now, if you'll come—"

"The rug is thin, and it lies too low for the door to touch it. And these tack marks are new. See, the hammer struck this corner one glancingly, and the bright spot on the dent hasn't even a grain of dust on it. The rug itself is dusty enough."

He pulled up the two tacks on the end nearest the door and rolled the rug to one side, against the sheeted body. In the middle of the newly revealed space the hardwood flooring was marred by a huge stain. Something had burned away the shellac and bitten deep into the maple parquetry. The place looked as though a coal fire had been kindled on it.

"That's what I was looking for," said Keeler in gentle triumph.

"The deuce you were!" exclaimed Pyne. "And now that you've found it, what do you make of it?"

"Just this: Suppose I throw vitriol on you. Only part of it can strike you. What becomes of the rest? It must spatter or else land with a splash somewhere, mustn't it?"

"Why—why, I never thought—"

"Pour a glass of water over a man. The water doesn't all stick to him, does it? Some of it must reach the ground or the walls. And the wet spot will show where the watered person was standing. It's the same with vitriol. I've been looking for the spot. And now that I find the vitriol mark, it is in a pool, not spattered. Milwood must have been lying on the ground when the murderer poured it on him. His face was just above that charred spot. So much of Ichi's story is true. The body *was* found lying against the door."

"Mr. Keeler," said the chief, "I don't mind telling you I felt a little sore at your being sent to horn in on this case. I take it back. It's a pleasure to work with you. Go ahead with what you were saying."

"This rug was not on the spot when Milwood was killed," resumed Keeler, vastly pleased at the unaccustomed praise, "that's evident. There was no rug here, or it would have been burned through. For some reason, the murderer took the rug from another part of the room, spread it over the stain, tacked it down so it couldn't be kicked aside by accident, and then laid Milwood's body on it."

"But why? *Why?*"

"Chief, I'm not Sherlock Holmes. I'm only a poor dub, working in the dark. I don't know why the murderer did such an unnecessary thing. I don't know, either," he added, a sudden pucker in his narrow forehead, "why the body should have been put so close to the door that a person from outside couldn't get in without pushing it away. I don't see how the murderer did that, and then got out of the door himself. He—he *couldn't!*" finished Keeler, looking up apologetically at the chief.

"Will you look at the body, Mr. Keeler?" asked Pyne, with a new respect, pulling aside the sheet as he spoke.

Keeler looked, withdrew his eyes with something very like a shudder, then forced himself to look again.

The merciless acid had done fearful mischief to the cameolike face. It had seared the wavy yellow hair like living flame. It had cut into the firm, bronzed flesh even as it had cut into the hardwood parquetry. After a single brief scrutiny of the almost unrecognizable head and face, Keeler drew a corner of the sheet across them.

The body was clad in a handsome and well-cut sack suit of light gray, the cloth riddled, about neck and chest and shoulders, with vitriol burns. Part of one shoulder of the coat was almost burned away.

The left arm, its fingers convulsively clenched, was flung across the chest. The right hand, open, its fingers asprawl, was at the dead man's side. The hand was long, muscular, shapely; the hand of a man who works his brain rather than his body. The nails had been newly cut, not roundly, as with knife or scissors.

Keeler's glance roved to the corner of the table, where lay the patent nail clipper, the two or three parings still strewn, untidily, near it. Pyne's glance followed his.

"Even if all the rest of his body had been burned away," remarked the chief, "that would be enough to identify him. He gave a dinner last night, you know. Clipped his nails, I suppose, to groom up for company."

Keeler visualized the love scene between Milwood and Mrs. van Vleck. Little as he knew of women, he realized that neither Milwood nor any other man would make love across a table on which nail parings lay.

"No," he decided, "he cut his nails after his guests went away."

"How do you figure that?" asked the chief.

"And," went on Keeler, abstractedly glancing at the open right hand as he spoke, "he dressed in this gray suit afterward, too. He would have been in evening clothes at a dinner. I have reason to think, chief, that Milwood planned to leave here very suddenly, either last night or early this morning. When his guests had gone, he made ready for flight by changing into traveling clothes, by trimming his nails, and by cleaning out his desk over there. Before he could pack, he was murdered."

"But why should a man making a get-away stop to cut his nails?"

"He— Chief!" broke off Keeler excitedly. "Would you mind taking a look out of each of those windows and seeing if there's any way a fairly active man could have climbed in from outside?"

The chief turned toward the nearest window. Keeler, with a succession of swift motions, seized Milwood's clenched left hand, forced it open, snatched from its clammy palm something tiny and glittering, thrust the object into his own vest pocket, and re-clenched the lifeless hand.

"This first window," called Pyne over his shoulder, "has a straight drop of twenty feet or so to the—"

"Never mind," said Keeler. "I'll look at the rest of them afterward."

A queer note of ill-suppressed excitement in his voice made Pyne turn to look at him. Keeler had picked up the dead man's right hand and was blinking at its newly manicured fingers.

"What's the matter?" asked Pyne. "What's the idea of staring so close at the nails? Are you nearsighted?"

"Y-yes," babbled Keeler, rising dazedly to his feet. "I—I suppose I *am* just a trifle nearsighted. I must be."

"You look like you'd seen a creditor," said Pyne inquisitively, "or had about two drinks too many. Are you sick? The look of Milwood been too much for you?"

"No," denied Keeler, by a supreme effort steadying his voice and forcing a nonchalant manner. "No, I'm all right. Bending over made me dizzy, that's all."

"Then shall we look at the rest of those windows?"

"Yes. Yes. Of course. If you don't mind. And—and, chief, you can let Ichi go free as soon as you like. The sooner the better. He didn't kill Milwood!"

CHAPTER X.
The Mud's Story.

"No; Ichi didn't kill Milwood," reiterated Keeler.

"Oh, he didn't, eh!" snapped Police Chief Pyne. "Then who in thunder did?"

"I don't know. I don't believe anybody will ever know." He was staring, slack-jawed, at the body.

Gradually the new look of admiration and respect on Pyne's face was beginning to fade.

"Well?" queried the chief.

Keeler did not answer. Stupidly he stood there; his eyes dull.

"Does that mean you're going to quit, Mr. Keeler?" inquired Pyne, trying to revive the other's interest by elephantine sarcasm. "You've found this case harder than you supposed when you first tackled it? And you don't feel called upon to tax your brain by struggling with such a tough problem? I don't blame you."

Keeler mumbled something unintelligible.

"I've only this to say," Pyne went on, the sarcasm gone from his voice, leaving it peevish—"I've only this to say, and that is, you've fooled me. I thought you were 'there.' That's because I watched you playing a game I'm no good at. I don't claim to be particularly brilliant or quick-witted. So those pretty tricks of observation and rapid-fire deduction you produced for my benefit took me in. They made me think you were just the man to push this case through to a conviction. But now you're playing *my* game. The 'plug, plug' kind. As a sure-fire detective, you're only a false alarm, after all."

Keeler glanced slowly around at him.

"I never claimed to be a detective," he said. "I'm just—"

"You can back out of this now, if you like," Pyne continued, with mounting heat, "but I'm going to stick till I find out who murdered Milwood. I've tackled it. And I'm going to see it through. Not only because it's my job, but because it's my *way*. That's what's earned me the place I'm in: the fact that I don't let go of any case I once take hold of until I've gone as far as the trail goes."

"Chief!" Keeler broke in.

The other, partly in anger, partly in illustration of his boasted tenacity, had clenched one beefy fist.

"Do that again, will you?" Keeler requested, with charming irrelevance.

The chief stared blankly at him.

"Do what again?"

Keeler pointed to his hand.

"Just close that once more for me," he repeated.

Pyne's eyes went slowly to his hand, now hanging relaxed at his side. And slowly, with brows bent over the task, he covered his palm with his fingers. The result was the loose, awkward grip in which a man might hold a live sparrow. Following the operation intently, Keeler nodded.

"What's the idea?" asked Pyne.

"Thanks," Keeler said, with a return of the absent-minded glaze to his eyes. "That's what I thought."

"Thought *what?*"

"Nothing," was the abstracted reply. "I—I'm trying to think."

"You asked me to clench my fist," persisted the chief. "Was it a trick or a joke or—what? What's it got to do with—"

Keeler started out of his reverie once more.

"I guess it hasn't anything to do with it," he agreed.

"Well," grunted Pyne. "I've no time to loaf around asking fool questions. I'm going to get busy here. As long as you're out of it—"

"Out of it?" repeated Keeler, looking blank.

"You said," retorted the chief, "that you didn't know who murdered him. And that you didn't think anybody would ever know. The case is too much for you. So if that means you're going off it—"

"Chief," Keeler earnestly assured him, "I was never more 'on' it than I am at this minute. Please believe that. You've got me all wrong. But," he went on, with a timid man's willingness to share all the blame in a conversational misunderstanding, "that's my fault. I should have expressed myself differently. I—I shouldn't have said that at all. I should have kept it to myself. But it was sort of jarred out of me by the surprise I got—"

Pyne was eying him; his scorn for Keeler's supposed quitting under fire changing to a frown of mystification.

"I'm glad you aren't dropping out," he said encouragingly: "Because you made a hit with me by the way you took hold. I can't see what makes you think this case is going to be so difficult to solve, anyway. You haven't been here twenty minutes. In that time you've discovered that the rug under the body, there, was tacked down. That it was done by the murderer, to hide where the spattering of the vitriol, that cut his victim's face away, had burned the floor beneath him. And—well, that's about all, isn't it? Except the good tips you gave me on Ichi. But what about the silver bullet? And what about the murderer's get-away? You said the body's lying so close to the door that Ichi had to shove it aside when he came into the room would keep the murderer from going out through the same door. You're sure—"

"That is true," Keeler assented. "You see, chief, if the body was found lying almost directly against that shut door, the murderer couldn't have passed through it, shut the door, and laid the body where it was discovered."

"Well?" prompted Pyne.

Keeler glanced around the room. His eyes traveled to the raftered ceiling of cement, and thence to the four latticed windows.

"Sure," nodded the chief, following the direction of his glance. "That's the only way he could have taken. The window I looked at has a sheer drop of twenty feet to the ground. Now, let's see—"

"Then," said Keeler briskly, "the same thing must be true of the window beside it. A man—er—couldn't jump twenty feet without breaking something, I suppose?"

"Both legs, probably," the chief curtly agreed.

"Yes," said Keeler thoughtfully. "Then it's the other two windows we'd better investigate. There may be a drainpipe, or something of the sort, that he could have used to climb down by."

Pyne, crossing the room a step or two in advance of him, pushed up first one and then the other of the two latticed windows on the north side of the room. Keeler, as he put his head and shoulders through one window, beheld the same amount of Pyne's anatomy extended, Punch-and-Judy fashion, through the other. And Pyne, in significant silence, was pointing a stubby forefinger at a tin pipe which ran down the side of the house, between them, to the ground.

"Would it hold a man's weight, do you think?" Keeler questioned.

By the way of answer, Pyne grasped the drainpipe in both hands and shook it—or exerted all his strength to do so. The pipe gave back not a tremor to the strenuous tugging.

"That's the way our man took," commented Pyne, with grim conviction.

Keeler, leaning farther out over the sill, was looking down at a moistly trampled space on the turf of the side lawn at the end of the drainpipe. The chief's eyes followed his.

"Look!" Pyne exclaimed suddenly. "This is the way he took. See the muddy footprints going down the side of the pipe?"

Keeler shook his head.

"What's the matter?" blurted the chief. "That's the way the man took, I tell you. But you don't have to take my word for it. Use your eyes. You don't want any more evidence, do you, that this is the way he went down?"

"Chief," said Keeler, with an unwonted touch of impatience, "why don't *you* use your eyes? There's mud on the ground, down there. But there's none in this room."

"What of that? He—"

"And another thing. When a man climbs a pipe, or anything of that sort, he uses his feet to aid his hands in making the ascent. But when he comes down, his legs are usually wrapped around the pipe to steady him. His feet don't need to come into it at all. Those muddy footprints don't show me that a man went down this pipe. But only that a man most certainly came *up* it!"

"And never came into the room at all?"

"He brought no mud in."

"But why, man? *Why?* It's silly! We're looking for the way the man got out. And—"

"And, instead, we've found the way he got in? Fifty men may or may not have shinned down that pipe, to get out. But it's a certainty they all did it before the murderer climbed up."

"How do you make that out?"

"Once more, chief, if you won't mind my suggesting it, why not use your eyes? It isn't a Sherlock Holmes problem. It's just a bit of observation. See that mud? The patch of it just below you, for instance."

"Yes," grumbled Pyne, staring sullenly at a thick smear of dried earth the size of a man's palm. "What about it?"

"It is nearly half an inch thick, and its edges on one end are curled upward, almost to a sharp line."

"Well?"

"Would it look like that if a man's body or even a child's body had rubbed against it, sliding down the pipe?"

"N-no," vouchsafed Pyne. "It'd be flatter'n a sheet of paper. I see. But— but I *don't* see."

"Don't see what?"

"It's all impossible!" snorted the chief. "We've shown the murderer couldn't have gotten out by the door unless he'd reached his arm in afterward and pulled the body up close to the jamb. And there'd be no motive in doing that. Nobody but a fool would have thought of doing it. So he got out by the window and the water pipe. It's the only other way out. And here you've proved, clear as day, that he *couldn't* have slid down by way of the water pipe, without his body rubbing off the mud marks. And the mud marks aren't rubbed off."

"Yes," assented Keeler dully.

"Then," fumed the chief, "the case stands like this: A man shinned up the water pipe. His shoes were covered with mud. He stopped outside the sill and rubbed every bit of mud off his shoes, so that not a scrap of it could get on this floor. Then he killed Milwood and poured acid on him and tacked a rug over the acid stains and laid the body close to the door; and—and melted away, or else made his trip down the pipe again, in the dark, dodging every piece of mud he'd left there. It's a dandy story, isn't it—for the foolish house!"

"It's an impossibility," supplemented Keeler. "And yet—it's the nearest possible solution. Unless—"

He pulled forward a chair, stood on it, and pushed at the transom above the door. He could not move it. He fumbled at its catch. It did not help him to stir the glass-lined frame.

"Transom, hey?" cried Pyne. "Good idea!"

"No," contradicted Keeler. "It isn't a good idea. It isn't even a bad idea. It's no idea at all. The transom won't move."

He carried his chair out into the hall and mounted it again.

"Nailed shut," he reported. "Putty all over both nails, to keep the light-gray tone of the woodwork from being broken by the rusty heads of nails. So much for that theory."

"That proves it," said Pyne, in heavy irony. "He didn't get out by the door or by the transom or by the window. So he just stood in the middle of the room and flapped his arms a couple of times and crowed; and then vanished. It's simple."

"Chief," said Keeler plaintively, "did you ever read any of our great detective stories?"

"Sure! They're the nicest fairy tales ever. I love 'em. Why?"

"Because," said Keeler, in genuine regret, "I wish I was one of the marvelous detectives in those books. With a magnifying glass and a set of deductions and the dust on the floor, I'd have the whole thing worked out by now. And," with a heartfelt sigh, "I don't even own a magnifying glass. And I wouldn't know how to detect clews with one if I had it. I'm just a dub. As Milwood once told me I was."

CHAPTER XI.
CRAIG TALKS—AND WON'T TALK.

Leaving the house of death, Keeler declined the chief's invitation to ride back to headquarters with him in his car—a sore temptation, for he had not ridden in an automobile four times in his colorless life—and, saying he had an appointment and would return later to headquarters, set off down the street afoot.

At the first drug store he turned in and made for the solitary telephone booth the place contained. A fat woman was occupying it. And she continued to occupy it for an interminable time; making grotesque mouths as she talked, and now and then tossing her head coquettishly.

Keeler mentally cursed the dire disease of telephonitis and fumed like a leashed dog that is balked at the very start of the scent. After an æon or so, the woman emerged, leaving the stuffy booth redolent of cheap perfume and a white dab of nose powder on the black rubber top of the transmitter.

Keeler bolted into the scarce-vacated cubby-hole as might a rabbit into its burrow; and actually summoned enough brazenness to shove aside a pasty-faced youth who was edging toward the booth. So harsh an action, on Keeler's part, was equivalent to a street fight to an ordinary man.

He was in the booth and had shut the door behind him before he realized that he did not know the "number" of the man he wanted to call; and the telephone book was on a stand outside the booth. Also that the pasty-faced boy was loitering alertly in the space between booth and book.

Keeler emerged from the booth. The boy bounded wrigglingly into his place.

"Excuse me," Keeler timidly addressed him, "but it's only fair to advise you to wipe off the transmitter carefully before you use the telephone. I'm supposed to be perfectly well again—in fact, I'm discharged as cured. But after smallpox there's always likely to be—"

The boy waited to hear no more of the faltering warning. If the booth had been in flames he could not have departed from it more promptly. He circled Keeler widely, and left the store at a rate no sprinter of the Half Moon Club's track team need have despised.

Keeler looked up Craig's office number in the gray telephone book. Then, this time carrying the book along with him, he reëntered the booth; right ungallantly taking precedence over a sweet young thing who had just come into the store, and, rapt-eyed, was bearing down upon the hapless telephone.

He called up Craig's office; only to learn that the metallurgist had not come to work that morning, but had sent word that a heavy cold would keep him at home. Keeler, fumbling the book's greasy leaves in the half light of the booth, managed to decipher the number of Craig's house telephone and called him up.

In a voice that bore no audible traces of a cold, Craig replied to his hail.

"This is Keeler," announced the little man. "Heard about Milwood?"

"I read it a few minutes ago," came the reply. "It's a ghastly thing."

"I've just come from his house," went on Keeler. "Can I drop over to your rooms, on my way back to New York? There are one or two new discoveries about the case I'd like to tell you."

"Why should you wish to tell them to *me?*" demanded Craig ungraciously.

"Only that we three were from the same place and he was a friend of yours, and—"

"He wasn't!" snapped Craig.

"And," mildly added Keeler, "you were one of the last people who saw him alive. I supposed you'd be interested to hear—"

"Oh, all right. Come on."

Keeler made his way to New York and to Washington Square, where, in a rambling old bachelor apartment house, Alan Craig had a suite of rooms. Craig himself came to the door of the apartment to admit him. If the host's voice gave no token of the cold he was supposed to have, his face, at least, was that of a decidedly sick man. It was gray and haggard, and his eyes were bloodshot.

He had not yet shaved, and there was a tousled air about him, as of one who has slept in his clothes. This supposition was, of course, quite untenable, since the evening suit he had worn at the Milwood dinner had been changed for loose brown tweeds.

Craig held the stump of a chewed cigar between his teeth. He seemed anything but glad to see Keeler; and his customary pleasant demeanor toward the little man was replaced by something very like gruffness.

"Come in!" he vouchsafed, leading the way to a living room that reeked with both fresh and stale smoke.

"You look sick," commented Keeler, as he followed the big fellow into the room and perched himself on the edge of the only comfortable chair in sight.

"I am. Touch of malaria, I think. I'm taking the day off."

"It was a heavy cold," meekly suggested Keeler, "when you phoned your office. Whatever it is, you look all in."

"I am," said Craig, adding irritably: "Dive into one of those leather chairs—can't you?—instead of balancing yourself on that torture seat like a measly canary."

"Thanks," twittered Keeler, shifting to the recesses of a big leather armchair, opposite the window divan on which Craig had just thrown himself. He did not add that he had postponed taking a permanent seat until he could first learn what Craig's own location was to be, and how the light would strike the latter's face.

"Now, then," pursued Craig, "what new things have you heard about poor Milwood? More than the morning papers told, I mean. And how did you happen to be over at his house to-day? You said you were going on vacation."

"I was. I am. This is it. I'm on vacation now. I'm taking it by doing a little amateur work on any own account in the Milwood case. It amuses me, you know, to dig into these things. And I can't do any harm, even if I don't unearth much."

"Queer taste! I'd as soon spend a vacation in jail."

"It wouldn't be a bad place to spend one," agreed Keeler, on reflection. "A fellow could pick up a lot in jail, if he used his eyes."

"What new things about the case did you want to tell me? The papers say his butler, or valet—that Jap—is held as a witness, and that Milwood was robbed."

"He wasn't robbed," gently corrected Keeler. "At least his clothes weren't."

"How do you know?"

"I don't say his watch and rings and cash weren't stolen. But I do say they weren't taken off the body. The vest buttonhole that a watch chain passes through was buttoned. A murderer in a hurry wouldn't unbutton the vest to take out the chain and then stop to button it again. He wouldn't pull the coat back over the watch pocket again, either. The hands were clenched, too. There were no rings on them. A man who opened the fingers to steal the rings wouldn't close them again. It's the same way with the pockets. They don't gape as they would if an outsider's hand had gone through them after the man was dead."

"Milwood may have been held up, first, and forced to give his valuables to—"

"And then buttoned his vest again and—"

"No. Probably not. You're a clever little cuss to notice such things, Keeler. You were always like that, even when you were a kid. You had a positive genius for seeing things that were in plain sight, but that nobody else ever bothered to see. I remember once, you saw—"

"Craig," shyly interrupted Keeler, "what were you quarreling about with Milwood last evening?"

Craig jumped to his feet.

"Who says I was quarreling with him?" he growled. "The police?"

"No. Oh, no. I didn't say anything to them about it. I thought I'd rather talk it over with you, first. That's the main reason I'm here."

"You said there'd been 'new discoveries'—"

"There have. I made them. I'll come to those later. But, first of all, would you mind telling me about that quarrel?"

"Why should I? What quarrel? Who's been blabbing?"

"Why, no one's been blabbing," Keeler soothed him. "No one heard it, except me. At least, I don't think any one else heard it. And I heard only snatches of it."

"Where were you?"

"Downstairs," answered Keeler, to whom it did not occur, for a moment, to make a mystery of his knowledge and thus strive to impress or scare his hearer. "I was waiting to see Milwood. I sat down in an alcove of the hall. There was a speaking tube right above me. I didn't know it was there," he hastened to say, in boyish apology, "till afterward. I didn't mean to be an eavesdropper or do anything sneaky. Honestly, I didn't. The words just seemed to come to me out of nowhere."

"And you heard—"

"I heard Milwood ask you to indorse some ore. And I heard you say it was 'salted'—whatever that means. And at first you wouldn't agree to indorse it—"

"At first?" echoed Craig, in wrathful surprise. "At *first?* What do you mean?"

"Well," said Keeler, with visible reluctance, and wiggling about in his voluminous chair seat, "I—I was pretty badly disappointed, I tell you frankly. I've—I've always liked you rather well, Craig. And I've always felt I could bank on your squareness and—"

"What on earth are you blithering about, man? As for 'squareness'—"

"It's none of my business," said Keeler deprecatingly, "so you needn't get sore. You asked the question, you know. You asked me what I meant. And since you *did* ask—I was a bit dazed at your saying you'd sell your indorsement, to that swindler, if you could get your price."

"*I?*" roared Craig. "Why, if you heard—"

"Yes, and I heard you, afterward, trying to salve your conscience with just such a rage as you're getting into now," added Keeler, standing manfully to his guns. "You said he was a 'yellow dog'—or he said you were; I couldn't make out which; and you said something about his using strong language and he threatened you—or—"

"What sort of rigmarole is this? Let's get back to the beginning. If you mean to say I consented to accept a bribe—"

"You did. You said you had your price. Then there was a buzzing and I missed some of the talk. But afterward I heard Milwood say: 'Then that's settled.' And a minute later the two of you were quarreling."

"Look here, Keeler," said Craig pleasantly, "you've got this all tangled. Will you believe me if I try to straighten it out for you?"

Craig had grown suddenly cool. Unnaturally cool, it seemed to Keeler, who was watching him closely. The man seemed to be putting a strong restraint on himself.

"Go ahead," adjured Keeler.

"Milwood wanted a statement from me. I refused. He offered me a bribe."

"I heard that much," observed Keeler.

"I told him I had my price. So he said: 'Then that's settled. How much?' And I told him: 'My price for doing the dirty work you want done is just exactly seven billion dollars.' "

"Huh?" queried Keeler, puzzled.

"You see, I'd answered him in the only language he'd understand. If I'd kept on being indignant, he'd have thought I was bluffing. I had to put the reply in terms he'd grasp. And he grasped it. Then I lost hold of myself a bit, and told him what a yellow dog he was. He warned me I was using strong language, considering there were several loaded guns in the room. And I laughed at his hint, and said I was safe enough, and that he wouldn't be such a fool as to start a murder scandal. Also that I could probably reach one of the guns as quickly as he could. It was windy talk, of course. But we were both excited."

"And that was all?"

"That was—about all."

"You're sure?"

"All that concerns anybody except a certain—"

"Miss Madge Carr?" asked Keeler innocently.

Craig turned on him in hot indignation.

"What do you mean by that?" he demanded.

"I? I don't mean anything by it. You seemed to forget the rest of your talk with Milwood, and I was trying to prompt you."

"What's that got to do with—"

"With Miss Carr? I don't know. I don't even know her, or who she is. But you and Milwood were quarreling over her."

Craig, with manifest difficulty, checked a fierce retort and said, in genuine pleading:

"Keeler, you're surely not going to tell this to the police? You're surely not going to drag her name into—"

"I'm not doing anything—yet. Except to get at so much of the truth as will help me unravel this tangle. If you care to tell me—"

"I threatened to expose Milwood's mine fake," said Craig sulkily. "He told me, if I did, he'd make trouble for me with Miss Carr. He had found out, I suppose, that I care for her. It's not an easy thing to talk about to another man. I told him to leave her name out of the talk. And I told him he soiled her name by the mere mention of it. Then I got out."

"Walking around a carboy of vitriol?"

"You saw as well as heard! You said you were downstairs in the hall!"

There was almost dread in Craig's voice, as at the supernatural. But it was no part of Keeler's plan to play on such a chord. So he answered:

"I heard him warn you not to knock it over."

"Oh!" laughed Craig, relieved. "Yes. That's so. He had it up there for experiments. That was all. I went downstairs then. Afterward—"

"Afterward?"

"Afterward," finished Craig, after a pause, "I went home."

Keeler rose with a sigh.

"Craig," said he, "I'm sorry you don't think it's worth while to be more honest with me."

"Honest?" flared Craig. "I—"

"Oh, you've been honest in all you've told me. I know enough of human nature to guess when a man's lying. But you haven't told me all, or even half. Why haven't you?"

"I've told you all you had any right to ask—and more. What in blazes do you mean, Keeler, by butting in on this case? It's no affair of yours."

"I'm trying to make it my affair—as far as you're concerned—to keep it from being an affair of the police. If they know what I know, they'll arrest you."

Long and earnestly, and with troubled doubt, Craig looked at the little man who blinked up at him so friendlily. At last he said, as if on impulse:

"Oh, all right! I'll tell you what little more I know. There's no good reason why I shouldn't. You'll give me your word it won't go any farther?"

"Why, certainly. I'm not a policeman."

"Very good. What do you want to know first? About my going back to Milwood's study after the other guests left, or—"

"Suppose," ventured Keeler, "suppose you begin by telling me how I happened to find *this?* It was placed in the dead man's hand."

He drew something from his pocket and held it out on his palm for inspection. Craig stared at it as if he were in a mesmeric trance.

"How did I come to find this clenched in his hand?" asked Keeler.

Craig's knees buckled under him. He collapsed, rather than seated himself, on the divan, and buried his blanched face in both hands.

"Go, please!" he muttered hoarsely. "Go!"

CHAPTER XII.
Craig Shuts Up.

Keeler hesitated an instant, his non-aggressive soul taxed to its utmost to make him remain where he was not wanted. Then he resolutely sat down again, and, with the harsh fierceness of a cornered baby rabbit, he made answer:

"I am not going. Not yet. I must get this business straight."

Craig said nothing. Overcoming his momentary emotion he straightened himself and turned a masklike, drawn face to his caller. It was evident he had himself well in hand once more; and it was also evident that his self-control was bought by tremendous will power.

"Craig," said Keeler persuasively, "you've got to tell me about this. I'm not asking through curiosity—though I'd be less—or more—than human, if I wasn't aching with curiosity about it. I'm asking for your own sake. To help you."

No reply. Keeler went on:

"Don't you see you're putting yourself in a hole? This thing I found in the dead man's hand—and your quarrel with Milwood, and your threat to kill him—and your refusal to say anything. All this is the sort of thing the police love to work on."

Craig shrugged his shoulders.

"Whatever you may say or may have said to me," promised Keeler, "I'll keep to myself. You have my word for it. But you've *got* to be frank with me. Can't you see that?"

"No," was the curt answer, "I can't! And I can't see that this affair is any of your business. You're not a cop. Keep out of it. In any case, you'll get nothing from me."

Keeler tried another tack.

"I never owned a dress suit," he said irrelevantly, "so I don't know all the wrinkles and rules of evening clothes. But I've often thought I'd like to own one if I ever get rich enough. That's why I read with a lot of interest a little pamphlet I found on a seat in the subway one night. It was published by a tailor concern and it was called 'Correct Costumes for Men.' It had pictures in it. Pictures of dandy-looking men who had no stomachs, and whose hair was brushed fine. I tried to brush my own hair like that," he added, smoothing his thinly bristling head, "but it wouldn't stay put."

Craig looked at him in frowning perplexity. Keeler continued:

"I read the part about dress suits two or three times, because I couldn't understand all of it. One thing, for instance: It said: 'Watches, watch chains and key chains are not worn with evening clothes.' That must be a misprint. Of course, a man could carry his key chain mussed up in his pocket along with his keys, where it wouldn't show. And he could carry a watch without a chain. But I'll bet anything he'd carry a watch. Now, wouldn't he? I've kind of wanted to ask somebody that knew, but I've always been afraid I'd be guyed. Don't you wear a watch with a dress suit?"

"No."

"Not at all?"

"Of course not. If you don't mind, I'd rather chat with you some other time, Keeler. I don't mean to be rude, and you're a good little chap. But I don't feel up to talking to any one to-day."

Keeler rose to go. At the door he stopped to ask:

"Then you didn't even wear your watch and chain to Milwood's last night? I don't see how you could tell what time to go home. You were in evening dress, but I'll bet you had a watch tucked away somewhere on you."

"Well, I didn't. Good-by!"

Keeler's hand dropped from the doorknob and he came back into the room. "Then," he asked, with unwonted abruptness, once more opening his hand and disclosing the object in his palm, "how did this—"

"You're right," broke in Craig, with sudden volubility. "Quite right. You'd win the bet. I forgot. I wore my watch. I remember now—in my waistcoat pocket. The chain was on it, and stuffed into the pocket, too. I remember I pulled it out to—"

"To see the time? No, you didn't, old man. Forgive me for contradicting you, but you didn't. When you stopped to talk to me at the Half Moon Club grill, you put your hand to your pocket the way a man does when he's feeling for his watch. And then you looked all around the room till you could get a sight of the grillroom clock. I noticed, because—"

"I was wearing my watch—and my watch chain!" rasped Craig.

Keeler shook his head hopelessly, and once more changed the subject.

"Your fists are both tight clenched," he observed. "I've noticed how men's fists clench when they're telling lies. It's a funny thing," he hurried on, as Craig took an angry step toward him. "It's a funny thing how little observation most people have. For instance: When a man clenches his fist he curls the fingers inward, so that the nails touch the palm. Yet, if you should try to close up another man's fist for him you'd probably close it so the balls of the finger tips touched the palm. Like *this!*"

Craig scarcely looked. In fact, to Keeler, it seemed as though he did not look at all. So the little man once more laboriously folded his right hand's fingers, nails outward, and thrust the awkwardly doubled fist in front of Craig's eyes. The gesture bore about as much resemblance to a threat as did the bunched fingers to an ordinarily clenched fist.

"Like this!" he repeated.

"Well? What of it?"

"If you were in a rage, or in pain or excitement, or—or in a death agony, you'd never think of clenching your fist this way. Would you, now?" pursued Keeler.

"No. No one would. What does all this idiocy lead to, anyhow? And won't you clear out? I want to be alone."

"You're right," beamed Keeler. "No one would. No one of his own accord would clench his fist like this. And yet—that's how the dead man's fist was clenched!"

He paused, with a mild effort at dramatic effect. Craig was scarcely listening. Disappointed, Keeler continued:

"His fist was closed like that. I noticed it. The police didn't. That's why I said, just now, how funny it is that most people have so little observation. The man never closed his own fist like that. It was closed for him!"

"Closed for him?"

"Yes. By some one else—after he was dead. And the same person who closed it, closed it over this thing I showed you. He put the thing in the man's hand and then closed the fingers over it. He put it there to be found. It's lucky *I* found it, eh, instead of the police?"

"And now you've found it," rapped out Craig, "what are you going to do about it?"

"*Do* about it? Why, nothing. I came here to ask *you* about it. What else should I do?"

"You're a white little man—a thoughtful little man, Keeler," said Craig. "I'm sorry I was so grouchy to you. It was decent of you to hide it and bring it away. It might have caused no end of trouble."

"It might."

"But," pursued Craig, "it won't."

Taking up the object from the table—where Keeler had momentarily laid it while he was illustrating the odd method of fist clenching—Craig tossed it into the very heart of the coal fire that smoldered in the grate. Keeler took an impulsive step toward the fireplace, then paused, shrugged his shoulders, and turned again to Craig.

"How did it come to be in his dead hand?" he asked.

"I've nothing to say."

"For your own sake—"

"I've nothing to say."

"Craig, in your quarrel with Milwood, you and he spoke of one Madge Carr—as maybe I've mentioned. She was one of the subjects of your quarrel. In fact, she seemed to be the very heart of it. Who is she?"

"Leave her out of this."

"I'd like to, but I can't. She's—she's quite important. I must find her."

"You must not!"

"Who is she?"

"I can't tell you any more."

"Not even under promise of secrecy?"

"Not under any conditions at all!"

"Where does she live?"

"I shall not tell you anything. She has nothing to do with this case. You hear me? She has *nothing* to do with it!"

"Craig," said Keeler slowly, "you're talking pretty loud, and your hands are clenched pretty tight—just to tell me she has nothing to do with this. Any fool would know she had, if only from your manner. I've got to find her. I wish you'd help me."

"If you try to—"

"Don't bother to threaten me, old man," begged Keeler. "Threatened men live long. Unless they happen to be named Milwood. And even then—Good-by!"

CHAPTER XIII.
Ichi Remembers Some Details.

A Fifth Avenue bus lumbered clumsily under Washington Arch. As it swerved to complete the circle, a small Italian boy jumped from the curb to pursue a tormentor. The chauffeur jammed on the rasping, crunching brakes and brought his ponderous vehicle to a swaying stop. Then he said things.

Shrill, nerve-wracked anathemas fell on Keeler's ears. He was balancing on the bottom step of the old-fashioned, high-stooped brownstone house where Craig had his rooms.

The interview had left him without his usual clean-edged deductions. He was vague and bothered by "theories" that were as fickle to one objective point as a flighty weathercock in a high gale. Craig, inclined to be more than reticent, acted as an unlooked-for stumbling-block.

"Lemme ever catch ye under me wheels again, ye little wop, ye! I'll grind ye to a paste! I'll go wreck ye father's banana stand! I'll—"

The wild threats died upon the shifting breeze. Keeler walked to the corner. He hadn't indulged in a bus ride since last Easter, when his Cousin Hetty, from Central Valley, came to visit. On one occasion she had been his companion in a delirious feast of stewed bananas and prune salad at a physical-culture restaurant. This revelry was supplemented by a bus ride, where, between trying to keep his derby on and extracting the tip end of a persistent feather from his watering eyes, he had pointed out the homes of various millionaires—and their shortcomings, as he knew them.

A bus ride now would be just the thing for him. He would take off his furry soft hat, rest it on his knees, and let the breeze sweep the cobwebs from his brain. A bus is an unbusinesslike vehicle, he decided. It is reserved for ladies who wish they owned automobiles and men who like to smoke on the way uptown. Being neither, he censured himself as he ascended the narrow, twisting steps. But on a working vacation one may indulge in indiscretions of the milder type.

The little registering machine, gripped in the grimy palm of the conductor, snatched his dime from him in one greedy gulp. It startled him. He resented its quick decision.

He lifted his hat carefully from his head and held it pinned to his knees. A playful gust tossed a lock of his fast-thinning hair. Automatically, he replaced his hat. He knew how easily he caught cold.

The bus rolled on past a squat, white hotel, where old-fashioned full-length windows opened on to tiny iron balconies. Within could be seen groups of animated young people bent on sampling the odd dishes for which the cuisine was noted.

Keeler's eye rested with horror on the trays laden with hors d'œuvres—those fascinating appetite enticers that are consumed mainly by those whose appetites need no enticing. To Keeler, food of that caliber savored of soda mints and sanitariums.

In a sudden, guilty revulsion to duty, he drew from his pocket the sheet of club note paper on which he'd jotted down his "suspected list."

He reread item No. I:

Man unknown—threatened to kill Milwood—unless—unless what?—quarters—eighths—fractions. Whatever they may mean.

Any one who was sufficiently calm and scientific to hold intelligible conversation in fractions wouldn't be likely to be driven to murder that same night. He had found that there were few cold-blooded, premeditated murders in so-called "high life." They were mostly the result of wine-drenched arguments, with here and there a freak affair, such as the strange disappearance of a member of a yachting party, or an automobile accident—presumably accidental.

And yet, the fraction man, whoever he was, might have been a personality erratic enough to combine, successfully, arithmetic and assassination. But who was he? Who?

Keeler tapped the slip of paper with the silver pocket pencil his mother had given him five Christmases before. He saw with dismay that the constant wear it had received had almost obliterated his monogram—and monograms were his almost one weakness. He forgot that the oftener he personalized his possessions by having those three letters engraved, the oftener was he likely to be asked what the middle one stood for.

The bus stopped with a sick jolt. Five seconds later, a breath of some strange perfume, suggestively Oriental, greeted his nostrils. A woman in something shimmering and pink had seated herself beside him.

Keeler shrank against the rail. His small, neat self assumed imaginary bulk and inelegance. He felt he was taking up too much of the seat; his collar button bored into his flesh; his feet, instead of resting comfortably on the floor, were balancing nervously on tip-toe. It was so that well-gowned, well-groomed, well-poised women always affected him.

He suddenly wondered whether, maybe, the surface car might not be more satisfactory; whether he could get off without disturbing anybody. He had about decided to stick it out when he caught the lady's eyes fastened on his hands.

Some one had told him, once, that he had the hand of an artist. Just at that moment he wondered how he could ever have entertained the idea. His hands were actually growing, under his horrified gaze, and the fingers had turned to the proverbial thumbs.

He did not know that a sheet of paper, covered with writing, acts as an irresistible magnet to the least curious passenger in a public vehicle. The lady had caught sight of the words, "threatened to kill," and upon this meaty nucleus had built, in one minute, a tragedy with all the weirdness of a Poe and the sincere brutality of a Gorky.

Keeler pressed the little electric button at his left and rose. He swayed down the narrow aisle, clutching his paper, bumping the shoulders of one passenger, then another, and finally reached the staircase.

Once on the curb he felt a great relief. What decision had he come to? None. He remembered that he had been shy on decisions that day. As he saw it, there was only one course to pursue.

The man who had threatened first was unknown to him. To progress at all he must discover his identity. Who knew him? Well, the only person who, logically, ought to know him was Ichi. A man's Jap servant usually knows all his friends, even those whom a master doesn't suspect he knows.

Keeler clasped the handrail as he descended the subway steps in quest of a Brooklyn express. He had tripped once, years earlier, and his accident insurance company had paid him twenty-four dollars a week for eleven days.

Chief Pyne looked up in frank surprise when the little man was ushered into his presence.

"Back again? Found something new? What's the main idea?"

Keeler looked apologetic.

"I'm sorry to report that I'm just angling, at present. I was wondering whether you'd object to letting me talk to Ichi for five minutes more. You see, I'd like to ask him a few questions which may—" he broke off suddenly. "That is, chief, if you don't think I'm imposing on your good nature. I—"

"Aw, ferget it! I'd stack you, ten to one, against the classy, gumshoe bunch I've had to deal with. Meaning no personal offense, I must say that you're the most unorthodox-looking detective I've ever seen. You look more like a—er—like a druggist, or something. But you got the goods! Sure I'll have that little brown eel brought out. Want me here?"

Keeler looked super-apologetic.

"I'd—I'd rather not—that is, if you have no objection," he added hastily.

A moment later the squat, sullen detention prisoner was brought in by an attendant.

When his glance fell upon Keeler his taut, yellow skin eased into a half smile. But behind his eyes lurked fear of the coming interview.

"I want to find out a few unimportant things, Ichi," began the little detective gently. "Nothing to get alarmed about. Just a few names. If you can possibly remember them, I'd advise you to do so, because, you see, the more names you remember the less chance—the less chance—"

Ichi flashed comprehension. His square, sinewy hands, with their square-tipped fingers, hung calmly at his sides. He was prepared.

"First of all," ventured Keeler meekly, "I want to know the name of the gentleman who was in Mr. Milwood's study at the time that you let me in—the first gentleman, Ichi. Now, his name, please."

"Which first gen'leman?"

"The one you let into the study some time *before* you let me into the house, Ichi. You're not thinking as briskly as you can. Remember, it is wise to do as I ask, if—"

"Not let him into study!" interrupted the Jap hurriedly. "Mr. Milwood let him in. When I hear them talking, inside the room, when they say about stocks, I—" He came to a horrified, gasping halt.

The incriminating evidence of eavesdropper had gushed from his lips when he was seeking vindication.

Keeler flecked a bit of dust from his own lapel and looked out of the window.

"As you say, Mr. Milwood let him in," he suggested blandly. "But maybe you let him out, Ichi. Did you let him out—out of the house—after the talk?"

"Yes. Let him out front door."

"Ah! Exactly. Now that's the way it should be. You let him out. So you saw him. You know who he is. You know his name. And you're going to tell it to me. What is his name, Ichi?"

"Vandiver. People call 'Colonel Vandiver.' Mr. Milwood call 'Vandiver.'"

"Colonel Vandiver. Ah, yes. Young? Old? Old, I guess, eh?"

"Old."

"Just so. Now, I wonder, if you thought very hard, whether you could remember just where this Colonel Vandiver lives, Ichi?"

"Emperor Hotel, New York."

"Really?"

Keeler scribbled the name on the back of the "suspected list."

"Now, before we leave Colonel Vandiver's name, Ichi, I'd like to know—I'd like to know, very much, whether Mr. Milwood has seen much of the colonel lately; whether they've been in communication."

Ichi showed signs of becoming more voluble.

"Colonel Vandiver call Mr. Milwood many times during week. He call on telephone. Mr. Milwood say, angry, 'Ichi, tell blamed old fool I not here, at home.' And I tell. And blamed old fool say: 'Tell him, Milwood, call up Vandiver, Emperor Hotel.' And I tell. But he don't."

Keeler rubbed his hands in glee.

"Well, that's fine. That's the way to testify. Right out with it. See? You're a very smart man, Ichi!"

The Jap's sturdy chest became a trifle more prominent. He stood eager for another onslaught of interrogation.

"Now that we know all we want to know about this gentleman, thanks to you," commended Keeler, with flattering emphasis, "we'll turn to a lady visitor. Among the guests at dinner that night was there a Miss Madge Carr?"

"Miss Carr? Very beautiful lady, with silk dress?"

Keeler coughed discreetly.

"I—er—the fact is, I have never seen the lady. We will presume she's beautiful—very beautiful because Milwood knew only beautiful women. Beauty was one of his weaknesses. And the silk dress—yes, she would have on a silk dress, certainly."

"Beautiful lady, in silk dress, gold color, very expensive," volunteered Ichi, warming to his description.

"Yes—lady in gold-colored, expensive silk dress," urged Keeler. "What then?"

"She was guest for first time. Never see her in house before. Don't eat soup."

"Doesn't eat soup?" parroted Keeler in blank amazement. "Why—"

"Don't know why. I serve beautiful mushroom soup. Beautiful lady not touch. Everybody eat. Beautiful lady she disdain."

"Oh, yes, I see. She hurt your feelings because she didn't eat your soup. And she was Miss Carr?"

"Don't know name." Ichi lapsed into bare facts.

"Didn't you hear any one call her anything? 'Madge,' or 'Miss Carr,' or perhaps—"

"Don't know front or back name!" declared the Jap decisively.

"And you don't know where she lives?"

"No. Don't know."

"Do you know if she *is* Miss Carr?"

"No. Maybe. I don't know."

"I see. Well, you've done very nicely. Thank you."

Keeler summoned the attendant. The interview was ended.

On the way out he met the chief in the corridor.

"Find out all you wanted to know?" inquired Pyne with the inflection of deep respect that had lately tinged his conversations with the little man.

"Not all. Not quite all."

"Well, do you think you found out as much as he knew?"

"I think so."

"H'm! Maybe if you call me up in a couple of hours I'll be able to add a couple of explanatory notes. Maybe not. Anyhow, it wouldn't do any hurt to call me up."

Keeler looked dazed.

"You're going to third degree him?"

"That's it, Mr. Keeler. I don't trust those little frogs. They're too blamed eager for education and the inside workings of things to be wholesome. Why, gosh, if I didn't know one once who took care of a bachelor's place, down here on Columbia Heights. The daughter of the superintendent of the building was found with her skull crushed in, down one of the air shafts; and he was star suspect, because one day a hallboy heard the girl call him a yellow rat when he spoke to her.

"I examined his belongings, to get a line on his habits, and in his stack of books, would you believe it, there wasn't one that was written in plain English, that a gentleman could understand. Lots of 'em were Latin—and the others put out by these fellows, Sudermann, Ibsen, Hauptmann—those were some of the names, I remember. Not that I guess they mean any more to you than they did to me. Well, as I was saying; no reg'lar man could make it out. So we got a chap who had graduated from Yale and was working with us then, to read 'em. We called him our 'millionaire detective,' because he was papa's boy. And he reported that the stuff was very morbid and likely to drive any one to drink—or murder. So we held the Jap."

"And was he convicted on the evidence?" gasped Keeler.

"Oh, no. But he came mighty near being. Would 'a' served him right too—reading that junk when he should 'a' been waxing floors and making beds. No. Later on, her father confessed that he'd pushed her off the roof because he couldn't get her to stay in nights. But ever since then I've been suspicious of the breed."

"Well, I don't think you're going to get anything more out of Ichi," declared Keeler. "When are you going to put him through?"

"Now. See that door?"

Keeler looked down the corridor. At the end was a metal door, painted black.

"Come with me," said Pyne cordially. "I'll show you something."

Their footsteps rang hollowly on the stone floor. Pyne knocked on the door, in cipher code, then motioned to Keeler to open it.

The interior of the room, black as the depths of night, was pierced by two powerful, dazzling rays of electric light. One fell on a cocked revolver lying on a table; the other on a huddled, twisted object, covered by a sheet. It was the same size, the same shape, and in the same position as Milwood's body, when it was found murdered.

Guiltless as he was and familiar with third-degree tactics, Keeler experienced a sudden sense of suffocation. It was such a simple and forceful argument: two lights, the weapon, and the victim! And all the rest—blackness.

Pyne stepped into the corridor again and pulled the door shut behind them.

"You noticed that the body—that's Tim Rafferty, our hotel man—was lying against a door, on the farther side of the room. The Jap'll be brought in that door. We'll make him open it. He'll have to shove the body aside to get in. Then we'll push him from behind. That'll make him stumble over it. Then we'll slam the door and leave him in there alone for two seconds. See?"

Keeler edged toward the nearest exit. He was suddenly conscious of the dryness of the roof of his mouth and the sandpaper surface of his tongue.

"I'll call you later," he promised shyly. "I guess I'll go now."

As he went down the steps he heard Pyne's voice, sharp and decisive:

"Bring the Jap!"

CHAPTER XIV.
On the Trail of Vandiver.

Coming out of the Poplar Street station, Keeler's eye fell on a fascinating sight. Across the street a wide plate-glass window bore in white enamel lettering the name "JOHNSON'S." Inside the window, a man in white, with chef's cap and spotless cotton gloves, was pouring a viscous material from a silver pitcher.

The material fell in round spots, on a black surface, under which burned rows of tiny blue gas flames. In a very short time these same round disks turned a delightful brown—and fluffy—and were transferred to a plate, together with a tiny pitcher filled with maple sirup.

Keeler stood on the curb opposite this den of enchantment, and watched. There were three other people watching. But they watched just from curiosity. Keeler was watching because within him was born a desire that was searing his brain.

He had not eaten buckwheat cakes since the last Thanksgiving morning that he had gone home for a visit. He had not wanted buckwheat cakes, because they had never been shoved under his nose like this, and because they were not listed in the dietary of "Delectable Dinners for Dejected Diners."

But now he wanted buckwheat cakes more fiercely than he ever had wanted anything. And, what was more, he knew that, even though he was hesitating, outside, while his will power fought with his digestive apparatus, he could pick the winner of the contest right off.

But it was not until he had given the order to a dryad in white linen collar and apron, and heard it echoed from the front—"Plate of wheats! Four!"—that he was sure he wasn't going to get cold feet and order dry toast and tea with lemon, instead.

This was the second time in one day that he had succumbed to hysteria—the bus ride, and now this short cut to dyspepsia. He ate slowly, "fletcherizing" with stop-watch calculation. The aroma of a cup of coffee beside the plate of his neighbor sent his brain reeling. But no—not that! He still had a shred of his former Spartan will left to him.

A man entered, slapped his hat on a peg, thudded heavily into a chair opposite, and shook out an evening edition of a newspaper with businesslike briskness. Keeler caught the headline:

''MILWOOD MYSTERY DEEPENS!"

And here he was devouring buckwheat cakes, while others, cleverer than he, were ferreting out this thing! It would serve him right if they got in ahead of him and cleared up the whole case till a simple child could gaze into its limpid depths.

But he didn't think they would. They were on the wrong track. They were all on the wrong track! Fortified by the warm, nourishing food, his confidence in himself returned. He called for his check.

The dryad looked with scorn upon the empty plate and punched a contemptuous ten cents on the bit of white pasteboard. Keeler hid a nickel under the plate edge, rose, took his hat, and said "Good afternoon!" because he thought she looked hurt. At the cashier's desk he refused the customary toothpick and hurried into the street.

"Hotel Emperor," he murmured to himself. "Let me see. That's on Columbus Avenue in the eighties. Subway to Seventy-ninth. Ought to make it in three-quarters of an hour."

Forty-seven minutes later Keeler walked into the main lobby of the Emperor. A weary-looking clerk, immersed in the intricacies of the New Orleans racing charts, raised one eyebrow in bold interrogation.

"Is Mr.—er—Colonel Vandiver stopping here?" inquired the little man timidly.

"Yep."

"I'd like to send up my card."

"Give operator the name. She'll phone up." Once more he sank into the complexities of Brown Betty, odds seven to one, for place, coming in a neck ahead of Ali Baba, the favorite.

Keeler approached the operator's desk.

"Will you be kind enough to send my name up to Colonel Vandiver's apartment?"

He leaned toward the switchboard and smiled gently at the blond damsel with the rhinestone sunburst and the Brazilian pearls.

"Vandiver?"

"Just so," said Keeler.

"Got a card?" she catechized peremptorily. "He can't hear over the wire. He's deaf as a—as a—Oh, excuse me, are you a friend of his?"

Keeler hastened to put her at ease.

"No, I'm not a friend of his. In fact, he doesn't know me at all. I want to see him on business. So he's deaf?"

"Fierce deaf over the wire! He c'n hear pretty good when you're talkin' to him in his ear—an' what he don't hear he makes up."

"Just wait a minute," said the little detective. "I'll be back."

He went across to the news stand, purchased a forty-cent box of mixed chocolates, and, returning, placed them on the operator's desk.

"Gee!" she looked at him with startled admiration. "I didn't think you were that kind of a guy at all!"

"I'm not!" spluttered Keeler helplessly.

"Oh, cutey!" she encouraged. "Let little Connie tell you your methods are regal!"

"How long has Colonel Vandiver lived here?" stammered Keeler, getting scarlet between where the barber cut his hair too short and the top of his collar.

"Bashful boy, eh?" urged Constance softly. "Talks about old, deaf fogy. Gee! Honest, when I seen you come in here I had you down for an agent for illustrated hymn books. But now that I got a good squint at you, I see the 'pep' behind your eyes. Believe me, kid, you're all to the chili sauce!"

"Listen, miss," said Keeler, gulping hard. "You've mistaken my purpose, I fear. I wanted to bother you and take up your time for a few minutes, asking you a few questions; so I thought the least I could do was to buy you a little box of sweets. I didn't think you'd care to talk to me unless you got something for your trouble. No one, much, does."

"An' you didn't fall victim to my dazzling smile and 'perfect thirty-six'? You didn't feel a flutter in your affections when you looked into my eyes? You're a queer fish!"

"Yes, I know," agreed Keeler simply.

"Want to know how long the old colonel's been here?" she repeated curiously. "What'd you want to know for? Say! You can't be a trailer, are you? A bull—a central-office gink y' know? Oh, of course you ain't! They don't come your pattern! Well, I'll tell you. The colonel's been comin' here for six years, off 'n' on—but this is the longest stop he's made. He's been here 'most seven weeks, I guess. He's a Civil War guy, y' know. Anything else you'd like to know?"

"No, nothing, thank you. If you'll just send up my card."

Keeler breathed more freely at the thought of a possible quick release. He would rather have been Ichi in the somber third-degree chamber, over at detective headquarters, than the victim of this girl's Broadway banter. He scribbled hastily, under his name:

In regard to the new War Pension Bill. I wish your opinions.

A few minutes later the boy directed him to room No. 410, on the fourth floor.

A man, of perhaps seventy-three or four, but looking five years younger, stood at the door. His frock coat, whose silk buttons bore the glaze of faithful service, crinkled in deep folds about his thin frame. His white beard and mustache hid the expression of his mouth.

In his eyes was the perpetual mild questioning that is found in the eyes of the habitually deaf. He extended a thin, vein-knotted hand in cordial greeting.

"Ah, Mr.—er—," consulting the card which he still held in his left hand, "Mr. Keeler, I am delighted to make your acquaintance. Won't you be seated?"

As Keeler's hand closed around his host's, he experienced a peculiar shock. His impulse was to look down at the hand that lay in his. Not wishing to appear rude, he restrained that impulse.

When he was seated and had refused both a nip of fine old Bourbon and a choice Havana cigar, he let his eyes wander to that right hand.

What he saw caused him to start almost imperceptibly; but, slight as it was, Colonel Vandiver caught the movement. He smiled sadly.

"I lost those two first fingers on my right hand," he said slowly, "at the battle of Malvern Hill. You see, they're shaved down pretty close to the knuckle. It was a short, hot argument between a young Confederate officer and myself. When the war was over and I came back to my home town, I was twenty-three years old. I died a thousand deaths over those shorn fingers, Mr. Keeler. Somehow, you're a hero when you lose a leg or arm in battle, but when you lose a couple of fingers you're only an object of pity—and of morbid curiosity."

"I can readily see how true that is," agreed Keeler gently.

The old gentleman laughed.

"Oh, of course, I've gotten used to it now. In fact, I never think of my poor, distorted hand until a stranger, like yourself, draws my attention to it. But in the young days, when the eyes of a pretty girl would rest upon it, and I saw the ill-concealed horror she felt, my heart was cut to ribbons. I never married," he added simply.

"Colonel Vandiver!" Keeler looked squarely into the dimmed, steel-blue eyes before him. "I came up here, sailing under false colors!"

"Your name is not Keeler?"

"Yes, my name is Keeler. But I have nothing to do with the new War Pension Bill. I don't even know if one has been proposed."

"Nor I, Mr. Keeler. I had hoped there had been."

The detective drew a folded newspaper from his coat pocket and handed it to the colonel. The grimly scarred fingers closed on it.

"Have you seen the evening paper, colonel?" he asked quietly, keeping a keen eye on the seamed face.

"Yes, sir. Why, yes. I have a copy here."

He went to a small stable and took a mussed-looking newspaper from the under shelf. He held it up in his right hand.

"Oh, you were reading it, when I was announced," remarked Keeler indifferently.

"Yes. I believe I was sitting next to the window reading, when the boy knocked at the door."

"I see. How long had you known the dead man?"

The long, wasted thumb wrapped itself convulsively around the two remaining fingers. The old man breathed with a dry rasp in his throat.

"Dead man? What dead man?"

"The one at Bay Ridge."

"I really hadn't seen the account. I—"

"Colonel Vandiver." Keeler spoke softly.

The old man cupped his palm into a sounding board and leaned forward so that his right ear was toward the detective. Keeler raised his voice.

"A man couldn't ignore a headline in three-inch type," he said. "Also, a man who is summoned to the door while he is reading a newspaper will either carry that paper to the door with him, or else throw it carelessly on the nearest article of furniture. Only a painstaking housewife, who prides herself on being able to 'eat off the floors' in her home, will think of folding it and putting it on an under shelf before admitting a visitor. You were reading that first-page story, colonel, and you didn't want any one to catch you reading it. Why?"

Keeler had not risen from his chair. He sat, carelessly swinging one leg over the other; looking with mild, inquiring eyes at the gasping old man before him.

"Sir!" breathed the colonel.

"Oh, dear! I knew you'd say that!" complained Keeler plaintively. "It isn't that kind of a case at all. I'm not trying to offend you—I beg you to believe that. Now that I've seen you, you make me think of my own grandfather—and he was a hero to me. Sit down, sir, won't you, please? I want to tell you something."

"You come to my apartment, sir, and accuse me of attempting to deceive, or falsifying, of—"

"Of course I do!" grumbled Keeler. "Because you were doing it—them—both. You attempted to deceive me and you falsified; but I don't bear any ill feeling, anyway. Now, let's get together on this, colonel. You sit over there on the other side of the table, and I'll sit here."

After a moment's consideration Colonel Vandiver dropped into the designated chair. His watery, light eyes bulged from their sockets until the entire iris was visible. His shrunken hands clutched each other till the feeble throb in his gray-blue veins was plainly perceptible.

"Did you ever see a silver bullet, colonel?" asked Keeler suddenly.

"No, sir, I never did, sir."

"No," mused the detective. "They're not common. I didn't think you'd ever seen one. I never had until—until—"

His voice trailed off into an indistinct syllable. He rose from his chair, walked to the mantelpiece, and examined a curious bit of bric-a-brac. It was a small, crystal vase, with a beautifully sculptured bronze dragon coiled around its transparency.

"Odd bit," he observed, picking it up in his fingers.

"Yes, my young nephew, who is an officer in the United States navy, sir, brought it to me from Japan. I have a peculiar feeling about that little vase. I feel that if I lost it my health would fail. I entertain no superstitions or fetishes of any sort, yet I have that strange presentment about a bit of crystal."

"Oh!" shrieked Keeler as the vase dropped from his grasp.

With a lightning movement the old man jumped to the spot. His maimed right hand shot out spasmodically to save his mascot from destruction. But with a skillful dive Keeler rescued it before it struck the floor.

While the colonel was still panting from the exercise, the little man began to speak rapidly, distinctly. For fear a word would be lost he bent over until his lips all but brushed Vandiver's ear.

"Colonel," he stated calmly, "you were in Mr. Milwood's study a few hours before the body was found. You threatened to kill him, unless he did something that you wished him to do. You repeated your threat. You said: 'I'll kill you!' three times. What did you want to kill him for, colonel?"

"I didn't kill him! I didn't! I swear to God I didn't kill him! You must believe me!"

The old man had slid to his knees. He clung to Keeler with hysterical tenacity.

"I know you didn't," declared Keeler calmly. "What I want to know is, why you had the desire to kill him. What was your grudge?"

Vandiver muttered vaguely to himself.

"I'm not trying to accuse you of anything, man," explained the little detective. "I am doing my best to eliminate you. There are too many characters in my play. I have to get rid of a few. And you're next in line. I tell you what I'll do. A fair exchange, et cetera, you know. You tell me why you wanted to kill Milwood, and I'll tell you how I know you didn't kill him. Now, is that a bargain?"

"I'll tell you the whole thing!" moaned Vandiver, half beside himself with worry and senile terror.

Keeler lifted him to his feet and placed him gently in a chair. Then he sat down himself.

"I went to his home last night, bound to get some satisfaction," confessed Vandiver, holding out his hands in earnest supplication. "He'd robbed me! He'd ruined the few years I have to live! But I didn't kill him! I didn't!"

"There, there!" soothed Keeler, reaching over to pat his arm reassuringly. "It's all right, colonel. I'll stand by you. Go on with your story. There's nothing to fear."

The old man's head sank forward on his outstretched arms. His spare body shook with a violent spasm of dry coughing. Keeler ran to the small wash closet, filled a glass with water and held it to the colonel's lips. After a sip or two the coughing ceased and the exhausted man wiped his streaming eyes.

"I had a little money," he continued, with a great effort. "The interest from it was an income sufficient for my needs. I have always had a passion for games of chance, sir. Not heavy gambling, because I never had sufficient funds. I did not stop to realize that, at my age, any chances I took might prove fatal. And so, when this man came along, I—"

"What man?" interrupted Keeler sharply.

"Milwood. He had a lot of dead stocks he wanted to unload. Some one told him of my little money and he sought me out. He told me to go to a broker and buy all the X. R. & T. stock I could get. He said, inside of ten days, it would go up twenty points and I'd clear a fat sum. I did as he said. I bought at thirty-two and a half. In ten days it was down to four and an eighth.

"I went to him, almost demented by the terrible tragedy that had overtaken me. I was an old man, alone in the world, my eyesight failing, my hearing seriously impaired—and my money gone! He promised to do what he could. Needless to say, he didn't keep his promise.

"I got people to telephone for me. They were told he was not at home. Yesterday I went to Bay Ridge with murder in my heart. I took up my stand outside his beautiful home. He had invited me to dinner, to 'talk things over.' I refused. But I went to his house. I waited until I thought they had finished dinner, then I walked up the steps and rang the bell.

"The door was ajar; the guests were just coming from the dining room into a sort of reception hall. Milwood's Japanese servant was passing around cigars and cigarettes. Milwood came to the door himself. I stepped into the hall before he had a chance to close the door. He motioned me upstairs and followed immediately.

"He led me into a peculiar room, all filled with guns and books and strange chemicals—then left me there alone. A half hour later he returned. Because he laughed at my pleadings, because he scorned the idea that I could find redress in the face of his financial power, I threatened to kill him. And I *would* have killed him—"

The old man rose, trembling; his clenched hands raised above his head, his dim eyes blazing vindictively, his voice shrill and rasping.

"I would have killed him, only—"

"Only what?"

"Only at that moment the Japanese servant knocked at the door and announced another visitor."

"Who? A Miss Madge Carr?"

The colonel shook his head uncertainly.

"I am very deaf," he said. "I did not catch the name. But it was a lady. I saw the edge of her skirt in a doorway off the hall, as I went downstairs."

"And she was his next visitor? You are sure?"

"I—I think so. At least—well, I passed a man on the stairs. It may have been—but I thought—"

"And the first you heard of the finding of the dead man was what you read in the papers this morning?"

"Yes, yes! I swear to that!"

"You needn't swear it to me," said Keeler kindly. "You couldn't have murdered him. I'll tell you why. You've lost the fore and middle fingers of your right hand. Nevertheless, you have not become left-handed. I proved that to my own satisfaction when I saw you shake hands with your right hand. You took the newspaper I handed you with your right hand; you held up the edition you had been reading with your right hand, and, last of all, when you were taken off your guard, you endeavored to save your crystal vase with your right hand.

"According to all the laws of nature, a man acting on a murderous impulse would use the hand he was accustomed to using every day—the hand in which he had confidence and power. A man lacking the first two fingers of his right hand could not fire a revolver with that hand—and the dead man was killed by a bullet! That's how I know you are not the assassin, Colonel Vandiver. Let me congratulate you on the fact that Ichi, the Japanese servant, knocked at the door exactly when he did."

"Who killed him, Mr. Keeler?" asked the old man, firm in the belief that the genius before him could read the stars if need be.

"I'll call you up when I find out," replied Keeler absent-mindedly, as he drew his pencil through Item No. I on the "suspected list." "Good afternoon, colonel."

Down on the main floor he crossed the lobby in a brown study. The blond goddess at the switchboard bit into her ninth chocolate cream and watched him disappear, his lips moving noiselessly, his brows knit.

"Nut!" was her terse estimate.

The doorman caught his murmurings as he passed.

"Woman—Hilda van Vleck—love scene—she threatened—struck him! H'm! Hilda van Vleck!"

The doorman gazed open-mouthed at the retreating figure.

"Bughouse!" he summarized.

CHAPTER XV.
Traveling in Circles.

Keeler stood on the corner of Columbus Avenue and Eightieth Street. Another man, as puzzled, as excited, and as hindered as he, would have paced up and down with his hands behind his back, or jingled his loose change and his key ring. Keeler did neither.

His gaze was focused on a window across the street. It was the second shop window he had taken a keen interest in that day—but this one was devoid of buckwheat cakes.

It displayed, instead, a full assortment of soaps and wash rags. The center feature was a huge, presumably hollow, cake of purple bath soap, that was intermittently illuminated and darkened. In the full light the name, "Super-Violette," was thrown into relief.

But Keeler was not looking at the display. Visible above the array of soaps was the cover of a cherry-colored telephone booth. He was making up his mind to go into that booth and call up Hilda van Vleck.

He had never met the woman; had never seen her. If she was the "very beautiful lady with expensive, gold-colored silk dress," of Ichi's narrative, he knew he would never have the courage to face her with sundry charges.

Anyway, wasn't it extremely rude to force oneself on a lady one didn't know? The possible etiquette of the detective business had never troubled him as much as right now.

No. He guessed the only thing to do was to call up, and approach the subject gingerly, on the basis of mutual friendship. He felt around in his pocket for a nickel. The most worldly Lotharian touch in Keeler's make-up was that he didn't carry a little pocketbook for his change.

He was the type of man for whom those queer little pin-seal and alligator-skin purses were manufactured. People watching him get on a car felt sure he was going to extract one, slide his silver into the flap of it, and pay his fare. They experienced the keenest disappointment when they found that he carried his money just like other men.

Keeler walked across the street, still searching for the elusive nickel, praying fervently in his heart of hearts that he would not find it. He was sparring for time, he thought. In reality he was sparring for that particular kind of nerve that one must have to face beauty in distress without succumbing.

Knowing full well that it was a necessity to mankind, Keeler had always looked upon the telephone as the curse of modern existence. He had been insulted more times, over the wire, than anywhere else. He had come nearer to inflicting insult, himself. He had sweated like a stoker in those booths in summer. He had been repelled by the stale odors of tobacco, concentrated lily of the valley and disinfectants, all pleasantly jumbled.

But here was an instance where the telephone was going to act as a shield, a buffer, a potent palladium. He could talk without being seen, without seeing. There would be no twin-pansy pools fringed with curling lashes. No twitching, moist red lips. In short, nothing to take his mind off the points of the case.

His fingers closed around a nickel. He could have sworn to its denomination by the queer little cold thrill that struck his heart. He entered the booth—his second telephone call of the day, but his life's first voluntary phone talk with a woman.

"River 10001, please," his voice faltered.

"What number, please?" insisted central.

"1-0-0-0-1 Riverside," elaborated Keeler.

"River 1—I beg your pardon!"

He heard the Columbus Exchange give it to the Riverside branch. He waited. An icy-cold moisture sprouted along the line of his spinal column. A Croton bug, wanderer and explorer, crawled slowly up the polished surface of the wood. Ordinarily, Keeler would have felt a keen disgust. To-day, he watched its progress, hypnotized.

There was a p-r-r-r, a deafening click that temporarily suspended his hearing.

"Busy!" reported central.

His nickel clinked into the little metal trough below. He pocketed it with a sense of exaltation that drove him to the soda fountain.

There, pasted in cubist geometrical designs on the mirror, he read of delicious drinks, such as "Frosted Delight," "Sugared Lime Whip," and "Raspberry Razzle." He felt foolish enough to sample them all. But a customer in distress stopped to order a draft of aromatic spirits of ammonia. That brought Keeler back to earth.

"I'll have some plain soda, with a dash of phosphate in it," he told the fancy mixer, who looked with disdain upon any order with less than six ingredients.

The unpleasant sting of his familiar drink cleared his brain. What a fool he was! Why was he so overjoyed when that number was reported busy? It was only postponing the agony, wasn't it? Of course it was. Well, then, what was there to be happy about? Nothing.

If the next booth telephone had been five miles distant he would have walked it rather than phone twice from the same place, right under the eyes of the clerks. He felt humiliated for no reason at all.

He walked three blocks south before he found another drug store, with the dark-blue-and-white bell suspended over the entrance. This time he strode in boldly. The same nickel was pasted to his hot, moist palm. He asked for the number. He waited.

"I'm ringing Riverside 10001—trying to get River 10001," came to him at automatic intervals of four seconds each.

Then a voice—a different voice—and a woman's, answered.

"Hello," it called softly. "Hello."

"Hello," answered Keeler, gulping hard. "Is this Mrs. van Vleck?"

"Monsieur wish to speak to madame? Ze name, please?"

"Oh—oh, er—this is Mrs. van Vleck's maid, I take it? Well, there's no use giving her my name, because she doesn't know it, you see. If you don't mind, ask her to come to the phone. Tell her it's a business matter. Tell her—"

"Just a moment, monsieur." The maid interrupted his explanations coldly. "I will inform madame."

She left the phone. Keeler began to feel brave, invincible. He even went so far as to whistle a few bars of "Die Wacht Am Rhein," which he always confused with the march from "Tannhäuser."

Suddenly, over the wire, he heard the little decisive click of high heels on a polished floor. A fumbling with the receiver came to him, and then the maid:

"Madame is reclining on her couch with a—oh, so miserable sick headache. Monsieur will have to excuse her. She is so sorry."

A noise that meant the slapping up of the receiver woke him from his reverie. Keeler stared in dismay at the unresponsive instrument. The conversation was ended. Once more he left a drug store. This time with all the latent Irish from the third generation back boiling in his veins.

What kind of a boob was he, anyway? he asked himself. Why hadn't he insisted on speaking to Mrs. van Vleck? Why hadn't he thrown a good scare into that maid? Why hadn't he—

An inoffensive carrot that had fallen from a vegetable stand in front of a grocery store lay in his path. He gave it a vicious kick that was intended to drive it into infinity. Instead, it rolled a short distance, pivoted on its long, thin point, and returned to him with the unerring accuracy of a trick hoop roller in vaudeville.

"That's what I've been doing all day!" muttered Keeler to himself, in frank disgust. "Traveling in circles! I've got to do something decisive. And first of all, I've got to speak to Mrs. van Vleck."

He consulted his watch, and was startled to find that it was a full hour later than he thought. At Sixty-seventh Street he turned through to cross Broadway. He had decided to try another phone call, this time from a switchboard. He wanted a woman's voice to greet the French maid. He wanted a woman's voice to insist upon speaking to Mrs. van Vleck.

With vivid memories of the gem-decked blonde at the Hotel Emperor still haunting him he shuddered at the thought of approaching another of the deadly species.

Midway between Columbus Avenue and Broadway, on Sixty-seventh Street, some one walked up to him and dug him playfully in the ribs.

"Say, didn't I wave day-day to you yesterday and wish you immunity from vacation madness? Ah, little did I suspect that one of your open countenance—I might say your guileless *gesicht*—was leading a double life! Where does she live—and what'll you blow me to if I don't squeal to the boys?"

Turner, the irrepressible, one of the younger men in the district attorney's office, hauled off and landed a resounding whack on Keeler's gray tweed shoulder. Without waiting for a response he rattled on:

"Honest! Listen! What's the main idea? Why are you prowling over asphalt lanes and through brick forests, when a babbling brook, a shady nook, and all the trimmings are singing their siren songs up in the mountains? I get mine a week from Saturday and I leave on the four-twelve that afternoon for Pompton, New Jersey. A friend of mine's got a dream of a place on the lake up there. Fishes for perch out of his living-room window and grows peacocks as a diversion."

"I'm—um—I'm delayed," stammered Keeler. Turner always got on his nerves. At this moment he frayed them to raw fringes. "I intended going this morning, but I was unavoidably detained in town."

"Well, say, take a tip from me, and don't get detained much longer. What's the use of going away for a couple of days? You eat up a bunch of car fare and all you do is try to make out the time-table, so you'll get the right train coming back. Nothing to it!"

He pulled Keeler over to the iron railing that ran around the armory on that block. From the way he pushed his hat back from his forehead and folded his arms Keeler knew he was going to hold him up for at least ten minutes and every minute had an hour's value to him just then.

"I imagine I'll have to be going on," began the little man timidly. "You see there are so many little things I have to settle up before I leave to-morrow—and I have to get some collars."

It was the wrong thing to say.

"Now, there's where you're all off!" declared Turner forcefully. "When you go away for a rest—anyway, a guy who works as hard as you do—you want to take nothing but flannel shirts with collars attached. Back to nature! That's the stuff."

"I dare say you're right," murmured poor Keeler, ready to agree to anything. "Well, I guess I'll be going. It's getting late. Good-by, Mr. Turner, I'll remember about the collars."

"Good-by, old top!" brisked the other, crushing the unresisting fingers in an iron grasp. "But, gee! Say—almost forgot it—what d' you think of the big Bay Ridge mystery? Isn't it just your luck, though, to be leaving town just when they're beginning to unravel a great, big, juicy one like that? I'll bet if the old man knew you were still in the city he'd send for you. Say, I'm interested in your idea of it. Just for fun—what do you make of it?"

"You mean the murder?" Keeler hesitated over the word.

"Sure, the murder! Great guns! What else is every one talking about? You don't mean to tell me you haven't gone over the thing? Why, it's just your style, Keeler. It couldn't have been more like you if it had been cut to your measure. Well, say, as long as you haven't gone into it, I'll tell you, confidentially, that the whole blamed thing is as plain as the nose on your face. Gosh! If they'd send me over there I'd clean up that muddle so quick that you wouldn't know it had—"

"Go down and tell the old man to put you on it," suggested Keeler, without malice. "It's good training for any one and the chief likes to see his men ambitious. Good-by."

This time he made a clean get-away, leaving Turner standing speechless in the center of the sidewalk, undetermined whether to be offended or inflated.

Keeler walked into the lobby of a quiet family hotel on Broadway. The switchboard operator, a small, frail girl, with eyes too large and too dark-rimmed for her tiny, flower face, smiled sweetly as Keeler bent over her desk.

"I want you to do me a favor," he began, hardly knowing how to approach the subject. "I want you to call a number for me. A maid will answer. I want you to ask for her mistress. Insist on speaking to her. Now, don't be afraid. You're not going to get into any trouble by doing this, at all. It's a er—a trick I'm playing on one of my friends. You don't mind, do you?"

The girl threw back her sleek, dainty head and laughed heartily.

"Why, no, of course not. I do that every day in the week. Sometimes two or three times day. And for every reason under the sun. What's the number you want to call, please? And the name of the party?"

Keeler could have embraced her on the spot. He felt she was not going to foozle things. He gave her the number slowly. She passed it on to the central with the distinctness and speed of an automatic machine. He added the name in full.

"Hello!" she said at length. "Hello, Marie! Is Hilda—er—is Mrs. van Vleck in? Yes, I would like to speak to her. Something about that rose-colored frock she saw. Yes, I'll hold the wire. Certainly."

She clapped her hand over the transmitter and turned to Keeler.

"How did you know the maid's name was Marie?" he inquired. Loving that particular form of wit, and despairing of mastering it, he was quick to recognize and admire the slightest trace of it in others.

"Most French maids sift down to 'Marie,' in time, no matter how high and mighty their original names may have been. If she had indignantly denied the 'Marie' I'd have apologized for having forgotten her name so soon. The Hilda, followed by a slight hesitation and the correction, proved affection, I think."

In Keeler's heart was a profound respect for all women. But this dark, wistful slip of a girl was the first of her sex to inspire him with confidence in her coolness and ability. He began to look around for a florist's stand. Candy wouldn't fit here, somehow.

She was speaking again.

"Hello! Is this you, Mrs. van Vleck? Just a minute, please!"

She motioned to the string of booths, jabbed a plug in firmly. No. 3 lighted up. Keeler took down the receiver.

"Hello!" he said. "Mrs. van Vleck, you don't know me. I'll tell you why I called you up. You see, it's about this Milwood affair over at Bay Ridge. I'm a friend of his and I know you are, so I thought I'd like to talk to you about it. Could you see me, now, if I came right up?"

There was no answer. Keeler listened intently. He knew he was still connected. To his trained ear came the sound of little, gasping breaths.

"Mrs. van Vleck," he called gently, "don't be alarmed. I assure you I come as a friend. I—"

"Who are you?" was wafted to him faintly over the wire. Then again:

"I want to know who you are!" This with plaintive inflection.

"Oh, you wouldn't know me, anyway," Keeler's nervousness lent an assurance and air of bonhomie to his voice that he was far from feeling. "You didn't see me and I didn't see you. But I know you were in Mr. Milwood's study last night and I heard what you said when you were there."

A low wail, ending in a gasp, struck his ear. There was a thud, followed by a knocking sound, that was caused, probably, by a receiver swinging loosely on a cord.

"Mrs. van Vleck!" he shouted into the transmitter. "Mrs. van Vleck!"

No answer. He heard a clock, evidently in her apartments, strike the half hour. Then the same high heels clicked into hearing.

"Madame! Madame! Qu'avez-vous? Mon Dieu! Qu'avez-vous? Madame!"

The exclamations, gaining in intensity, ended in a terrified shriek. Then the receiver was snapped into place.

Keeler dashed out of the hotel. He had a vivid picture of the probable scene in Mrs. van Vleck's apartment, at that moment. She had fainted. Fainted or something worse. The terror in the maid's voice suggested almost anything. A lady's maid must be used to fainting spells. In Keeler's hazy knowledge of the accomplishments of women, fainting occupied a prominent position. He had heard frequent lapses in that direction was the prerogative of the gently bred, the neurotic, and the super-temperamental woman. Therefore, either the maid had been in the employ of the more stolid, bourgeois type—or else Mrs.

van Vleck was in a serious state.

There was not a taxi in sight. Usually, at this point, where Broadway and Columbus Avenue cross, there is a continuous procession of them, each with its soliciting chauffeur. If Keeler took the surface car he would have to walk three long blocks. The subway would be even less convenient.

Coming through the side street, fresh from the livery stable, appeared the type of vehicle that infests the entrances of Central Park; in which one can tour the length and breadth of the park with authentic information concerning the mall, the casino, the reservoir, McGowan's Pass Tavern, et cetera, thrown in for one dollar! This carriage, a miniature, loose-jointed imitation of a victoria, is a shred of the New York of thirty years ago—unchanged.

The horse looked less dejected than he should have been, to be absolutely in the picture. The driver was sober, and the upholstery was fairly intact. Keeler stepped to the curb and raised his right hand.

His foot was on the step, his hand gripping the slippery cloth, when a man, familiar in outline, darted from the shade of a side entrance and ran across Broadway. Keeler blinked just once—and looked again.

It was the man he had found lurking in the bushes outside Milwood's home the night before. It had been dark then. But the exaggerated squareness of the mold in which he was cast, and the massive joining of his neck and shoulders, left no doubt in Keeler's mind.

The man was not a yegg. In the daylight his clothes appeared to be of good quality—and neat. His face, though of the florid, bulldog type, bore traces of refinement. A surface car came along. It stopped. The man got aboard; the doors snapped closed behind him. The car went on.

Keeler thought with lightning speed, then.

"Follow that car!" he commanded the coachman. "The red one. Keep about a half a block behind it."

Then he shrank into a corner of the vividly odorous carriage seat, covered with confusion, at having spoken so peremptorily. He would have to make it up to the driver in the tip.

His mind swerved back to the man in the car. What was he? Who was he? Where had he been between the time of the chase, on the previous night and now? Had he just now been trailing Keeler himself?

Keeler crimsoned at the possibilities that came crowding into his brain. Could he have been shadowed without knowing it? He began to wish with all his heart that he had gone on his vacation. His lips tightened involuntarily; his limp fingers stiffened into a half-threatening fist.

"I'm going to get him," monologued Keeler, "if I never do anything else worth while! That is, I'd be very pleased if I *did* get him," he added characteristically.

The driver was following directions beautifully. Whenever the car stopped to take in or let off passengers, he would slow his speed to a bare walk—always keeping the required half block behind. The man was still in the car. Even if it had been possible for him to put on a disguise in a public vehicle, he could never have cloaked his bulk sufficiently to deceive.

The thing was getting on Keeler's nerves! He'd been blocked so much; in such unexpected places. A traffic policeman held up his hand! The red car slid by, in time to ignore the warning.

His driver had to pull up or be arrested. Keeler jumped to his feet, his eyes glued on the fast-disappearing spot of red. He looked impatiently at the cross-street traffic—and knew he could not wait for it to pass.

Crushing a two-dollar bill into the welcoming palm of the driver, he jumped from the cab, ran to the upper corner, and waked a dozing taxi driver by slamming the door of his machine until the glasses shivered in their frames. He called excitedly through the little round hole in the window before him.

"Catch up to that uptown car. I don't care what you do to get it—and I'll pay the fine if there is any."

In the upper nineties the taxi was a little over a block behind. Keeler saw the car stop. A figure swung from the front platform, dashed in front of the car, ran across the street, and disappeared through the doors of a German restaurant.

"Stop right here!" Keeler shouted to the chauffeur.

Five seconds later the little man walked into the same restaurant, sat down at a table, and ordered a split of Apollinaris.

There were six customers in the place—and an average of four waiters apiece. Over in a corner, partly screened by a dusty, frayed near palm, was the object of Keeler's curiosity. Before him, on the cloudy-looking table-cloth, was a seidel of Münchener beer.

Keeler counted the bubbles in his Apollinaris; because he didn't want to appear too vindictive toward this mysterious Unknown. A waiter added to the beer a raw-beef sandwich, with crisp lettuce cup-filled with finely chopped onions.

The man was going to eat real food. Keeler told himself that he would have known that raw meat was the man's diet. The brute looked it!

Suddenly, through the frayed palm leaves, across the full width of the restaurant, their eyes met and clashed. If the Unknown had endeavored to explain his presence; if he had even appeared to be apologetic for being there, nothing would have happened.

Instead of an expression of humility, however, his eyes seemed to flash defiant challenge! He stared brazenly into Keeler's inquiring face, his eyes bulging, his lower jaw set and grimly undershot, until he looked like some famous "pug" ready to send out tickets for a ten-round scrap.

The look stung Keeler to the core. He motioned a waiter to his own table and whispered a few words to him. The waiter, open-mouthed, incredulous, bent closer and asked him to repeat them. The little man, his gaze never wavering from his object of prey, repeated his request now distinctly.

The waiter disappeared through the short, swinging doors that led into the café. In a few seconds he returned. In his wake trailed a policeman. The two approached Keeler's table.

With a strange, weird cry, the mysterious Unknown jumped from his seat and, almost knocking down a waiter carrying two orders of pig knuckles and sauerkraut, leaped through the doorway into the street.

Keeler grabbed his hat and seized the wrist of the unsuspecting cop. He pulled him through the door just in time to see the victim cut through the side street, down toward Riverside Drive.

"This way!" bade Keeler shrilly, and started in pursuit.

"What's he done? What's he done?" inquired the policeman as often as he could get his wind.

In the two very short blocks to the river, they accumulated quite a pursuing party. Corner idlers, a waiting chauffeur, two delivery boys who shed provisions to the right and left in their progress, and several excited women, who shouted directions that were not practical.

The pursued dived into Riverside Park. The policeman running down one winding path and Keeler running up another, cornered him. He offered no resistance. All three were so breathless that, for a minute after the impact, they made no move at all.

The Unknown's face was strained to apoplectic blues and purples. His prominent veins throbbed visibly. He breathed with the irregularity and unpleasant sound of an automobile exhaust that is sadly out of order. The policeman was the first to recover his normal state. He laid a heavy hand on the collar of the suspect who was a good four inches taller than the top of the bluecoat's hat—and brandished his nightstick.

Keeler stood by, still panting; and trembling with the little convulsive thrills of a rabbit which has been driven from his hole in the stone ledge by a ferret. Now that he'd made good on his muttered threat of less than a half hour ago, he felt no triumph.

"What did he take off'n you?" demanded the cop of the little man. "Has he got it on his person, d'you think, or did he get rid of it?"

"Why, he didn't take anything from me. He just—he—"

"Lift your hands from my collar, or I'll break every bone in your body!" the Unknown thundered.

"Here youse, now, none of that! See?" The cop punctuated the admonition with a forceful tap of the stick and awaited further explanation from Keeler.

With one mighty shake the suspect cast the officer from his person and strode over to Keeler.

"You fool!" he bellowed. "You blunderer! You poor, little, underdone shrimp! Do you know who I am?"

The open-mouthed audience drew closer in frank hero worship of the big man and frank contempt of the little one.

Keeler mouthed some unintelligible syllables.

The Unknown flapped back his coat. There on his vest flashed the badge of the United States secret service!

From his pocket he drew his certificate bearing his photograph. Then he snapped his thumb and forefinger under Keeler's nose—twice.

CHAPTER XVII.
The Van Vleck Chauffeur.

"WHY didn't you tell me you were a secret-service agent?" said Keeler. The distressing thought had just come to him that all this trouble and tomfoolery, all this conjecture and complex suspicion might have been avoided if only the man before him had stated the facts of the case.

"Why didn't I tell you?" echoed the secret-service man, his voice breaking in shrill sarcasm. "Why didn't I tell you? Why should I tell you, little one? Is your job in life just hanging around loose, waiting to be confided in? None of this guff now! See? What's the main idea? And are you spooffin', or were one-half your ancestors squirrels and the other half nuts, huh?"

"It would have been so much simpler, don't you see?" persisted Keeler. "All this could have been done away with and the time wasted could have been employed in furthering the elimination process. We could have worked together and—"

"Worked together!"

The big man's gaze traveled in underestimating appraisal from the tips of the little man's vici-kid, broad-toed shoes to the frayed edges of his wing collar. Then to make sure he hadn't slighted any point that would bear criticism, he made the return trip just as faithfully.

"Say what's eating this guy?" he appealed to the policeman, who had become a silent member. "Can't he sublet that top apartment of his? It's a shame to leave it vacant all year round."

"Here youse; clear out!" warned the bluecoat, passing along the gathered crowd. "This here ain't no moving-picture comp'ny, and it ain't a fight. It's a little mistake between two gentlemen. Now beat it! The whole bunch—or I'll get lively with my stick."

"Say, who are you, Percival?" asked the secret-service man as the hangers-on dispersed. "What are you?"

"I'm a detective," asserted Keeler as unostentatiously as most people confess to menial occupations.

The former suspect howled. His hilarity was deafening. Besides that, it was disturbing and goat getting.

"You a detective!" he jeered. "A little soda-fountain habitué like you! A poor little simp who spends all his time barking at the foot of a flagpole when he knows blamed well there ain't any branches on the darned thing to conceal anybody! You a detective!"

"On the district attorney's staff," added Keeler. "Please do not laugh. I do not like it. I am going back to that restaurant now and pay my check."

"Are you?" mocked the other. "For that elaborate feed you had? Well, so long, Sherlock! Better luck next time."

"Oh, I see!" observed Keeler quietly. "That means that I'll have to pay your check, too, my friend."

The gentle little sting didn't penetrate the hide of the secret agent. He and the bluecoat walked off together, chuckling, their heads close together. Twice they looked back at Keeler, and he looked at them. There was no venom in his heart. Just a great, overwhelming self-reproach—and humiliation.

A little way down the path, under an overhanging bush, he caught sight of an empty bench. Slowly he sought its rest. A deep sigh escaped him. The low afternoon light was coating the river with layers of crimson gold. The black little tugs, chugging away with their heavy tows, cut through the reflected radiance of the setting sun.

Keeler looked cautiously to the left and right. He stared down the grassy slope before him. He even turned and deliberately examined the bush directly behind him.

Then, when he was absolutely sure that there were no eavesdroppers, he drew the "suspected list" from his pocket and very shamefacedly drew his monogrammed silver pencil through the fifth item, the item beginning: "A big, ugly-faced chap hiding in bushes on lawn."

Just a moment longer he sat there. It was quiet. The peace of it soothed his soul. He thought he would like to stay longer. Maybe some evening when this case was all cleared up he would bring a couple of chicken sandwiches and an apple with him and sit there under the trees and watch the day die and the night dawn and listen to the river sounds and pretend the shifting boat lights were modern fireflies who had found that it paid to advertise. Yes, if he should bring a couple of newspapers to sit on—to protect him from the ground damp—and a light sweater he imagined it would be a very pleasant thing to do.

Two children, roller skating, slid into his line of vision. They were calling gayly to each other. Suddenly the larger of the two stumbled, and tried to save herself by catching hold of a tree trunk, but was unsuccessful.

As she fell, and the cry of dismay from the other child reached his ears, Keeler jumped guiltily. The thud and scream that he had heard over the wire that afternoon had until now entirely escaped his mind.

First he looked to see if the child had injured herself. Evidently not, for already she had picked herself up and was almost out of sight. He wondered if Mrs. van Vleck had recovered so quickly.

If she had—her suspicions aroused by his phone message—and all this time having elapsed between! He shook himself impatiently. If the woman had a vestige of guilt concerning the whole affair she might have disappeared before now. Even if she were not guilty, a woman of her standing would wish to avoid all such notoriety.

Well, if she were the criminal he had bungled it good and plenty. "Latest methods in shadowing crooks," he scoffed, "is to call them up and let them know you're coming." He scorned himself with caustic ridicule. He wondered what the "old man" would think of him now. He dwelt on the profound respect and admiration for his ability that Chief Pyne had professed.

Away down deep he knew he would never breathe the details of his comedy of errors. A green amateur could not have mussed things up into a classier hodgepodge. If that big secret-service man went and blabbed he'd never hear the end of it. The boys would be sending him field glasses, microscopes, bottles of soothing sirup, and rubber heels forever.

"I'm going to make a try at this lady, anyway," he confided boldly to a miserably thin and mangy-looking squirrel that had suddenly become his neighbor on the bench. He felt in his pockets for a possible edible crumb, knowing very well that he had nothing but fountain pens, erasers, and quill toothpicks.

"You're a wretched little beast, aren't you?" he pitied softly, and the tiny thing crept closer in more urgent supplication. "I tell you what I'll do. If you wait here I'll go up to Broadway and get you a bag of nuts."

And the strangest thing about it is that Wayne Keeler would have done just that thing if the squirrel had not scampered away, in cold disdain, at that moment.

The waiters eyed him with undisguised suspicion when he walked into the German restaurant for the second time. The place was practically empty. Alone in one corner a bush-bearded patron was deep in the war humor of *Simplicissimus*. The waiters stood in little, excited groups, discussing the late happening and offering a weird variety of solutions.

He called for the two checks, and paid them in a deprecatory manner that completely outwitted the bunch of open-mouthed, conjecturing Teutons. He left a quarter in the palm of the man who brought his change, and walked out of the place.

In front was a string of taxis stationed there to catch the patronage which issued from the subway station.

He picked out the sanest-looking chauffeur and gave him the number of Mrs. van Vleck's home. Then he changed his mind.

"Just drive me to the corner of that street and West End Avenue," he countermanded. "Stop on the southwest corner. And don't blow your horn unless it's absolutely necessary. In those quiet residential side streets a horn sounds like a blast to rouse the dead—and I don't want to rouse anybody."

Keeler leaned his head back in the shadow of the cab, and closed his eyes, while the chauffeur cranked up and puttered around the radiator.

Something had happened to Keeler that had never happened before. The keen edge of his enthusiasm was blunted. He was still interested and eager to be the first to unravel the tangled threads. But the avid zeal with which he had entered upon the mystery was gone.

Of course, running up blind alleys and butting into stone walls will knock the ardor out of almost anybody. But it had never knocked it out of him before.

He hoped that he would stumble across something at the van Vleck home to stir the smoldering embers into a brisk blaze again. The taxi started from the curb with a vicious jolt. The man had neglected to throw off his emergency brake. Keeler slid back on the seat and braced his feet in preparation for another upheaval. But the cab rolled along right smoothly for at least three blocks.

Then it began to act queerly. The engine missed, sputtered, and finally throbbed away madly, as if it were suffering from too high blood pressure. The chauffeur seemed trying to pick out a tune on the gears, if one could judge from the number of times and the rapidity with which he shifted them.

Keeler began to get nervous. Not that he feared an accident. But the jolting and thumping and spasmodic progress was making his head ache. He did not want his head to begin to ache right then, because he never took headache remedies, on account of their heart-depressive properties; and his own cure that had never failed him—great drafts of very hot boiled water, followed by a short nap—was not wholly feasible at the moment.

He leaned out the side window, took a good look, and then, knowing less about an automobile than almost anything else in the world, he addressed the chauffeur.

"What seems to be the matter?" he asked gently.

Every one who has driven a car knows that any tirade of scorn or even mild abuse from a passenger is easier to stomach than that maddening phrase: "What seems to be the matter?"

"Just a minute! She'll be all right, sir." The chauffeur spoke with a caustic assurance that was not even skin deep.

And when after a few more minutes of broncho busting, interlarded with a couple of fancy fox-trot intricacies, the machine came to a dead stop, Keeler decided that the van Vleck house was within walking distance.

He stepped out quietly, and came alongside the engine, displaying great concern.

"It's very hard to keep a car in good running order, isn't it?" he inquired. Not because he wanted the information, but because he felt sorry for the chauffeur.

"Yeh, it's fierce!" was the fervent retort. "But she ain't never done this before—that is, not 'xactly. There may be somethin' wrong in the cylinders—full of carbon, perhaps; or then again the valves may need grinding; yuh can't tell whether the oilin' system's workin' up to snuff; and the carburetor may need adjustin', or the mixture's too rich. Even the distributing plug could make it act like this, or maybe water in the gasoline. Perhaps it's been standing too long—and then again it's just possible that a couple of bolts are loose. See?"

"Say!" exclaimed Keeler in honest admiration. "For one set of symptoms exhibited I'll bet you could put it all over the best diagnostician in the medical world—as far as a list of possible causes goes. You're a wonder!"

The man smiled in sheepish appreciation.

"Well, yuh see, I understand a car. I c'n take down and assemble any car that was ever manufactured!"

"Really!" marveled Keeler. "Well, what I want to know is how you're going to locate which one of these dire things is the direct cause of the sudden fatigue felt by the machine. Is there such a thing as an automobile stethoscope or a motor thermometer or—"

"Oh, sure, sure! We got all the tools goin' at the garage. It won't take more'n half to three-quarters of a day to fix her up. Yuh see, yuh just begin an' fix everything that might be the matter an' you're sure to hit it. See?"

Keeler overpaid him and hastened away. The dreariness of that chauffeur's outlook and the hopelessness of his methods of discovery formed the needed impetus to his own case. If it consumed all that imagination, perseverance, and hard labor to locate a clew in an automobile—why, detectiving was a cinch.

He turned in at the van Vleck corner five minutes later. The house was lighted from basement to attic. Keeler felt a wonderful flood of confidence sweep over him. She had not left the city, even though she had had hours of warning. Why? Was it because she did not know anything about the murder? Or because she did—and thought it wiser to allay suspicion by remaining?

He stood across the street, in the fast-gathering gloom, and watched for a moment. The shades were all drawn. Every few seconds a black shadow flickered across the windows on the second-floor front. On no other floor was there a sign of life, although nearly all the rooms were brilliantly lighted.

Keeler tried to discover whether the shadow was thrown by the figure of a man or woman. Whichever it was, the person did not pass close enough to the window for him to determine positively.

A few seconds later the figure stopped directly in front of the window and raised its arms. It was a woman. Transparent sleeves fell away from the rounded elbows, and rebellious little curls softened the smooth outline of the head.

Maids are not in the habit of wearing negligees—Keeler only surmised this—so the figure must be that of Mrs. van Vleck. He crossed the street.

He had mounted two steps of the brownstone stoop when the front door of the house was thrown open and the reeling figure of a man shot out into the vestibule and caught at a doorknob for support. Then the door slammed behind him.

Keeler shrank into the shadow of the post at the bottom of the stoop. He wanted to get a good look at the man without being seen. He soon found how futile his hope had been. He was already discovered.

The unsteady figure flopped from the vestibule to the top step and leaned forward at an angle dangerous to its present powers of equilibrium.

"I see you! I see you!" it prattled as if they two were participating in a game of hide and seek.

Keeler stepped into more prominent view, and mounted a few more steps. At that the irresponsible man flung himself into the little detective's arms and clung to his neck in affectionate abandon. The force of the impact of a heavy body falling from a height almost threw Keeler backward to the sidewalk. By hanging to the stone railing with his left arm he kept his balance.

"Yeh, I see you an' I know all 'bout you!" effused the stranger. "I know who—who—y'are an' everythin'!"

"You have the advantage over me," murmured Keeler coldly.

"'Vantage nothin'!" expostulated the other. "Y'are a reporter—a newspaper reporter. Yessir! An' you've c-come here—hic—you've c-come here to find out all about a scandal in high life. An' I'm the guy—I'm the guy that put the 'can' in that scandal! Ha! Lissen! Joke—didn't I make a joke? Y' didn't laugh."

Keeler bolstered him up more firmly. "You know a lot, do you?" he asked cautiously.

"Lot? Sh'd say I do. Sh'd guess yes! I know most! Yessir, I know most. An' I'll tell yuh b-because I like yuh. I like y'r style. See! I c'n tell a reporter a mile off. I—I saw one once. He was just like you, friend."

"And who are you?"

"Me? I'm—why, I'm the ch-chauffeur. V-Van V-Vlecks' chauffeur. I ain't! I *was!* Yeh, I'm the ch-chauffeur! An' I'm goin' to tell you. Tell whole story. Then maybe they'll think twice before they fire me again."

CHAPTER XVIII.
Getting At the Secret.

Keeler supported the practically helpless man down the remaining steps and propped him up against the round stone post at the bottom. For a moment he was puzzled. He felt an instinctive loathing at contact with this disgustingly intoxicated creature, but he realized that if he withdrew his support there would be a total collapse, and then he could whistle for his information.

The point to be decided quickly was whether it were wiser to deposit the man in some place where he would be safe and quiet, and interview Mrs. van Vleck first, or whether the information the man was so eager to give would be an asset in the eventual interview with the lady.

Evidently she was not going to make a get-away. There was nothing to indicate that the bird was going to try her wings. A second advantage in postponing the talk with her was that it would give the woman a chance to get over her hysteria on the subject—and look at it all in a sane light.

Keeler decided.

He attempted first to persuade the chauffeur to walk a few steps. The attempt was unsuccessful. The man admitted frankly that he "guessed he'd go to sleep right there." Keeler shook him.

"Say, do you want a drink?" he buzzed loudly into his ear.

"F-foolish question number two m-million one hundred an'—" The indistinct syllables trailed off into nothingness.

"Well, now you listen to me and you'll get one."

There was a cold, would-be threatening note in Keeler's voice that carried conviction through the alcohol-steeped tissues of the chauffeur's brain. He looked startled.

"I'm going to leave you here while I look for a taxi," Keeler went on hurriedly, though with exaggerated distinctness. "Then I'm coming back to get you and we're going down to a decent cafe, where we can get some swell booze. See?"

"What'll y' have?" murmured the submerged one, cordial, though semi-conscious. "Make it a little c-clam broth for me."

"But you must promise you won't go away until I get back. Remember, if you do, you're going to get into serious trouble. You need somebody to take care of you for a few hours, because you aren't able to take care of yourself. And most likely if I let you go you'd be in jail, or under a third degree before morning. Remember, if the police get hold of you it'll be more than a week-end trip."

"Say, cap, mind my cush for me, will yuh? I just g-got paid, and th' fellers might swipe it on me, see?"

He dragged out a badly crumpled wad with a yellow wrapper. This he stuffed loosely into Keeler's hands.

"Th' cab an' th' supper's on me," he insisted stubbornly.

"We'll talk about that later," announced Keeler.

He settled him snugly into a little niche at the curve in the railing. Then he went in search of a cab. He found one rolling slowly along West End Avenue, jumped in, and drove back to the van Vleck house.

Through the fleecy dusk no dark shape was visible at the bottom of the stoop. Keeler nearly swore. Where on earth had the fellow gone to in those few minutes?

He could not have stumbled back into the house, because his late assisted exit did not denote exactly that they were going to keep the lamp burning in the window for him any more.

Keeler explored the areaway and the vestibule; he even went through the basement to examine the back yard. No trace of the chauffeur could be found.

He was just about to run up the steps and ring the front-door bell when a voice from across the street stopped him.

There, diagonally opposite, in exactly the same position that he had assumed on the van Vleck's stoop, was the chauffeur.

"The moon was too strong in my eyes," he explained. "Had to move across the street. Oh, please, please lead me to 1-liquid refreshment. I am perishing with thirst."

The "moon" turned out to be a huge arc light that had just burst into bloom at the corner. Keeler tried to make that point clear as he assisted his newfound informant into the taxi. The first stupid daze was beginning to wear off. The man was getting querulous.

"What's your name?" demanded Keeler curtly.

"Dave. The madam used to call me a 'prince' up to a few days ago. Well, she knew she had a g-good—hic—thing. There ain't so many these days that c'n keep their mouth shut. Don't you know there ain't?"

"That's right. Especially when there's anything to keep your mouth shut about."

The little man jumped in, and gave the signal to start. Dave had settled into his corner. He was maintaining a dignified silence.

"I say, especially when there's anything to keep your mouth shut about," repeated Keeler, anxious to get him started.

"Oh, I had plenty I could 'a' squealed about, don't you fret! What I ain't got stored up under my hat! Say, take it from me that set is rotten!"

He lurched sideways, and became extremely confidential.

"I always thought so," gossiped Keeler, without the faintest idea of what set he meant.

"Yessir. You thought right."

Dave looked out of the window and endeavored to keep his head stationary long enough to get a clear focus in the passing scene. He gathered that they were going out of the neighborhood.

"What're we goin' downtown for?" he grumbled peevishly. "There's lots of good booze right round here. Leave it to me, I c'n lead you to it."

That was exactly what Keeler did not want. He thought it about time to begin to sober up the ebullient spirit beside him. A drunken man's evidence—although it may be gospel truth—cannot be relied upon. The little man gripped Dave's forearm firmly.

"I want you to get this," he said slowly, and waited till the shifting eyes sought his. "I'm taking you out of the neighborhood for two reasons. One is because if the police come looking for you they'll go to your old haunts, of course. The other is that I don't want to be seen with you at those places. Your old cronies would surely think something was up if they saw you hob-nobbing with a stranger. You see how I'm trying to protect you—don't you, Dave?"

"You sure are a sport! You're—you're a prince!" exclaimed Dave, using the most extravagantly flattering term that had ever been bestowed upon himself. "What're going to have when we light, eh? I think I'll start in pr-prelim'naries with a rye high. What's yours, eh?"

"Oh, I'm just going to take a glass of Apollinaris if you don't mind. You see, I want to have a clear head for the next few hours."

"Say, lissen!" Dave expostulated. "I had a hunch right along that you was leading me to a seltzer lemonade. Have a heart, can't you?"

"I think, when I've explained things to you," Keeler told him gently, "you'll can the drink for to-night of your own free will. Because you've got a good head, Dave. The shape of your forehead indicates a clever brain."

Dave swallowed bait, hook and all.

"I want to impress upon you," continued Keeler, watching closely the effect of every word, "the very important position you occupy in this case. Just think of all the things you know about it that other people don't know! Things that they want to know—and who's going to tell them? You! Only *you!* Do you begin to see how necessary it's going to be for your brain to clear up?"

"Aw, just one dinky little rye high ain't going to spiff me! You don't know your Cousin Hiram's capacity. I think my hat's inflamed my head. It feels feverish. The band must be too tight and stopped the circulation."

"And another high ball will stop it some more." Keeler was being a deliberate kill-joy. "Now, see here, be sensible for a half hour, anyway. I'm interested in the story you're going to tell. And I know that if you'll only keep your head clear you'll tell it with the art of a born dramatist."

From that moment, Keeler could have asked anything, to the half of his kingdom, from Dave, and have the request granted on the spot.

The taxi stopped in front of a Longacre Square hotel. Keeler started to get out. A little farther down Broadway, a fascinating green-red-and-yellow electric sign, made up of queer-looking dragons that did things, denoted a chop-suey joint.

"Say, if yuh don't mind," suggested Dave, "let's go up to the chink's instead and eat a trough full of that prize feed of his. They don't give you nothin' but tea up there, anyway," this last sheepishly.

They found a table for two in a little alcove, hung with wistaria blooms and tiny Chinese lanterns. They were completely isolated from the rest of the diners. No one could hear their conversation; and from only two tables—in direct line with theirs—were they visible.

Dave ordered by number instead of risking the complicated names that meant pork, lobster, and chicken. Keeler had never eaten chop suey. He never would. There wasn't any doubt about it in his own mind. The rice that they served in little, green-sprigged bowls was going to be his life-saver.

"Why are you sore on the van Vlecks, Dave?"

The question was so abrupt and so unexpected that it stunned the man opposite him. Keeler watched his hands. Sure enough! They closed spasmodically on each other.

"Because they fired me like a dog, without a word of recommendation. Kicked me out! Van Vleck did! And when I went back to get my pay, I tanked up a bit so that I'd have courage to smash him if I needed to. And then the darned stuff got me—and he kicked me out again! Wait till I get him by the throat! Wait till I tell all I know! I'll have him kissing my feet before I'm through."

"You knew Milwood, of course. Didn't you?"

"Did I know him? I used to drive the madam there a couple of times a week. Drove her there last night, anyhow."

"So you were there last night?"

"Sure I was there."

"But you didn't know until late this morning that the body had been found?"

"No. Gee, it scared me stiff when I read it."

"What time did you and the madam reach home from Bay Ridge?" questioned Keeler.

"Now, look here," interrupted Dave, "I gave you my word that I was going to spiel the story. So you better let me tell it in my own way. It won't take long."

"That suits me," muttered Keeler.

"In the first place," began Dave seriously, "I want to tell you that I was always glad to take the madam over to one of them dinners that Milwood used to give so often, because the chauffeurs used to get swell feed, too—and plenty of booze.

"Last night word was sent down for me to get ready and bring the car around almost three-quarters of an hour too early; and it was pulling teeth then to get the madam away.

"We made the trip over in good time. There wasn't a holdup or an unpleasantness all the way into the city. The cook over at Milwood's—he's a Jap—had gave me a small flask for my hip pocket. And while I was waiting for the madam, a rotten night wind blew up from the bay down there. I drank a little more'n was good for me—and when I pulled up at the door I guess I was pretty well fixed.

"Well, the madam ran up the stoop and disappeared into the hall. Just as I was goin' to start for the garage, I found something on the floor, tangled up in my feet. It was the lace scarf my madam had worn over her head to the dinner. I knew how she valued it. I heard her tell one of her friends one day that it had been brought to her from Spain by a man who was an old friend of her father's.

"I heard her say that it was one of the finest specimens of Spanish lace there is, and that she'd rather lose her diamond bracelet than lose that. So you can imagine I was good an' particular the way I ran right into the house with it.

"The front door was open. A carelessness of the madam. She was the last one to go in that way. Of course, when the door was open that way, I went in without ringing.

"I heard sounds of folks quarreling in the library. The doors was shut. I crept along the hall, just for fun, to listen. It was the natural thing to do," he added, in defiant self-defense. "There was a terrible fight going on between the madam and Mr. van Vleck. And then, when it was over and—"

Keeler leaned across the table and let his hand fall heavily on Dave's working fingers.

"You say Mr. and Mrs. van Vleck were having a violent quarrel. Did you hear the subject of that quarrel?"

"Sure, I did!" exclaimed the chauffeur, undismayed. "I heard every word spoke by both of 'em. Why, gee! The quarrel was over where the madam had just come from—Milwood's. He hated to have her go there. I figure it out like this: She got home and maybe found that he was there before her; so I s'pose she thought it'd be easier to lie and say she'd been somewhere else. So she did. But it didn't go down. See? The boss was on to her. And he told her a few plain facts about her actions.

Oh, gee! It was a reg'lar hoopla scene, like yuh see in plays, y' know!"

"Were there any blows exchanged?"

Keeler watched Dave with an eye that missed nothing—not even the smallest shade in the man's expression. He felt that he was telling the truth. And yet he had known so many cases where a person, unaware of any story-telling ability on his own part, becomes carried away by his unsuspected eloquence, and rushes on and on, adding any stray, little embellishment that he thinks will add to the dramatic value of the recital.

"D'you mean did he hit her? Aw, no! She'd 'a' killed him if he had. You don't know the madam. She's prouder'n a queen—and a temper like a hail-storm. Hit her? I should guess not! God help the man who ever insulted or struck the madam!"

Keeler looked at this man across the table from him. He had spoken of great hunger after they entered the place, yet there lay his little silver dish of chop suey and uncovered bowl of rice, untouched and cold. There was something he did not understand, something that would have to be explained before he could believe the man absolutely sincere.

"You imply great admiration for Mrs. van Vleck in your tone, Dave," he remarked, with elaborate indifference. "All the way through, you have seemed to admit with some reluctance that she is an unusual woman. If you have that exalted opinion of her, why are you so anxious to tell all you know—instead of shielding her?"

"Because she didn't shield me when she could have!" snarled Dave, with the religion of "pay back in kind." "She could always hold her own in scraps with her husband, and many's the time I lied myself blue in the face—yes, an' took a callin' down, too—to save her a minute's unpleasantness. But never again! She egged him on when he started to kick me out! Yes, sir, egged him on!"

"Did he accuse her of being too friendly with Milwood?"

Dave grinned.

"Did he? Say, what he didn't say about Milwood could be printed on the head of a pin! I only got a word here and there, but I guess I got enough. When he got through listin' his shortcomings, believe me, I felt like little Eva, next to that kind of a reputation. He ended up with a pleasant little remark that ran something like this: 'If you've got to get stuck on some one, why don't you pick out a man, not a dirty-fingered crook like him?'

"Then, when she didn't give him no answer to that, he says something I don't catch. Then he flings open the library door; and there was I, balancing on one foot, too late to make a getaway."

"Did he—er—did he attempt to do you bodily harm?" suggested Keeler gently.

Dave's lower jaw shot out vindictively. He ground out his answer through his grimly set, irregular teeth.

"No, he didn't 'attempt'! Why, look at me! I'm all smashed up. But then I forgot you didn't know me when I was natural looking. Don't fret, though. He's going to pay—and pay dear—for every one of these bumps and bruises, no matter how small!"

"Eat!" said Keeler. "You must be hungry."

Dave followed the suggestion with ravenous obedience. For two minutes he ate, without once laying down his fork. Keeler watched. There was nothing to indicate that this man was holding back anything. To all appearances he was spitting out, in an ecstasy of willingness, everything that could be used against the van Vlecks.

But Keeler knew that there was something more to come. Something that couldn't be forced from the chauffeur. He decided that the only way he could hope to find out would be not to refer to it at all. It was the same spirit that he had employed where, as a child, he had sat moveless on the back-porch steps, after he had been told four times by the cook that he positively could not have any ginger cakes! He had always found that if he sat there long enough and quietly enough, with never another reference to the lovely things, cook would come out and carelessly slip him a few.

The fervency of Dave's appetite began to get on Keeler's nerves. Then suddenly the chauffeur put down his fork, pushed his empty plate into the center of the table, and smacked his lips.

"Great stuff!" he observed.

"So they say," replied Keeler, who had always entertained a rabid aversion to this bizarre dish that we Americans have wished on the Chinese.

As they took their hats from the grinning Celestial at the top of the stairs, the little man said cordially:

"Well, Dave, you've given me a good deal of information. I may be able to use it. I may not. But you haven't told me one thing that I couldn't have found out from some one else—from one of the other servants, for instance. They could have told me of the van Vlecks' frequent quarrels and their cause. Surely they know as much as you. As to Mrs. van Vleck's presence in the Milwood home last night, I had fastened that fact early this morning—Milwood's Jap man, you know. You haven't given me any mystery news. See what I mean, Dave?"

They were descending the marble steps, their hands sliding along the polished brass rail.

"Mystery, eh?" echoed Dave. "Well, don't you fool yourself. I got a prize little mystery up under my hat, mister. Something nobody knows— something nobody could know very well, except me. Something I wouldn't tell van Vleck no matter how bad I needed money. See?"

"Good for you! I admire your spunk," commended Keeler.

"Yeh. I wouldn't tell van Vleck—but I'll tell you."

They stepped from the glass-inclosed vestibule onto the sidewalk. The Broadway crowds were beginning to swarm into the streets. Dave moved up close to Keeler and talked right into his ear.

"It's just this: Last night, when I'd driven a couple of hundred yards away from Milwood's house, I was told to stop the car. *And a woman got out and went back there!*"

"A woman?" echoed Keeler. "Mrs. van Vleck?"

"Woman!" repeated Dave, in drunken secretiveness. "Never mind naming names."

Keeler took hold of his elbow and swung him about violently. Then he looked deep into his eyes.

The man was telling the truth.

CHAPTER XIX.
THE SILVER BULLET.

"Let's walk down a little way and get some air," said Keeler hastily. "It's pretty lively around here just at this time."

Dave looked at the little chap with an expression of mingled wonder and contempt. Here was a New York newspaper man extolling the white lights as if he had but lately arrived from Wayville, Illinois. He was afraid that Keeler's next suggestion would be "Let's look in the windows."

The chauffeur was suffering from that peculiar nagging grouch from which the too quickly sobered always suffer. He did not want to walk down Broadway. He did not want to look at people who were bright and happy and bound for a good time. He did not want to encourage mirth within himself.

What did he have to be jovial about? He'd lost his job. He'd been kicked around far more insistently than the hound of popular-song fame. He was entwined in the coils of a murder mystery—and he felt rotten!

The inventory of his "things to be thankful for" was disheartening. And besides that he was saddled with a man who, though a New Yorker and of the press, had the instincts of a tank-town tourist. Although he had taken a violent fancy to Keeler when semiconscious, the man's neatly cleaned-and-pressed mannerism was beginning to get on Dave's nerves.

He cast about in his still cloudy mind for a plausible reason to "break loose." All he could think of was that his mother didn't know he was going to stay out. But, as he had not had any mother since he was fourteen; and since when he did have her she didn't care whether he went out and forgot to come back or not, he didn't have the nerve to spring it, even on Keeler.

"Everybody looks kind of gay, don't they?" Keeler sighed, with a happy sense of well-being and the love of all mankind.

"Yeh. None of 'em looks like they've had anything happen to spoil their day yet," agreed Dave, indulging in a mental sob at the raciness of the conversation.

"I wonder where all the people get the money to maintain automobiles."

Keeler made the remark as if it were an utterly original foundation for debate.

"I guess they get it left to 'em," Dave filled in, to keep the conversation from lagging.

"Let's stand here a minute and watch the people going to the theater," proposed the little man. "There are so few good plays, aren't there?"

"Oh, I don't know," criticized the other; "the Columbus puts up a pretty good show every once in a while. There was a crackajack there last week—'The Crimson Queens'—it was a riot! In one part the soubrette runs a boarding house for I. W. W.'s, and every time she comes for their board they hand her a bomb and she hotfoots it downstairs. In another part a college boy gets stuck on her, and—"

"Ah, yes, there's always a college boy and a soubrette and pale-blue-ribbon ingénue and a brace of Hebrew comedians and a Percy with a wrist watch—isn't there?"

Dave gasped.

"You don't mean to say that you've never been to the Columbus, do you?" he spluttered. "*I* always did, till I got sore when they started to ring in the same companies with the name changed, every three weeks or so. Then I quit."

"Let's go in here for a minute," Keeler steered Dave to the door of a large drug store. "I want to get something."

All the clerks were engaged at the moment, so they hung around the counter, waiting.

"They have very good chocolate-fudge sundaes here." Keeler imparted the information with a shade of gusto. "I really think they're the best in the city. Will you try one on me?"

If some one had offered Dave a cyanide sandwich, he could not have looked more horrified.

"What d'you do with 'em? Smear 'em on your hair?" he came back with the snappy patter.

He waited for the laugh that he was sure must follow. Instead Keeler made a serious retort:

"They're pleasant to the taste, and also very nourishing, due to the chocolate. They are, in fact, not a bad substitute for a meal, if one is rushed for time."

Dave groaned.

"Say, what're you going to get in this joint? A teething ring or a box of talcum?"

"No; I want to telephone."

Keeler walked over to a telephone booth and dropped a nickel.

Before central answered, he slid the door shut in its semicircular slot. Then he asked for Riverside 10001.

Lounging against the perfume case, Dave watched him. The conversation of two men, dawdling near the counter, drifted into the chauffeur's meditations. He listened, even though he wasn't particularly interested. They were evidently discussing some one within their line of vision. Dave's curiosity got the better of him.

"No, that one over there—right in front of you."

"Where? At the cigar counter?"

"No, the little man in the gray tweed suit in the telephone booth. The one with the foolish face—the kind of pleasant, foolish face."

"Oh, that one! Who'd you say he was?"

"Why, he was pointed out to me one night at the Half Moon Club. His name is Wayne Keeler—one of the most brilliant detectives in New York. No man knows it, though, except the men who work right with him. He's a member of the Brooklyn district attorney's staff, you know."

Dave's blood began to congeal, starting at his heart and working outward. Then he mentally kicked himself around the block. Those men were talking about somebody else—another man who was telephoning, most likely. He looked around for another booth. Yes, there was one next to the stack of note paper. But its occupant was a brown-eyed girl, wearing a huge red hat perked at a saucy angle. The two men were still talking.

"I'd never take him for a detective."

"Nobody ever does. Maybe that's one secret of his great success."

"What does he work on?"

"Oh, anything he's assigned to. But his specialty is murder stuff. He has the most uncanny faculty of being able to fasten crimes on people least suspected. A man once said about him that he'd bet Keeler could make an absolutely innocent party appear damned beyond salvation if he wanted to do it. He's a wizard, I tell you—and he looks like an agent for grape juice."

Just then Keeler slid open the door of his booth for some air. He was having some trouble getting his number. He had reached the stage where a person does hysterical things with the hook.

"I said Riverside 10001," he insisted, "and you gave me—" The door closed again.

Dave did not stop to consider. He did not hesitate. With one agile bound he cleared the space between where he stood and the main entrance. Then he sprinted.

Fifteen minutes later, Wayne Wisconsin Keeler, dog-tired and mentally depressed, dragged his weary feet up the front stoop of his boarding house.

In the dark of the vestibule, where no one could see, he rested his head against the outer door for a moment before he fitted his key in the lock.

From the front parlor came the strains of the latest fox trot. The new Third Floor Back was teaching its latest possibilities to the Second Front Hall Room. There was a lingering odor of pot roast floating through the door.

Keeler let himself in. Midway between the parlor and the floor, a board creaked under his cautious foot. From the basement rose a plaintive voice:

"Mr. Keeler, is that you? Mr. Keeler!"

Above the barber-shop chords and the forced laughter of the dancers, the call rose, insistent. He had hoped for immunity from persecution for just this one night. He was so tired—and there was so much to do.

"If I don't answer and sneak up the rest of the way, maybe she'll think she was mistaken," plotted Keeler.

No such luck. The music had stopped. The Third Floor Back, in a dripping perspiration from his herculean task of a moment before, came out into the hall to stand in the brisk draft at the front door. The Third Floor Back was young enough to get away with that sort of suicide stuff. At the worst, he would have sniffles the next day and wonder how on earth he got them—when he was "so careful, too!"

Following his example, the horde of young folks trooped out after him. Keeler was discovered.

"Oh, Mr. Keeler, something terrible must have happened!" the blonde with the sparkling green pin in her hair and the putty-colored crêpe de Chine shirt waist exclaimed.

"Is that Mr. Keeler?" rose again from the depths.

"Yes, Mrs. Moody, it is," chorused the "extras."

"Oh, Mr. Keeler! How terrible!"

"Three policemen!"

"It's very important, they said."

The phrases surged up to him where he stood, halfway between the parlor and the second floor. He was confused and provoked.

"You'd better go right around," advised a young man who had thought of studying law but decided to compromise on traveling for a twenty-five-cent-neckwear house. "From the looks of the thing, it must be a pretty urgent matter."

"What?" said Keeler. Then: "When?" And: "How?"

By this time Mrs. Moody had succeeded in working her way to the front row. She came up two or three steps. Keeler noted that she was laboring under a sense of injured pride.

"Oh, Mr. Keeler! what have you done? What terrible thing have you been led into? They've sent three policemen after you!"

"Yes, three!" echoed the mob.

"Where are they?" asked Keeler simply. He spoke as if having three policemen on one's trail was just an ordinary occurrence.

"Why, they're gone!" breathed Mrs. Moody. "You don't suppose for one minute that I'm in favor of having three policemen hanging around my house! What would people think? Why, why, my goodness, they could think almost anything! They went. But they left word that you're wanted around at the station house the minute you come in."

"Then you can be sure I'm not under suspicion of having committed any crime, my dear lady—nor have I disgraced your house. The police are not in the habit of leaving word for crooks to come around and give themselves up, you know."

"Why, Mr. Keeler, the idea! As though I ever called you a crook! Or even told anybody what was in my mind! I was only saying that I'm worried for you, poor boy."

A spasm of fear shook Mrs. Moody's black mercerized moiré. Here was a boarder who paid every Monday, never ate butter on his bread, and went light on red meats. Besides that, he lent caste to the dining room. He was always introduced to guests, company, and new boarders as "Mr. Wayne Keeler, of the district attorney's office." And she had almost insulted the man!

"Maybe a member of your family has gotten into trouble—a black-sheep brother, or even a cousin. I know how those things happen in the tastiest families. If I can do anything at all to aid you, Mr. Keeler, I hope you won't hesitate to call upon me."

"Thank you. But I trust I shan't find it necessary. Will you please give me the message just as you got it, Mrs. Moody?"

Mrs. Moody settled herself for her recital.

"Well, at first a great big policeman came to the basement gate and asked for you. Said you were wanted at the station house. Of course I didn't let him in, so I guess he thought the only polite thing to do was to go away when he wasn't wanted and all.

"Then, not more than twenty minutes later, a little smaller policeman came to the front door with the same message. And about fifteen minutes ago the third little fellow came and said to be sure to tell you the minute you came in."

Keeler turned to descend the stairs. The hushed throng watched him go—the hero who had three policemen after him!

At the station house the lieutenant greeted him cordially.

"You're in demand over in Brooklyn," he told him. "Chief Pyne, of Poplar Street headquarters, got your address from the Kings County district attorney's office. When he found that the house you lived in had no phone, he called up here and asked at three different times this afternoon for a policeman to be sent around to tell you he wanted to speak to you."

"And the three of them came," smiled Keeler. "I'll call from here, if I may?"

"Certainly! There's a booth over in the corner."

Keeler took down the receiver. The old, nervous excitement burned his cheeks a dull red.

"Poplar Street headquarters!" came to him briskly over the wire.

"Chief Pyne," said Keeler meekly.

"Hello!"

"Hello, chief! This is Keeler."

"Oh, Keeler! Say, have you heard?"

"Heard what?"

"You haven't heard, then? Great news!"

"What?"

"The Jap told everything. Under the third degree."

"Told what?"

"The whole thing. The night session. How Milwood was threatened. Everything!"

"Yes? Well?"

"Say, don't sound so glum! You don't believe in professional jealousy, do you?"

"No. Have any arrests been made?"

"Sure! What do you think we are over here? Say, just because it's Brooklyn, you know, is no reason why you—"

"How many arrests?" interrupted Keeler laconically.

"One, of course. The man who killed him."

"What's his name?"

"Craig."

"Craig!" The receiver rattled sharply against the instrument.

"Yeh. The case is all over. Simple. Come in to-morrow. I'll talk it over with you."

"No!" begged Keeler. "Tell me now! You say you've arrested a man named Craig?"

"Alan Craig. Lives in Washington Square, over in Manhattan."

"On what grounds did you—"

"Ichi made a clean breast of it. He didn't want to talk very much at first. But we ripped it out of him. Pretty soon he was glad enough to jabber."

"And the little liar implicated Craig?"

"Liar nothing! It's straight. Straight enough for an arrest, anyhow. And we'll easy get the rest of the evidence."

"Tell me—"

"Jap swears he heard Craig and Milwood quarreling the evening before the murder. Heard Craig threaten to kill Milwood. Saw Craig go back up to Milwood's study after the other people went home."

"That proves nothing."

"No?" sneered Pyne. "But maybe this does: Ichi swears that Craig always wore on his watch chain a funny little charm in the shape of *a silver bullet!*"

"Y-yes?" faltered Keeler.

"Yes!" exulted Pyne. "And Milwood was shot with a silver bullet.

Maybe now you think we have no grounds for arresting him?”

“Did—did he say—”

“Who? Craig? Won’t open his head. Won’t even get a lawyer. Won’t explain about the bullet or anything. We searched his rooms. No silver bullet anywhere there. Good reason! It’s in Royce Milwood’s head.”

“The Jap is lying!” flared Keeler. “Craig never did it. You put Ichi in mortal terror, and he told the first lie that occurred to him to save himself.”

“Not a chance!” crowed Pyne. “Not a chance! You’re jealous, friend. That’s what’s the matter with you. Drop over next time you’ve got a new batch of theories.”

CHAPTER XX.
The Hunt for “M. C.”

Craig was trying to enjoy a very good cigar in very bad surroundings. On the edge of his shelf bed in his gray-lit cell he sat, smoking, poring dully over the morning paper.

His scarce-tasted breakfast had been taken away. And he faced a day whose unbelievable length can be guessed at by no one who has not been a prisoner. For one entire week Craig had faced such days.

His cigar was as dried maple leaves for flavor. His newspaper held not a word to which his interest could cling. His heart was dead. He was as a man new wounded by a bursting shell—dully aware of his mishap, but with nerves still too numb to feel pain.

It was not fear, it was not remorse that gripped and deadened his every faculty. It was utter grief, a grief that blackened his very soul. At his examination he had refused to testify. He had refused to employ counsel. He had refused to see his friends. For the present, until the machinery of the law should take its next step, he was left pretty much to himself. The “third degree” had left him unscathed. A visit from Keeler had been received in sullen grimness, and the little man’s assurance that he was not responsible for the arrest had fallen on deaf ears.

To-day, as on other days, Craig sat waiting—always waiting—for nothing.

At last, with a groan of impatience, he laid aside the paper, tossed away the cigar, and threw himself on his cot.

In a cell on the same corridor a "drunk and disorderly" awoke to find his liquid exultation had not been stolen from him by slumber. And he awakened the somber echoes in an improvisation on "Tipperary." The words presumably were his own:

> "It's a long way, upon the Erie,
>   Wherever you go.
> It's a long ride and a dreary,
>   As all commuters know.
> Say good-by to comfort.
>   Just sit back and swear.
> It's a long, long ride upon the Erie,
>   To get anee-where!"

"Can it!" roared an invisible voice of authority.

And the warbler was mute. For a moment silence fell. Then a man in the cell just across the corridor from Craig all at once broke down and began to cry in a strangled medley of coughs and sputtering sobs.

Craig's nerves began to curl. He picked up his paper again and tried to read it. And just then a blue-coated tier turnkey came to order him out. Craig followed the man, neither knowing nor caring whither he might be led.

In the same drugged apathy he let himself be ushered into a dingy "reception room" with barred windows. There he found Keeler awaiting him. Craig halted with a frown. Keeler came forward with smiling cordiality. But Craig ignored the deprecatingly outstretched hand.

"What do you want?" he growled. "Haven't you done harm enough? Can't you let me alone?"

He was well aware that he was speaking like a cross schoolboy, but his wonted cool nerve had been put to undue strain.

"I haven't harmed you, old man," Keeler assured him, speaking as to a fretful baby. "Honest, I haven't. I've tried so hard to make that clear to you. And, besides, you ought to know me better by this time. I wouldn't harm a fly unless it lit on me when I was trying to get sleep. That isn't kindness, but just because I can't get any fun out of making folks unhappy. Some can. *I* can't."

Craig did not answer, but stood heavy-eyed, listless, uninterested, still unconsciously holding in one flaccid hand the newspaper he had been trying to read when the summons had drawn him from his cell.

"I wish I could say something," went on Keeler, in genuine distress, "to make you believe I don't mean any harm to you—or to any one. Not even to—to whoever did that killing. That's *true.*"

"What did you come here for," asked Craig, softening instinctively at the other's appeal, "if you—"

"I came to ask you once more to tell me how to find Miss—or Mrs.—Madge Carr. No, no"—as Craig's face darkened and he turned away—"don't take it like that! And don't shut up like a clam. I tell you, I've *got* to know where she is, and how to find her. I've *got* to! It's for your sake more than any one else's. It'll help clear things up a whole lot, unless I'm very much mistaken. It'll certainly help to get you out. You didn't do this crime any more than—than I did. Madge Carr can—Now tell me where Madge Carr lives."

"Find her yourself!" said Craig gloomily. "You'll get nothing out of me."

"Find her?" echoed Keeler. "D'you suppose I'd have come back here and risked a jawing from you if I hadn't first tried every other way of finding her? I've looked through the city directories and telephone books and called up dozens of Carrs and gone to see dozens more and gotten the cops to ask—"

"You have mentioned her name to—to the police?" gasped Craig, his lips ashen and dry, his apathy gone.

"I didn't tell them why. Anyhow, it didn't do any good. We couldn't find her at any of the Carr addresses in New York or Brooklyn or in the suburbs. There were plenty of Carrs. Carrs to burn. But no one in any of their families was named Madge."

The tenseness in Craig's face lessened.

"Then," pursued Keeler, garrulous in the tale of his vain quest, "I wrote three letters, and addressed each of them to 'Miss—or Mrs.—Madge Carr.' One in Brooklyn, one in New York, and one to New Jersey. The post-office people are awfully good about tracing people that letters are addressed to. But all three letters came back to me stamped 'Not Found.'"

"Give it up, then. It's no concern of yours, or of any one."

"Give it up?" repeated Keeler, in wonder. "Why, man, I can't give a thing up until I've seen it through. Night before last I tried one more move. I put a 'display ad' in the 'Personal' column of the *Chronicle* for yesterday morning. It went something like this: 'If M. C. knows or wants to help Alan C., will she communicate at once with W. W. K., *Chronicle* Office, Box 6447?'"

"You put *that* in the Chronicle? You little—"

"It didn't do any good. At least, it hasn't yet. I called at the *Chronicle* office yesterday and again on my way here this morning."

"And there were no replies?" said Craig, in visible relief. "Good!"

"Oh, yes," insisted Keeler, with patient literalness, "there were replies."

"What!"

"Yes; three of them. One was a printed form saying the *Diurnal* is a much better advertising medium than the *Chronicle* and I'd get better results by advertising in it. There was a list of advertising rates inclosed, and some testimonials."

"Oh!"

"Then the second letter was from a man who runs a detective agency in Hoboken. He said that for a twenty-five-dollar retainer and seven dollars a day he would guarantee to find 'M. C.' for me inside of a month. And"—Keeler hesitated and blushed, fidgeting a little— "the third letter was—was almost improper. It was from a person who called herself 'Goo Goo' and who said that as 'W. W. K.' seemed lonely she would be glad to correspond with him. Object, matrimony. It had a picture of her along with it. I seriously doubt, though," he added conscientiously, "if 'Goo Goo' is her real name. It seems such an absurd name for a grown woman. And the woman was grown. She had the little lateral lines under her chin, in the picture, that don't come till thirty."

"If there's nothing else you want to pump me about—"

"There is. One thing. You still won't tell me how that silver bullet happened to get out of your possession?"

"No."

"If I'd told the police I found the bullet in the dead man's hand, they would have known it wasn't the bullet that killed him. I didn't tell them. For the fact of its being found in his hand would have been as bad for you, in their eyes, as if you'd really shot him with it. There'd have been the same old story of a struggle and of his snatching it mechanically from you in the death struggle. So I didn't tell. Besides, I'd promised you."

He sighed lugubriously and picked up his soft hat.

"Well, old man," he said, "I wish you'd be sensible and tell me things that would let me help you. But since you won't—By the way, is that this morning's *Chronicle* you're holding?"

"Yes, I believe it is. Why?"

"I told them to keep on inserting that M. C. ad every day till further orders. Can I have the paper a minute, please? I'd like to see what place they've given it to-day in the 'Personals.' "

Craig handed the paper over to him. Keeler fussed through its labyrinth of crackling pages until he came to one whose third column was headed "Personals."

There he halted, turning the sheet toward the unwashed barred window for better light.

His forefinger ran down the column, then checked itself.

"Here we are!" he said. "Third from the bottom. Might have given it a better showing, I should think. Yesterday it was next to the top. See?"

And in his precise, dry little voice he proceeded to read aloud the advertisement, thrilling slightly at the perusal of his first literary production.

> "If M. C. knows or wants to help Alan C., will she please communicate at once with W. W. K., Chronicle Office, Box 6447?"

"That ought to fetch her if she sees it," he added, with modest pride. "She can't help knowing who Alan C. is. I wish they'd put it up nearer the top, though, as they did in yesterday morning's paper. I—*Hello!* Right under it, to-day, there's one beginning—"

He thrust the paper closer to his eyes. His lips mouthed silent words grotesquely as, over and over, he read something. Craig looked at him, first idly, then in faint surprise. Never in all their lifelong acquaintance had he seen Keeler so profoundly, so hysterically moved.

The little man's face went green yellow and sweat ran down his cheeks. Presently, his wabbly knees refusing to support him, he slumped jarringly into the nearest chair and sat there, panting, as after a hard run.

"It's all up!" he moaned brokenly. "Oh, good Heaven, *it's all up!*"

CHAPTER XXI.
A Rabid Lamb.

Craig, dumfounded, roused out of his own dumb misery, watched the writhing Keeler in real concern.

"What's the matter?" he demanded. "What ails you?"

Keeler could not reply. Craig strode over to him and took the paper from his nerveless hands. Keeler made a feeble and belated effort to recover it. But already Craig had found the "M. C." advertisement in the "Personals," and, recalling Keeler's half-uttered sentence of "right under it," glanced at the paragraph immediately below. He read:

> To WAYNE WISCONSIN KEELER, whose ad I read in yesterday's Personals: I know who all those initials stand for, including your own, you see. That is all I have to say. M. C.

"She never wrote that!" burst out Craig indignantly, speaking on hot impulse. "She couldn't. It isn't like her."

Keeler, brought back to himself by the sound of Craig's voice, started up, shaking, and, for once in his life, beside himself with anger.

"He'll pay for this!" he shrilled. "Oh, he'll *pay* for it! I might have guessed, but—but how could I dream he'd know? How *could* I? Tell me that! But he'll pay. I was beaten," he raged on hysterically, "clean beaten, though I wouldn't own up to it, even to myself. But I'm not, any more. I'm in this to stay. And I see light, too. Oh, what a fool he was"—rapping the paper fiercely—"to turn back like this to kick a beaten man. I'll let him find out whether the joke's on him or on me. He'll pay for showing me up—"

"He?" queried the bewildered Craig. "Who is '*he*'? Who on earth are you jabbering about? Have you gone daffy?"

Keeler pulled himself together, with a quiver of his whole small body.

"Did—did I say *'he'?*" he faltered, his old meek self once more. "I meant 'she.' Or maybe 'it.' Just forget it, won't you, please, Craig?"

"I think," said Craig, in crass perplexity, "I think this case has turned your brain. Better rest up. By the way"—to lead the talk to what he deemed calmer channels—"I never knew before that the 'W. W.' in your name stood for 'Wayne Wisconsin.' What a queer—"

"Neither did any one else, as far as I know," cried Keeler, his wrath breaking forth anew. "I've guarded it all my life. I'd rather have lost one of my arms than have people get on to that horrible, crazy name. It's been my secret. The secret I've kept hidden the way—the way you're keeping mum about Madge Carr. And for a blamed sight better reason. Because I didn't want to be everybody's laughingstock. It wasn't any one's business, either. Not *any one's!* And now he's let all the world know."

"He?" asked Craig again.

But Keeler shut up and glowered sulkily out of the dirty window. Nor could Craig's gloweringly indifferent efforts wrest another word from him. Presently the little man jammed his hat down over his eyes and slouched out of the room and out of the building.

Napoleon, calm and self-poised at the crisis of Austerlitz, was wont to burst into tears of weakly babyish rage, it is said, when the imperial barber nicked him in shaving. And Keeler, who in all his uneventful life had not twice lost his temper, found himself in a fuming, half-delirious frenzy at this revelation of his shameful name secret. The blow had shaken him to the very soul. Laugh if you will, you who do not know that a tiny life secret or shame is as zealously guarded by its owner as would be a national scandal.

A handful of dry grass burns quite as fiercely as does a prairie fire. And Keeler's rage blazed as hotly as did the betrayed Othello's.

But as he tramped aimlessly across the bridge back to New York, the exercise and the air and his years of calm reasoning gradually concentrated his flaming anger into a single mighty impulse of vengeance.

The methodical clockwork in the back of Keeler's brain was too firmly established in its workings to be shaken by even the direst mental earthquake. Wherefore, even as his purpose of revenge was crystallizing, he found himself instinctively following out the program he had arranged for the day.

From the bridge he dived down into the bowels of the earth and boarded an uptown subway express. A little later he was walking toward the van Vleck house. He mounted the steps mildly wondering at himself for following out his original routine for the morning, instead of seeking a more alluring road suggested by the advertisement he had read.

The servant who answered the door responded to his almost inaudible query for Mrs. van Vleck—Keeler had mortal cowardice in face of supercilious livery—admitted him to a little reception room, and deigned to take his card. Ignorant of such usages, the visitor could not determine whether the lofty personage's action in admitting him was a sign that Mrs. van Vleck was at home and visible or not. So he nestled uncomfortably on the sharp corner of a spindly chair and waited, hat in hand.

He had clearly mapped out what he wanted to say to Mrs. van Vleck and what he had hoped he might lure her into saying in reply. But the past hour's events had quite unsettled his line of action and had thrown into disarray his neatly drilled cohorts of eloquence. So that the swish of the skirt in the hall outside found him stammeringly unprepared to open battle.

A woman came into the reception room. She was tall, lightly built, decidedly attractive.

Keeler scrambled to his feet, his felt hat squeezed in both hands. It was his first conversation face to face with a woman of her semiexalted class. He did not know what the first move should be. On the stage, at one of his few visits to the theater, he recalled seeing such a grand lady as this sweep into a drawing-room as this woman had just entered. Memory also served to remind him that on the stage one of the characters had greeted her advent by saying:

"Heaven bless your ladyship's bonny face! 'Tis a proud day for us tenantry. Will you condescend to join in our simple revels on the castle lawn?"

Keeler, on memory of this speech, dismissed it at once from the list of possibilities. It did not seem, somehow, to fit the present crisis. Instead, he bobbed his head jerkily, clutched his hat tighter, and, in a burst of loquacity, whispered hoarsely:

"How do?"

Meantime the woman had come straight toward him not at all like the haughty countess in the play, but with a rather winsome smile and with her right hand outstretched.

"Mr. Keeler," she said, before the guest could make up his mind to release his hat long enough to touch her proffered hand, "I am so glad to see you! I've been trying so hard to find you."

She spoke with a quick earnestness and with a sincerity and warmth that were unmistakable.

"Trying to find *me?*" he echoed. "But I've called—"

"And," she went on, "not ten minutes ago, I wrote to you."

"Wrote to *me?*" he gasped, parrot-wise.

"Yes. At least, I was certain it was to you."

"I—I don't understand, Mrs.—"

"Wasn't it your personal in this morning's *Chronicle?* I happened to notice it half an hour ago. I don't generally see the personals. But, as I was turning over the pages, my eye happened to light on such a funny —I mean such an unusual name, 'Wayne Wisconsin Keeler.' And I—"

She checked herself momentarily, for she saw the man flinch as though he had been cut by a dog whip. Then, as he gave no further sign of distress, she seemed to assume that his action was due to some nervous affection, and she continued:

"So I read the personal that began with your name. It didn't make any sense to me. For I didn't associate it with the Mr. Keeler I had heard of. But it was odd, and it interested me because there seemed to be a mystery behind it. And so I read the other personals in the column to see if I could find any more that were interesting. And right above the one I'd first read I came upon a personal *you* must have written. Though I don't quite see how it could have been in the same edition as the one underneath that was an answer to it."

"I had it printed yesterday, too. So the—"

"I see. Well, I read it. And when I came to the part about 'Alan C.,' I knew it must be you who wrote it. So I sat down to answer it. Why did you ask—"

"How can the personal interest you?" he demanded, breaking in bewilderedly. "Unless you can by any chance give me the address I want. I—I believe you *can!*" he cried, in sudden hope. "What a ninny I was not to think of it sooner! You and she were both friends of Milwood."

"I and—who?"

"Mrs. van Vleck," he asked eagerly, "can you tell me where or how to find a Miss—or Mrs.—Ma—"

"Pardon me," she interposed, "I am not Mrs. van Vleck. She is out. That is why I chanced to see your card. I thought—"

"Not Mrs. van Vleck?" he almost groaned. "Am I never to see her?"

"But I gathered that it was *I* you wanted to see. I thought, from the ad—"

"You? Why, I don't even know who you are."

"I am Madge Carr. Mrs. van Vleck is my sister."

CHAPTER XXII.
REVELATIONS.

Keeler stared, bottle-eyed, at her for a full half minute, his gaze as starkly imbecile in its astonishment as though he had just seen the girl change into a coach and four. Then he spoke.

"No," he said, very decidedly, "that can't be. Luck wouldn't come over to my side like that. Not so suddenly. I hate to contradict you, Miss Carr. I mean Miss Somebody. But it can't be—"

He caught himself up, realized he was thinking aloud, and that she must think him a blithering idiot, and regained some sort of control over himself.

"Excuse me," he begged. "I—I wasn't quite prepared for you. You see, I've been looking and advertising so—"

"And I've been trying just as hard to get hold of you. But all I could find out about you was that your name was Keeler and that you came to see Mr. Craig just before he was arrested, and that he seemed excited and miserable after you had gone. I got that from the hallboy at the apartment house where he lives—lived. I didn't think so much of it till I said to Mr. Craig that I'd heard of your call on him and I asked if you had anything to do with the case. He snapped out: 'He has *everything* to do with it.' Then he fell back into that horrible silence again and wouldn't say another word. But I wanted to find you, to see if you knew anything that could clear matters up, or if your visit to him had anything to do with his arrest or—"

"It hadn't. He is a friend of mine. I wanted to help him. He won't let me."

"He won't let *me*, either," she complained. "He wouldn't even *see* me of his own accord when I went to that prison place over there. I had to tip an attendant to get me an interview with him. He seemed to shrink from me. He wouldn't talk at all, except to beg me never to go there again. Oh, it is so *horrible!* I hear he won't make any explanations to the police, either; and he won't even hire a lawyer. *What* do you make of it?"

"Forgive me if I am impertinent," said Keeler, regaining strength and composure under the piteousness of his appeal. "But I want to ask you some questions. Will you answer them? Beforehand, let me say I'm Craig's friend, that I *know* he isn't guilty, and that your help may give me a chance to set him free. I'm in the district attorney's office, but I'm working on this case as a free lance. I won't repeat anything you may say. Will you answer my questions?"

Her big, dark eyes were fixed on his own mild blue orbs, and she was reading deep into his very soul. What she read satisfied her. For, on impulse, she made reply:

"Yes, I'll tell you everything I know about it. Gladly."

"Good! First—you won't be offended?—why did Craig and Milwood quarrel about you?"

"About *me?* Did they?"

"Yes; the evening of Milwood's dinner. Milwood wanted Craig to go in with him on some crooked, deal. Craig refused. Then, a little later, Craig, as far as I can gather, seemed to be threatening Milwood, because Milwood said something about you. I—of course, I don't know whether Craig had any right to—"

"He had every right he chose to take. We love each other."

"Oh, excuse me!" muttered Keeler, as distressedly as if he had chanced to blunder into her bedroom. "I didn't mean—"

"Mr. Craig and I are engaged," she continued, with perfect frankness. "It is not announced. We became engaged only a day or two before he was arrested. That is why I went to his apartment to inquire about him, when he didn't answer any of my telephone calls, the morning after the murder. I was afraid he might be ill. That was why I was so determined to see him at headquarters, and why I bribed my way to him. I *had* to see him. He was in trouble, and he needed me. He needed me terribly at such a time. But when I saw him, he—he would hardly speak to me. I—I don't know—"

"And Milwood?" Keeler mustered courage to ask. "Was he in—in love with—"

"With *me?* Why, no; he—of course he wasn't. I'm certain. I have every reason to know."

"Then it wasn't that kind of a quarrel?"

"It couldn't have been."

"But why else should two men quarrel about you?"

She did not answer at once, and seemed to be pondering. Presently she said:

"I think I can imagine."

"Please."

"It is rather a long story. I'll make it as short as I can. My father is quite ill. His health broke down through money worries and through dreading that he might be disgraced in the financial world. The doctors said that if his cause for worry—*they* didn't know what it was—could be taken away, he might get well."

"But the quarrel between Craig and Milwood," suggested Keeler, trying to lead her back from a supposed digression.

"I'm coming to that. Mr. Milwood had induced my father to become an investor in some of his schemes and to lend the use of his name and influence to them. Father thought they were honest and aboveboard, of course—"

"Of course," assented Keeler mechanically.

"When he found they weren't, and when he found in what peril he stood, it broke him down. He is old and he's not strong. Not only his own money is mixed up in it, and the money of people who invested on his advice, but most of the inheritance left me by my grandmother, and some of my sister's money, too."

"I'm so sorry."

"It's all right. If it goes, it goes. People have lived happily without much wealth. It isn't the money we've been so unhappy about. It's father."

"'We?'"

"My sister and I."

"Mrs. van Vleck? Oh!"

"That was why we went to Mr. Milwood's dinner."

"Because he had cheated your father?" asked Keeler, puzzled, ashamed of himself for so silly a question and looking doubly deprecating after he had asked it.

"Yes," she said. "Indirectly. My sister had written to him to ask for an interview. She and he knew each other well. And she thought she might persuade him to release father from the hideous tangle. Mr. Milwood wrote inviting us to dinner, saying he and Mrs. van Vleck could get a chance for a private chat that evening."

"They did."

"What did you say?"

"Nothing. Go on. But you said a while ago you could guess why Milwood and Craig mentioned your name in their quarrel."

"Yes, I was coming to that. You said Mr. Milwood wanted Alan to join him in some dishonest deal, and Alan refused, and then they quarreled and my name was used. It would have been like Mr. Milwood to hint covertly that unless Alan consented to do as he wished he would wreck my little fortune. It was in his power. And he probably thought that Alan, caring for me, might be brought to terms by such a hint. I don't wonder Alan was angry and threatened him."

"And you think that was the cause of the quarrel?"

"I can't think of any other explanation for it."

"Milwood knew Craig cared for you."

"Probably. He had seen us together often enough."

"H'm!" commented Keeler, only partly convinced.

"Can you think of any better theory?"

"No."

"They arrested Alan because the Japanese servant swore he heard the quarrel, the papers said. Was that enough pretext for so outrageous an arrest?"

"No," returned Keeler, "it wasn't. That wasn't all the Jap told the police."

"But the papers said—"

"The rest of the Jap's statement was kept from the reporters, for some reason best known to Pyne. Ichi also said that he'd seen Craig wearing a queerly mounted silver bullet on his watch chain. And, you remember, the victim was shot with a silver bullet."

"I remember. I read it. But I didn't connect it with—it *wasn't* the same silver bullet Alan used to wear on his watch chain," she declared, with sudden positive assurance.

"I know it wasn't. I have every reason to know it. But how do *you* know it, Miss Carr?"

She seemed startled by the suddenness of the little man's question. She hesitated, then she said slowly:

"Because Alan was not wearing the silver bullet on his watch chain that night—if he wore a watch chain at all. Because he didn't have the bullet in his possession at that time."

"He didn't?" asked Keeler, atremble. "What makes you think that?"

"Because," she answered, her eyes calmly meeting his, "he had lent it to me two days earlier."

"Lent you his watch charm?" asked Keeler, although he saw she was telling the truth. "Why should he do a thing like that?"

"Because I'm silly enough to be superstitious. So is Alan. He was calling here one evening, a couple of days before the murder. I was looking at the bullet, and I asked him where he got it. It was such a queer thing—a silver bullet. He told me Mr. Milwood had picked it up, among a lot of other odd curios, somewhere in Europe or in the East, and had given it to him. I believe he told him the silver bullets used to be made with strange ceremonies, and were blest, too. Alan said, the very day he got it, he had a raise in salary and the next week he recovered a debt he had supposed was hopeless. So he looked on the bullet as a mascot and had it mounted and hung on his watch chain. He told me it was always bringing him good luck."

"Well?"

"Well, father's affairs and ours were at their worst just then. And the foolish notion came to me that perhaps a mascot would improve our own luck. So I asked Alan to lend it to me for a while. He took the bullet off his watch chain and snapped the fastening of its ring around this thin gold bracelet I always wear."

"He did? Then— By the way, he knew of your family's trouble with Milwood, I suppose?"

"No, I decided not to tell him. In the first place, he and Mr. Milwood were old acquaintances and seemed to like each other. I didn't want to cause trouble between them—certainly not until we had made sure Mr. Milwood was not going to be man enough to help my father out of the trouble he had gotten him into. And, besides, father had begged us not to tell any outsider about the affair. He dreaded its being known."

"I see. And now if I'm not tiring you—to go back to the silver bullet. What did you do with it?"

"I lost it."

"Lost it? Have you any idea where?"

"Either at Mr. Milwood's or on my way home."

"You are sure?"

"Yes. At dinner that night it caught in the lace insertion of the tablecloth. I remember Alan disentangling it for me. He sat at my left. And when I got home I noticed it was gone. The fastening had come open."

Keeler got up nervously and began to walk up and down.

"So, now," continued Miss Carr, in sudden inspiration, "we can go to the police and I'll tell them my story about the bullet. That will clear Alan from any possibility of having shot—"

"No," dissented Keeler. "I'm afraid not. But—but I begin to see several things much more clearly. At least, I'm quite certain I do. Very clearly, indeed."

"But *why* won't it help Alan to have me tell?" she persisted.

"Be patient with me a few minutes more, please," he entreated, "and I'll tell you. I've still one or two questions to ask you, if you'll let me."

"Certainly," she replied, her earnest sincerity unmistakable. "I want to help. Oh, I *do* want to help him!"

"And you're doing it by every word you speak," he said gratefully. "Please believe that. Lord! If I could have met you the day after the murder! First—you and Mrs. van Vleck dined at Milwood's. Some of you played cards or had music or something downstairs after dinner.

One or two others went up singly to Milwood's study to talk to him. Do you know who some of the people were who went up?"

"Is it really necessary?" she asked, with visible reluctance, "for me to tell you that?"

"Miss Carr," he answered, with a quite phenomenal burst of eloquent metaphor, "in this case everybody seems to be trying studiously to strike the wrong clews. Everybody except myself. And the only reason I happen to be on the right path—or on one of two right paths—is because I know something—a big something—that nobody else knows. Just before I came here this morning I was going to give up looking for the other of the 'two right paths,' and follow the path I was on to a very quick ending. But seeing you has given me a better idea. You've set me on the second path now. I'm only at the outset of it. But I'd be miles away from finding it at all if it hadn't been for you. And but for you I can't take a step along the path you've helped me find. *Won't* you help me? On my honor, you won't regret it. For it's a path that leads to Craig's freedom, among other things. To his exoneration, too. Say, Miss Carr, I'm no good at making speeches or persuading ladies to do anything they don't want to. But—but—"

"I will tell you anything I know," she broke in, with a new decision. "You ask who some of the people were who went up to Mr. Milwood's study that night. Several people left the living room, for one reason or another, from time to time. I didn't notice who they were. I was playing auction at the time. But later I found out who *one* of them was. She told me. It was my sister."

"Mrs. van Vleck?"

"Yes. I knew our reason for going to the dinner was so she could have a private talk with Mr. Milwood. As I told you. But I didn't see her leave the room. It was only when we were getting into our car that she told me she had had the talk."

"She told you—"

"You have promised never to repeat what I say."

"I have," he panted eagerly. "She told you—"

"She told me she went to beg him to help my father. And—and that he made shameful love to her. He—oh, it is vile to have to repeat such things of a man who is dead!—he said he would reinstate my father if—if she would run away with him."

She spoke with head averted, every word forced from her lips by manifest effort.

"Good!" thought Keeler, exultant, even while he fairly wriggled with bashful distaste for discussing such a theme with a young girl. "Good! She's been telling the truth all along. This proves it. Poor thing!"

Aloud he ventured:

"So your sister told you that?"

"Yes; as we got into the car and started off. I—I was so indignant, so sorry for her, so disappointed at her failing to help father, that I did a very rash and very wrong thing."

"Please," he protested, the vital facts arrayed in full before him, as he thought; and, unwilling to torture her further, "Please don't go on if it makes you unhappy."

But, unheeding, she continued:

"On a crazy impulse, I ordered the chauffeur to stop. I had made up my mind to speak to Mr. Milwood myself. To make one last wild plea to him. I see now how useless it was. But it meant everything to me."

CHAPTER XXIII.
A Divine Lie.

"You—you mean you went back?" exclaimed Keeler. "You mean—oh, you surely don't mean it was you who got out of the car and went back into Milwood's house?" gurgled Keeler.

"Yes; I was almost beside myself. My sister implored me not to. I wouldn't listen to her. The front door was still open. The Japanese servant was holding it ajar for a man who came down the front stairs—from the study, for all I know—as I reached the veranda. It was Alan Craig."

"Craig? He went up to the study, then, after the guests left?"

"I suppose so. We—Mrs. van Vleck and I—had been the last to go. I hadn't seen Alan to say good night to him. I supposed he had gone until I saw him come down the steps and out through the front door."

"He saw you?"

"Yes, he stopped me. But I told him I was going to the dressing room for something I had left. I didn't dare tell him the truth. I knew if I did he wouldn't let me go up there at that time of night to talk with Mr. Milwood. He asked if he couldn't get what I wanted for me. I said no. And then he told me I was as white as a ghost and that I was trembling. And he asked if I were ill. I laughed—or I tried to—and I told him I was all right, and not to be silly, and I said good night to him and waited till I heard him go down the veranda steps. Then I asked the Japanese to take me up to Mr. Milwood's study."

"All alone, and—"

"I tell you I was frantic about father. And I'm forever doing foolishly rash things. I went up there. Mr. Milwood must have heard me on the stairs, for he met me at the study door. I don't clearly remember just what I said to him. But I remember pleading with him to save father from disgrace. I almost went on my knees to him. And oh, how I hated myself to have to beg favors from such a man! I hated him— *hated* him—for the way he had just behaved toward my sister. At last he said he'd think it over and let me hear from him the first thing in the morning. So I came away. There was at least that crumb of comfort to offer my sister. There!" she finished. "That is all. You—you despise me, don't you?"

"Despise you?" he repeated, almost reverently. "I—I think you're— you're—I don't know the right word. You're splendid! But," he added, "you're wrong when you say that's all. That's only just the beginning."

"It *is* all, Mr. Keeler!" she insisted. "Honestly it is. We came straight home and I went to bed. I was so exhausted I went to sleep at once. I didn't even hear Mr. van Vleck come home. Next morning at breakfast I read about the murder. And—"

"You misunderstood me," he hastened to say, in almost frightened apology. "I didn't mean you hadn't told me everything you knew about. You did. I'm certain of that. I meant there is much, *much* more to tell. But it's not by you. Let me thank you with all my heart for telling me all this. And now, in return, I'll tell you something: I can explain why Craig has taken this thing the way he has; why he shut up so, why he didn't want me to find you, or you to find me; and why he didn't want to see you when you went to headquarters. I can explain all that from what you've been telling me."

"But how? What I've told you was only my own—"

"It was Craig's part, too. Brace yourself for something of a shock, Miss Carr. And forgive me beforehand for having to say this—"

"What?"

"Craig thinks you killed Milwood."

"Alan—Alan Craig thinks *that*? Oh, you are mad!"

"No," asserted Keeler, "I'm sane. Craig believes you killed Milwood. That is why he won't deny the crime, why he won't retain counsel, why he looks as if his whole life was broken."

"Alan Craig could never, *never* believe such a horrible thing about me!" she flashed. "I won't listen to such a—"

"He does believe it," doggedly persisted Keeler. "And, to shield you, he is risking his own life. He is prepared to take the blame on his own shoulders to save you. If suspicion should point toward you, I verily believe he would confess to save you. It would be a lie, of course. But it would be a divine lie."

She was listening to him, wide-eyed, incredulous, well-nigh stupefied with amazement. But she found breath to say:

"Will you please explain, if you can, what twist of brain leads you to think that Alan Craig can possibly believe for one instant that the girl to whom he is engaged could possibly sink to such a crime?"

"Perhaps," suggested Keeler shamefacedly, "perhaps he thinks you *rose* to it. There are some forms of homicide that are as praiseworthy as to put a mad dog out of the way."

"I—I don't understand you at all," she murmured, in utter perplexity.

"No? I'll try to explain. Craig saw you go back into Milwood's house late at night, just as he was leaving. After all the other guests had left. He saw you were deadly pale and shaking all over. Next morning he read that Milwood had been found, a little later, murdered. Craig knew you were perhaps the last person, except possibly the Jap, who saw him alive, if you saw him at all."

"And you think, on *that* flimsy thread of evidence, Alan would suspect me?"

"No, I don't. Though it would set him to thinking, to worrying. And it did. When I went to see him in the morning, he was sick with worry."

"But—"

"Then," proceeded Keeler, "I showed him the silver bullet. The one he had lent you. The one he had seen on your bracelet at the Milwood dinner."

"You—*you* showed him the bullet? But how did you ever—"

"The minute he set eyes on it he was struck all of a heap. He was on the point of telling me about his going back to Milwood's study after his quarrel. But when he saw the bullet, he shut up. He threw the thing into the fire and ordered me out of his rooms."

"But where did *you* find the bullet?" she asked once more, in crass astonishment.

"I found it," said Keeler, with slow solemnity, "in the dead man's hand. And I told Craig so."

"In his hand? In Mr. Milwood's hand?" she babbled, aghast. "But—"

"And now, Miss Carr, you know why Craig thinks you did the killing. And you know he *does* think it."

"In his hand!" she kept repeating vacantly. "But I lost it in—"

"I know you did. I know perfectly well you did. You are as innocent as Craig is or as I am."

"But how could the bullet have gotten—"

"I think I know. I have thought so all along. And now I am practically certain."

"Tell me."

"I can't—yet. Very soon I can tell you and every one else; including my wise friend, the chief of detectives. Or, better still, I believe I can make the person who put that silver bullet in the dead man's hand tell it himself."

"The person? Who?"

"The person I'm looking for, Miss Carr. Thanks to you, the 'two paths' I spoke about have at last merged into one. A very few more turnings of that path, and I believe I'll be at its end. I'm sorry I haven't the right to say any more just now. Good-by. I won't wait to see Mrs. van Vleck. There's no reason any more for my seeing her."

"But what am I to do?" she protested. "How can I let Alan go on thinking that I—"

"You can't. You can't let him go on thinking anything of the sort. Here!"

He scribbled a few lines in his neat, cramped little handwriting on the back of one of his cards and handed it to her.

"A note to my friend, Chief Pyne, at detective headquarters," he explained. "Present that, and the chief will see you have an audience with Craig—alone. Tell Craig you didn't commit the murder. Tell him I say so, and that I know who *did* commit it. And that I'll have the murderer trapped inside of one week at the very most. Tell him, too, just why you went back to see Milwood and all that happened. Unless I'm mistaken, Alan Craig will sleep better to-night than he has in a long while. That is, if he believes you."

"*Believes* me?" echoed the girl, from far deeper knowledge of nature. "Why, he *loves* me!"

CHAPTER XXIV.
Another Hopeful Suspect.

Keeler turned to go. Pausing at the door, he methodically drew out a somewhat soiled sheet of paper and a pencil. Opening the paper, he crossed off two names—the names of Mrs. van Vleck and her husband.

"If you need me for anything, at any time, in connection with the case—which you probably won't," he said, "I am employed in the district attorney's office, as I told you. I go back to work there in a few days. And," he added, under his breath, "you can thank your lucky stars, young lady, that Ichi didn't happen to know your name and *did* happen to know Craig's. Otherwise you'd have been a much likelier suspect for him to lay the blame on."

"Good-by," Madge Carr was saying. "And I thank you more than I can say."

He bowed himself awkwardly out of the room—and against some one who had just come into the house and was passing down the wide hall.

Overcome with confusion, he whirled about, stammering apology to a large woman of the Junoesque type. She stared in no great favor at the somewhat shabbily clad little visitor. Madge, who had followed Keeler to the doorway of the reception, threw herself into once breach to relieve the man's squirming embarrassment.

"Mr. Keeler, you wanted to see my sister," she said, with intentional informality. Then, to the large woman: "This is Mr. Keeler, of the district attorney's office."

Keeler was struck by the ludicrously sudden change which swept over Mrs. van Vleck's face.

Mrs. van Vleck became positively ghastly. The full curves of her figure seemed to shrink. She looked at Keeler as might a rabbit at a boa constrictor.

That so large and palpably self-assured a woman should, in her own house, bestow such an abjectly terrified stare upon meek little Keeler was quite unbelievable. Keeler bowed gawkily, and began to shuffle backward toward the front door.

At his first move, Mrs. van Vleck recovered herself sufficiently to bleat nervously:

"From—from the district attorney's office, did you say?"

Prompted by a quick impulse, Keeler answered, in a tone that he tried to pattern after Chief Pyne's:

"Yes, Mrs. van Vleck, from the district attorney's office. In connection with the Milwood murder case."

A gurgling, wordless noise issued from Mrs. van Vleck's lips— lips that had all at once turned yellowish-white, along with the rest of her face. She glared with glassy-eyed fascination at him. Then, before either Madge or Keeler could speak, she braced herself, and, still keeping her twitching face averted from her sister, forced out the words:

"Madge, I—I sent to ask Mr. Keeler to come here this morning. I wanted to see him—to see him on a very important matter. Would you mind leaving us alone together for a few minutes?"

Wondering at this new tone of her usually well-poised sister, Madge made as though to speak. Then, catching Keeler's eye and reading its request, she turned and went upstairs, leaving the little man and Mrs. van Vleck confronting each other.

Mrs. van Vleck, with steps that actually tottered, led the way back into the reception room, the puzzled Keeler following. Once inside the room, she collapsed into a chair and looked up with sodden hopelessness at him.

"Madam," began Keeler, still striving to speak majestically, "you told Miss Carr you had sent for me. Why did you say that?"

"To—to get her out of the way. I don't want her to know till—till she must. I understood why you had come as soon as she said 'from the district attorney's office.' You didn't tell her anything about—"

"No."

"I've been waiting—and dreading this—"

"If you will be frank with me, Mrs. van Vleck," he urged, in his best Chief Pyne voice, "you will find it greatly to your advantage."

Keeler was delighted at his own hitherto unsuspected gifts as a bully; though, with his wontedly precise self-knowledge, he realized he could not have mustered the assurance to speak thus to any one who was not badly frightened. He judged that Mrs. van Vleck, in her normal state of mind, would have awed him into scared silence by a single look—even as could his horrible landlady.

But the woman was far too frightened to note the spuriousness of his majestic tone.

"I am waiting," he said loftily, as she fought for words.

"What—what do you want to know?" she whimpered.

"Pray don't dodge the issue, madam," he retorted. "I think you understand quite well what I came here to learn."

This was a case where the wish was father not only to the thought, but to the hope as well. Keeler was all at sea. But for the woman's manifest terror, on learning whence he came, and upon what business, he would not have dreamed of suspecting anything amiss. Indeed, she was already crossed off his list. He was conducting the interview at a mere venture, hoping to discover he knew not what.

"It will be wiser for you—and better for every one else concerned," he continued sternly, "to begin at the beginning and tell me everything. Everything," he repeated, clearing his throat and looking upon her in cold suspicion. "I will even stretch a point," he added, "and promise that if you will be wholly open and aboveboard with me, I will not report to my office any confession you may make."

Too frightened to note the glaring inconsistency of his pledge, the woman sighed in relief.

"I will tell you," she said shakily.

"Pray do!" he barked.

"I dined at Mr. Milwood's on—"

"I know all that," said Keeler, with a fine show of impatience. "I also know every word of the interview you had with him in his study. Why you went there and the alternative he offered you. Proceed from that point."

"We came home," she said unsteadily. "About half an hour later, Mr. van Vleck returned from the business trip he had been on. He found me crying. He insisted on my telling him why. I didn't mean to tell. I tried not to. But he wrung the truth out of me. He—my husband—is a very determined man. He flew into the most fearful rage I ever saw, and he—"

"Yes, yes! Go on!"

"He swore he would kill Mr. Milwood for daring to make—"

"To make love to you," brusquely amended Keeler, marveling at his own brazenness. "I know all that. Go on!"

In growing astonishment at this man who seemed to know everything, she blundered ahead.

"He said he would kill Milwood. And he said that no jury on earth that heard the story would convict him for doing it. Then he left the house."

"Ah! Taking a pistol along?"

"I—I don't know. I suppose he must."

"He had a pistol in the house?"

"A pistol? *A* pistol? He must have had forty. He has picked them up all over the world, just as Mr. Milwood used to. He got the idea of the pistol-collecting fad from Mr. Milwood when they were associated in business together years ago. He has all types of pistols, from the earliest makes to the latest. I hate the sight of them. They always frighten me. So he keeps them put away in a case in the library."

"Did any of them shoot silver bullets?"

"I don't know what they shoot!" she exclaimed, irritably.

Feeling that her fear was giving place to crossness, Keeler cleared his throat ponderously and declaimed:

"I will hear the rest of your story, madam. He left the house. Well?"

"I watched for him till he came back. It was a quarter of six in the morning when he got in. He was soaked with rain and mud-stained, and his boots were thick with mire. I didn't dare question him then. And he hadn't a word to say. Afterward, when I read the account of the murder, I—I—"

"And he has never touched on the subject since then?"

"Never! And—and I've been afraid to. But every minute I've been dreaming that one of you policemen would come—"

"I can set your dread at rest for the moment," said Keeler. "He will not be arrested yet. Perhaps not at all. Good day!"

He quitted the house abruptly. In the street he carefully rewrote the crossed-off name of van Vleck on his "suspected list."

"As soon as I get this thing all straight in my mind," he muttered plaintively, "some one has to come along and tangle it all up again. But"—with renewed optimism—"the *next* step's plain, anyhow."

CHAPTER XXV.
CAT AND MOUSE.

Half an hour later, Keeler walked into Chief Pyne's private office at detective headquarters in Brooklyn. The chief looked up with a pleasant grin. He had grown to like the modest little chap who had so odd a gift for "seeing things." And, despite the fact that Keeler's earlier discoveries in the case had not been followed by complete triumph, the chief nourished a great, if unwilling, respect for the man's judgment.

"Well, Mr. Keeler?" he hailed him jovially. "Back already, hey? I hoped you'd blow in here again, after our chat with Craig. But when I asked about you, you'd gone. Got anything new?"

"Yes, sir," replied Keeler apprehensively. "I've got a big favor to ask of you. And I don't like to, for fear you'll turn me down."

"Anything short of my pay slip," the chief assured him largely. "Pin a label on it, and it's yours. Spiel away. How much?"

"If one of your prisoners was turned loose—" began Keeler evasively.

"I'm sorry you're at that subject again," grumbled the chief. "I won't stir one finger to help you in your crazy idea of getting Craig out. He's as guilty as—as Benedict Arnold."

"He is as innocent as you are," retorted Keeler, with unexpected spirit. "And I'm going to prove it mighty soon now. But, chief, you're barking up the wrong tree. I'm not talking about Craig."

"Who *are* you talking about, then?"

"One moment! If you were to turn loose one of your prisoners, and if you tipped off two or three of your best men beforehand to be on the watch for him as he left here and to follow him wherever he went, keeping close to him but not letting him know he was trailed— what chance would that prisoner have of making a clean get-away?"

"What chance? About as much as Craig has of getting acquitted."

"I'm sorry. For the sake of my plan. Because Craig is going to be acquitted. Or, rather, he's going to be set free long before his trial."

"Don't let's jaw over that," laughed the chief. "You were talking about the old cat-and-mouse trick. It's been tried a hundred times. Setting a man loose, trailing him to some pal of his that we want to locate, and then nabbing the two of them. It's old stuff."

"How often does such a prisoner give your men the slip?"

"He doesn't. He never does. In books maybe. Not in the New York detective force. Why, how could he? We turn him loose, him not sus- picioning a thing. See? And a handful of men who've been trained to such work for years shadow him. What chance has he? The chance of the good old tallow dog chasin' the asbestos cat through hell. He's *gotta* get caught."

"You don't think you're running a risk, then, of losing a prisoner that way?"

"When the boys are tipped off and waiting, no."

"Then," pursued Keeler, "we come to the favor I was working up my nerve to ask you. About an hour from now will you turn Ichi loose?"

"Turn the Jap loose! Why?"

"Under your usual cat-and-mouse terms. He ought to be easy to follow. And any one of your men is strong enough to catch him again."

"But what's the main idea?"

"If I tell you," responded Keeler, hesitating, "will you give me your word to do as I ask? Or, at any rate, will you promise me, on your word of honor, not to interfere with what I am going to try to do?"

The chief thought for a moment, then answered:

"You're on. I can't be overlooking any bet on getting myself in bad by a promise like that. I won't butt in on your game whatever it is. And, if you can show me a good reason for turning Ichi loose for an hour or two, I'll do that, too. Fire away!"

Hitching his chair close to the chief's desk, Keeler began to speak in a low-pitched, confidential tone. At first his words came haltingly, almost incoherently. But as he warmed to his theme, he talked faster and with the quiet authority of a man who knows he is in the right.

Chief Pyne's face, as he listened, was a study—first of dawning interest, then of amazement, then of frank and grinning incredulity. But finally, as Keeler talked, the mocking grin faded from the detective chief's mouth and eyes, and was replaced by a look of almost blank irresolution. When Keeler had finished, the chief sputtered:

"I don't believe a word of it. You're dippy!"

But he said it without the slightest conviction, half defiantly, half doubtfully. Keeler made no answer. He was satisfied. Presently, with a grunt of surrender, Pyne blurted out:

"You're ripe for the foolish house. And so am I for helping you. But I've got a hunch. And I'm going to follow it just for a flyer. Go ahead. I'll let Ichi loose in an hour, and tell three of the slickest boys to shadow him and to grab him when the time comes. Will three be enough?"

"For Ichi alone they'll be more than enough. Yes, they'll be enough for—for any emergency, I think."

"So do I. And to make things surer I'll send a hint to the central office, in Manhattan, to look out for—"

"No. You gave me your word not to interfere."

"Oh, all right!" growled the chief. "And, anyhow, the whole idea's bughouse. I'm not keen on being laughed at. I won't say anything."

"Not even to the men who are to trail Ichi," exhorted Keeler. "Just tell them to have him followed, and, when I give the word, to take him."

"If he's where you are so you can 'give the word,' " answered Pyne. "Which it's fifty to one he won't be."

"Will you wager fifty dollars to one on that?" asked Keeler.

"N-no, I won't. But it's so. All right, then, Mr. Keeler. Trot along.

And in an hour I'll tell Ichi we've decided to let him go, because we believe he won't try to give us the slip when he's wanted to testify. Good luck. But—oh, it's a fool idea!"

"If it was a fool idea, chief," said Keeler pleasantly, "or if you really thought it was a fool idea, you wouldn't go in on it."

"I'm not going in on it," hastily disclaimed Pyne. "I'm letting you go ahead with it—as—as a favor to you. Just as I might buy my kid a popgun to shoot bears in Borough Hall. And—speaking of guns—you're heeled, of course?"

"Heeled?"

"You carry a gun, don't you?"

"A gun? A pistol? Oh, dear, no. Of course not."

"You—you mean you're horning into that mix-up without a gat! Here, take this along."

He pulled from a drawer a squat, black automatic. Keeler backed hurriedly away from the ugly weapon.

"No," he stammered. "Please. No. I—I don't want it. It might go off. I never handled one."

"Well, I'll be—" ejaculated Chief Pyne. "You're the bravest coward I ever ran up with. Or the sissiest hero. I ain't sure which."

CHAPTER XXVI.
KEELER WATCHES A MOUSETRAP.

AT a tiny card table in one corner of the big living rooms in the house that had been Royce Milwood's, Wayne Wisconsin Keeler was seated. On the floor beside him lay his discarded shoes.

The house remained as it had been on the night of the murder; pending the arrival of heirs-at-law or the appointment of an executor of Milwood's estate—or some other legal process.

Milwood had left no will. And, as no relatives had come forward, his affairs had been allowed to remain in abeyance. Thus, the house was untouched. Its shades were pulled down, its shutters were closed, and a policeman was posted, day and night, in front of it.

The policeman's presence was for a double purpose: to guard

the vacant premises from thieves or morbid hunters of relics, and to provide for an off-chance that an old and asinine tradition might be fulfilled—that "the murderer might return to the scene of his crime." This last despite the fact that the police were smugly certain they had the murderer in a cell.

This afternoon, for some reason, the ever-present policeman had temporarily left his post. The early thrill of the murder being swallowed in later sensations, the staring little crowd that for the first few days had loitered on the sidewalk outside the grounds had melted. Perhaps, to-day, the falling of a cold, drizzly rain may have had something to do with the vacant condition of the street before the house.

For more than half an hour Keeler had been there. He had entered the side door by means of a key supplied by Chief Pyne. And he had purposely left this door unlocked. As he had wished to be on the spot in good season, he had not taken time to lunch before coming thither. Instead, he had stopped at a corner delicatessen, bought a "health lunch," and carried it to the house with him.

This repast he had set out on the little table which he found near a corner window. The shade was down and the room was gloomy. But there was light enough for eating; and, consulting his watch, Keeler decided there was ample time, too. So, after taking off his shoes, he made ready for clothing the inner man. He always felt braver and cooler on a full stomach; as do most people.

But perhaps few people would have chosen the menu which just now graced Keeler's impromptu banqueting board. His midday meal consisted of five cents' worth of zwieback in a paper bag and a half-pint bottle of Kumyss.

Drinking out of the bottle, which he held right sportily in one hand, Keeler dived from time to time into the rattling paper receptacle with the other, fishing out a flinty morsel of the zwieback and crunching it conscientiously. He was quite content with his surreptitious feast, there in the big, dusty room, with its eerie silences and clustering shadows. He counted twenty chews to every swallow of the dry zwieback; and he was duly careful not to swig his Kumyss, but to sip it with true hygienic slowness.

In the *Health Journal* which had converted him to these horrible diet orgies of his, he had also read that a patient, while eating, must keep his mind from all serious or disturbing topics. Wherefore, he shoved out of his brain all save lovingly inane thoughts and sought to become, for the moment, even as a ruminant cow.

Long practice had made this feat surprisingly easy to him. But long practice had not yet taught him to gauge the exact flight of time during these much-chewed and scanty-mentalized meals.

Thus, by mere chance now, did he hear, in an interval of hailstorm-like munching, the faint creak of an outer door.

He set down the bottle and the half-gnawed chunk of zwieback with the guiltily shamed haste of a child caught red-handed in the jam closet. He got noiselessly to his feet, drew out and glanced at his battered nickel watch, and realized, with horror, that in the gross delights of gluttony he had miscalculated the time by a full twenty minutes.

"To think!" he wordlessly scourged himself. "To think that the pleasures of the table should have made me risk the loss of everything! I'm a worthless, bestial gourmand, that's what I am!"

Even as he berated himself, he was speeding on stockinged soles to the wide doorway of the room. There, between the drawn folds of the portieres, he crouched, ready to dodge back or forward at the slightest cause. The hallway, into which he peered through the half-inch opening of the meeting curtains, was even darker than the living room where he had been sitting. But his eyes, fairly well accustomed to the dim light of the house's interior, could make out the scene in front of him.

The hall was vacant. If, indeed, he had heard a creaking of the side door, and if that creaking betokened some one's entrance into the house, there was certainly no sign, yet, of such an intruder.

Keeler knew the lay of the ground floor from several previous visits. He knew that every room on that floor opened into the hallway. And, though two or three of the rooms, on the side opposite the living room, led into one another, yet no one was likely to use so roundabout a method of traversing them, when the hallway provided a shorter cut from one side of the house to the other. To reach the stairs, it would be absolutely necessary to come out into the hall.

Keeler waited, tense, breathless, his mouth open, that he might hear the more distinctly. But, save for a rat scurrying between the walls and the muffled hoot of an automobile horn far down the street, no sound greeted him.

And, on the spur of the moment, he decided that his carefully planned position was a strategic error. There was a door leading into the living room from the rear. Suppose some one should enter the room, silently, from that quarter—the watcher would at once become the watched. Keeler was aware of a nervous tingle at the thought. The situation seemed to call for a change of base.

On velvet feet, he slipped between the portieres and sped down the hall, running close to the side wall to lessen the chance of a board creaking. The journey was scarce fifty feet in length; yet to his over-strained senses it consumed hours of time. Every door he flitted past seemed on the point of flying open and disgorging some hidden and terrible foe. A myriad unseen eyes watched his progress.

Yet in a second or two he reached his goal—the closet wherein he had sat, waiting, on the evening of his call on Milwood. Once there, he breathed again. Now, at least, no secret lurker could creep up on him from behind.

In that hiding place he could, by leaning forward, command a full view of the hall, clear to the front door. And he could not be seen. For he was in the hallway's very darkest part.

As he stood there, a very low and nasally sighing sound assailed his ears, causing him to start ever so little. It came from just behind his head. Then, with an impatient shake of his puny shoulders, he recognized the noise. It was the wind buzzing and droning in the broken speaking tube—the tube through which, before the tragedy, he had heard and half heard the scraps of talk in Milwood's study.

But, that night, the wind had been blowing in sharp gusts. To-day, there was only a vagrant breeze stirring. And the buzz was scarce audible.

For a minute longer Keeler waited, his eyes patrolling the hall and its short double line of closed doors. Then, as he watched, a room door halfway down the hall slowly opened.

No sound accompanied the turning of the knob or the moving of the hinges. The door simply opened; very slowly, indeed. Keeler had to strain his eyes to make sure they were not tricking him; so slowly, so impalpably, in that shadowy gloom, did the neutral-colored portal swing outward.

Inch by inch, the door opened; still with no sound; still with no one coming through its slowly widening aperture. For perhaps eighteen inches it opened, pushed with the utmost care from an unseen hand at its farther knob.

Then the motion ceased. The door stood ajar and moveless for a long half minute, while Keeler crouched and waited for the invisible person behind it to issue forth.

Just as he was assuring himself that the latch had been imperfectly fastened, and that an eccentric wind current from somewhere had pushed against the panels and forced them ajar, the door began to close as slowly and as noiselessly as it had opened.

Little by little it shut. There was no click of the hasp as the door edge came flush with the jamb. It closed firmly and without a trace of sound; a manifest impossibility unless the steadiest of guiding hands chances to be manipulating the knob.

Keeler's thin hair began to ripple along his scalp. He had prepared himself to expect any one or *anything* to come through that mysterious opening. But the uncanniness of a door opening of itself, then closing and latching itself again, was too much for his nerves. He could almost feel a new presence in the gray-dim hall; as though an Invisible had come out when the door was ajar and had closed the portal after It. A gentle sweat began to dampen the watcher's forehead and his palms.

Then, in a way that seemed to him, by contrast, almost business-like and thunderously noisy, the closed door of the hall's rear room, just opposite him, swung wide. A man came out.

Even by that faint light, Keeler had no trouble at all in recognizing the stocky little figure and sallow face of the Japanese servant. And at once the fear of the unseen fell away from him; to be succeeded by a mild ecstasy of relief.

This was no longer a matter of ghosts. Keeler understood. Ichi had prowled around the outside of the house; had found the side door unlocked, and had entered. He had gone through to the middle room, just behind the big living room; had started to open its door; had then gone back into the rear room for some reason, and had, at last, come out of the latter into the hall.

In the reaction, Keeler was so ashamed of himself for his momentary panic, and so anxious to atone for it, that he would willingly have atoned by stamping into a French camp just then, bawling: *"Deutschland Uber Alles!"*

Ichi paused for a moment, glancing furtively around him, as he stepped out into the hall. Then, with quick, light tread, he crossed the wide passageway, opened the door next to the closet against whose rear wall Keeler was pressing, in the darkness, and passed into the rear room on that side.

Keeler waited for perhaps two seconds. Then he left his hiding place and glided after the Jap. The latter had left open the door whose threshold he had just crossed. Keeler stood in the doorway. This was the dining room; as he not only remembered from his former inspection, but as the sight of dustily polished table and sideboard told him.

But the room was empty. The Jap had evidently passed through it to another.

On one side was the kitchen extension; on the other the library. The doors leading to each were open. Which way had Ichi gone?

So little time had elapsed that the Jap could scarce have left the dining room by the barest fraction of a second before Keeler reached its threshold.

Keeler started to follow, meaning to take the direction of the kitchen as the more likely goal of a servant than the library.

He raised his right foot to step forward. As he did so, the dim room suddenly burst into a billion flashes of many colored lights. Lights that crackled and stabbed into Keeler's brain.

The walls contracted with a rush. The ceiling collected itself into one tremendously hard lunge and fell, with a crash, on the top of his head. The floor sprang welcomingly upward to meet him. It hit him a fearful blow in the face.

Then the whole house gently melted into nothingness. And Keeler, for the first time in his life, discovered he was a wonderful swimmer. He was swimming dreamily, but at incredible speed, through a cool, jet-black ocean of nothingness.

CHAPTER XXVII.
Whose Knock-Out?

Keeler vastly enjoyed his cool swim through the blackness of the eternal seas. But presently—or in a century or so—some impertinent meddler reached down a hand from the unseen heights above, caught him about the neck, and lifted him bodily from the delicious caress of the waters.

Though the swim through darkness had been a rare delight, yet the emerging from it into the light of day was a matter of agonizing torture. His head, which had been so drowsily comfortable, was gripped by hideous pains that pierced and rent him.

Billows of deadly nausea swept his very soul. Uncouth babblings smote upon his aching ears. And these coarse babblings gradually began to group themselves into clumps of meaningless words. Then the words took on meaning, and he heard some one eighty miles off remarking complacently:

"He's comin' around all right. I saw him bat an eyelid; and he's breathin'. Once more with the water!"

An icy dash of wetness deluged Keeler's racked head, sluicing out the last sweet remnants of drowsiness.

"Good!" went on the unwelcome disturber of his rest. "Now with the flask!"

Keeler felt his locked teeth pried apart, none too gently. Something—stinging, sweetish, and burningly painful—filled his dry mouth and gurgled like liquid flame down his throat.

Snorting, sputtering, strangling, he tore open his eyes and struggled to his full senses.

He lay on the table in Milwood's dining room. But now the shades and shutters were wide open. Above him leaned a thick-necked man who held a flat, brown bottle in one hand, while with the other he supported Keeler's head. A second man stood close by, grasping an empty pitcher. From the sides of the table onto the floor rug, little rivulets of water were dripping.

Keeler sat up dizzily. The man with the flask put an arm around his swaying shoulders. And now Keeler recognized the thick-necked flask wielder; yes, and the man with the pitcher, too. He had seen them both, dozens of times, at detective headquarters.

And in the doorway of the dining room stood another man he knew—no, *two* men. One had the other by the collar. One was a plain-clothes man of Pyne. The prisoner whose collar he hung to, bull-dogwise, was Ichi. A scared and pitiably abject Ichi, who bore scant resemblance just now to his fearless ancestors, the Samurai.

"All right, Mr. Keeler?" queried the thick-necked man. "Another swallow of the old stuff will put you on your feet."

Keeler summoned all his wabbly and scattered strength to push aside feebly the advancing flask.

"No!" he mumbled. "Alcohol's a poison. I—I read it contains—It—"

Suddenly his memory and his dogged will power came back to him in a rush. Lurching free of the detective's supporting arm, he slid to the floor and stood reelingly, gripping at the table edge for support.

"Quick!" he muttered thickly. "Search the house. Don't let him get away. Search the house and the grounds."

The detectives laughed tolerantly at his almost incoherent vehe-mence. "Easy, Mr. Keeler!" laughed the thick-necked man. "Easy, there! We've got him all safe. Don't you worry!"

"Got him?" croaked Keeler, trying to concentrate his mind once more, and scarce able to control his dazed faculties into a semblance of sanity. "Got him! Thank goodness! Where is—"

"He bolted out of the house at a dead run, looking like the devil was after him," explained the officer. "We nabbed him, and then we came back to see what had scared him so. And to look after you, too, like the chief said we must when he sent us to shadow him. We found you all crumpled up on the floor there, by the door. I put you on the table, and Harris ran to the pantry sink for some water. And—"

"Where is he?" demanded Keeler, unheeding.

"Where?" echoed the plain-clothes man. "Why, right there in the doorway. Kivlin's got him. Are you too groggy to see that far? He—"

"Not the Jap!" cried Keeler, impotent fury surmounting his diz-ziness and nausea. "The other! Quick! Go through the house. The grounds. Turn in an alarm."

"An alarm?" laughed the thick-necked man. "Who for?"

"For—for—I don't know," replied Keeler drunkenly. "Oh, search the house, can't you? He may be here, yet."

"Listen, Mr. Keeler," interposed the detective, speaking as though to a sick child. "You take a good big hooker of this booze and you'll feel more like yourself. We've got the measly Jap. No use searching the house for him."

"The—the other—"

"There ain't any other!" declared the man, a whit less patiently. "I tell you, there ain't any other. This guy was the only one that came in. We was close behind him. And—"

"But the other!" persisted Keeler, his thick speech gradually growing clearer. "Search the house, men! Search every room, every closet, every corner. He may not have gotten away yet. He may still be hiding somewhere here."

"I was like that oncet," volunteered the man in the doorway who held Ichi. "The time the gas-pipe crowd laid for me and put me out. For pretty near an hour after they'd brought me around I could 'a' swore I heard little birdies singin'. And I thought the amb'lance surgeon's whiskers was purple. That's straight. I did. I—"

"Search the house!" entreated Keeler, wholly unimpressed by these interesting glimpses into hallucinary psychology, and staggering toward the door as he spoke. "Do as I say! Come! We'll start with the ground floor. He may—"

"Hold on there, Mr. Keeler!" interposed the thick-necked man. "Go easy. You're liable to harm yourself if you don't keep quiet for a spell."

He laid a detaining hand on the little man's shoulder as he spoke. Keeler couldn't any more have shaken loose that grasp than he could have pushed a stone wall down. He understood for the first time what must have been the feeling of Æsop's shepherd boy when that sensational youth yelled "Wolf!" for the last time. He saw there was no immediate hope of making his meaning clear to these well-meaning numskulls. Forcing his dazed mind to think collectively, he started on another tack.

"Did you leave anybody on guard outside?" he asked.

"Outside?" answered the man with the flask. "No. Why should we? We nabbed this Jap outside. There wasn't any one else to watch for. So we all came in to see where you were and to—"

"The policeman who's usually on duty out there? Chief Pyne told me he'd have him ordered away for a couple of hours. Is he back yet?"

"Not him. His two hours ain't near up. And he won't waste time comin' on peg-post dooty here till he's got to."

"Then any one could have gotten out—could be getting out *now?*"

"Anybody could. But anybody isn't. There's no one to—"

"Listen to me!" commanded Keeler, striving to curb his wild impatience and speaking with almost unintelligible softness. "This Jap didn't knock me senseless. It was some one else. Won't you search the house, *please!*"

"Some one else?"

"Yes. The Jap crossed the hall and came into the dining room. I followed. I was barely a second or two behind him. He had hardly had time to go through one of those two doors. And just then I was struck. It must have been from behind. For there was nobody in front of me. He—"

"That's simple enough. He'd heard you followin' him, and he skipped around to that next room and out into the hall and come on you from behind. It's an old trick."

"He couldn't have done it. There wasn't time. I tell you, he wasn't more than two seconds ahead of me. Some one else—"

"*I* see how it was," spoke up the man who had discoursed so learnedly of songbirds and purple-whiskered ambulance surgeons. "I had the same thing, that time I was tellin' you about. Last I remembered I was turnin' into Waverly Place from Sixth Avnoo. And they found me halfway down Macdougal Alley, where I'd been done up. I didn't remember one thing about gettin' there; nor I don't even yet. The amb'lance surgeon says that's most always the way when a guy's knocked cold. Their mem'ry stops quite a spell before the time when they get hit. The last few minutes or seconds before they falls asleep is always a blank to 'em. Tom Sharkey told me he was in a fight once when—"

"There was some one else!" fiercely protested Keeler. "Search—"

"Kivlin's right," decided the thick-necked man. "I've heard of a dozen cases like it. The last thing you remember was followin' this chap into the dinin' room. That ain't sayin' it's the last thing that happened. Why, for all you know, he may 'a' turned on you, and you had a mix-up with him, and he put you out—all without your rememberin' anything that happened after you—"

"Wait!" implored Keeler, thrusting his hand into his cash pocket and fishing out a little wad of bills. "Here's six dollars. It's all I have with me, except some change. Take it for your trouble in searching the house. Now go and *search!*"

"We don't want any dough from a friend of the chief," stiffly returned the thick-necked man. "If it'll help chase the bats out of your mansard, we'll search the place."

And search it they did, with tolerable thoroughness, Keeler insisting on going with them, in spite of his dizzy weakness and headache. Kivlin alone remained in the hall with Ichi, who by this time had won back his usual cold stolidity.

The search was fruitless. So was the cross-examination through which Keeler sought to put the Jap. Ichi would say nothing, save that he had come hither to collect some of his clothing, and that he had seen no one there. Not even Keeler.

"Then why did you run out?" demanded Keeler.

"Because I had hit you. I thought maybe you dead," replied the Jap, his mask of a face breaking up into a grin of pure mischief.

"Because you had hit me?" insisted Keeler. "Why, man, you just said you didn't see me."

"Maybe I hit you with eyes shut," explained the Jap, his grin broadening into a snicker.

CHAPTER XXVIII.
The "Display Ad."

It was dark that night when Keeler reached the far-uptown and far-upstairs bedroom that he miscalled "home." He was so dead tired that he went straight to bed and to sleep, without so much as taking his regular "fifty deep breaths" at his bedroom window before turning in. He had had a busy day. And he was looking forward, on the morrow, to a busier.

From the Milwood house, he had returned to the Poplar Street Headquarters with the detectives and Ichi. There, when the Jap had been locked up again—this time not as a "material witness," but on a charge of felonious assault—Keeler had gone straight to Chief Pyne.

The chief, having heard the detectives' report, had received Keeler with jocose sympathy. But, after a half hour of earnest conference, the little man had departed, leaving the chief once more battling between intention and common sense, and had even forced from him a decidedly reluctant promise concerning the morrow.

From Brooklyn, Keeler had gone to the *Chronicle* office, and had written, for insertion in the next morning's paper, an advertisement for which he demanded and bought "display space" far in excess of the item's apparent value.

His day's work done, he realized all at once that he was sickeningly tired, that his head ached deliriously, and that there was a bump on the back of his thin-thatched scalp the size of a pigeon's egg. He had been through a wakeful and strenuous day; a day rife with shocks and nerve rack. And he yearned mightily for bed.

Keeler's sleep was miles too deep for dreams. It was the glorious beast slumber of utter exhaustion. And from it, early in the morning, he emerged as from a cold plunge—still stiff and a trifle sore; but wholly refreshed.

As was his wont, he made a pilgrimage to the door at once, and came back bearing the spoils of the brief foray in the shape of a copy of the *Chronicle* and a letter.

Crawling back into bed, he propped up the paper in front of him, and then tore open the letter. It was signed "Hilda van Vleck." It had been sent to him early the previous afternoon, as the envelope showed, by special delivery, and addressed to the district attorney's office. Thence it had been forwarded to his home. He spread wide the stiff page and read:

Dear Mr. Keeler: You promised to respect my confidence, and I am still holding you to that promise. Though, thank Heaven, I am *wholly* convinced, now, of my dear husband's innocence.

As soon as you left here, this morning, I telephoned to him at his office, to come home at once. He reached the house half an hour ago. I told him of my talk with you, and that the district attorney's office and the police suspect him of murdering poor Mr. Milwood. He was terribly overcome. At first I could hardly prevent him from going straight to the district attorney, but I persuaded him he was in no immediate danger. Then he broke down and told me all about that awful night. And I believe *every single* word he said. For he never tells me lies. *Never!* Not once in a year.

Mr. van Vleck admits he left home with every intention of thrashing Mr. Milwood within an inch of his life, if not actually killing him. When he got to Brooklyn, it was very late, and there was a thunderstorm. He is not familiar with Brooklyn, and he got on the wrong car.

He got far out into the suburbs before he found out his mistake. The car conductor told him how to get to Marken Street. It was a mile. He had to walk. Part of the way was across vacant lots and fields.

Mr. van Vleck got to Mr. Milwood's just in time to see two or three policemen hurrying out of the house. He asked what was the matter, and they said there had just been a murder.

My husband waited around in the rain for an hour or more, to learn the details of it. Then there was a block on the cars. The current was affected in some way by the electric storm, he says. And he had to walk all the way to Brooklyn Bridge.

He was still so upset and so ashamed of himself for having gone to thrash a man who was already being murdered by some one else, that he wouldn't say a word about it to me or to any one—till to-day.

He thanks you for promising to keep quiet about it, if possible; but he says, if necessary, the testimony of the car conductor and of the policeman he spoke to will give him an alibi. So while he hopes he won't have to appear in court he is *sure*—and so am I—he will be vindicated. I thought you'd like to know. So I'm writing at once. Very truly yours,

Hilda Van Vleck.

Keeler read the letter. Then he reread it. Then he laid back for a space, with his eyes shut and his scanty eyebrows puckered. Then he sat up, reached for his coat, drew out the "suspected list" and a pencil, and crossed off Van Vleck's name.

"Leaving," he mused, glancing down the overscored names, "only the Tramp. And to-day will end *him!*"

He put back the list in his pocket and picked up the *Chronicle.* Riffling the paper's voluminous pages, he came presently to what he sought. On an inner page, in display type, and surrounded by a "bull's-eye border," was the following advertisement, full four inches in depth and across the width of two columns:

MILWOOD HOUSE TO BE DESTROYED TO-DAY.

The dwelling house at 9999 Marken Street, Brooklyn, formerly owned and occupied by the late Royce Milwood, will be torn down to make way for a storage warehouse to be built on its site. The work of demolition will begin promptly at two p. m. to-day, at which time the J. D. Lowerie Company's wreckers will take possession of the building and set to work at once destroying it.

Bids for timber, firewood, bricks, et cetera, from the house may be made at the afore-said company's offices.

This notice is inserted in accordance with Section 746 of the Building Code of New York State.

By Order of the Court.

CHAPTER XXIX.
ARRANGING A SENSATION.

Keeler read his carefully composed advertisement with gentle satisfaction.

"I wonder," he said, half aloud, "if there *is* a Section 746 of the Building Code. Or if the Building Code has that many sections. Or if there's a wrecking firm named 'Lowerie.' Also, just what is the penalty for inserting a fake 'ad' in a reputable newspaper. As a lawyer, I suppose I ought to know the last answer."

He got up and made ready for the day.

He went, first, to the district attorney's office in Brooklyn and obtained leave for a word or two in private with his chief.

"Well," the district attorney hailed him, "how is the vacation coming on? Let me see—you wanted leave to mix in the Milwood case, didn't you? They seem to have the man who did it."

"No, sir," denied Keeler respectfully. "Not yet. But we hope to before night."

"But Craig—"

"Craig will be free before night, sir. Unless I am very much mistaken, we shall have the real murderer within a very few hours. I called here to ask another favor. Would you mind giving orders to have him brought directly here when we get him?"

"But—"

"You see, sir," explained the ever-apologetic Keeler, "you were good enough to let me 'mix in,' as you call it, on this case. I'd like to have the satisfaction of proving to you, first-hand, that you didn't make a mistake in giving me that permission. Also, sir, to show you that members of your staff are sometimes even more competent than the police. And," he finished, "I think I can promise it will be interesting to *you,* too, sir, to hear the story."

"All right," assented the district attorney, impressed in spite of himself with his subaltern's desperate earnestness. "I'll give the order. But who is the man, if it isn't Craig?"

"Do you mind, sir," begged Keeler, wiggling in his chair and smiling across at his chief in the propitiatory fashion of a puppy that seeks to dodge punishment; "do you mind very much if I keep that back, as a surprise to you? You see, sir," he added, in explanation, "I've spent a lot of thought and all my annual holiday on this business. And I'd like it to wind up with a sensation. I've—I've always wanted to be the center of a sensation. All my life, sir. And I've never been. If you don't really insist—"

The district attorney chanced to be in a genial—almost expansive—mood. The morning's papers had not hammered him. In fact, one of them had devoted a half-column editorial to chanting his praises. And he was in high good humor. He placed no implicit faith in Keeler's far-fetched prophecy of success. But he liked the little fellow, and the latter's eager appeal mildly touched him.

"All right," he vouchsafed, "suit yourself. If I hear the crowds cheering and the salutes fired some time this afternoon, I'll know the sensation's on its way here and that you are in the center of it."

"Oh, no, sir!" the ever-literal Keeler reassured him. "There'll be no crowds and no cheering. I promise you. We'll bring him here very quietly, without any fuss."

"I see," observed the district attorney tolerantly. "Well, as I used to know Royce Milwood pretty well, I hope, for his memory's sake, the sensation will be worthy of such a sensational chap as he was. I don't think I'm betraying any secret when I tell you that I've learned a few things about Milwood lately. I've had a talk with some of the Washington secret-service men. It seems, if Milwood hadn't made such a sensational exit from life, just when he did, he was due for a still more sensational entrance into a Federal prison. He had been under surveillance for days before his death. The case against him was completed at last. He was to have been arrested the very next day. The very day after he cheated the law by dying. There is every reason to believe he knew it, too. He had made plans for flight. The secret-service people found out that much."

"Yes, sir," said Keeler, "I know. And now—"

"*You* knew? How?"

"I made a few inquiries."

"H'm! And now run along and let me get to work. Is it spoiling the effect of your 'sensation' to ask where and how you expect to catch the murderer?"

"There is an advertisement in this morning's *Chronicle*," said Keeler, feeling his way around possible conversational snags, "that work on tearing down the Milwood house is going to begin this afternoon at two. At twelve, the policeman on duty there is going away. I—I think, some time in the next two hours after that, a man is going into the Milwood house. If he *does*—he will be the man we want."

"Keeler," replied the district attorney, "you don't need a vacation; you need a course at some really good sanitarium, under the personal supervision of an alienist."

"Yes, sir," admitted Keeler, in no wise offended, "perhaps so."

"And you have the nerve to tell me this rigmarole about—"

"Just wait till this afternoon, sir," entreated Keeler, "before you pass judgment. And give the order I ask you to. To have him brought straight here. He will be the right man. I'll stake my job on that."

"Yes," was the grim reply, "I rather think you will."

"It's a bargain, sir. Good-by—till this afternoon."

CHAPTER XXX.
THE TRAMP.

Marken Street, Bay Ridge, drowsed in the midday sunshine, like a sleepy cat on a warm doorstep. In front of the Milwood house loitered the solitary policeman to whose presence the neighborhood had grown quite accustomed.

In the disused garage barn, back of the house, sat two men. They had sat there since before sunrise. Burly men they were, in ready-made dark suits and derbies, and with square-toed and super-polished boots.

In the living room of the house, behind the lowered shades, a third man of like aspect sprawled on a leather divan. He, too, had been on duty since before dawn. So had another man who nodded in the one comfortable chair in the reception room across the hall.

A covered grocery wagon, driven by a bony youth, and drawn by an equally bony horse, turned into the street and rattled along the roadway, drawing up, with jolting suddenness, in front of a house opposite Milwood's and two doors farther down. The driver jumped to the ground, moored his steed by means of an iron weight on the end of a rope, dived one arm into the inclosed body of the cart, yanked forth a basket of groceries, and disappeared around the rear of the house.

Which, as any watching neighbor could have testified, was odd. For the house was vacant. Its occupants had moved out two days earlier. And, equally odd, was the fact that the boy did not reappear.

But the good folk of Marken Street are not overcurious or given to idle deductions. And a genuine mystery on that very block—in the Milwood house across the way—had more than sated their inquisitiveness, for the time being. So no one disturbed the somnolent horse or the deserted wagon.

This was just as well, perhaps. For, on piles of empty sacking in the bottom of the cart reclined no less noteworthy a collection of groceries than Wayne Wisconsin Keeler and a very grumpy, sheepishly self-disgusted celebrity, Chief Pyne by rank and name.

"Yes," the chief was grunting under his breath, his cross words barely audible to Keeler, "we're a pair of walleyed fools. But I'm foolisher than what you are. For I've got more to lose. Gee, if the noospapers ever get onto my hidin' in a grocery cart, with my eye to a torn place in a canvas cover, why, I'd be laughed out of the department."

"If we lose, I lose my job," returned Keeler, in the same tone. "I told you that. And my job means as much to me as yours means to you. But we're not going to lose."

"So you said. But—"

"And so you believe, in spite of all your grumbling!" snapped

Keeler, with an unexpected show of spirit. "If you didn't believe it, way down in your heart, you wouldn't be here. And you wouldn't have posted those men in the barn and in the house."

"Huh!" sneered the chief, in lofty disgust.

But he did not continue the argument. An argument which had just had a tenth repetition in two hours. He and Keeler put their eyes anew to worn spots in the ragged sides of the canvas. And silence brooded over their odd vigil.

Presently the policeman in front of the Milwood house looked at his watch, yawned, stretched, and made off down the street, with the air of a boy at the end of a school day.

For a space, stillness and midday calm held the block. A cat crept toward the middle of the street in a laudable effort to stalk a bevy of sparrows. Two little girls came in sight and, arms about each other's waist, ascended the steps of a near-by house. A man rounded the next corner, glanced idly along the street, and slouched down the block.

"There he is!" whispered Keeler.

"Who?" queried Pyne. "Him? The guy that needs a shave and has fringe on the feet of his pants? Gee! He's just a hobo."

"Watch him," returned Keeler.

The prospect that met the newcomer was not one of startling interest. The block dozed in the midday sun. Its men were at business in New York; its women and children at luncheon. Midway between the two intersecting streets a cat stalked sparrows, and a bony horse attached to a grocery cart switched flies with his semibald tail. For the rest, there was not a human being in sight.

The man whom Pyne had so slightingly referred to as a "hobo" scarcely deserved the title so far as looks were concerned. True, his felt hat was dusty and had lost most of its nap, his chin bore the growth of several days' beard, and his black suit was shiny and frayed and grease-spotted, with an ill-mended rent here and there.

But his shoes—first sign of sartorial deterioration—were of good leather and fitted well. Nor, though they needed polish, were they old. Keeler alone noted this fact.

But Pyne himself saw that the man did not bear himself after the hopelessly collapsed fashion of a human derelict. He slouched; but his shoulders were squared, and he gave the appearance of latently lazy strength rather than of bodily degeneracy.

The "hobo" came down the block in half-aimless fashion, glancing now and then from a soiled card in his hand to the house numbers he passed, as though to verify an address.

He passed the Milwood house—Pyne nudged Keeler in contemptuous triumph—then hesitated, turned back, and, card in hand, passed hesitatingly up the walk leading to the veranda, seeming to seek a better view of the house number.

He mounted the steps, with the same hesitating yet perfectly open demeanor, and crossed the width of the porch to the front door. There, feeling for the bell with his left hand, he glanced rapidly up and down the street and, with a key that had been held in his right palm, swiftly unlocked the door.

He swung open the door, stepped inside, and closed it behind him. So swiftly did he do this that the three successive motions seemed one. It was achieved with the deft speed of a conjuror's trick.

A half second later, the muffled toot of a police whistle sounded from just inside the house.

Pyne and Keeler threw themselves from the wagon back, tore across the street, and, abreast, raced up the walk. Keeler could hear thudding feet along the paved way that led around from the rear, and he knew the garage's two occupants were hurrying on their way to the scene of action.

As he and Pyne dashed up the walk, other sounds rose above those of the detectives' running feet. Sounds of scuffling, of stamping, of swearing, of hard-flung bodies banging against walls and furniture. Fifty men seemed to be battling in the hallway there, if Keeler might judge from the racket that came from the house's interior.

Then, of a sudden, the double front doors flew outward beneath a crashing impact, and three writhing bodies were precipitated bodily upon the veranda floor.

Keeler had but the briefest vision of this new stage of the encounter. For, on the instant, one of the trio shook itself free of the other two, leaving a ripped coat and waistcoat in their grasp.

It was the "hobo." By a feat of strength worthy a professional wrestler, and with all the lightning skill of a football half back, he had wriggled free of the two men who were grappling him.

Coatless, his vest and dirty collar gone, his soiled shirt torn from neck to waist, his unshaven face livid, the fugitive cleared the veranda at a stride, and, easily dodging Pyne's cumberous effort to tackle him, cleared the porch steps in one beautiful leap. Ahead of him lay the empty street and—freedom.

Yet, alas, that so splendid a bound for liberty should have so disastrous an ending! Instead of landing lightly and safely on his feet in the middle of the unobstructed walk, the "hobo" came to ground right ingloriously and on all fours.

And this for the reason that Wayne Wisconsin Keeler, close behind Pyne on the steps, had hopped upward at precisely the right moment and had clutched with both hands the only portion of the fugitive's flying body which chanced to be within his reach.

He had grabbed the man by the left ankle, and he hung on. The swinging foot caught him square in the chest, knocking him breathless. The impact of the hurtling body swung him off his own feet and into the air. But he hung on.

Keeler described a parabola through space and struck the flagged walk with the broad of his back. *But he hung on.*

A frantic kick from his sprawling captive lifted him bodily into the air again and brought him back to the flagging with a resounding and agonizing thwack. The imprisoned ankle twisted and jerked with a spasmodic force that sent the blood spurting from Keeler's finger nails and shook him as a puppy worries a dishrag. But—*he hung on.*

Breathless, tumbled about, battered, dragged along the walk, in anguish of body and in deadly fear, he hugged the writhing ankle to him, and endured the fearful punishment inflicted by its attendant leg and by the leg's mate.

All this for a hundred years or more. At least, for the second of time required for four husky detectives to launch themselves upon the madly tugging "hobo."

In fiction alone can a Hercules, prone on the ground, defend himself against a quartet of powerful opponents. And in a half minute, the grossly unequal struggle was ended. The fugitive lay on his back on the flagged walk, his wrists snugly handcuffed, two plainclothes men sitting on his legs, Pyne's black automatic shoved against his panting stomach.

The man lay there, his broad chest heaving, his eyes ablaze with helpless murder light, his shirt and undershirt in ribbons. Pyne, seeing the prisoner was beyond chance of escape, turned his attention to a huddled little figure close by. Keeler, his eyes shut, every instant expecting death, and not at all aware the battle was over, lay asprawl on the ground, breathing in moans and still clinging tenaciously to the captured ankle. He was dully grateful, through his stark confusion of senses, that the hand-wrenching motions and kicks had momentarily abated.

The chief, with the gentleness of a woman, pried loose the thin, tight-locked fingers and lifted Keeler to his feet.

"Mr. Keeler," he said, his voice hoarse and choked by a sudden emotion very foreign to him, "you've done it. We've got you to thank. You're—you're a dandy little hero, that's what you are! I want to beg your pardon for ever thinking you weren't the cleverest, nerviest guy on top of the earth. Ain't badly hurt, are you, sir? Paint's a bit scratched, hey? But cylinders all right. Lord, but you're a *man!* A he *man!*"

Then the prisoner found voice. "You little shrimp!" he snarled. "But for you I'd have won free!"

Keeler drew an agonizing but needful volume of air into his lungs. Then—

"Thank you, Milwood," he managed to say.

CHAPTER XXXI.
Hero Keeler.

The district attorney of King's County sat in his Court Street office. On his usually heavy face was such a look as a matinee girl wears just as the curtain is about to go up. A half hour earlier, a telephone talk with Chief Pyne had put him in possession of decidedly startling facts—the skeletonized story of the capture, the identity of the prisoner, and the announcement that the captors, with their prey, were on the way to his office in Pyne's car.

"And little Keeler was the man to down him," the district attorney was repeating to his secretary. "Meek little Keeler, who never had the spunk to hurt a fly. Hung onto him by the leg till the rest could catch up. Look at the way he worked up the case. How he did it, I can't—"

An attendant came in with word of Pyne's arrival. And presently into the room came five men. Pyne led the way, ushering in his exhibits with true showman pride. After him came two plainclothes men, with a prisoner between them, his wrists shackled to theirs. The captive had secured from some charitable officer a coat which was wrapped closely about him, buttoned up to the very throat, masking his tattered undergarments.

Keeler brought up the rear. There was a walnut bruise on his forehead. One of his eyes was blackened. His under lip was badly swollen. So was his nose. His usually prim neatness of costume had given place to dishevelment that was almost rakish. His hands were bandaged; and through one of the bandages showed bloodstains.

The district attorney rose—actually rose—and came forward to greet him. He sought to shake his battered aid by both hands. Finding the hands shapeless with bandages, he shook Keeler's wrists.

"My boy!" he declared effusively. "I'm proud of you. *Proud* of you. The whole staff is proud of you!"

And this from the saturnine district attorney! Keeler could have wept aloud—more through utter rapture than from the pain occasioned from the emphatic pump-handling to which his sprained wrists were subjected by his chief.

It was his hour!

The district attorney turned to Milwood.

"Well, sir," he remarked. "It seems you weren't content to stay dead? I can't say I commend your choice."

"No?" queried Milwood, with perfect courtesy of voice and manner. "Oddly enough, that is just what I said about the people of Kings County last year when I heard they'd elected you. I suppose you wish a statement from me, and all that sort of thing?"

"Presently," answered the district attorney, flushing. "Just now I prefer to hear from the man who thrashed you. Mr. Keeler, I—"

"Thrashed me?" repeated Milwood. "'Thrash' is such an ugly word. I recall thinking so when they used it about the man who beat you so badly for State senator. May I sit down?"

"Keeler," said the district attorney, presenting his back to the pleasantly smiling Milwood. "This morning I said I wouldn't press you with questions till you were ready to talk. Are you ready now? If you are, I should like very much to know how you discovered this was not the man who was murdered—when every one else, including the whole detective force—declared he was."

Keeler, drunk with joy, and eager as a child to recount his triumphs, straightway forgot the deferential shyness that always gripped him in his chief's presence. Speaking with methodical dryness, he began:

"I knew, sir, because the man who was killed was not a tennis player."

"A—Wasn't a—"

"A tennis player, sir. Perhaps you've noticed, people who play very much tennis always have a callous ridge—right along *here.*"

He indicated the space between the middle knuckle of his right forefinger and the crotch between forefinger and thumb.

"I haven't one myself," he added, "because I don't know how to play tennis. But all players have. Milwood plays tennis all summer, and he plays squash all winter. Look at the ridge on his right hand. It's the biggest I've ever seen. I've noticed it lots of times. Just as boxers have a—"

"But what has that to do with the murder?"

"The man who was murdered didn't have any such ridge on his right hand, so I knew it couldn't be Milwood."

The other men, except Milwood, were looking at the speaker with the admiration children lavish on a conjuror. Such mute tribute after years of snubs and good-natured neglect was as a glimpse of paradise to Keeler. He went on:

"I saw it when I bent to see why the dead man's hand was closed so queerly. It was closed that way because some one had put a silver bullet in his palm—after he was dead. I'll explain that part later, if you'll let me, sir. Well, it was then I knew Milwood was alive some-where. And I set to figuring out where he could be and why he had wanted people to think he was dead. He must have wanted people to think he was dead, you see, or he wouldn't have dressed the other man in his clothes."

"Well?" as Keeler for the first time hesitated.

"Well, sir," answered Keeler, somewhat less vaingloriously, "it was then I started out on the wrong one of the two roads that were open. I wasted a full week on it."

"How do you mean?"

"I started out to find who did the killing, instead of looking for Milwood, sir. I thought if I could get an idea who did that, I could hunt up Milwood himself later on. He'd keep. The body was in a suit of Milwood's clothes, you remember. And the face was destroyed by acid. I knew several people had threatened to kill Milwood. My idea was that Milwood expected to be killed that night, and that he had gotten someone else to dress in his clothes and perhaps make up his face like Milwood's, and then stay at the house that night while Milwood ran away. I still think that is probably what happened. Milwood's clever. We call him 'the man who can do everything.' "

"Thanks," said Milwood.

"Then, I thought, the person who came to kill Milwood killed this other man by mistake and escaped. And that Milwood perhaps came back and put acid on the victim's face, so people would think it was he who was dead. And so the person who had tried to kill him would think so, too, and wouldn't hunt for him any more."

"Good theory," approved the district attorney. "A little tangled in spots. But not bad, for you."

Keeler winced at the last two words. They seemed to wabble his new-built pedestal. But he resumed:

"Then I set out to discover who had killed this unknown man by mistake for Milwood. And I wasted nearly a solid week in proving to myself that none of the people I suspected could possibly have done it. I was about at the end of my tether yesterday morning. Then Milwood put an insulting—a damnably insulting—advertisement in the *Chronicle* about me."

"About one Wayne Wisconsin Keeler," interpolated Milwood.

Keeler shrank from the words as from a blow, and he glanced at the district attorney in terror. But the chief only said:

"Go on, man! Go on!"

And Keeler, with fresh courage, obeyed:

"It made me lose my temper, sir. I'm sorry. But it did. And then I did what I ought to have done a week back. I set out to find Milwood. I believe he killed that man—whoever it was—and made it seem he himself was killed. By his advertisement, I knew Milwood must still be somewhere near New York. And it looked queer to me that he shouldn't try to get farther out of the way. The only reason I could think of for his hanging around here was that he didn't have any money. I knew he was well off. And I knew he'd been getting ready to disappear. So I put two and two together and I figured that he had realized on all his investments before the murder, and had the money in the house, ready to carry off with him. I don't know yet why he didn't take it along the night he went away. But it's clear he didn't. So I guessed he was looking for a chance to come back and get it, and that he didn't dare to while there was a policeman watching the house."

"Good!" said the district attorney. "Very good!"

Keeler beamed delightedly and continued:

"The thought came to me that perhaps he had given it to Ichi to hide somewhere for him and bring it to him. You know, sir, the Jap's story was fishy. I thought he might be standing in with Milwood. But Ichi was locked up, and couldn't get at the money, if he'd really hidden it. So I told Chief Pyne, here, my idea, and got him to let Ichi out—"

"On a string," supplemented Pyne.

"And I got him to have the policeman taken away from in front of the house for a while. Then I went there and hid, waiting to see if Ichi would come. He did. But some one else had gotten in, too, while the policeman was away. And that 'some one' came up behind me and knocked me in the head. I knew a sneak thief wouldn't do that. A sneak thief would want to keep out of the way till both Ichi and I had gone. It would only be some one who didn't mind Ichi's being there, and who did mind my being there. Some one who wanted a word with Ichi. That description didn't fit any one but Milwood."

The district attorney once more nodded approval.

"The man got away," said Keeler. "So I asked Chief Pyne to help me set another trap for him. He 'planted' men there. And I put an 'ad' in the *Chronicle*—I knew from his own dastardly advertisement that Milwood reads the *Chronicle,* and would be on the lookout for 'ads' in it—I put an 'ad' in the Chronicle saying that wreckers would begin tearing down his house at two o'clock to-day. And the policeman had orders to go away at twelve."

"But—"

"If he saw that 'ad'—as I knew he must—and if the Jap had really hidden the money somewhere in the house—Milwood was certain to go for one last look for it before the place was torn down. And—he did."

Keeler cleared his throat, tenderly caressing his fast-closing blackened eye, and finished:

"That is all, sir. Except that Craig couldn't have fired the silver bullet, because the silver bullet he wore on his watch chain was the one I found in the dead man's hand. Where you put it!" he flashed, wheeling melodramatically on Milwood.

"Wayne Wisconsin, my boy," said Milwood, almost respectfully, "in thoughtless moments, from time to time, I have now and then referred to you as a 'dub.' Even as a 'shrimp.' My apologies. That is the highest praise I can give you. You have intervals of almost human intelligence. You're about the only man of my acquaintance who has."

CHAPTER XXXII.
MILWOOD TALKS.

Keeler bent his head awkwardly, in recognition of the compliment. Milwood, in the same tone of lazy banter, added:

"But it seems a pity that so much mind should have so little body to cover it. Why, man, your intellect is almost indecently exposed. By the way, gentlemen, you've forgotten the good old formality. I feel slighted. No one has taken the trouble to tell me that 'anything I say may be used against me at my trial.' It's one of those white lies that—"

"It *will* be," snapped Pyne. "Remember that!"

"I hate to contradict a police official," said Milwood. "It's such a waste of words to do it. Give them time, and they're certain to save one the trouble by contradicting themselves."

"That's a pretty bum joke, Mr. Milwood. I—"

"I hardly expected a policeman would see the point. A family skeleton has no funny bone. But we are wasting the time of our admirable host, the district attorney. The very fault the taxpayers are forever laying at his door. Do you wish a statement from me, Mr. District

Attorney, or do you not? I'm quite ready to talk."

"It is optional with you," said the district attorney coldly. "As Chief Pyne has just warned you, anything you may say will be used against you at your—"

"At my trial? You are mistaken. As the people of King's County have a way of hinting—there will be no trial."

"In a murder case—"

"Murder case? This is no murder case. There was no murder committed."

"Homicide, if you prefer."

"Homicide? Not even that. I didn't kill the poor fool. No one killed him. There was no homicide. There wasn't even suicide."

"The man died of old age, I suppose?" suggested Pyne, with mammoth sarcasm.

"The man died of rush of silver to the head," amended Milwood. "But he wasn't murdered. He didn't even attempt to kill himself."

"Is that also one of those 'white lies' you spoke of just now?" asked the district attorney, derisively incredulous.

"Most lies start out by being white," responded Milwood. "But they get tanned by exposure. However, as it happens, this isn't a lie at all. I didn't kill Parkman. No one killed him. He didn't even commit suicide. I'm rather tired of repeating that."

"And I'm tired of having my intelligence insulted," rapped the district attorney, "by such—"

"I don't insult imaginary quantities. I'm telling the truth. Sometimes I do. I told it, for example, the day I called here to see you last year, and you showed me all through your new offices; and I said—"

"I remember what you said," sharply interrupted the district attorney. "I warn you, Milwood, this insolent flippancy is not doing you any good. You are here on a charge of murder. And you—"

"You say the dead man's name was Parkman?" asked Keeler, so interested as to commit the unforgivable rudeness of interrupting his revered chief.

"Yes, Parkman. Shall we drop this airy chit-chat and get down to facts, gentlemen? I'm quite willing to tell you anything you may want to know. But my time is valuable. I have an appointment in lower Manhattan in an hour."

"An appointment in—You'll be lucky if ever you are free to keep appointments again. It won't be for some years, at—"

"It must be inside of an hour. I always keep my appointments."

"This is cheap bluffing."

"Wait till the hour is up before you say that, please. And now, do you or do you not want my version of the affair? I'm ready to give it without prejudice and without asking immunity. Do you or don't you want it?"

"Oh, *please!*" begged Keeler, in childish eagerness. "Please, Milwood!"

"Go ahead!" grunted Pyne.

"I'll be as brief as I can. You've probably heard I was in trouble with the Federal authorities over what they chose to call a misuse of the mails and one or two other silly charges. There was a leak—a leak I paid well for—and I got the tip. One afternoon I had word the government case was ready enough for an arrest. And I was to be taken into custody next day. It was time to get out. I was prepared, as Keeler guessed. I had gotten together, in cash and negotiable securities, about twenty-two thousand dollars. I had it in a steel strong box in my desk. When I got the tip, I made my plans to take the steel box on a journey, and to start just before dawn. The route was all planned. They wouldn't have found me in a thousand years. Anybody got a cigarette?"

No one answered. Milwood continued:

"I had a dinner on for that night. The night before I was to start. The night before the day they had arranged to arrest me. That afternoon, as I was leaving the Half Moon Club, I ran into Parkman."

"The tramp?" asked Keeler excitedly.

"I fancy he looked enough like one. These are some of his clothes I'm wearing now. So you can judge. Though how you happened to know I met him is more—"

"Who was Parkman?" demanded the district attorney.

"A chap I'd been associated with in a mine deal, some years back. We were old chums, Parkman and I. It was more by luck than skill that I was able to jump from under when the crash came. He was slower in dodging. And they got him. For a five-year term. He was turned loose only a month or two ago. And he started on a still hunt for me. He traced me, by and by, and came up to me that day. I don't mind confessing it shook my nerve. He was the last fellow on earth I wanted to see, just at that critical time. I gave him the slip. But he followed me. He found, somehow, where I lived. And that night he paid me a call."

"That night?" echoed Keeler. "But I saw—"

"After the people had gone. I was in my study. I had just changed from my evening clothes into a business suit. I was getting ready to go. But I was worried, for I had had word that evening that some one was hiding in the grounds. And a—a friend in the government employ had just called me up and told me there was a secret-service man watching the house to keep me from going away in case I might have a notion to leave before they could arrest me. That complicated matters. I couldn't very well walk out with my steel box under my arm—it weighed like lead, and it was a foot square—without being caught. My only chance was to get out in disguise. But any secret-service agent would suspect if a man should sneak out of my house at such an hour carrying a big bond box. And if I should be caught going out with all that money on me, it would amount to a confession. I was wondering how to—"

"But Parkman?" broke in Keeler, impatient.

"Quite so. Parkman. Forgive the digression. I was in my study there, alone. Ichi had locked up and gone to hod. I heard a window open behind me. In crawled Parkman. He'd climbed up the waterspout. He didn't see me at first. I was in the other corner of the room, with part of a bookcase between him and me. He sat on the sill and kicked off his shoes. I heard them drop onto the turf below. That was a cheap burglar trick he had picked up in prison, I suppose. A fool trick, at that. He was always an ass. He kicked off his shoes and then swung himself into the room in his stockinged feet. That was when he saw me."

"I see!" shrilled Keeler, in delight. "*I* see! That's why there was mud on the waterspout, and why there was none in the room. Remember, chief?" he appealed to Pyne. "And no one slid down that pipe afterward. For the mud was still on it in the morning. The mud from Parkman's shoes."

"By all means," smiled Milwood, "keep it up, sonny. The busy little brain is never still."

"Go ahead!" ordered the district attorney, as Keeler purpled with mortification at the tone of merry patronage. Milwood complied willingly enough.

"We had an unpleasant five minutes, Parkman and I, till I persuaded him I'd not been to blame for his bad luck and that I was willing to help him all I could. I took the cringing tone that all weak idiots love. And he began to think he had the whip hand. I let him think so. And, very gently, I was steering him to suggest what I wanted him to suggest—or, rather, to demand. You see, he and I were pretty much of a size, and we weren't unlike in looks. I wanted him to shave, groom up a bit, put on a suit of mine, take a big suit case full of worthless stock certificates and so on, and go away. He would be certain to be nabbed by the secret-service man in front of the house. By that dim light, in the storm, he'd easily pass for me. Especially to a stranger who barely knew me by sight. The secret-service man would either nab him or else trail him. In either case, the coast would be clear for me to escape with my bond box before the secret-service agent could find out his mistake. I was sure he hadn't been able to see Parkman shin up the waterspout. It was too dark. And, besides, it was at the other side of the house."

"Now, that was clever!" applauded Keeler, in reluctant admiration.

"It was," modestly agreed Milwood. "I have a way of being so. That's what makes me different from the rest of you. No offense, Mr. District Attorney. Well, I jockeyed Parkman into ordering me to do that very thing: To fit him out with clothes and cash and send him, rejoicing, on his way. I consented—after a deal of whining and begging him not to be so harsh and implacable in his treatment of a dear, old friend. I gave him a suit of mine. He put it on. I was just going to get some shaving things for him when he caught sight of a nail clipper in a drawer of my desk. He took it out and began to cut his nails. And, while he was cutting them, he began to notice a lot of old weapons that hung on the wall. 'I may as well be heeled, too,' he said. 'I'll just help myself.' And he did. He happened to be standing just under a little 'gag' pistol I'd bought in the Black Forest. It was one they'd used in the seventeenth century for shooting witches and warlocks and sorcerers and werewolves and such mythical vermin. You may remember reading—but, then, you wouldn't, for it is *literature,* and not in daily newspapers. Anyhow, people used to think that demons inhabited witches and werewolves, and that an ordinary weapon had no power to harm them. So sacred guns and pistols were made, and 'sacred silver bullets' molded—a leaden bullet could not harm witches. The weapons and silver bullets were blessed by the local priest.

"This was such a pistol—the one above Parkman's head. When I bought it, it was still loaded—it's a flintlock, of course—with a silver bullet. And a second silver bullet was in a sort of box in the butt. By the way, I once gave that second bullet to Craig, the man you've very brilliantly locked up for murdering me. I—"

"You say the pistol? How—"

"It was loaded when I got it. I never took the trouble to draw the load. There was something quaint in the memory of an unsophisticated old German having loaded it, in the firm belief it would kill some one 'possessed by devils.'

"The light was not strong in the study that night. I suppose Parkman thought it was a more modern pistol. Anyhow, he reached up for it. It was hanging on a nail by the trigger guard. Parkman gave it a yank. The trigger must have caught on the nail. Anyhow, the pistol went off.

"It made a tremendous racket and a lot of smoke—with all that old-fashioned black powder, such as our ancestors made. Parkman tumbled in a heap. He struck against a vitriol carboy as he fell. It upset. The pistol had been directly above him. And the silver bullet drilled a hole clean downward through the top of his head. A queer shot. I never saw one just like it."

"Never mind that. What—"

"Ichi came running in in his pajamas. The shot had waked him. He caught sight of the body—lying, face down, in a puddle of vitriol—before he saw me. And he set up a yell. I saw he mistook Parkman for me. That gave me my idea. Up to then I'd been cursing my luck that the man I'd counted on to fool the secret-service agent had passed beyond the chance of helping me. Now I saw a loophole."

"And," intervened the district attorney, "that was your first thought on the death of your old friend and dupe?"

"I'm not a hypocrite," disclaimed Milwood. "I thought 'if Ichi can be fooled into thinking it's my body, perhaps other people can.' I brought Ichi back to his right mind and I made him turn the body over. Then I saw my plan was feasible. The vitriol had—had done horrible things to the face. No one could have recognized it. I worked out my plan of campaign and explained it to Ichi. He is devoted to me—"

"The blazes he is!" mocked Pyne; but Milwood paid no heed, and resumed:

"I thought I'd try to confuse the trail just a little. So I had a rug tacked down over the vitriol on the floor. Then I put in Parkman's hand something I'd picked up on the stairs a half hour earlier. I had a slight grudge to pay—"

"Against Craig," supplemented Keeler. "And the thing you found on the stairs was his silver-bullet watch charm. It had fallen from some one else's bracelet."

"Yes? I fancy so. Next, I arranged for the body to lie close to the door. So close that the door couldn't be opened unless the body was shoved away. I told Ichi where to hide my bond box—in a cupboard of the attic. Then I rehearsed him in the story he was to tell. From what I read in the papers, he seemed to have told it pretty well. I advised him, if they tried to give him the third degree, to break down and say he'd heard Craig threaten to kill me, and to tell about the silver bullet Craig used to wear."

"You mean to say—" broke in the district attorney; but Milwood went on serenely:

"Last of all, I made Ichi lower me by a rope from the study window to the ground. It was dark. No one could see. I told him beforehand to climb out of the room through the transom, then nail the transom shut and put putty over the nail heads. I thought all that might give the police a little something to puzzle over."

"It did," vouchsafed Pyne.

"I put on Parkman's clothes and stuffed a hundred dollars in his vest pocket. Ichi lowered me to the ground. I went around to the other window and groped for Parkman's shoes. I found them; and I dropped them, with the pistol, down the corner sewer. Ichi had already taken the vitriol carboy to the cellar before I left. The coast seemed clear. The secret-service man hadn't seen me. I was sure Ichi would be turned loose in a few days. I had told him where to find me with the bond box. Then the bad luck set in."

"There seems to have been just a little bad luck already," ventured Keeler, in a laudable effort at irony. "For Parkman, anyhow."

"Bad luck, as far as I am concerned," politely corrected Milwood, "means bad luck to *me*. It began twenty minutes later, when I thought I was far enough away to venture on boarding a trolley car for Flatbush Avenue. I was bound for Great Neck. Or, rather, to a pleasant little hotel near there. I had given Ichi the address and had told him to bring me the bond box to the hotel as soon as he could get off. I boarded the car and felt for the roll of bills I had just put in my vest pocket. It was gone."

"Gone?"

"It must have fallen out when Ichi lowered me, or else when I leaned over the corner sewer mouth."

Chief Pyne chuckled aloud, as at some pleasing thought.

"I hadn't a cent with me. I couldn't go back for money, for by that time the alarm would probably be raised. I got off the car and walked for the rest of the night. In the morning I pawned an old Etruscan ring—the only thing of value on me. I got two dollars for it. I've been living on that ever since.

"Of course, I had to give up the Great Neck idea. I went back to Marken Street as soon as I dared. A policeman was in front of my house. I kept near there, off and on, every day afterward. But yesterday noon was the first time the policeman was off duty. I got into the house and went to the attic cupboard. The bond box wasn't there."

Again that mysterious and jovial chuckle from Pyne.

"I ransacked the whole house," said Milwood. "In the middle of my hunt, I heard some one else come in, and I hid. Then I heard a third person come into the house. I peeped out. I saw Ichi go into the dining room from the hall. Keeler was just behind him. I wanted to get the bond box from Ichi. I cracked Keeler over the head from behind. Ichi heard him fall and came out into the dining room. But at sight of me, the idiotic Jap bolted before I could stop him. I got out as quickly as I could, for I heard men shouting in the yard. To-day I came back, and after I'd passed the corner once or twice I saw the policeman leave his post. I went in for a second look for the bond box. That's all."

"Not quite all," contradicted Keeler. "That abominable advertisement you put in the *Chronicle's* 'Personal' column yesterday!"

"Oh, that!" laughed Milwood. "I picked up a copy of the *Chronicle* at a branch Y. M. C. A. reading room the day before. I always read

'Personals.' They amuse me. I hit on yours. Any fool could have known who 'M. C.' and 'Alan C.' and 'W. W. K.' stand for. I judged you were meddling. So I went without two free-lunch meals to put that other 'Personal' in the next day's paper. Just a gentle rebuke. And as a goat capturer. I remember, as a kid, how you hated to have people know your funny middle name."

"It was dastardly!" blazed Keeler. "But—but I got even. It was my advertisement about your house being torn down that got you there to-day."

"About my house being torn down?" echoed Milwood, in astonishment, whose genuineness could not be doubted. "What do you mean?"

"Didn't you read this morning's *Chronicle?*"

"No. I never read the *Chronicle* unless I happen to pick it up by chance. What's this nonsense about tearing down my house?"

Keeler could have wept.

"Hold on," spoke up Chief Pyne, coming to his relief. "Now that you've talked so freely to us, Mr. Milwood, turn about is fair play. I'll just give *you* a bit of news. The rest of you, too," he added, glancing at the district attorney.

CHAPTER XXXIII.
"The Man Who Could Do Everything."

The intermittent and oft-repressed chuckles wherewith Chief Pyne had punctuated the last phases of Milwood's story now broke bounds in a genuine guffaw. The district attorney looked up in cold and wondering disapproval at the detective chief's unseemly mirth.

"'And therein is the Scripture fulfilled,'" quoted Milwood, in a pietistic whine, "concerning 'the laughter of fools'—or am I thinking of what Goldsmith says about 'the loud laugh that speaks the vacant mind'?"

"The 'loud laugh' is on *you*, friend," grinned Pyne, no whit offended. "Listen—to begin with, you overlooked a big bet in thinking that hundred-dollar roll fell out of your pocket. It didn't. Ichi lifted it. Lifted it out of your vest pocket just as you grabbed the rope to climb down from your window to the ground."

"Ichi?" repeated Milwood, with crass incredulity.

"That same Little Brown Brother," Pyne assured him. "The one who is 'so devoted to you.' He's just about as devoted to you, Mr. Milwood, as he'd be to an attack of smallpox."

"Rot! I ought to know. He's been in my employ for years. As for his stealing—"

"My friend, you may recall that we stopped the car at detective headquarters on the way here, and I left you people and went in there for a few minutes? Well, I learned a lot while I was inside. I had the Jap hustled into the front office. I pointed you out to him. I told him you'd just confessed."

"Confessed? Confessed what?"

"That he was the murderer. I told him we'd have him in the chair inside of two weeks on your testimony. That loosened him up with a vengeance. Lord, how he talked! Gave me the whole thing, and straight."

"I wish you had told me," yawned Milwood. "It would have saved me the trouble of talking so much. I regret I cast so many of my verbal pearls before swine."

"Blaze away!" chuckled Pyne. "He substantiated what you've told us, all right. But he said a lot more. For one thing, that he hates you like poison, because you knocked him down that night. He was planning to kill you himself—quite a passel of people seem to have had that pleasant ambition in life. He was meaning to creep in and do it when you went to sleep."

"Ichi?"

"It appears, from what he says, that he comes of good folks, back in Japan. A family, I take it, called 'Sammy Rye.' "

"Samurai," corrected Keeler.

"Yep. Just as I said. And it's a killing matter to hit one of them with the fist. So Ichi was layin' to get you, when, all of a sudden, he hears that shot and runs in to see what's the row. When he finds out what's happened and that you're meditating a sneak, he thinks he's got his revenge dead easy. Easier than by killin' you. He says, out in Japan, when men go dead broke or are fugitives from justice or anything like that, they have to sell themselves out as servants or go to the hills. It makes 'em outcasts. And he says it's a heap worse to be an outcast than to be dead. And Brother Ichi cast *you* for the alloorin' rôle of outcast."

"He told you all this? The little cur!"

"All this, and more. To make sure of havin' you be an outcast, not only from the law, but by bein' broke, he lifted your wad. Then, when your back was turned, after he's done the stunts you told him to with the transom, he takes the bond box and hides it. Not in the cupboard in the attic, but up behind an old-fashioned fireplace in your back kitchen. No wonder you couldn't catch him!"

"He—"

"When I turned him loose yesterday, he makes a break for your house to see if, by any chance, you'd found the box. And maybe—for all I know—to help himself from it. Just as he gets to the kitchen he hears a bump. He turns around and sees Mr. Keeler, here, layin' on the dining-room floor and you standin' over him. Ichi thought you suspicioned him. He thought you'd killed Keeler and that you'd be killing him next. So he's scared stiff and makes a get-away. Right into the arms of my men. Now, then, is 'loud laugh' on you, or isn't it, Mr. 'Man who can do everything'?"

Milwood sat back in his chair, exhaustion and defeat writ plain in every line of face and body. Slowly he turned to the district attorney.

"I'd like to ask a favor of you, sir," he said, in a humility as pathetic as it was unusual. "I am beaten. Will you let me telephone to—to a very dear friend—before I am locked up? I want one private word with her. Surely it can do no harm," he urged, pitiful in his defeat. "You've got me fast enough. I want to—to say good-by to her. May I? There's a telephone booth in the anteroom, if I remember rightly."

To Keeler's amaze, the district attorney answered:

"Yes, Mr. Milwood, you may do that. I see no harm in permitting it. But, of course, a detective will go into the anteroom with you to guard you, and will stand outside the booth while you are talking. He will not be able to hear you. But he will see you don't escape."

"Just as you like," said Milwood, with courtly dignity. "I thank you from the bottom of my heart. And—and I beg to apologize for the language I used toward you to-day. If you will order my handcuffs removed—I can't very well talk privately in a booth when I am manacled to two detectives—I shall be your debtor. Chief Pyne himself can go along, if he wishes, to see I don't try to escape."

At a word from the district attorney, the handcuffs were removed; Pyne ostentatiously drawing a pistol at the same moment and covering the prisoner. The district attorney picked up the telephone on the table in front of him.

"While you are gone," said he, "I will just call up the Federal authorities and tell them you are here. They want you rather badly, you know."

"I know, sir. And—I thank you again."

Milwood crossed the door of the adjoining room; Pyne, pistol leveled, at his heels. Milwood opened the door.

"Wait!" barked Pyne. "I'm taking no chance on your bolting. Let me go through first."

He backed through the doorway into the anteroom, warily keeping the prisoner covered. Milwood followed; at an order from the district attorney, shutting the door behind him.

On the same instant, the district attorney's manner underwent a change.

"Hello!" he called eagerly into the transmitter of his desk telephone. "Switchboard operator? Connect this wire with the anteroom phone. Quick!"

Turning to Keeler, he said:

"It will do no harm to find out who his possible accomplice is, and to hear what he says. He'll talk freely, because he will think nobody can overhear."

Delighted with his own acumen, he raised the receiver to his ear. In the same gesture, he motioned Keeler to pick up a second appliance for the right ear. Keeler, now understanding his chief's unusual clemency in granting Milwood's favor, hesitated. He was not minded to do any more eavesdropping. But the district attorney commanded sharply:

"Put the other receiver to your ear. It may be necessary to have you as witness."

Keeler reluctantly obeyed. He lifted the little cap of rubber that dangled from midway down the green cord running from the wall apparatus to the telephone. Thus, each with a receiver to his ear, the two waited.

It seemed to Keeler that they waited an interminable time, without hearing a sound. To him, the fever of the chase being spent, this spying on a man's private talk over the telephone was distasteful.

All at once, Milwood's voice sounded through the double receiver. The dignity, the pathos, the proud humility were gone from his tone. It was gay, mocking, debonair.

"Mr. District Attorney," came the scoffing voice. "You're there, aren't you? I felt quite certain you would be. I told you I wanted to say good-by to a dear friend. *You* are the dear friend. A man is known by the company he keeps. That's why I'm leaving yours. A man is also known by the company he promotes. That is why I am forced to dodge the Federal authorities, too. Good-by. Would you mind quoting to Pyne from the old wheeze about 'he laughs best who laughs last'? My regards to the excellent Keeler. Perhaps he and I may have another merry little bout, some day. If he—"

The district attorney, recovering from his astonishment, dropped the receiver as though it burned him and made a dash for the anteroom door. The door was locked. It required two minutes' time and the combined efforts of Keeler, his chief, and the two wondering detectives to break it open. At last the lock broke, and the four men piled, pell-mell, into the anteroom.

On the floor beside the empty booth lay a writhing man, clad only in underclothes, and who was snugly bound with his own suspenders and shirt, and gagged with his felt hat and his necktie. The door leading out into the corridor was also locked on the far side.

"Slugged me in the jaw and put me out!" sputtered the chief, as they pulled away his gag. "When I came to I was like this. Clothes, gun, cash, watch—all gone. He stumbled. I tried to catch him from falling. And it was then he slugged me. Where is he? Let me get at him! He's done—*me!*"

"He's the man," muttered Keeler, with a note of awe in his mild voice—a voice lost in the tumult about him—"he's the man who could do—*everything!*"

THE END.

Appendix
Original source publication

This novel was serialized in four issues of *The Popular Magazine,* from the May 23 1915 issue through the July 7 1915 issue.

May 23 1915

Chapter I through IX

Front text:

Author of "The Fate Chaser," "An Amateur War Lord," Etc.

The most bashful and retiring man on the district attorney's staff— a young fellow who fills his leisure moments with the cheery study of criminology—takes a vacation and spends it uniquely: by delving into a murder mystery! Like "The Phantom Shotgun," which brought us many congratulatory letters, this novel of Terhune's absolutely defies solution till the closing pages. Here you will find all sorts of clews, and it will be curious to know how many readers will reach the heart of the mystery before the young attorney does.

(In Four Parts—Part One)

End text:

TO BE CONTINUED.

The second part of this story will appear in the issue on sale two weeks hence, June 7th.

Editorial changes

overhead was changed to overheard

sulphuric was used in this story and has been retained, as opposed to the more modern and common sulfuric

heterogenerous was changed to heterogeneous

thoughful was changed to thoughtful

Not wishing to appear rude, he restained that impulse.
was changed to
Not wishing to appear rude, he restrained that impulse.

June 7 1915

Chapters X through XVI
Front text:
Author of "The Fate Chaser," "An Amateur War Lord," Etc.
SYNOPSIS OF OPENING CHAPTERS
Of the three men, only Milwood attracted notice in the metropolis
for brilliance and enterprise. Craig was a promising metallurgist, while
the other man of the trio, Keeler, was in the district attorney's office,
his hobby criminology, but his disposition diffident. The same night
that Milwood invites Craig to a dinner party, Keeler calls. Being shy,
Keeler tells the Japanese servant that he will wait in the back hall until
Milwood is disengaged. While there Keeler suddenly becomes aware of
a tiny, far-off voice threatening to kill someone. He is startled into listening for more. Nothing but a buzzing noise rewards him. Then, quite
as suddenly as before, he hears an echo of fierce altercation. Near as he
can judge they are the voices of his two friends, Craig and Milwood,
hotly arguing over a crooked deal. Again, there is a threat of death,
and Craig leaves the distant room, apparently. Now a woman's voice
is mingled with that of Milwood. She pleads for her father. Milwood
answers by making violent love to the woman; suggests that they run
off together. She replies that her husband would kill Milwood if he
knew of his treachery. At this moment Ichi, the Jap servant, interrupts the tense dialogue to tell the woman—Mrs. van Vleck—that
her sister suggests it is time to leave. Keeler hears the woman swish
out of the room and then hears Milwood curse Ichi and knock him
down. Thoroughly alarmed, Keeler leaves his place in the back hall
and slips away, but not before discovering that he had overheard all
these things through a disused speaking-tube. Interested in just such
problems Keeler makes notes of the extraordinary number of threats
and dangers hanging over Milwood's head. Nevertheless, he is startled
next morning to read glaring headlines announcing the murder of
Milwood, whose body has been found with a silver bullet through

the head and the face disfigured beyond recognition from sulphuric acid burns. Keeler makes up his mind to try his hand at solving the mystery. Ichi is being held as suspect. Going to headquarters, Keeler requests Chief Pyne to accompany him to the scene of crime. Keeler examines the body and the premises and makes a discovery. He turns to Pyne with the conclusion that the Jap is innocent. "You can let him go free!" he says to the bewildered chief of police.

(In Four Parts—Part Two)

This story began in the POPULAR dated May 23rd, still procurable at the news stands.

End text:
TO BE CONTINUED.
The next installment of this novel will appear in the issue on sale June 23rd, two weeks hence. Reserve your copy.

June 23 1915

Chapters XVII through XXV
Front text:
Author of "The Fate Chaser," "An Amateur War Lord," Etc.
SYNOPSIS OF PRECEDING CHAPTERS
Of the three men, only Milwood attracted notice in the metropolis for brilliance and enterprise. Craig was a promising metallurgist, while the other man of the trio, Keeler, was in the district attorney's office, his hobby criminology, but his disposition diffident. The same night that Milwood invites Craig to a dinner party, Keeler calls. Being shy, Keeler tells the Japanese servant that he will wait in the back hall until Milwood is disengaged. While there Keeler suddenly becomes aware of a tiny, far-off voice threatening to kill someone. He is startled into listening for more. Nothing but a buzzing noise rewards him. Then, quite as suddenly as before, he hears an echo of fierce altercation. Near as he can judge they are the voices of his two friends, Craig and Milwood, hotly arguing over a crooked deal. Again, there is a threat of death, and Craig leaves the distant room, apparently. Now a woman's voice is mingled with that of Milwood. She pleads for

her father. Milwood answers by making violent love to the woman; he suggests that they run off together. She replies that her husband would kill Milwood if he knew of his treachery. At this moment Ichi, the Jap servant, interrupts the tense dialogue to tell the woman—Mrs. van Vleck—that her sister suggests it is time to leave. Keeler hears the woman swish out of the room and then hears Milwood curse Ichi and knock him down. Thoroughly alarmed, Keeler leaves his place in the back hall and slips away, but not before discovering that he had overheard all these things through a disused speaking-tube. Interested in just such problems Keeler makes notes of the extraordinary number of threats and dangers hanging over Milwood's head. Nevertheless, ha is startled next morning to read glaring headlines announcing the murder of Milwood, whose body has been found with a silver bullet through the head and the face disfigured beyond recognition from sulphuric acid burns. Keeler makes up his mind to try his hand at solving the mystery. Ichi is being held as suspect. Going to headquarters, Keeler requests Chief Pyne to accompany him to the scene of crime. Keeler examines the body and the premises and makes a discovery. He turns to Pyne with the conclusion that the Jap is innocent. "You can let him go free!" he says to the bewildered chief of police. Keeler resolves to search out Mrs. van Vleck. He telephones to her, with startling results—she faints. Keeler is on his way to her home when he sees a suspicious-looking fellow; a man he had noticed lurking about Milwood's place. Keeler shadows him, only to discover the chap is a secret-service agent!

(In Four Parts—Part Three)

This story began in the POPULAR dated May 23rd, and can be ordered at the news stands.

End text

TO BE CONCLUDED.

The final installment of this novel will appear in the issue on sale July 7th.

July 7 1915

Chapters XXVI through XXXIII
Front text:
Author of "The Fate Chaser," "An Amateur War Lord," Etc.
(In Four Parts—Part Four)

This story began in the POPULAR dated May 23rd, and can be ordered at the news stands.

Editorial changes
For a minute longer Keeler waited, his eyes patrolling the hall and its short double line of closed door.
door was changed to doors

Publisher's general notes:
References are made in dialogue to two then-popular newspaper panel comics by cartoonist Rube Goldberg.
First is "I'm the guy who put the ___ in ___." Besides the newspapers, this fad took the form of pinback buttons and sheet music.
Second is "Foolish Questions," which were numbered (though not consecutively).

The upper/lower case of the name **van Vleck** was inconsistent throughout the story. For this edition, the lower case **van** was used, except when it started a sentence.

This serial was not illustrated.

Turn this book over for another complete novel
by Albert Payson Terhune!

When *Liberty* Was *Born*

Albert Payson Terhune

When Liberty Was Born

SCP Tête-bêche
Book IV

Silver
Creek
Press

2021

CHAPTER I.
I Lose My Temper.

I STARED down open-mouthed, dumfounded, at the mischief my clumsiness or stupidity, or both, had wrought for me.

There, strewing the muddy snow of the gutter, lay the scattered sheaf of great scarlet roses.

The bonbons, too, were everywhere—soaked, spoiled. The pretty porcelain-and-gold box that had held them was smashed to a hundred pieces against the ground.

And there, barring my way, with arms akimbo and fire-flashing eyes, stood the daintiest, fiercest atom of girlhood my country-bred eyes had ever beheld in city or country.

For a space we stood looking at each other—I, looming up bulky and gawk-like in my homespun suit, coonskin greatcoat, and long, muddied boots; she, indescribably lovely in her scarlet silken cloak and hood, her little flower–face aflame with wrath and her great brown eyes ablaze.

Then it occurred to me I had somewhere read or heard that 'twas monstrous bad manners to gape openly at strangers. Now, for manners, in those days, I gave scant care. Yet an unknown something (that annoyed as much as it perplexed me) suddenly made me averse to the idea that this little town-bred aristocrat should think me the uncouth and unsophisticated youth I was.

So I contrived to drag my eyes from hers, and made shift to step past her along the Beacon Street footpath to my destination.

But it seemed I had reckoned without my host (or hostess). For she halted me at my first move.

"*Wait!*" she commanded. And even in its anger, her voice rang as sweetly clear as a silver bell.

I stopped, involuntarily, at the imperious summons.

Wait!" she repeated sharply. "Is Boston a howling wilderness like your own native woods that you think you can blunder against a gentlewoman in Beacon Street, upset the precious things she is carrying, and then plod onward without one word of excuse?"

"I—I was not looking," I muttered, bashful as any unbirched schoolboy; "I did not see you until I chanced to jog your shoulder with my swinging elbow in passing and—"

"And knocked from my arms the first winter roses Boston ever saw!" she caught me up. "The roses Sir William Howe himself sent me this morning. Yes, and my comfit-box of Milan porcelain! There is not such another in the Colonies."

"Well," growled I, glancing down at the shattered box and bedraggled roses, "'tis done. Why make such pother over it?"

"*What?*" she gasped, as though doubting her own ears.

"I say," repeated I still more sullenly, "why make such fuss over a handful of weeds and a few bits of sugar? As for the china box—if sixpence will make good its loss, I—"

"Oh!" she broke in, a little whirlwind of fury. "You *lout!* You trapper of the forests! Must you destroy my pretty gifts—and that without a word of civil regret—but you must also seek to thrust a coin upon me? Spend your sixpence on a 'Book of Polite Manners.' They are for sale at the bookstall in Milk Street. And 'twill profit you! Or stay out of Boston until you have learned the ways of civilization."

"We be as 'civilized' in my home at Wilbraham," quoth I hotly, "as are you Boston folk. We do not frill our speech with fal-lals and spend our good money for china boxes and roses. But, for all that, it ill befits you to make mock of my home. Even if we cannot boast a populace of seventeen thousand as does Boston, we teach our women to hold their tongues and not rail at their betters."

"Their *betters?*" she repeated blankly, evidently taken aback by my sudden torrent of heavy sarcasm.

"Yes, mistress," I retorted, "their betters. Is not man ever the superior of woman? Doth not St. Paul say—"

"*Oh,*" she cried again in impotent rage, "if only one of my father's lackeys had escorted me abroad this day! He should cane you until—"

I broke into a laugh of honest amusement.

"On Springfield Fountain," I interrupted, lazily flexing the mighty

muscles of my arms and chest, "I net a black bear last year, when Lieutenant Merrick's son and I had robbed her lair of its cubs. Merrick ran at her onset. *I* killed her with my naked hands."

"You did?" she gasped, unwilling admiration for the instant replacing wrath in her bright face. "I believe you could. You are a giant!"

Then, suddenly catching her breath, she returned to the attack:

"And the bear doubtless bequeathed to you her manners," she flashed. "Though had she manners such as yours, she richly merited death. Here! Even bears may be trained, by the will power of a human being. Take your first lesson from me. Pick up those roses and give them to me!"

I stared at her, bewildered. In my farm country it was an unheard-of thing in those days for a woman to dare order a man about.

We naturally expected our womenfolk to wait on and otherwise obey us. That this slender slip of a Boston girl should give me orders—

"Pick up my roses!" she commanded again. "Every one of them. And hand them to me."

"Do you take me for a slave?" I roared, all at once finding my voice and my dazed wits.

"Every true man is a slave to courtesy," she returned. "A gentleman would have been restoring my scattered treasures to me ere they fairly touched ground, and would have overwhelmed me with humble apologies. But," she added, "for the matter of that, a gentleman would not have been so clumsy as to knock them out of my—"

"A *gentleman!*" I mocked boorishly. "Thank Heaven, I am no fop! As for parlor tricks and pretty speeches, I have sense enough to regard them as time wasted. Whereas—"

"Whereas," she caught me up, "they are the divine oil of life's wheels. But we digress. Pick up those roses!"

"I will not!" I snapped. "I am no—"

"Pick them up!"

"Pick them up yourself, if you value the silly weeds. I—"

"Pick them up!"

"Enough of this childish folly! I—"

"You will pick them up, bear! *At once.* Do you hear?"

Her sweet voice was calm, steady, low-pitched. Yet it angered me more than had her first gust of temper. That she should have the insane

audacity to order *me,* a *man,* to—

And then (to this day I know not how it came about) I suddenly found myself on my knees in the slush, awkwardly scraping together the red roses from snowdrift, walk, and gutter.

My face was purple with self-contempt and with a wild, unreasoning fury against the little lady who stood triuimphantly above me directing the task.

Oh, if my patient, toil-bowed mother or my buxom, obedient sister could have seen *me,* Roger Sessions, at that moment! I thanked Heaven that Wilbraham was a full hundred miles from Boston, and that no visiting neighbor was like to behold me.

"There!" ordered my scarlet-clad little tyrant. "Over there to the left! Behind that snow-ridge. There are two roses you've overlooked. So! Now wipe off the stems. They are all wet. Oh, not so roughly! See, you have broken one of them."

Red, mortified, raging, I scrambled to my feet, gripping the recovered sheaf of roses in my huge fist.

I had made no effort to arrange them. They stuck out in every direction from my fingers like hay-wisps.

"There! Take them!" I snarled, thrusting the disordered handful of flowers toward her.

To my further chagrin, she recoiled a step in pretty disdain.

"A service is robbed of its grace if courtesy go not with it," she rebuked me primly, as if teaching a simple lesson to some stupid child.

"What more do you want?" I grumbled. "There are your foolish roses! What—"

"Foolish enough the poor blossoms look, as you hold them now," she agreed. "Arrange them. No, not that way, but with the heads together. *So!* Now—"

"Oh, take them and let there be an end to this farce!"

Again I shoved the flowers at her. But once more she drew back.

"When a gentleman offers me a bouquet, he does so with a bow," she chided. "Not as if he would thrust it down my throat. Try again."

"I will not!" I fumed. "I am no 'gentleman,' and I have told you so. I have debased myself enough for you. Oh, well, here then!"

Impelled again by that same annoying, incomprehensible force, I bobbed my head, ducked my shoulders, and held the flowers sheep-

ishly toward the girl. This time she was graciously pleased to take them. The wrath in her big brown eyes had softened to a twinkle of mischief.

"Did the bear teach you that bow?" she queried innocently. "There! I was wrong to mock you. For, after all, you have made such amends as you could. And you hate me. I can see it in that glower on your face. You would not be ill-looking, sir, if you could wipe away that scowl and learn to square those giant shoulders of yours."

"Never mind my looks," I broke in, embarrassed. Then, against my will, I added:

"What was amiss with my bow? It was not a cringing, dancing-school salute, but—"

"What was *amiss* with it?" she repeated. "Everything! I cannot explain. You would not understand. But see you the gentleman who has just turned the corner? Observe him. And when he bows to me, you will see the poetry that true breeding can put into so simple a salute."

I glanced ahead. Toward us was walking a tall, rather heavily built man whose gorgeous major–general uniform was but half hidden by the military cloak he wore. From the frame of powdered wig looked forth a handsome, whimsical, tired face.

And it was a face I knew from many a picture in the print-shops. I drew back instinctively into the angle of a wall, eying the newcomer with respectful admiration.

For this was General William Howe, most dashing of English offi-cers. Gambler, duelist, man of pleasure, fearless soldier, and coffee-house wit, he was the envied model of every provincial dandy.

The general's tired eyes brightened as they fell upon the girl. He quickened his rapid pace, advancing, hat in hand.

Halting before her, he bowed low, until the brim of his chapeau brushed the snow at her feet.

It was the exaggerated salute of that time. Yet, as he performed it, it seemed but natural—the very poetry of motion.

She responded with a graceful curtsy, as though in a ballroom. Even at the moment, it struck me as odd that a great general should thus demean himself before a mere woman.

And I wondered if it were possible that my ideas of man's superior-

ity could have been wrong. Then, shamelessly, I listened to their talk.

"Venus has sure forsaken Olympus to brighten the provincial soil of Boston!" cried Howe gaily, as he rose again to his full height.

"To thank Mars for his gift of roses," she replied in the same exaggerated vein.

"They are royal red to match your cloak," said he, "but your cheeks put their blush to shame. Truly, our men may rejoice to wear his majesty's red coat when lovely Mistress Marjory Winthrop sets the fashion in color."

Marjory Winthrop! So that was the dainty, fiery damsel's name? Daughter, no doubt, of old Simeon Winthrop, who was the richest Tory in Boston, even as mine own father was the richest Tory in Wilbraham.

"His gracious majesty should be pleased," Sir William went on, "with such loyalty in dress. It is a comfort to find it in the hotbed of provincial rebellion."

I was watching her, and I saw a shadow as of disapproval cross her sunny little face at his flattering words. Very deliberately she tossed aside the scarlet cloak she wore, and let it hang across her arm, with its white fur lining turned outward.

"You strike your colors?" cried Howe in mock dismay.

"The morning grows warm," she answered. "Spring will soon be here."

"Spring!" sighed Howe. "And that will mean the pestilent rebels will make some silly demonstration. And, as legal servant of King George, I shall have to order the poor wretches mowed down."

"You do not enjoy the prospect?" she asked in a curiously muffled voice.

"I am a soldier, Mistress Marjory. Not a butcher. I have fought in China, and in Europe as well. But I scarce relish marching my men against a rabble of farmers and shopfolk. These American peasants will never show fight. A riot, a charge by the regulars—and their puny insurrection will be at an end."

"Or fanned into a flame that all King George's power can never quench!" she cried impulsively.

As the impetuous words were spoken, I could see her bite her lip in sharp vexation as though at some imprudence. Howe's surprised

reply I could not fully catch. For, side by side, they had moved out of my hearing. And, like the country yokel I was, I stared stupidly after them.

Yes, I could see now the difference between gentleman and lout—between townsman and farm lad. The feeling sent a new rush of rage through my blood.

A moment later, I had taken a sudden, illogical resolve that was to change the whole current of my life. Yes, and a resolve that was to change the current of history as well.

CHAPTER II.
I Meet With an Adventure.

I AM Roger Sessions, farmer's son. My father was the one man of note in our tiny community who was not a rabid revolutionist. He remained stanchly a Tory, a devoted admirer of King George III and of Lord North. And I, his only son, had been raised to think and believe as he did.

It was not until the week after my twenty-first birthday that, for the first time, I strayed more than ten miles from my home. Then (great event of my ignorant youth) I was sent to Boston to transact some business for my father. The task accomplished, I had wandered about the streets to fill in the few remaining hours until the stage–coach should set out.

Boston, in the early spring of 1775, was a vast and teeming metrop-olis. At least, so it seemed to my country-bred ideas. It contained full seventeen thousand inhabitants. Often one might see full twenty or thirty folk on a single block of its narrow, twisting streets.

Not only plain burghers, demure maidens, and farm visitors, but everywhere the smart, white-wigged, red-coated British soldiery as well. For almost three thousand of his majesty's regulars were gar-risoned there.

It was these soldiers, above all the things I saw, who roused my admiration. They were bronzed men who had seen many lands. Their uniforms were gorgeous. They bore themselves with a haughty dis-

dain toward the townsfolk. I longed, secretly, to be one of that glittering band.

I had read and heard that Boston was a hotbed of rebellion. Here, in 1770, had turbulent citizens been shot down by the troops in the public streets for insurrection against the king.

Here, too, in 1774, a party of patriots had shown their disapproval of his gracious majesty's tea tax by disguising themselves as Indians and hurling a ship's cargo of tea overboard.

I had been prepared to find brawls on every corner. But, to my surprise, a quiet, even a gloom, hung over the city. Men glanced darkly at the swaggering troops, it is true, but spoke not aloud of mutiny.

I was disappointed. I had hoped to thrash some rebel for speaking ill of the king ere I returned to Wilbraham. It would have been a fine tale to bear back to my Tory father.

I had been longing for such adventure, and had also been lost in wonder at the town's lofty buildings—some of them full three stories high—when I had blundered into Marjory Winthrop at a corner of Beacon Street, just above the Common.

And now back to my story.

My meeting with the girl, her open scorn of my hitherto self-satisfied self, the brief glimpse of Howe—all had filled me with vague resentment of my uncouth plowboy ways and of the simple backwoods life.

Why should I spend my golden youth on a farm, the laughing-stock of city folk, when I had brains and strength that would make me the equal of any man?

A soldier, strolling just ahead of me, elbowed a portly merchant off the narrow walk into the gutter. Why should I not become such a lord of creation as this redcoat? I knew there was ever a demand for recruits. I could turn my back on the farm, enlist in King George's army, and earn the right to look down upon mere civilians.

Even Marjory Winthrop might, perchance, think me less like a bear when she should see me clad in a smart scarlet coat and with powdered hair. Yes, for good or for bad, my resolve was taken. I quickened my pace, seeking to catch up with the trooper in front of me. From him I would inquire the way to the nearest barracks, there to enlist.

When Liberty Was Born

If you who read are inclined to sneer at me for the impulse to give up my life as a rich farmer's son and heir for the hard, ill-paid lot of a common soldier, I will ask you to remember that I was but twenty-one, that militarism was in the very air about me, that I still smarted from Marjory's gibes at my uncouth country ways. Also, that it was my first sight of soldiers and of town life.

Out of Beacon Street into a narrower thoroughfare swaggered the trooper. By this time I was close behind him.

He came abreast of a wide-windowed shop above whose door hung a goldsmith's sign. As he passed the doorway a soberly dressed, stout man of about forty emerged from the threshold.

In his outstretched hands the newcomer carefully bore a long peacock feather fan, such as those that were in use among ladies of quality. Its sticks were of wrought gold, daintily chased and carved, inlaid with tiny seed pearls and other gems of price.

The fan was a treasure, and the holder bore it as carefully as though it had been a sick child. He moved toward a coach that stood in mid-street and from whose open door a neat lady's-maid leaned.

Doubtless, thought I, this portly man was the goldsmith himself. The fan had been sent to him for repairing, and he would allow no 'prentice hand to return it to its owner's envoy.

But I had scant time for surmise. Even as I gazed, the soldier I was following cunningly tripped up the goldsmith, sent him asprawl to the ground, snatched the precious fan from his loosened grasp, and made off with it at top speed.

Before the overturned merchant could gasp "Stop, thief!" I had cleared his scrambling body at a bound, and was in full pursuit of the fleeing soldier.

That so barefaced and wanton a theft should be achieved in open daylight in a city street acted like fire on my honest country blood. I behaved on impulse, as I should have done had I seen a wandering tinker making off with one of my father's prize geese.

Down the twisting street fled the soldier with his prize. And after him I rushed. I was fleet of foot in those days, and few of our village lads could cope with me in racing.

Ere the thief had traveled a furlong I was upon him. Feeling my grip on his arm, he dropped the fan and whirled about on me, draw-

ing the short bayonet he wore at his belt.

But I was too quick for him. Even as he thrust at me with the weapon, I threw out my left arm to ward off the murderous blow. At the same time, I struck with my clenched right fist.

The bayonet, deflected, ripped through coat, shirt, and skin, plowing an ugly little cut in my forearm. But my right fist had caught the soldier on the jaw, and had dropped him limp and sputtering in the frozen mud of the roadway.

I picked up the fan, rejoicing to see it had apparently come to no hurt from its rough handling, thrust it into my pocket, and turned to the fallen redcoat.

Swearing, writhing, threatening, he was slowly staggering to his feet.

My blow had been a hasty and glancing one, else he had lain long where he fell.

I caught the struggling thief by the collar of his uniform, jerked him angrily to a standing posture, and, turning, propelled him roughly before me as I retraced my steps toward the goldsmith's shop.

He was a powerful fellow, and nearly my own size. But, tug and twist as he would, he could not shake off my grip. Nor had his appalling threats moved me.

So onward I drove him, for my rustic brain was still full of resolve to take him back to the place of his theft and there to turn him over to the authorities.

We rounded a corner and came face to face with the excited goldsmith. One or two apprentices, shopkeepers, and idlers had joined in the chase.

At sight of us the hue and cry halted in amazement.

Looking back on the scene, I can well understand the reason of their astonishment. In those days the military were undisputed masters of Boston.

It would have been safer for a Colonist to raise his hand against a magistrate or a reverend clergyman than against a redcoat.

Yet here I was, a strapping Yankee yokel in homespun, roughly propelling before me a squirming British regular in full uniform.

Scant wonder the sight transfixed the group of pursuers!

"Here he is!" I cried, exultant, shoving my captive in front of the

goldsmith. "And here is the pretty gewgaw he stole. Now, which of ye be the town constable? I would fain turn this cutpurse over to the law. For contact with him soils an honest man's hands. Take him, one of you."

"The man that lays hands on me," howled the wriggling soldier, "shall answer to General Gage or to Sir William himself. Yes, and my fellows shall burn the roof over his head. Loose your hold on me, you Colonial boor!" he snarled over his shoulder at me, seeking in vain to tear free from my grasp. "Zounds! But things be at a pretty pass when a soldier of his majesty's service may be manhandled by any low Colonial!"

"Things are at a worse pass," quoth I, "when his majesty's uniform is disgraced by such as you. Here, Mr. Goldsmith, is your thief. Take him. My part in the task is done."

"Your part is that of a gallant, if rash, man," answered the goldsmith, speaking in a pleasantly modulated voice. "And from my heart I thank you. The fan could not have been replaced for a hundred guineas; a loss I could ill afford. And I could still less afford to note the grief its loss must have cost Mistress Marjory Winthrop, who left it with me for mending. If—"

Marjory Winthrop again!

And I, thick head that I was, had unwittingly prepaid her scorn by doing her this monstrous great service! Once more my tanned cheeks grew red with anger. And I vented some of my rage by giving my fuming prisoner an extra shake to still his struggles and his profanity.

"I want no thanks," I made surly answer to the goldsmith. "I but wish the constable or some other to take this scoundrel off my hands. I—"

"Turn him loose," requested the goldsmith, in a voice whose outward gentleness seemed barely to mask some ill-concealed emotion.

"Turn him loose!" I echoed, while from the little crowd that had gathered arose a murmur of angry disapproval. "Turn him loose? Is it thus the great city of Boston deals with criminals? If so, I thank my stars I be a rustic. Is there no justice in this town of yours?"

"*No!*" bellowed a shock-headed blacksmith in the crowd. "None for free-born Americans. For such as we there is but—"

"Silence!" ordered the goldsmith.

He spoke quietly. Yet there was a ring of authority in his deep voice that stilled the blacksmith and hushed the increasing murmur of the crowd.

"You treason-breathing dogs!" howled the soldier, getting his breath at last, after the mighty shake I had given him. "Soon enough ye shall taste good British justice, one and all of ye! And there shall not one stone of your miserable Boston town be left standing on another. A century hence the very name of Boston shall be forgot. As for this outrage upon a soldier of King George—"

"Down with tyrants!" was shouted.

A stone whizzed through the air. The missile grazed the soldier's powdered head, and struck me full on the shoulder.

Again in impotent fury, stung by the pain, I shook the redcoat until he hung, limp and gasping, in my grip.

The goldsmith had turned suddenly upon the crowd.

"Shame!" he cried. "Is this the self-control I and the others have sought to teach you? Would you spoil all? Do you want to spend the rest of your days in the barracks prison while your wives and babes starve? Have done, I tell you, and disperse!"

"My father," I remarked, as the men hesitated, "has told me the Boston rebels are but windy cowards. Now, I see 'tis true. There is no danger to the king's peace from such timid folk who can be cowed into peace by one tradesman's word and by sight of a redcoat. Where is the constable, Master Goldsmith?"

"As I have told you," urged the goldsmith, "let the fellow go. Thanks to your courage and strength, I have back what he stole. Seldom is it that Boston men receive even so much redress from those who pillage them. Were we to hale him to the guard-house, his word would be taken before ours. He would be set free, and some of us would sleep in jail this night. You are from the country, young sir, and you do not understand. But *I*—"

"But you are a pack of cowards," I stormed. "If none of you will aid me, I shall take this cur to the guard-house single-handed. In which direction does it lie?"

"No, no," begged the goldsmith, "be warned. If—"

"I say I shall do it!" I raged. "If there is justice in Boston—"

"There is not. And—"

"Hallo!" spoke up a sneering, authoritative voice from behind me. "What treasonable coil and brawling have we here? Odzooks, *canaille*, stand aside, I command you, and let me through to see what all this rumpus is about!"

CHAPTER III.
I Change My Mind.

AT the scornful command the crowd sulkily gave way. A man and a girl had just emerged from a cross-street leading down from Beacon Hill. Though it was the man who had spoken and who now came forward ahead of his companion, yet it was the girl on whom my eyes first fell.

And as our gaze met—I knew her for Marjory Winthrop. The big eyes widened from amused recognition to an admiration not unmixed with trouble as she saw that I held captive a wriggling British soldier.

Meantime, her companion, Sir William Howe, had made his way to where the goldsmith, the soldier, and I were standing, pushing his path through the press as though through a kennel of dogs.

"What does this mean?" he cried in haughty wonder.

"It means, Sir William," I retorted, too angry to be cautious, "that one American is not too cowed at sight of a red uniform to catch a thief and bring him to justice."

"May it please you, Sir William," sputtered my prisoner, "this Yankee brute grabs me as I'm going along peaceful-like and—"

"Silence!" ordered Howe curtly. Then, to me:

"What do you mean, you young Goliath, by choking a king's man? Unhand him!"

"He is a thief," I said doggedly, "and—"

"If you undertook to choke all thieves, those big hands of yours would soon be worn off at the wrist," answered Howe. "Let him go, I say!"

"I will not. He stole a gold-handled fan from this goldsmith. And he shall go to jail for it."

"It's a lie, Sir William!" squealed the soldier. "I just—"

"If he has been at fault," said Howe, "the provost marshal will know how to deal with him. It is not for a pack of Yankee rascals to lay hands on his majesty's uniform. Let him go free!"

"And encourage every other redcoat thief to steal, unpunished?" I returned. "Not I."

"Do you know who I am? I—"

"I know. But you are not *my* master. And I hold this scoundrel until the constable comes."

"Then you will hold him till doomsday, you Yankee rebel! I say, let him—"

"I am no rebel!" I flashed. "I am as stanch a king's man as yourself. This soldier stole a valuable fan. There it is"—indicating the trinket the goldsmith was still holding—"and I—"

"Oh, *my fan!*" cried Marjory, catching sight of it. "My fan!"

She hurried forward. Sir William glanced whimsically from her to the fan, and then back to me.

"This puts a new face on the affair," he observed carelessly. "Mistress Marjory, I am at your pretty feet imploring fifty thousand pardons that a man of mine should have laid sacrilegious hand on aught you cherish. Believe me, he shall be punished."

The general set a silver whistle to his lips and blew a shrill note thereon.

"As for this shaggy Hercules," he went on, "I suppose, for your fair sake, I must reward him instead of letting him cool his heels in the city prison. A proper fine giant he is, I confess. But—"

Three troopers, summoned by the whistle, came down the street at a run. Howe broke off in his careless speech, turned to them, and, indicating my captive, said:

"Take him to the provost. Say that I order for him fifty stripes on the bare back and fifty days in the guard-house."

The men moved away with the cringing soldier. Howe again turned toward me.

"You have done an ill thing," quoth he, "in venturing to lay hands on a soldier of the king. If such acts were to pass unpunished, you Yankees would soon get the notion you were human beings. And then where would the sacred authority of England be? Nevertheless, you say you are loyal. And you have been so lucky as to do this fair lady a

service. So take this instead."

He flipped a golden guinea toward me. I caught it and flung it into the mud at his feet.

He reddened at the bold act. Then, with a shrug, observed:

"As you will. Mistress Marjory, the sight of your face is so great reward that mere gold seems to him as dross by comparison. Shall we continue our walk? I fear the sight of so many rebels has spoiled your morning. In summer, the flies; in winter, the rebels. I know not which are worse."

She took his proffered arm without a word, and they moved away. But, as they went, she cast over her shoulder a look—not at the fan the goldsmith still held, but at my surprised, confused self.

Again our eyes met. I could not read the look in hers. Yet, somehow, it set me all atingle.

And the goldsmith spoke to me twice before I could draw away my own dazed glance from the dainty little retreating figure. As she passed out of sight the world seemed strangely dull.

The goldsmith was leading me toward his shop, a few doors away.

"You are hurt," he was saying. "Come in and let me stanch the wound."

I glanced down at my left arm. Through the slash made by the bayonet drops of red were spreading.

In my excitement I had taken no note of the injury. Even now it seemed to me too petty a matter to call for such solicitude.

Nevertheless, I suffered myself to be led into the quaint, dim interior of the shop. The goldsmith made me sit in a big chair while he bustled off in search of lint and warm water.

The crowd had melted away. Only one or two clerks and apprentices remained.

I glanced about the shop in real interest. The walls were hung with odd prints, save where shelf-space was taken up with rows of gold and silver ornaments that gleamed lividly from behind their thick glass cases.

Bits of filigree work, rings, fans, and other trinkets were piled high on a table behind the counter. In a rear room stood a tiny forge, and near it a printing-press. At a window was a bench with a set of engravers' tools. And, through that same window I could read the swinging

street sign's legend:

PAUL REVERE,
Goldsmith and Engraver.

The next moment my host had returned, his arms full of bandages and such stuff.

He deposited his burden on the floor, stripped off my coat, and with the tender touch of a woman proceeded to lay bare my throbbing arm.

The cut was not deep nor in any way dangerous. But the sharp east wind of Boston had gotten into it and it stung cruelly.

Also I was a trifle dizzy from loss of blood and from so much excitement.

Therefore I willingly allowed the goldsmith to wash and bind the wound, leaning back, meanwhile, and watching with admiration his deft skill as a surgeon.

"This is not the first hurt you have dressed," I hazarded.

"I wish I might hope it would be the last," he made answer. "No, it is not the first. I learned this sort of work in the Crown Point campaign against the French, in 1756. I was a lieutenant of artillery there."

"A lieutenant of artillery in '56?" I queried. "You can scarce be above forty or forty-five now."

"I am but forty," he said, working as he talked. "Great events bring forth the men to meet them. And those men often are mere lads. I was scarce twenty-one at the time of Crown Point campaign. Yet, our captain was but nineteen. Like myself, he was promoted from the ranks."

"For bravery?" I asked, suddenly interested.

He laughed.

"In the rough days of the French and Indian war," he answered, "there was scant political preferment. Men were promoted for bravery—or not at all."

"I have oft heard of that great campaign against Crown Point," said I, watching his busy fingers tie the last knot in the bandages. "My father has told me how a handful of sturdy New England Colonists went forth into the hostile wilderness, how they fought starvation, wild beasts and fiercer Indians, and at the last against fearful odds captured France's strongest fort. Is it so?"

"It is so," he agreed gravely.

"Yet," I pursued, "to-day, you—the man who dared such perils—shrank in fear from arresting one British soldier. Do advancing years bring cowardice?"

"Young man," he said sternly, "it is ever the way of youth to judge a jewel casket's contents by its exterior. Therefore I overlook your insult. The name of Paul Revere may not live in my country's history; but if it does not 'twill not be because I am a coward. Let that suffice."

"I ask pardon if I offended," I muttered, half ashamed, "yet to see a Crown Point hero cringe before a thieving redcoat irked me. The jewels must be over fine to justify as tarnished a casket."

Yes, it was a boorish, brutal speech. I know that. I had the grace to realize it, vaguely, even then.

What better can one expect of a farm lad on his first contact with real men? To my surprise, almost to my disappointment, Revere did not flare up. Instead, he said gently:

"The rustier the casket, the less will thieves be likely to rifle it. But, for that matter, is there no shame to yourself, my friend?"

"For accepting a service from you?" I suggested, glancing down at my neatly bandaged forearm. "And then berating you for a coward? It may be so. I spoke in haste."

"Not for that," he corrected me. "That is forgotten already. It was but the thoughtless churlishness of youth."

"For what, then?" I asked, genuinely curious.

"You are an American," he answered, after a moment's pause. "A New Englander of the old stock. Massachusetts bred. Yet I heard you boast loudly to General Howe, a few minutes ago, that you are a stanch king's man. Is that no cause for shame?"

"For *shame?*" I retorted hotly. "No. For *pride.* Are we not all subjects of King George? Is loyalty no longer a virtue?"

"Loyalty is no longer a virtue," he answered, "when its object is no longer worthy of loyalty. We Colonists settled this land. We conquered its savages. We turned a dreary wilderness into a country of untold riches. For whom? For England's king. When France menaced him here, we overcame France. We yearly swell the royal revenues. In return we are abused, ill-treated, robbed right and left. We grovel under the heavy, unjust taxes the king's ministers have saddled upon

17

us. We have no representation in Parliament. We slave for a country that despoils us."

"This is treason!" I cried. "Rank treason!"

"Treason and truth, just now, walk hand in hand," said he. "So, can you think hard of me when I am saddened at seeing a son of America, like yourself, turn his back upon his suffering fellow countrymen and shout, 'I am a king's man'?"

"You speak over-bravely now," I taunted. "Yet when that blacksmith in the crowd did much the same thing you rebuked him to silence."

"Had I let him speak as he would," answered Revere, "there would soon have been a riot. Then, a file of soldiers, a volley fired into an unarmed throng, and the blood of dozens of innocent men would have dyed the snow. And to what good purpose? It is what I and my fellows are working night and day to prevent. The time is not yet ripe. But it is at hand!"

The last two sentences were murmured under his breath to himself rather than to me.

"What is to prevent me," I asked, rising, "what is to prevent me, as a loyal subject of Great Britain, from going to the authorities and denouncing you? You are speaking treason. You are hinting at an uprising against the king. You should be in prison."

"According to Tory ideas, perhaps," he calmly assented. "But it will not be *you* who will send me there."

"Why not? I—"

"I have the gift of reading faces, my friend," said he, "and yours is as an open book. You could not denounce any honest man. Least of all a man whose poor hospitality you have enjoyed. It is for that reason I spoke so plainly. For that and because—because you seem too much a *man* to remain a Tory. Yet, as matters now stand, you will go back to your country home, thinking—"

"You are wrong," I contradicted. "I am not going back home. On that I have firmly decided. When I met you a half hour ago I was on my way to the nearest barracks to enlist. Now that my hurt is dressed, I will e'en thank you for your kind courtesy to a stranger, and go on my way thither."

"To enlist?" he exclaimed, agape.

To my amaze, he ran his hand through his long thin hair, in bewildered fashion; then broke into a hearty laugh.

"To enlist?" he repeated. "Man, have you no wits? You would go to the barracks, where by this time every trooper has heard how you maltreated their comrade and how you got him fifty lashes? What reception would you get there? Enlist? Why, they would tie you up, flog you and then 'lose' you in some black cell!"

I halted, irresolute, half-way to the door. I knew he spoke truth. My rashness had barred me forever from joining the king's army.

And I had so eagerly longed to wear a red coat and to have my yellow hair cued and powdered!

"None the less," I growled, "I shall not go back home to be a country lout forever. I shall find employment here in Boston town."

"Well said!" he agreed. "But what employment, if I make so bold as to ask?"

"I can plow, fell trees, shoot, trap, ride, and—"

"All excellent accomplishments," he assented, "but not likely to win you employment in a city. Listen! My watchman fell ill yesterday and is in hospital with a quinsy. While you are looking about, will you take his post? The wage is small. But I take it you are not pressed for ready money. He has a comfortable room in my loft, and the duties are light. Wilt take the position?"

"And keep ward over your gold and silver?" I asked. "How know you I will not steal it? I come unvouched for."

"I have told you," said he, "that I read faces. The post is yours if you will accept."

I hesitated. And at that instant a figure darkened the doorway and fumbled with the latch.

"'Tis Mistress Marjory Winthrop come for her fan," said Revere, looking up. "Doubtless she fears to trust it a second time to a maid's care."

"Mistress Marjory Winthrop!" I echoed, vexed that the sight of her should so oddly affect me. "Does she come here—*often*—Master Revere?"

"Why, yes," he answered in some surprise at my query. "Well-nigh every week for some trinket or other. Sometimes twice or thrice in a week. Will you think over my offer? Or—"

"No," I made sudden answer. "I have no need to think it over. I accept!"

"But the wage is only—"

"No matter!" I broke in eagerly. "I accept!"

CHAPTER IV.
I Turn Eavesdropper.

IT was four weeks since I had taken my new position. The work was light, consisting chiefly in patrolling the shop and outbuildings two or three times during the night and in helping to arrange and tabulate the stock.

I had much time to myself, and I spent it in trying to rub off my rough country ways and in seeing the wonders of Boston.

Marjory Winthrop I had met but twice during that month. Each time an imp of bashfulness had held me well-nigh tongue-tied. She, on her part, had scarce accorded me a glance. I half repented my useless ruse to be near her.

I had much to observe in those days. The seemingly quiet, gloomily submissive city, as I speedily found, was, beneath its dull surface, a seething hotbed of rebellion.

Men who bore openly a peaceful bearing secretly whispered together. These whispers ever died away as I drew near. Yet I felt that the air was surcharged with trouble.

It was early one morning (when I had retired to my attic after a night's vigil in and around the shop) that I met with my first positive inkling that something was brewing.

I had gone to bed and was half asleep when something bright—far brighter than sunshine—flashed across my closed lids and set me wide awake.

As I opened my eyes the flash of light was sliding out of the window. I saw it was the reflection of a bit of looking-glass.

Street boys, in my youth, had a mischievous way of using such bits of mirror to flash the sun's rays into the eyes of passers-by. I imagined that some such youngster across the pavement was amusing himself

by flickering little shafts of light athwart my attic walls with a view to awakening me.

Cross at the disturbance to my slumber, I got up, seized a water-pitcher and moved stealthily toward the window, with the idea of drenching the young mischief-maker.

As I neared the low casement, I saw the spot of white light flickering across a signboard on the opposite side of the street.

For a moment I watched it idly, then more curiously. For, instead of flashing on the sign and then off again, it jumped from letter to letter of the inscription in a most erratic fashion.

Once in every few moments it would leave the sign and dart off elsewhere. But always it would return.

It had doubtless been in one of these random departures from the sign-board that the reflection had accidentally cut across my eyelids.

Wide awake now, and thoroughly inquisitive, I sat down on the window-sill and followed the motions of the dancing beam of light with real interest.

The sign-board stood on a street corner. Just beyond was Market Square. It was market day and the square was full of drovers, truck farmers, and hucksters; mingling with produce buyers from the city.

As I looked I noted that here and there in the jostling crowd a face was turned toward the sign. Not with the idle interest of one who glances at a queer flash of light, but with absorption as keen as it was furtive.

One little man in glasses was even moving his lips as if spelling something.

Then I looked again at the sign. There was nothing remarkable about it. On a whitewashed board were large black letters reading:

Zealous, experienced men are wanted for the king's grenadier service. Quick promotion. Bravery rewarded. Join the army! Apply at barracks for details.

It was one of many signs of like sort with which Boston was studded. Yet as I looked closer down into the Market Place, I could still see more men eying it attentively.

I turned again to the sign. The little white shaft of light was once

more moving quickly from letter to letter.

It rested a moment on the letter "I" in the word "Grenadier;" then skipped to the "S" in "Service."

Then it wandered off the board and directly returned to touch the letter "A" in "Army." And then again to "T" in "Wanted."

Another vanishing of the light speck and it reappeared on "H" in "The," on "A" in "Are," on "N" in "Experienced," and on "D" in the same word. Then it whisked away.

"'Is—at—hand,'" I found myself muttering absently. I was more interested than I would admit.

Was the light speck spelling out words from the sign? And did each removal from the board signify the end of a word?

If so, what sense did the words "is at hand" make? I resolved to put the idea to the test. I reached over to my coat that hung on a chair.

As the light flickered back I drew an old letter from the pocket, along with a stump of pencil, and prepared to jot down each new letter as it was touched by the light-ray.

Again the bit of mirror was at work. Without moving my eyes from it I wrote out the letters, with a space between when the flicker vanished.

It was amusing, even if not so profitable as a good sleep. I now no longer toiled to spell the words mentally; but simply copied each letter as it occurred on the paper I held.

For a full ten minutes I sat there, absorbed in my self-appointed task. So engrossed was I that I scarce noted the fact that the sign chanced to contain all the letters of the alphabet nor to wonder from what near-by vantage-point an unseen hand was signaling this queer message—and to whom.

At the end of ten minutes the light disappeared and did not come back. I waited a little longer. Then, cramped from my awkward position, I rose; observing that the stray faces in the crowd which had been watching the board had now turned away.

I looked down at the hastily scrawled, irregular words on my letter-back. This is what I had transcribed and now read:

"Is at hand. The report is ready. Let all who are concerned meet at the malt-house cellars at eleven to-night. The password will be 'Probitas.' Come singly.

If a hint reach the authorities the cause will suffer. Remember, above all—"

Here the writing had stopped in an ugly tear. My pencil point had broken, and in my absorption I had written on, not knowing of the mishap.

And meaningless indentations on the rest of the paper were the sole result.

What did it all mean?

What conspiracy was afoot, whose members could not safely be notified by word of mouth, but must trust to such odd means of communication?

I tumbled into bed. But for the first time in all my twenty-one years sleep avoided me.

I lay for hours staring at the low grimy ceiling, and wondering.

Then, boy-like, my inspiration came. What adventurous lad of one-and-twenty was ever able to keep away from that which concerned him not—the more especially when excitement promised?

I knew where the wrecked old malt-house stood, at the southern corner of the Common in a deserted tract of ground. I had the password of the meeting. Why should I not go thither?

Youth loves to run its head into hornets' nests. And only age and a long succession of stings can cure that desire. I was no exception to my age.

And the adventure promised much. Whether the mysterious conspirators were plotting to burn Boston, to massacre its citizens, to turn the Indians loose on the city or merely to play hide-and-seek in the big, rambling cellars of the malt-house, I knew not nor cared.

But in any event I would be there.

I went on duty as watchman at eight every evening. By nine the street was usually dark and quiet save for the passing of groups of roystering soldiers; and the Revere family were all abed.

On this night I made an extra round of the premises as ten-thirty boomed from the old North Church tower on the hill. Then, making all fast, I slipped away into the street.

Through lanes and byways I made my way. Boston at that time of

night was as dark as the wilderness itself. There were no street lamps. Such pedestrians as were compelled to travel abroad carried lanterns. But the town was virtually asleep by ten.

I was a woodsman born and bred. From childhood I had learned the art of finding my way, in the blackest night, through the forests of my native mountains.

Hence, it was with no unsure step that I now hastened on to the malt-house. Once I passed a couple of the city watch, clumping along with staves and candle lanthorns.

But I lurked in the shadows, and they saw me not. Again, by stepping back into an alley-mouth, I eluded six noisy redcoats who swung down the roadway arm in arm, taking up the whole street from wall to wall.

Another time, in the darkness, I passed a muffled, cloaked man groping along in the gloom and in the same direction as myself. But except for these few encounters, the streets of Boston were as silent and deserted as a midnight graveyard.

As I rounded a turn that should bring me out upon the Common, a dim bulk of a man loomed up before me from a wall-angle, and croaked:

"Stand and deliver!"

It was one of the swarms of highwaymen that infested the night thoroughfares to prey on drunken soldiers and timid belated burghers.

But I was more at home in the darkness than he. So, as he peered forward uncertainly and sought to focus his wavering pistol-muzzle on my half-seen body, I ducked nimbly, struck his wrist a smart blow that sent his weapon flying; and leaped for his throat.

But he was evidently out to prey upon the defenseless and not to fight. For he took to his heels with ludicrous speed, before my arms could close about him.

I gave chase for a few yards; then tripped over a barrow and came to earth with a bump that shook the breath from my body.

As I got to my feet, bruised, muddy and wrathful, I could hear the sound of his running feet die away on the soft turf of the Common.

I gave up the pursuit and again turned my face toward the malt-house. But the various delays had taken up much time. The North

Church clock had already chimed eleven. I was late. Yet on I hurried. At last I came to the entrance where the half-ruined building stood. There was a wide gap in the crumbling wall. The house itself was falling into decay. Yet the wide cellars, once used for storing quantities of malt, were still intact. An ideal place for a secret meeting.

As I crept through the wall-gap, onto the turf-crusted, broken flagstones of the yard, I could see no glimmer of light, could hear no faintest whisper. Yet all at once I had the feeling, so strong in woodsmen, that I was not alone.

I felt the nearness of many people, the magnetic presence of an excited throng. And, at that late hour and in the dead silence, the sensation was uncanny.

I moved forward to where I knew the sloping, rusty iron doors of the cellar-way were. My hand came in contact with one of them.

I ran my fingers along the groove, seeking for some vantage-point whereby to raise the rusted portal.

At the edge, my grip found purchase, and I heaved at the metal slab.

But all my strength could not stir the door. I rose, gasping from the effort, and as I stood up, strong arms pinioned me from behind.

Before I could brace myself to shake off that hold or to grapple with my unseen foe, the cold circle of a pistol-muzzle was clapped to my face.

CHAPTER V.
I Learn Great News.

It is one thing to meet a stronger enemy face to face, in honest, broad daylight. It is quite another to be seized by invisible, soundless assailants at dead of night.

For an instant, as I felt the heavy grip on my arms and the pistol muzzle at my head, I confess I was abominably frightened. But on the moment my fighting blood was up.

My giant muscles leaped to the command of my will. I would pay these midnight ruffians for the scare they had given me.

Sanity came to my aid, however; barely in time to save a life or two—including my own.

"Probitas!" I whispered.

As by magic, the hands fell away. The pistol rim was removed from my forehead. The sloping half door of the cellar swung open, revealing a faint glow of light from beyond.

No word had been spoken by my antagonists. I had not so much as seen them, save as vague shadows against a paler sky.

Now that the darkness of the close-clouded night was relieved by that glimmer, I glanced cautiously about for my late foes.

They had vanished.

Before me lay the steep stairway leading to the cellars. Driven onward by the same pulse of adventure that had drawn me thither, I passed the threshold and picked my way down the rough, uneven steps.

As I entered, the iron door swung silently shut behind me.

I paused, midway on the steps, to note this odd phenomenon. Then, for the first time, the gravity of what I had done broke upon me.

I had blundered on the secrets of a midnight meeting; unlawful and in a spot where help could scarce reach me.

That the conspirators not only guarded their rendezvous jealously, but were not the sort of men to stop at anything, I was convinced by the way I had been treated before I gave the password.

Should the plotters learn that I, an inquisitive stranger, had stolen in upon them, I had scant doubt as to the fate that would await me.

I glanced back once at the closed iron door. Escape was cut off.

I could not crouch on the short stairway where the next late-comer would see me and might discover that I had no rightful place there.

No, I had rashly entered upon this affair, and now I must see it to an end.

And when I realized that escape was cut off, the love of peril and of wild adventure once more surged in upon me. The blood danced through my veins. My strength came back tenfold.

I ran down the remaining steps, turned a sharp corner and—found myself in a vast, low-ceiled, dim-lit vault of a place, packed with cloaked men.

A fitting scene and setting for the darkest of story-book conspiracies.

I should not at that moment have been astonished to hear the muffled, strange assemblage shout aloud their intent to cut the throat of every sleeping citizen of Boston town.

But, as my eyes and senses grew accustomed to the spectacle before me I began to observe the absence of all dramatic effect.

True, the place was lighted only by a half-score candles grouped on a desk-table that stood upon a dais at one end of the room. And the conspirators, as I have said, were cloaked.

But in all other respects the meeting bore an orderly, businesslike aspect, better fitted to a town council than to a nocturnal conspiracy.

The audience stood quiet and deeply attentive, listening to a man who, from the dais, read in low, mechanical tones from a long sheet of paper.

So dim was the light at the far end of the place where I stood, that I could neither recognize nor be recognized by those who stood nearest me.

I was half disappointed at the tameness of it all. Then I recalled the scene at the doorway above; and I listened to the slow droning voice of the reader.

From the first words I caught my sense of disappointment became deepened to utter chagrin.

Was there ever such anticlimax? I had come expecting some blood-curdling revelation. Here is what I actually heard:

"Rice, 35,000 pounds. Salt fish, 17,000 pounds. Beef and other cattle on the hoof—"

I growled my disgust. Was this a Board of Trade conference? At the next syllable my interest quickened:

"Gunpowder, 17,441 pounds. Bullets, 22,191 pounds. Flints, 144,696. Bayonets, 10,108. Field pieces, 12. Firearms, 21,549."

Rice and gunpowder! Beef and bayonets! What did it mean?

The reader was rolling up his list.

"These are all the provisions and munitions," said he, "that Massachusetts has thus far been able to collect. More could doubtless have been gathered, had not strict secrecy been so urgent. The stores of arms and food are now hidden and well guarded, near Concord. Little

by little we are adding to them. When the struggle comes—as come it must—we shall not therefore be wholly unprepared."

He sat down. Scarce had he done so, when a short, slender man in a brown bob-wig and snuff-colored suit, sprang to the platform.

"The committee's report," he cried, "is doubtless most interesting!

"But it merely proves one thing: namely, that we are ready for war and that every added day of waiting means a day of weakness. The land is ready. The eyes of twelve suffering Colonies are turned upon Massachusetts. When Boston strikes the first blow, then will the country rise as one man and cast off the galling British yoke. But as the days drag by and Boston lies dormant, submitting ever to worse and worse oppressions, the country grows to doubt our courage and to weary of waiting for us to act. I say: *Strike! We are ready! Strike!*"

He sat down. A low rumble of mingled applause and disapproval swept the tense mass of listeners. Another man, broad-shouldered, plump of face, mounted the platform. It was Paul Revere.

"To fire a gun before it is loaded," began he, in homely, drawling diction, "seldom scores a mark. Each day that we wait makes us stronger. Our committee's report proves that. At this rate, in another year we shall have laid in enough weapons and food to warrant us in crying 'To arms!' But to throw down the gauntlet now, scarce half prepared, would either ruin all or at least force us to drag along a conflict where our chief enemies would be starvation, scanty clothing, and insufficient arms. What hope could such equipment have against the strength of England?"

He paused; then continued:

"Our stores are piling up at Concord. In every village within twenty miles of Boston, the Minute Men are secretly drilling. Daily their ranks are swelling. Daily the food supply grows larger. All are ready to fight the moment the word goes forth. But why shed the blood of brave men in vain; when by waiting long enough, their numbers and strength will be sufficient for the strife? Even now we are so far committed that if the British learn of our plans we shall be forced to fight. We cannot turn back. Why press the issue when delay means gain?"

He left the platform. And again that mingled murmur arose. It changed to eager interest as a tall, handsome young man sprang to

the rostrum.

He was clad in black, and wore his long dark hair unpowdered. I recognized him even at that distance as young Dr. Joseph Warren, a Bostonian whose name was already known from one end of the Colonies to the other.

"What Master Revere has said," he began, "I indorse. Every word of it.

"It is by his advice as much as by that of John Hancock and of Samuel Adams and of my humble self, that we have held in check every premature uprising. Revere and his thirty 'Watchers' have kept us apprised of British plans. They have checked premature riot and open sedition, until the British call us all cowards.

"They have kept their fingers on the pulse of the people. They know better than any of the rest of us exactly how matters stand. If Revere says 'Wait!' then I, too, say 'Wait!' Hancock and Adams are at Concord, overseeing the supplies. Were they here, they would echo the word. If the spark be prematurely struck, then will our half-ready patriots fight to the last breath. But why strike that spark before the powder mine be laid?"

Others spoke. But I heard no more. My mind was in tumult. Truly I had stumbled on a rare conspiracy.

I was like the man who went forth to trap a fox and caught a lion. I had come hither to listen to some petty piece of secret criminality. Instead, I had unearthed a mighty plot against King George himself.

This parcel of rebels were actually preparing for war. Preparing to raise treasonable hand against the Lord's Anointed. They were drilling bands of villagers to the use of arms. They were collecting weapons, provisions, ammunition in vast quantities, and hiding it near Concord.

They were daily growing stronger, and but awaited the hour when they should be able to throw off the mask of submission and strike at the very heart of the king's American power.

As a loyal Tory, my blood boiled at so terrible a conspiracy. I longed to fling my self bodily on the traitors and to avenge with my very life the insult to my sovereign.

Yes, and Paul Revere, my own friend and employer was one of the band! The man whose service I had taken, whose bread I had eaten.

The man who had ever seemed to me noble and good—save for his disloyal sentiments toward the king.

Biting my lips to keep back my rage, I waited until the meeting should come to an end.

My course of duty was clear. The moment I could get free from that gang of treason-hatchers, I would hurry to British headquarters and tell my story. Perchance it was not yet too late to nip the traitorous plot in the bud.

Howe had sailed, a week agone, for New York. General Thomas Gage was commander of his majesty's forces in Boston. To him I would go, forthwith, at Government House, with my tale of arrant treason.

After an endless delay, the meeting ended. I, with the rest, filed out, up the narrow stairs past the rusty iron doors, into the warm, overcast spring night. The moon had risen, behind the clouds, casting a faint weird light over the dispersing groups of conspirators.

I got clear from the rest and, turning to a narrow alley, ran at top speed toward Government House.

If Gage had gone to bed I would have him awakened. Surely, such news as I bore warranted a breaking of any man's rest.

But when I turned the last dark corner and came out into the little square before Government House, I halted suddenly; struck by the blaze of light that greeted me. The square was full of coaches and sedan-chairs; among which shouting link-boys passed, waving their torches. Every window of the mansion was lighted. Stately figures passed ever and anon by the long casements.

In the great ballroom on the second floor, to the right, a minuet was in progress. The squeal of violins and the thrumming of a harpsi-chord plainly reached me.

I could see satin-clad beaus and powdered, flounced, beribboned belles bowing to each other in graceful fashion or gravely pirouetting through the mazes of the dance.

The broad steps leading to the open front doors were lined with gorgeous torch-bearing flunkies. At the top of the flight stood a fat major-domo.

Thus, it was that the king's loyal followers were dancing away the night of April 17, 1775, while, within a mile of Government House,

treason was rearing its head. And I alone could avert the disaster!

Thrusting my way, by main force, past the lines of footmen, I cleared the steps at three bounds; and, shoving aside the indignant major-domo, rushed into the house of gaiety.

CHAPTER VI.
I Find Myself in Strange Company.

ONCE past the wide-flung doors of Government House, I paused irresolute. In another moment, I knew, the discomfited major-domo might readily summon a brace of footmen to turn me out.

In fact, the semimilitary cut of my new Boston-made coat was, I believe, the sole passport that enabled me to make my way into the house at all.

It was a time when soldier-messengers and special couriers were constantly arriving at headquarters. Doubtless my dress and my imperious haste led the guardians of the place to believe me some such emissary.

There, in the broad hallway, guests were ever tripping to and fro in a bewildering kaleidoscope of colors. Men in white satin, in peach-blow silk, or in the garish dress uniforms of the British army; women in brocaded and many-flounced gowns of every hue; liveried servants—all seemed to circle about me in amazing fashion.

I, in my sober suit of dark blue with its brass buttons, looked like a jackdaw among peacocks. My loose yellow hair, too, felt oddly unkempt alongside the snowy periwigs that bobbed all around me.

As my eyes accustomed themselves to the gay scene, I singled out a servant and beckoned him to me.

"Where is General Gage?" I demanded. "I have urgent business with him."

The fellow looked me over superciliously. Being evidently a body attendant of the general, the sight of a supposed courier did not impress him as it had the other servants.

"His excellency is dancing the minuet," he replied in lofty reproof at my haste, "and after that he will be in the supper-room. He cannot

be disturbed."

"But my business is of deepest import," I protested. "It will not brook delay."

"Then tell it to the officer of the day," insolently suggested the fellow. "He is in the library, drinking punch."

He pointed carelessly to a room farther down the hall.

"The officer of the day?" I repeated. "Perhaps it will be as well. At first breath of my message, he will take me to General Gage. Which is he?"

"The officer of the day is Major Pitcairn," was the reply.

And the servant scurried off about his business, leaving me to find my own way. I hurried on to the library. It was deserted save for two or three gaily dressed men and one woman.

And, before the latter turned her dainty, aristocratic little head in my direction, I recognized her as Marjory Winthrop.

Very beautiful and winsome did she look in her fluffy white ball gown with a splash of scarlet roses at the belt. She was standing in animated, gay talk, between two uniformed gallants.

Not waiting to see if she would deign to recognize me or not, I walked past her and up to the taller of the two men at her side. He was a fine-looking, soldierly young fellow, with florid face and dancing gray eyes.

"Major Pitcairn?" I asked.

He favored me with a half-haughty, half-amused stare. Then he nodded his head carelessly toward the man on Marjory's other side. The latter was shorter, darker, less distinguished looking than his companion. I did not like his face.

"I am Lord Percy," said the taller officer. "There is Major Pitcairn."

"What is your will with me?" asked Pitcairn, noting, with a sneer, my simple dress. "You are a Colonial, are you not? Who admitted you?"

"I am a man who may save King George from the Colonials," I rapped out, nettled by his insulting tone. "I bear news of grave import to General Gage. Will you take me to him immediately?"

Pitcairn laughed in my face.

"I should like to see his excellency's countenance were I to break in upon his dance or his supper with news that a beggarly, nasal-

voiced provincial demanded speech with him!" he scoffed. "Come, man! Give me your message and begone."

"My message," I retorted, choking back my wrath for the sake of the cause, "is of treason. A meeting was held to-night by the rebels, who—"

"Another treason plot!" broke in Pitcairn. "This is the hundredth. And all equally false. As well expect the sheep to rise against the shepherd or the lamb against the lion. Let us hear it, and then be off with you!"

"Pardon, major," interposed Marjory, speaking for the first time. "May a mere lass break in upon so weighty a matter, and crave a boon from one so important as the officer of the day?"

"If you would make the dance music sound rough and discordant by comparison," said Pitcairn with a low bow, "pray speak, Mistress Winthrop."

"'Tis absurd," she faltered in apparent mortification, "and I crave your pardon that such an incident should mar our evening. But—this much-excited yokel is a country dependent of my father. He is well meaning; but his brain is touched by an early sunstroke. Of late, his mania hath been 'rebel plots.' He sees one in every bush. And my father is much put to it to keep him from running ever to General Gage with his wild stories. I am ashamed that he should thus intrude at his excellency's ball."

I stared, dumfounded, at her. At that moment I make no doubt I looked enough like the village idiot she described me.

Her strange speech robbed me of sense and of words. All I felt was a dull ache at the heart.

"Is it your wish that we have him thrown out?" asked Lord Percy.

"By no means," she made haste to answer. "But I crave your indulgence to leave me alone with him for five minutes. I can manage him when none other can. And I can persuade him to leave the place in peace."

"But—"

"Grant me this favor, I pray you!" she begged.

The two men obediently drew away and left us standing face to face.

For a moment neither of us spoke. The girl seemed to be thinking.

My own surprise and pain were too great for immediate words. It was she—as it is ever the woman—who broke the silence.

"Your message?" she asked anxiously. "Your news? What is it? Speak quickly, sir."

"What is it to you?" I retorted. "You make public mock of me. You stamp me an idiot. You tell these men grievous lies about me. What is your will, that you seek speech with me after such treatment? Have you not insulted me cruelly enough?"

"I crave forgiveness," she answered, speaking in rapid undertone and avoiding my eye. "It was needful. You heard what Major Pitcairn said about rebel plots. Had your news been of ever so great import he would have laughed it to scorn. And the message would never have reached General Gage. 'Twas for that reason I interrupted your tale."

"But why make mock of me as an idiot?" I demanded, still more angry and hurt than I wished to admit. "Surely—"

"'Twas my one chance for a word alone with you. No other excuse could have insured me five minutes in private with an ill-dressed outsider, at an affair like this. Cannot you understand?" she queried.

Despite myself, I felt my wrath ebbing. Yet I made one more futile stand:

"Why do you wish to speak alone with me?" I asked crossly.

"To learn your news," she replied "Don't you see? If you give me your message, I can take it in person to General Gage and tell it in such fashion that he *must* believe. None other would do that. It is because I believe in you—because I believe you have tidings of real import to his majesty's government, that I give you this chance.

"Now, will you tell me what your message is? You spoke of a meeting of the rebels to-night. What of it? Tell me, I say!"

It was evident her eager excitement was not one whit assumed. And, looking into those compelling eyes of hers, my last trace of sulks and resentment died.

It was plain I could not hope for personal word with Gage. I had but just received proof of Marjory's claim that the officers around us would deride my story.

Even should I find one who would listen to it, had not Marjory Winthrop just proclaimed me an imbecile? Who in that glittering assemblage would believe the tale of a man thus branded?

No, my one hope of warning Gage was to let Marjory carry my tidings to him. Her father was the stanchest of Boston Tories and was high in government councils.

Surely his daughter must have the king's welfare close at heart. What better messenger could be found?

My mind was made up. In any case, under the command in those wondrous big eyes of hers I could scarce have refused her.

Beginning with the mirror's sun-flashes on the signboard, I told her my whole narrative of the day's events; briefly, yet in full.

I repeated a second time the list of arms and provisions at Concord, the daily swelling roster of armed rebels, the decision to wait until sufficient strength was amassed, before striking the first blow at the government.

"If a strong force of soldiers be sent secretly and by night to Concord," I finished, "the rebel supplies may be readily seized, the two arch-traitors, Hancock and Adams, be captured, and the uprising be forever crushed before it can make its first move. But the raid should be made suddenly, privately, and with no hint of warning. Otherwise, the Minute Men will swarm down upon the troops and there will be bloodshed. If a blow be struck, it means more blows. But if the rebel stores all be quietly seized, the revolutionary movement will become a world's laughing-stock."

She listened with burning cheeks and flaming eyes. Never had I seen a woman so stirred. Never had I seen one so beautiful.

Yet, until I was done, she spoke no word, but seemed to drink in every syllable. Then:

"You did well to tell this to me, instead of to some official," said she. "It is all so impossible—so strange—that none would have credited you."

"*You* do not doubt?" I cried.

"No. For I am American by birth and I know what Americans can do. But his excellency would scarce believe the tale, unless some one such as myself should tell it to him."

"I claim one reward for my services," I said awkwardly.

A glint of contempt shot into her brown eyes. She drew back from me as though from some loathsome thing.

"I did not understand," she replied coldly. "I thought you came as

a loyal king's man to do your sovereign a service. And for that I gave you much credit. But if you crawl here to barter men's lives and hopes for money—why, then, I have wronged myself by speaking so long to so vile a creature. What may be your price, Master Informer? Thirty pieces of silver?"

I felt myself go white to the very lips. It was by no means the least fierce battle of my long career that I just then waged with my temper. Yet by mighty effort I forced myself to say quietly:

"It is not yourself you wrong, Mistress Winthrop, but me."

"Is it possible," she sneered, "to wrong a man who betrays human beings for money? Perchance, though, I was amiss in naming thirty pieces of silver as the price? A larger sum, I doubt not—"

"The reward I claim," I interrupted, still keeping fierce grip on my madly struggling resentment, "is not in money. I—"

"You ask office? I fear that my influence is scarce—"

"I ask," I flashed, "in full reward for my information, that Paul Revere's name be not mentioned by you in your report to General Gage."

She took a step forward and glanced up at me, startled, incredulous.

"I—I do not understand," she faltered.

"I scarce expected that you could," I retorted bitterly. "Our lines of life lie far apart, yours and mine, Mistress Winthrop. I could not understand, some weeks ago, why you should expect me to grovel in the snow for the roses you had dropped. You cannot understand, it seems, how a man may be loyal to his king and yet wish to save a friend from harm. 'Reward' and 'blood money' doubtless mean the same thing to you."

"You misjudge my words!" she cried, but there were tears in her silver voice. "You have no right to say such things."

"I crave pardon," returned I; "but what a mere yokel and sunstruck idiot may say can scarce matter to you. Let me, then, explain briefly my request, and leave you to carry the warning to his excellency:

"Paul Revere is my friend. He is my employer. He is a good and gallant gentleman. He has been drawn into this treason plot because he falsely believes the rebels are in the right. I would cut off my hand sooner than that he should suffer for his mistaken zeal. Therefore, I

entreat you to make no mention of his name in your report to General Gage. Do you give me your word?"

"Yes! Oh, yes!" she cried brokenly, "and, sir, I—"

"There is no more to say," I broke in.

I bowed awkwardly, turned on my heel and hurriedly quitted the room, leaving her staring after me with a look such as never before had I seen in her eyes.

As I reached the great front doors I glanced back once more at the bright scene behind me. For the remotest part of a second, I saw, through a momentary gap in the crowd, two figures in earnest consultation at the far end of the long hall.

One of the two I recognized as General Thomas Gage, acting commander-in-chief of King George's army in Massachusetts.

He was leaning forward, listening with eagerness to something a little bob-wigged man in snuff-colored clothes was saying to him.

And I recognized the little man, too. He was the impassioned orator who, at the secret meeting, barely an hour earlier, had made so fiery a speech urging the rebels to strike at once.

This man, who apparently stood high in secret revolutionary circles, was now conversing on earnest, even intimate terms with General Gage.

That he was telling the general news of deep import was evident.

"My wonderful tidings," I muttered to myself, "will be stale by the time they reach Gage through Mistress Marjory's red lips. It seems the government has efficient spies. Those supplies at Concord will not remain long in rebel hands. And the village Minute Men have been drilled in vain. The war is over before it begins. I wonder what it was that Mistress Winthrop sought to say to me when I rushed away from her just now."

CHAPTER VII.
A Nocturnal Adventure.

WHEN Paul Revere came into the shop next morning I was busy arranging goods in the cases. He had not the air of a man who had engaged in midnight plots, but looked as though he had slept a dozen

hours. I could scarce find words to respond to his cheery greeting. For my mind was troubled on his account. I had made Mistress Marjory Winthrop promise to leave his name out of her report to General Gage. But would not the snuff-colored spy have babbled it to the general?

Might not my patron even now be in danger of arrest and prison? And how could I warn him?

Were I to tell him of his peril, he would assuredly guess at the rest of the facts. He would know the secret of the rebel stores at Concord was discovered. He would have those stores moved at once.

Thus the treason plot would be scarce momentarily checked. And yet—

I could not let this friend of mine be seized for treason. Oh, it was a fine mess wherein I found myself!

I strode to the door and out into the street, to be alone and to think. I could not bear contact with my employer's jolly, bright presence in the shop.

I stood in the warm springtime air with knit brows, trying to form some sort of plan. Of a sudden I looked up from my reverie to find Marjory Winthrop standing before me.

It was a meek and chastened Marjory that I beheld. In no sense the haughty, fiery damsel whom I was becoming so accustomed to see.

"I was on the way to your shop," quoth she, "for a word with you. I am glad have found you."

I had removed my three-cornered hat and stood fumbling it, in embarrassment, between my big hands.

"I came," she continued, "to say what you would not wait to hear last night. To ask pardon of a brave, loyal man for so cruelly misreading him. Can you forgive—"

"'Tis forgotten, Mistress Marjory!" I exclaimed, sore distressed at her unwonted humility. "'Tis *all* forgotten. Do not shame me, I pray, by thinking more of it. You were right, from your view-point, to misunderstand. You had no means of knowing that I was not a scoundrel."

"I was wrong," she persisted, "for I had ever thought otherwise of you. That was why it shocked me into rage when I believed you sought

betrayal money. But—"

"You had thought otherwise of me?" I echoed. "Then you *have* thought sometimes of me? And I thought you regarded me no more than the stones under your feet. I—"

I brought myself up short. I was blundering too far. To ease the situation and to cool the sudden hot flush from her face, I hurried on to another theme.

"The message you promised to carry to General Gage," said I. "I fear we both had our trouble and excitement for naught."

"What do you mean?"

"A man who spoke for war at the meeting in the malt-house cellars was later closeted with the general. And I make no doubt he told him all. He was a government spy. I know not his name. A small man in bobwig and snuff-colored coat. I—"

"You are sure—you are *sure* of this?" she whispered between dry lips.

If I had sought to drive the blush from her cheeks, I had of a certainty succeeded. For her face was now white and drawn. Her great eyes glowed with a smoldering fire.

"You are sure?" she repeated.

"Quite sure," I answered; and I told what I had seen.

I marveled at her sudden emotion. In another woman I could have put it down to dire consternation, to panic dread. But I knew no cause why she should fear.

And I decided it was but feminine resentment that another should have forestalled her in relating a choice bit of news and in serving the king she loved.

Gage, no doubt, had listened gravely to her story, had thanked her for telling him, and had said not a word of the information he already held. Small wonder she was enraged!

I started to say something by way of condolence. But she pushed hurriedly past me and into the shop.

I was sure now that I understood her motive. She had pledged me that Paul Revere should be safe. Finding that Gage already must know of Revere's complicity, she had impulsively gone to warn the goldsmith, whom she greatly liked.

Well, if her warning should give the rebels an inkling that their

plot was known, it was no affair of mine.

It was a way out of my difficulty. Revere would be set on his guard, and the fault of the rebels' possible thwarting of government plans would not rest with *me*.

My mind at rest, and my whole body tired from a wakeful night, I ran up to my attic, flung myself on my cot, and in five minutes was sound asleep.

I needed that slumber. It was many hours before I slept again.

When I came on duty, refreshed and wide-awake, early in the evening, Revere was nowhere to be seen. The serving-maid who gave me my supper said he had ridden forth on horseback an hour agone.

This struck me as odd. For Paul Revere was not wont to ride abroad at night. I fancied the servant might be mistaken. So, on my first round of the premises, I glanced in at the stable-door.

There, in its stall, stood the young white horse that Revere had bought but a week before. But the great dapple–gray that he usually rode was gone. So was the newer of his two saddles.

Then an explanation came to me. Marjory had warned him of danger from the law, and he had fled.

Well, in any case, it behooved me, as his employee, to guard the house in his absence. So I resumed my rounds with extra caution.

It was an hour or so later, as I was reading in the back room of the shop, between my trips of inspection that there came a sudden beating and shaking at the barred front door. Some one of no great strength, but of tremendous purpose (to judge from the sound), was hammering fiercely for admittance.

I picked up my lantern, strode to the door, and prepared to fling back the bar.

Then, remembering the extra care I had resolved to take of the place in my employer's absence, I stopped, picked up a loaded and primed pistol from behind the counter, and thrust it into my belt.

Thus armed, and ready to face any foe, I unbarred the door and flung it open.

Across the threshold rushed a slight, muffled figure, caught the door from my hand, slammed it shut, and stood in the half-lighted shop, facing me.

It was Marjory Winthrop!

From head to heels she was covered in a dark, hooded cloak, under whose somber folds peeped forth the lace and silk of a white ball dress. In her hand she carried a lantern. She had been running fast. For she was breathing in labored gasps.

"Mistress Winthrop!" I exclaimed, aghast.

"Where is Master Revere?" she demanded. "Has he set out?"

"Yes. Some two hours ago," I replied in wonder. "Have no fear. He is safe beyond pursuit by this time."

"Beyond pursuit?" she repeated, puzzled. Then she cried:

"I could come no sooner. Not a minute sooner! I slipped away from the Copley ball the instant I heard. And he is already gone?"

What she said was Greek to me. Before I could frame a question, she hurried on:

"Where is his nephew?"

"He is at Dorchester, on business for his uncle," I answered.

"And his apprentices?"

"Are all away. I am alone here to-night. Why do you ask? Is aught amiss?"

"I cannot do it alone," she was murmuring. "I *cannot!* I am not strong enough. I know not where any of the others live. And whom can I trust?"

"I do not understand," I broke in on her half-tearful despair. "But I take it you are in need of some sort of aid. If *I* may serve you, I—"

"*You?*" she cried, her big eyes dilating. Then, with a new light in her excited face, she added, more to herself than to me:

"Why not? Any means is justifiable. And if *I* fail, *all* fails. You are strong. You are brave—"

"I am at your service in all you may command," I broke in, for it pained me to note the frightened distress in her face.

I suppose I am a fool. For a frightened child or woman has ever seemed to me the most pitiful sight on earth. And better men than I would sacrifice much to soothe away such fear.

Marjory Winthrop was still eying me with that doubting, panic-stricken look wherein a faint hope was beginning to dawn.

"Listen!" she said suddenly. "You are a loyal man! You are devoted to the cause! Then you can do your country great service this night. There is none other who can do it!"

41

"I thought it was *you* I was to serve," I stammered in perplexity.

"It *is*," she declared fervently. "Not only the cause, but *me*. The greatest service you could render me. Will you do it?"

"I have twice told you I am at your command," said I. "What do you require of me?"

"That you climb with me to the belfry of the North Church," was her amazingly unexpected reply.

I stared at her, agape. Was she mad? What did she mean? It surpassed the most freakish vagaries of nightmare.

Here, late at night, a beautiful girl, clad in ball dress, cloaked, and bearing a lantern, had burst into a goldsmith's shop in a state of panic fear, and had entreated the watchman to serve the king and her sweet self by climbing with her to the belfry tower of a distant church.

I furtively pinched myself to see if I were really awake.

I suppose my vacant, bewildered stare must have told Marjory what was passing in my mind. For she went on with fresh vehemence:

"Why do you hesitate? Is it too great a favor I ask of you? You who just now placed yourself unreservedly at my command! Do you fear the ghosts and hobgoblins in the churchyard, that you shrink back afraid?"

"I do not shrink back," I said stoutly, finding my tongue at last. "And I am not afraid. I do not understand. That is all. Will you explain?"

"Explain?" she mocked tremulously. "Since when has a true knight asked a lady to explain the quest whereon she sends him?"

"I am no knight," I retorted, "nor even a gentleman. I am a Wilbraham farmer's son. Yet, such as I am, use me as you will. I am at your service. If it pleases you that I should climb belfries at dead of night, or that I should tweak Major Pitcairn's nose in the street, or singe John Hancock's wig, say the word and I will obey."

She smiled at me through her gathering tears.

"Spoken like a gallant knight," she approved, in pathetic effort at lightness.

Then, with a return of her former fierce earnestness:

"I will explain all, later. I promise. It is enough now to know you are helping your country and—*me*. Will you come with me to the North Church belfry?"

"To the end of the world, if you do but give the command!" I

returned.

Sneer at me if you will, you older and wiser folk, for blindly following a mere girl's lead.

I was twenty-one. She was beautiful. And her eagerness had of a sudden infected me. I had, moreover, as you may have guessed ere this, a love for adventure and for dipping into affairs that piqued my curiosity. In any case—wise or foolish—I was ready to follow wherever the imperious little beauty might point the way.

"Come, then!" she cried, catching up her lantern, and drawing the dark cloak more tightly over her silken ball-gown. "We have lingered too long, as it is. Take your lantern. Oh, *hurry!*"

Already she had opened the door and was in the street. I locked it behind me and followed.

I had great ado to keep up with her as she hastened forward at a run, through the network of dark lanes and byways leading toward the hill whose summit was crowned by the North Church.

The town was still as death. But, once, as we halted at a turn, I thought I heard the far-off tread of marching men.

The moon had not yet risen, but all the eastern horizon was bright with its approach. My blood was stirring with the magic of the night and of the strange quest we two were pursuing.

I was serving the cause and her fair self, Marjory had told me.

For the time, that sufficed me. Later, explanation could come. At present I reveled in the mystery of it all.

We mounted the hill and entered the old churchyard. Before us loomed the black outline of the church with its tall tower.

Between the graves we hastened, Marjory ever in the lead, and around to a side door of the sacred edifice.

The girl fumbled in her cloak, drew forth a key and unlocked the door. I passed into the building, close at her heels, reverently removing my hat as I found myself at the pulpit entrance of the sanctuary.

Across the echoing auditorium sped my guide, her lantern throwing ghostly shadows behind her. She passed through another door and we were at the foot of a long flight of stairs.

Up I followed her into the darkness. At he stair-head she halted.

"Here begins *your* work," she said, speaking for the first time since we had left the shop.

She pointed to a long ladder that lay transversely along the bare space in front of us.

"Lift it and set it in place," she ordered.

Like a man in a mesmeric sleep, I dully obeyed. The ladder was heavy, even for so strong a man as I. But I bent my powerful back to the task, heaved the great length of wooden rungs from its moorings, balanced it and pressed its upper end against one side of the gray patch of light that glimmered far above our heads.

Marjory, who had stood beside the thick bell-rope, watching me and recovering her breath, now came forward as I tested the ladder's security.

"Up!" she cried. "Quickly!"

Slipping my lantern handle over my wrist I climbed the rickety ladder. I could hear Marjory close behind me on the lower rungs. The old ladder swayed and creaked under our double weight.

Presently we were at the top. We found ourselves on a shaky platform that ran about the central ladder-hole. Many feet above us hung the great bell. And even higher there were open squares of bluish light that showed where the belfry apertures were cut. Then—

Something struck me stingingly hard, in the face, something whizzing and hot.

CHAPTER VIII.
I Play the Fool.

I THREW up my hands with an exclamation.

"'Tis but an owl we have disturbed from its nest," explained Marjory. "There is nothing to fear. Oh!"

Her reassurance ended in a startled cry. A bat had swept past her head.

"I will take you for my model o' courage," said I dryly. "What next in this crazy quest of ours?"

"This ladder," she explained, pointing to a shorter, thicker length of steps that lay on the platform floor.

I tugged hard ere I could lift its solid bulk. Small wonder that Mar-

jory had needed the services of a man—and of a strong man at that—in her odd task!

At last I had raised the ladder and propped its top against the bell supports. I flashed my lantern upward.

"There is space on that ledge up there for but one," I reported. "Which shall it be? You or I?"

"How high is the window-opening above the ledge?" she asked.

"A full six feet," I answered, after another examination.

"Then it must be you," she decided, a note of sorrow in her voice. "I am sorry. But—"

"As you say," I assented. "At this rate I shall soon mount to the sky itself. And then I shall probably find out what this is all about."

I started up the ladder.

"Wait!" she ordered. "Take my lantern with you."

"I have my own," I objected.

"Do as I say," she insisted. "Take mine, too."

I laughed aloud.

"This is the merriest, maddest, most senseless game any sane man ever played," said I. "Give me the lantern. I shall no doubt wake up anon and find myself dozing over the table behind the shop."

A lantern slung over each wrist, I made my way up the ladder.

When I had reached the ledge, I paused. The air, of a sudden, was full of whirring, clapping wings. Clouds of fluffy feathers rained down about me. I had dislodged a whole colony of pigeons from their nightly roost.

"I am up here," I called in mock resignation. "What's the next weighty move?"

"Can you raise your hands as high as that aperture?" came her voice from the dark platform below.

"My head tops it by full two inches," I made answer.

"Then raise both lanterns to the opening and swing them!" was her whimsical command.

"This passes the veriest bounds of lunacy," I protested. "To climb the belfry top at night and there wave two lanterns above my head! You are sure jesting."

"Your promise!" the sweet, imperious voice reminded me from below.

"As you say," I grumbled, giving in as usual.

As I started to lift the lanterns I became aware of a jutting shelf of stone, some three feet above where I stood. I stepped up on this, and, balancing myself, looked out through the belfry arch.

The moon had just risen, and hung huge and red in the east. Below me lay the silent, sleeping city, stretching out on every side beyond the churchyard's solemn space.

The moon silvered the waters beyond and, bulking grim and black against the silvery gleam, I could see the British war-ship Somerset, riding at anchor, a ghost ship in a ghostly sea.

More, too, I could behold as I gazed out at the ribbon of silver water stretching between Boston and Charlestown.

My eyes, keen as a hawk and trained from babyhood to see in dark forests at night, could make out a line of military barges silently crossing the stream. They were laden to the gunwales with armed men.

My foot slipped ever so slightly on the smooth ledge. Instinctively I threw my arms up to catch my balance.

The lanterns, one on each wrist, swung upward with the gesture, and waved frantically.

I had, unwittingly, done just what Marjory Winthrop bade me. I had waved both lanterns from the aperture. The spell of the night had for the moment made me forget to do so. And now I had done it involuntarily.

Something darted forth from the shadows on the Charlestown shore, burst through a clump of budding willows, then swept out into the white line of road leading to Medford and Concord.

It was a fast-galloping horse, whose rider urged him madly forward. The steed had an oddly rolling gait that even at so great a distance was plainly noticeable.

A dozen times in the past month I had noted that odd manner of galloping, and knew of but one saddle-horse in all Boston which had it.

Yes, and I knew of but one rider who sat his horse in that peculiar Indian-like fashion.

The flying equestrian was Paul Revere! And the horse was his huge dapple gray charger I had missed from the stable that night.

So he was at last in flight! But why (since he had started two hours

earlier) had he lingered until now upon the Charlestown bank? And why, having waited so long, did he now ride at so furious a pace?

The foremost of that creeping line of military barges presently came into full view of him. I could hear a distant cry. The barge was halted, and I saw tiny sparks of flame leap from the rocking boat. A moment later the report of musketry reached my ears.

The soldiers had seen Revere and had opened fire upon him.

But the bullets must have flown wide, for the horseman dashed on, out of my range of vision.

Why should the regulars have fired at Paul Revere? It was an impossible absurdity that a whole fleet of military barges should have been put across the river by night, simply to catch one unimportant rebel.

No, the soldiery were crossing for some other purpose. And with evident effort at secrecy.

But why had they fired, then, at Revere? And why should hundreds of armed men, in time of peace, be secretly ferried across to Charlestown late at night?

The solution came to me, in a flash. They were the martial force sent by Gage, as I had advised, to march privately on Concord and seize the store of weapons and food hoarded there.

The work was as good as done. The revolution was over ere it began!

Lightly I hastened back to the lower platform where Marjory still crouched trembling in the dusty darkness.

"I could not see you," she said. "The ledge shut off my view. You gave the signal?"

"The signal?" I repeated, "I know of no signal. I waved the two lanterns from the arch, if that is what you mean. Was it a signal? I might have known, had I not been such a thickhead. A signal of some sort, to those troops who were crossing to Charlestown, of course."

"The *troops?*" she panted. "They are crossing? Already?"

"A whole flotilla of them," I retorted cheerfully. "Bound for Concord, I doubt not. To surprise the whole—"

"Oh, if it should be too late!" she murmured in panic.

"Too late? Never fear. The road lies empty before them. They will be at Concord before the alarm can be spread. They will catch the

rebels and all their stores."

To my dismay Marjory burst into a passion of tears. The gallant spirit that had sustained her through that gruesome climb now utterly collapsed.

She rocked back and forth on the dusty floor sobbing uncontrollably. I stooped to comfort and reassure her as best I could. But I have scant skill in dealing with women.

She was sobbing forth some incoherent, broken words; and among the rest I caught the name "Revere."

"Do not weep for him," I exclaimed, glad to find some crumb of consolation to offer her. "He is safe. I saw him gallop away. From one of the boats they fired on him. But he was far out of range."

I had hoped, I say, to comfort her. But I was all unprepared for the electrical effect of my simple words.

For, scarce had she heard them when she was upon her feet, her tears and weakness gone, her slender form a-thrill with rapture, her face transfixed. She had the air of an inspired prophetess.

"*Safe!*" she cried, her silver voice ringing like a trumpet. "Thank Heaven! *Thank Heaven!*"

Her cloak had fallen away. Her white, clinging ball dress glimmered like a sunset cloud in the lantern light, brightening the dusty belfry loft. I looked at her in wonder.

"Yes. Revere is safe," I said, faintly jealous at her wild joy over my employer's escape. "Does it mean so much to you?"

"Revere?" she echoed, puzzled. "Oh, yes! But it was not of him I thought. It is the cause—the holy *cause*—that is safe!"

"You mean that the rebellion will be forever crushed, by the seizing of the stores tomorrow? You are right. Every loyal soul should rejoice. And—"

"They will *not* be seized!" she cried, ablaze with excitement. "They will be *saved!* And the revolution shall never be crushed until America is a free land. It is not the *end.* It is the *beginning.* The glorious, heaven-blest *beginning!*"

"You are mad. Stark mad," I gasped. "That you, a loyal Tory maid, should speak so!"

"I am no Tory," she fiercely disclaimed, all caution cast to the winds. "I am an *American.* I am the servant—the loving, loyal ser-

vant—of my country."

"Oh, this night's mad work has turned your brain!" I muttered, dumfounded. "Your country is England. As is mine."

"My country—the country of every true Colonial—is America!" she retorted. "Man, don't look at me in that scared, sorrowful way as though my wits had fled! Cannot you understand? *This night Liberty is born!*"

"Come!" I begged soothingly, "let me take you home to your father. Careful nursing and the skill of a good doctor will soon make you well. In a few days, I doubt not—"

"I am as sane as you!" she replied, shaking off my restraining hand, and speaking still in that delirious tone of exaltation. "Must I explain all to you, as I would to a stupid child? Do you not yet see—?"

"Come home!" I reiterated, "I will send for a doctor and—"

"You poor blind, dull instrument in God's hand!" she broke in. "Listen to me. You came to Government House last night with warning of the patriot plans. Had you carried your warning to General Gage, the revolution would have stood in grave peril. So I made you entrust the message to me. Think you I repeated it to his excellency? Not I!"

"But you said—I thought—"

"You thought me a Tory like my father. So does many another. So do all the government officials in Boston. And in that way I have learned of many a government plan and have told it privately to Master Revere and to Adams and Hancock and the rest. And thus have I served my country."

"You—you have played the *spy?*" I gasped. "Oh, 'tis preposterous. You are moonstruck! Come—"

"I have played the spy, if you term it so," she assented. "I have given my life and my wits to the service of my stricken country in the only way whereby a mere weak girl could be of use to her."

"And you did not tell Gage what I learned last night?"

"No. And I thought he would never know. Then, this morning when I saw you and when you told of the spy who was closeted with him—then I knew the secret was in his hands. I went straight to Master Revere. He sent for Dr. Warren and some of the rest. At length we hit upon a plan."

"A plan? To—?"

"To save the Concord supplies and to save our country. Revere was to ride post haste through Middlesex, to warn the Minute Men and to give the patriots at Concord time to hide their treasured stores, before the British could reach there. For, we knew Gage would soon send an armed force to destroy them. But we could not act at once. For we did not know at what hour the British would set forth or whether they would leave Boston by the land or the water route. All depended on that. So I was chosen to find out, and—"

"*You?*"

"I. At the Copley ball this evening. I was sure to meet Gage or Pitcairn or Lord Percy or some of the rest who were in high authority. I was to get the secret from them and to let Revere know at once. At noon to-day I chanced to hear that this was the night chosen for the raid. I told Master Revere. We arranged that he should be mounted and ready, on the Charlestown bank, and that a signal should be flashed to him, as soon as I could learn whether the British were to go by land or by water."

"The signal?" I repeated dully. "And you were to—?"

"I was to find out, if I could, at the Copley ball. Then I was to tell a chosen friend of Revere's. He had pledged himself to flash the signal to Revere from the North Church belfry. The moment Revere should see that signal he was to set off to spread the warning. If the British were to go by land, one lantern was to be swung from the belfry arch. If by water, two lanterns."

"Oh!" I shouted, with late-dawning comprehension. "And I—"

"It was late before I could get a five minute chat alone with the general this evening," she went on, "I quickly found out from him what I wished to know. The British were to leave by the water route. I hastened to the man whom Master Revere had appointed to give the signal. He lay sick with a sudden attack of lung fever and could not rise from his bed. Thence I fled to Revere's shop and—"

"And for lack of fitting rebel material used *me* as your dupe!" I stormed, unable to keep my wild resentment longer in check.

"Not as a dupe," she pleaded. "As the instrument for liberty. For—"

"*Liberty?*" I snarled, wholly beside myself. "Say rather for sedition and foul black treason against the safety of the king's government!

I, who love my king, have been made blindly to do him a grievous wrong. I, who would give my life for England, have set in train a blaze that may cost hundreds of British lives. And you exult in your night's work! Oh, I blame you not that you laugh in your sleeve over the ignorant, loyal country lad whom you so finely tricked!"

"I would *trick* no man!" she protested earnestly. "The fate of my country hung in the balance. You—whether you wish it or no—are a man of that country. I used you—not for my own ends—but for *your* land's welfare. Blame me for that, if you will. But—"

"But you deceived me. You said service you required was for the king—"

"No," she corrected, "I said for your country."

"And," I raged on, "you said it was for the cause."

"It is," she answered, "for liberty's sacred cause."

"I cannot argue with you. Your crafty woman-wit makes easy mock of my stupid loyalty. But all the arguments on earth cannot blot out the fact that you made *me* give a signal to aid my sovereign's foes. For that I can never forgive you or myself. Sooner would I have cut off my hands at the wrists than that they should have been raised to carry that light to Paul Revere. I am—I—oh, you have made me a *traitor!*"

"No," she said, cringing under my torrent of harsh words as beneath a lash, "I have not even made you a *patriot.*"

"A *patriot!*" I scoffed. "Say rather a 'scoundrel.' Oh, the jest is upon *me!* You have made me a fool, a dupe, a blackguard! Laugh over it with your fellow rebels. Tell as a rare quip how one gloriously beautiful girl besmirched a silly, blindly devoted rustic's honor."

"Don't! *Don't!*" she pleaded, her sweet voice shaken with sobs. "I meant all for the best. I did indeed. Cannot you forgive me for what I make you suffer? I will make whatever atonement you demand. I will—"

"What 'atonement' can a man receive for lost honor—for ruined loyalty?" I sneered. "A 'gentleman' would, no doubt, bow and scrape before you and tell you with flowery speeches that all was well, and that you must not sorrow on his account. *I* am but a boor, whose ideals you have smashed. So I crave forgiveness if I cannot speak such words as should calm your mind."

"Don't! *Don't!*" she begged again, in that muffled, heart-broken

voice I found it so terribly hard to resist.

"What is done, is done," I said gently, her sobs cutting me to the very soul. "And what am *I* that I should judge any woman? I pray you, overlook what the bitterness of my chagrin forced to my lips. And I—"

Of a sudden I broke off and leaped to the ladder. An idea quickly flashed across my mind.

"It may not yet be too late," I cried, exultant. "Revere started from the *lower* road, at Charlestown's river bank, so that he might see this signal. If I mount and ride like mad, by the *upper* road, I may yet cut him off at the crossroads."

"*What?*" she panted, starting up in horror.

"I can save a full half-hour by taking the upper road," I said, swarming down the ladder. "And the white horse in Revere's stable is the faster of the two for a man of my lighter weight. I may cut Revere off. And if I do—"

"If you do?" she cried in terror. "Then—"

"Then I may yet undo what my blind folly has well-nigh caused," I retorted from the foot of the ladder.

"But he will not turn back?" she pleaded. "Oh, do not!"

"He *must* turn back. If not—"

And my hand closed about my pistol-butt.

"He is your friend," she urged, her voice shaking with terrified appeal. "Your *friend!* And—"

"My loyalty—like your own in a different cause—must come first. Good-by!"

"*Do* not go!" she shrieked wildly. "What ill have our patriots done you? I implore you! For the sake of pity—"

"For the sake of the king!" I shouted back over my shoulder.

The church door clanged shut behind me. Down through graveyard and the dark streets I rushed, running as never I ran before.

A government's safety depended upon my speed. Yet, through all my turmoil of excitement I could not shut from my memory the sound of heart-rending sobs, the sight of a white-faced, spirit-broken little maid, kneeling in vain appeal to me.

I reached the stable, flung a saddle on the waiting horse, and tore forth on my life-and-death ride.

A man's honor—a woman's heart—the history of an unborn nation— hung trembling in the balance.

CHAPTER IX.
Paul Revere's Ride.

So, through the night, rode Paul Revere.
So, through the night, went his cry of alarm
To every Middlesex village and farm.
A cry of defiance and not of fear!
A voice in the darkness, a knock at the door,
And a word that shall echo forevermore.
Longfellow.

THE April moon hung high above the eastern hills as I drew near the crossways where the two roads met.

I had not spared whip nor voice, and the white steed I rode had responded gallantly to the summons.

But the upper road was still deep-mired from the breaking up of the winter frosts, and the going was heavy. The lower road was firmer and more traveled.

So it was that, as I topped a rise of ground, I heard a thunder of hoof-beats through the stillness of the night.

Along the lower road, and flashing past the junction of the two, galloped Paul Revere. He was bareheaded. His thin hair flew loose in the wind. His great gray charger was already foam-streaked, but was going as gaily and powerfully as if his journey had but just begun.

I had lost my wild race by a bare two hundred yards!

I had staked all on reaching the crossways in time to halt Revere and to silence the warning that should set the Minute Men and the Concord folk upon their guard.

And I had lost!

I shouted a furious command to him to stop. Through the quiet of the night my voice boomed uncannily.

Revere turned in his saddle, without checking his horse's pace. Our eyes met, and even at that distance I knew he recognized me.

"Halt!" I bellowed.

He waved his hand at me in greeting, but thundered on.

"Halt!" I roared again, whipping out the pistol at my belt. "Halt, or

I'll bring you down!"

The moon's rays glinted blue on the pistol–barrel. Revere must have seen the weapon, must have heard and caught the import of my threat. Yet he did not draw rein. In fact, he turned his back on me and honored me with not another glance.

I fired. The man was out of range. I could not bring myself, in cold blood, to pull trigger on my friend and employer.

So I shot in the air, hoping to scare him into halting. His horse, as well as my own, leaped nervously forward as the reverberation of my shot split the stillness of the spring-time night.

Then, with a dogged resolve not to be beaten at my self-appointed task, I drove spurs into my steed's foaming flanks and darted onward in pursuit.

Revere was a heavy man, heavier by many pounds than I. His weight might well wear down even so powerful a beast as the gray charger he bestrode. With luck, I might overhaul him and by main force turn him back, ere he could reach Concord.

So, settling down in my saddle, I resumed the mad race.

But, struggle as he would, my white horse could not cut down the furlong's distance between himself and the gray. The deep-mired state of the upper road had told sadly upon his strength. He could barely keep up the space between ourselves and Revere.

Still, I kept on. At any time Revere's mount might play out; or, striking some inequality in the road, might stumble and fall. The chase seemed well worth while, on even so slight a chance of victory.

So, through the warm, moonlit night, heavy with the breath of spring, we galloped; our horse's hoof-beats waking the echoes from sleeping hill and dale. A strange race, with a strange goal.

Ahead of us, at last, lay a broad farmstead. Its low-lying, scattered buildings shone white under the moon. At sound of our noisy approach a dog barked. Then another.

Into the dooryard of the main dwelling dashed Revere. With his clubbed riding-crop he pounded upon the nearest window-shutters.

A sleeping voice from within growled some incoherent challenge.

"The British are coming! Wake!" trumpeted Revere.

And he was off again as I came almost alongside. On again we sped, he drawing more and more ahead of me.

At every farm or clump of houses he halted momentarily to repeat that loud call of warning. And each time the delay almost sufficed for me to overtake him.

But my horse, if speedier than his, lacked the gray's wondrous staying powers. Urge him as I would, he began to lag.

And now, as a larger group of houses loomed before us, I redoubled my vain efforts to catch up with the gray charger. For I knew we were drawing near to Medford. Once let a town of that size be aroused, and the mischief was not to be lightly quieted.

Down into the main street of Medford dashed Revere, just as the discordant bell of the town hall crashed out the stroke of twelve. A sleepy watchman with lantern and staff plodded out into the roadway, droning drowsily:

"Twelve—o'clock—and—all's—well!"

Then he caught the hammer-beats of our horses' hoofs. Like a giant fantom, Revere bore down upon the startled old man.

"Scrymegeour," hailed Paul, calling the watchman by name, "'tis Revere! The British are coming! Ring the alarm-bell!"

He swept on down the quaint old street. I spurred my horse toward the watchman to forestall his warning. But with a marvelous agility the old fellow had already scurried into the town hall.

As we left Medford the clangor of the big bell followed us. For miles its peals rolled forth through the midnight hush. From far ahead of me I could hear Paul Revere laugh exultantly at the sound, like a boy new released on holiday.

So on for another hour we rode. My horse was panting aloud and stumbling from sheer fatigue. Even the matchless gray was beginning to feel the terrific strain.

But for that and for the occasional halts at farm, village, and hamlet, where the warning was shouted, I should have lost him.

I can shut my eyes now, a half century later, and see Revere's broad shoulders, low-bent head, and flying hair, as he rode on his mighty errand of liberty.

I can hear his deep, magnetic voice in the oft-repeated cry, "*The British are coming! Wake!*"

The long, white, moonlit road, the budding trees, the clustered villages, and the tireless galloping rider are stamped forever in my

memory, as they are in that of the grateful land he saved.

Once, I remember, his horse's flying hoofs struck a red spark from a road-bed flint. And as I toiled wearily after him the fanciful thought came to me that Revere was striking a spark whose resultant flame might not be quenched by oceans of brave men's blood.

Now, I know that the spark was liberty. Then, in my blindness, I called it treason.

Through Lexington we tore at one o'clock. And, as Revere thundered over the bridge and on to the broad patch of village green, he raised his cry of alarm.

"Some drunken roysterers," snarled a voice from the upper window of a house. "Less noise there!"

"You'll have noise enough before long," cried Revere as he dashed past. *"The British are coming!"*

We had scarce left this village behind us, when, as ever, in our wake broke forth the clamor of alarm-bells and cow-horns.

On toward Concord we sped. For another half-hour I managed to keep my steed going. Then, with a final plunging stumble, he came to a standstill, and stood with lowered head and heaving shoulders, refusing to budge another inch.

In vain I shouted and urged. The poor brute was spent. He could not travel another yard.

I had long since lost sound of Revere's progress. He had passed on out of sight and hearing. Yet at this point I might do worse than to describe in a word or so, as I heard it later, the rest of his famous ride.

He was joined presently by two rebel patrols—one William Dawes and Dr. Samuel Prescott. Together the three spurred toward Concord. But at Lincoln, ere they reached their destination, they were halted by a group of British officers, who, suspecting their errand was one of sedition, made all three prisoners.

But Dr. Prescott swerved aside, leaped his horse over a wall, and escaped. He rode on to Concord and gave the alarm.

Revere and Dawes were marched back a mile or two toward Lexington by their captors; and then, for lack of evidence to warrant their detention, were set free.

As I said, I set forward afoot, when my horse broke down. But soon I halted. I was on a wild-goose chase. How could I hope now to

catch up with Revere? And, even if I should, the mischief was done.

The whole countryside, from Boston to beyond Lexington, was already aroused. From a dozen distant points the frantic pealing of alarm–bells reached my ears. Here and there glowed the red glare of signal fires. From everywhere came a faint buzzing sound as of countless voices.

And somewhere between me and Boston a column of British infantry were marching toward Concord, their cursing officers already aware that the country before them was awake and seething.

There must come a clash when that advancing red column should meet with its first resistance. And, turning about, I set off at a run in the direction of Boston, to be present at whatever excitement might befall.

It was only as I retraced my steps that I saw how fully the rebels were aroused. In every farmhouse lights were tossing. Men were running from opened doors and across fields, gripping long fowling-pieces, scythes, and other rude weapons. Now and then a farmer horseman, gun athwart saddle, pounded past me at full speed.

At each village the bells were tolling, and groups of armed men were forming in rude military order.

The Minute Men were out. True to their name, they were prepared on the instant to meet the British invader.

At one roadside house I saw a weeping woman strapping with trembling fingers a musket bandolier across her shirt–sleeved husband's shoulders. At another, three boys, scarce old enough to be out of the nursery, were hotly disputing as to which should carry the one gun their household boasted.

Again I passed a woman in widow's weeds, hurrying along, dragging a blunderbuss far too heavy for her strength.

As I reached Lexington gray dawn was breaking. The moon had paled before the onset of day. And a weird, shimmering half-light overhung the world.

On Lexington's village green a thin line of men was drawn up. Some were half dressed. Others were appareled in some attempt at military fashion.

There were less than forty of them in all. A big, hatless fellow in shirt-sleeves was trying to harangue them. But the hoarse jangling of

the meeting-house bell drowned his voice.

A half-grown schoolboy, astride a bareback farm horse, lumbered around the curve from the direction of Boston, crossed the bridge and drew up awkwardly in front of the little crowd of militiamen.

"Cap'n Parker!" he called, hailing the big bareheaded leader.

The latter ceased his speech to the men, and hurried toward the rider. The meetinghouse bell was hushed. The plow-boy's words came fast, and almost incoherent with eagerness.

"They're coming!" he cried. "They'll be here in another five minutes. I rode alongside in the field for more'n a mile. There was a hedge, and they couldn't see me. When they found the country was awake, Colonel Smith, their leader, split his force in two. He halted with one body, and he's sent back to Boston for reenforcements. But he sent six hundred men on ahead with Major Pitcairn. An' they'll be here in—"

A bugle call, then a military order, could be heard down the road beyond them.

"Best fall back," suggested some one. "There's less than forty of us here. We can't make a stand against six hundred. Fall back till we can join some of the other Minute Men companies. Then—"

"And leave Lexington to be burned to the ground?" retorted Captain Parker. "Not we. Here we are, and here we'll stay. Here at our own home. Boys, don't fire unless you're fired on. Remember Hancock's order that the regulars must fire the first shot. Let them fire first. *But if they want a war, let it begin here and now.*"

The handful of ill-armed men gave him a cheer. At his command they lined up in martial formation to face the bridge.

The growing morning light fell upon their resolute faces. Not a qualm, not a trace of swagger, no hint of nervousness or doubt could I detect.

Calmly, unafraid, this pitiful little line of untrained men were preparing to face more than ten times their number of the best-equipped troops of Europe. And not for fame, or for gain, or even because they were cornered. Simply to defend what they believed to be the right.

And as I watched I felt a mist spring unbidden to my eyes. My heart beat quicker.

These men were no traitors. They were heroes. And they were of mine own land, of mine own blood. A sudden feeling of keen, all-

engrossing pride in their heroism filled my mind and heart.

Around the turn came a line of red. Then another. Then a third. The British regulars, marching in files of eight, debouched onto the straight bit of roadway leading to the bridge and to the green. In the gray of early morning their scarlet coats blazed forth vividly.

At the column's head rode a dark, thickset officer in major's uniform. I knew him at a glance for that same Major Pitcairn who had so sneered at my provincial bearing and at my news on the night of the Government House ball.

I glanced back at the single ragged line of patriots drawn up on the green. Surely, at sight of this avalanche of redcoated regulars they must scatter and flee? But they stood as firm as their New England hills.

Across the intervening road and on to the bridge strode the regulars. Then they caught sight of the pathetic little patch of men drawn up to meet them. And, despite strict British discipline, a guffaw of laughter burst from the red-clad files.

"Silence in the ranks!" snarled Pitcairn. "Halt!"

The word was caught up by the subalterns, and was passed along. The scarlet column came to a standstill scarce a hundred feet from the handful of patriots. Pitcairn spurred his horse forward until he seemed about to ride Parker down, as the latter stood, cutlas in hand, in front of his men.

"Disperse, you rebels!" bawled the British major. "Disperse to your homes! In the name of the king!"

The line of Minute Men stood firm, expressionless. Pitcairn, wheeling his horse, dashed from between the two lines. Drawing up at the meeting-house steps, where his plunging mount dislodged and scattered a handful of frightened women and children, he drew his sword and waved it.

"Present! Aim!" he shouted.

The front rank of regulars dropped as a man to one knee, bringing their long-barreled muskets to a level. The men in the next rank aimed above their kneeling comrades' heads.

"Fire!"

A crashing report, like that of a single enormous gun, blared out on the still air of dawn, reverberating over hill and plain.

Yes, and that shot's report resounded to Boston, to New York, to Virginia, and to far-off Georgia; to England itself. Across the whole world it rang.

And as long as true manhood and love of freedom endures, its echoes shall never die.

CHAPTER X.
THE SHOT HEARD ROUND THE WORLD.

You know the rest. In the books you have read,
How the British regulars fired and fled—
How the farmers gave them ball for ball,
From behind each fence and farm-yard wall,
Chasing the redcoats down the lane,
Then crossing the fields to emerge again
Under the trees at the turn of the road,
And only pausing to fire and load.

Longfellow.

FROM the leveled muzzles of the redcoats' guns rolled forth, with that volley, a pall of gray, fluffy smoke that filled all the space between them and the thirty-odd Minute Men.

And through the smoke-reek I could hear Captain Parker's fearless cry to his farmer-militia:

"Fire!"

A rambling, ragged volley answered his command.

A front-rank grenadier lurched forward on his face. A second-rank man tumbled against his next-in-line. A soldier farther back and to one side dropped his musket and bent double over a shattered wrist.

Then a whiff of down-wind blew the smoke aside. And my eyes fell upon the line of Minute Men. Eight of them were lying sprawled on the young grass. A ninth was staggering backward into the arms of a frantic, bareheaded woman who had run forth from one of the houses that faced the pretty little church.

The gallant little line had been crumpled and shattered. Full a

quarter of its members were wounded or slain. The road to Concord lay clear and unopposed before the six hundred redcoats.

"March!" yelled Pitcairn.

The bugles took up the cry. The ranks reformed in marching order, the wounded grenadiers were swung into stretchers, and the ground shook with the tread of rhythmic, tramping feet.

The momentary check was at an end. On pressed the victors, unheeding the ravage they had wrought.

But a man (travel-stained, dusty, wild of eye) had sprung forth from the group of pallid onlookers on the meeting-house steps. Raging like a wild beast, he had darted among the slain, had caught up a fallen Minute Man's musket, clubbed it, and with a growling cry had hurled himself at the flank of the marching British column.

Three farmers seized him and dragged him back from the certain destruction his blindly insane act courted. Yet he was a giant in strength. The combined efforts of his three friendly captors could scarce restrain him.

He struggled furiously to tear away from them and to attack the indifferent passing redcoats single-handed.

"Let me free!" he screamed hoarsely, battling with the farmers who so kindly restrained his futile madness. "Loose your hold on me, I say! They are *murderers!* They have killed my countrymen! They marched against them, fifteen to one, and mowed them down! Oh, you craven *cowards* to let the red demons escape in safety like this! *Free* me, I say!"

Others of the Minute Men clustered around him, and by sheer force of numbers drew him out of danger. He still fought like a maniac, cursing the British, scourging the hero Minute Men for cowards.

Then, as the last of the British troops plodded by, the lunatic came slowly to his senses. And—shame on me to confess the babyish madness!—he was *I.*

Yes, *I!*

I, Roger Sessions, loyal Tory, son of a loyal Tory. It was I (in the blind fury bred of the massacre I had just witnessed) who denounced King George's troops as murderers and demons, and who sought to die killing them.

I wonder if, at this point in my tale, you who read will lay aside these pages with a sneer and say:

"Pooh! This is a sorry hero, after all. First he prated against liberty, and now, for no reason at all, he turneth rebel and hateth the loyalty he once practised. We will have no more of him!"

All that you may thus say of me is quite true. I make no defense. I state but the facts. I am, indeed, a sorry hero. Forsooth, I doubt me if I be a hero at all.

But I pray you cease not on that account from reading further into my story. For, though you may well despise me, yet the tale I tell is one that no true American can afford to despise. It is the tale of Liberty's hallowed birth, and of the events that made you all free men. Wherefore, read on, I entreat. The story of Liberty can never grow stale.

Many to whom I have told of the sudden change that turned me from rabid Tory to more rabid patriot, have shrugged shoulder and laughed their disbelief.

But a few others (who can read men's hearts as you and I read books)—General George Washington himself among the rest—have found nothing strange in the transformation.

It was Washington who, on a later day, explained it to me, saying mine was but one of hundreds of like instances in the early times of the Revolution.

Men who, by birth and training, deemed themselves loyal Tories, often realized, at sight of their brutally slaughtered fellow farmers, that they were, first of all, Americans; and that the blood-brotherhood of their own countrymen was far thicker than the water of a vague allegiance to an English king on whom they had never set eyes.

Be all that as it may, there I found myself clutching a musket, a bullet-pouch, and a powder-horn, and imploring thirty ill-armed Minute Men to let me lead them forthwith against six hundred British regulars!

As my brain cooled, none could have been so amazed as was I by my own madness. Yet, with calmer mind, my new-found patriotism did not lag.

I joined myself to the little party of survivors, resolved to strike at least one blow for liberty that day. And the chance was at hand.

When Liberty Was Born

Though the meeting-house clock marked only the hour of five, yet from everywhere farmers and Minute Men were flocking into Lexington.

Down roads and lanes and across fields they came; singly, by twos and threes, and by dozens. The village green was choked with grim-faced, armed men.

No thin line of desperate, hopeless defenders now; but hundreds of militiamen, farm-hands, and shopkeepers. White-haired, bent grandsires, and beardless schoolboys stood shoulder to shoulder. Muskets, fowling-pieces, horse-pistols, blunderbusses—every conceivable weapon bristled from those ill-formed, homespun ranks.

There was no confusion, no shouting, none of the disorder and clamor that marks a mob. Orderly, calm, deadly, the rough battalion formed itself.

A tall, old man in ministerial garb mounted the meeting-house steps overlooking the thronged green and the road beyond. He stretched forth his hands in brief prayer. Every head was uncovered.

Then, with a deep-muttered "Amen" from hundreds of throats, we formed into line, shouldered our weapons, and marched off down the Concord road in the wake of the British phalanx.

It was not long ere we came upon traces of their passage. The whole countryside was buzzing like a monster swarm of furious bees. At every crossroads new throngs of Minute Men and farmers joined us. We were too late to check the British attack upon Concord, but in ample time to avenge it.

Colonel Smith, Pitcairn, and the six hundred regulars, after leaving Lexington, marched upon Concord, meeting scarcely any opposition. But Paul Revere's ride had done its work.

Like so many beavers, the Concord patriots had been toiling for hours. And the carefully hoarded stores of provisions and arms were well hidden.

When the British reached Concord they found they had come upon a fool's errand. And furious enough they were at their outwitting.

Four hundred and fifty Minute Men were drawn up in front of Concord liberty-pole to check the British onslaught. They were headed by old Major Buttrick. Captain Isaac Davis (leading spirit among the farmer militia) had just marched in with a company of volunteers.

At the first volley from the British, Davis and many of his company fell dead. Buttrick shouted:

"Fire! For Heaven's sake, *fire!"*

Before the rifle-blast of the Concord patriots the advancing British wavered and fell back. They could make no headway against that force of quiet, coldly determined patriots. Here was a mere handful of thirty-eight defenders, as at Lexington.

Yet the British were too strong to be crushed. The patriots could but hold their own. The redcoats found and disabled a few old cannon; destroyed one or two barrels of flour that had not yet been hidden; set fire to the court-house, and hacked down the liberty-pole. Then they turned back toward Boston.

But it is easier to thrust one's head into a hornet's nest than to draw it forth again unscathed. Any fool may walk into a trap. But to walk safely out of it again calls for more wit and luck than Smith and Pitcairn possessed. The real excitement of that most glorious of days was but just beginning.

Back fell the British in good order; moving with stately tread, in solid phalanx, like some mighty, inhuman, irresistible machine of destruction.

And then, to the attack we rushed—we, the men of Concord and Lexington!

From every roadside stone wall we poured a deadly hail of lead into the prim red ranks. Not a bush, a tree, or boulder, or farmstead outhouse but hid a homespun-clad sharpshooter.

We were the men of woods and fields; men trained from childhood in the use of firearms; men who could drop a tiny squirrel from the loftiest tree-top, or stop the course of a distant deer in full flight.

Against such home-bred marksmanship what chance had the slow-moving mass of British infantry? Here was no case where undisciplined men were lined up and forced to fire straight in front of them at a scarce-understood word of command. We were hunters, all of us, from our youth up. And now our guns were trained at will on man's most thrilling quarry—his fellow men.

Still in every memory lay those huddled victims of the Lexington green. The dead face of Isaac Davis and his fellows was fresh in the farmers' minds. Fresh, too, was the recollection of burned houses, of

brutal insults, of long years of patiently borne oppression from these same powdered, red-coated British soldiery.

Can you wonder that we leaped forward, mad with eagerness to wipe out the black debt!

The British held to their stiff martial formation as best they might. But from every direction poured in the patriots' bullets. The farmers hung on the column's flanks like flies—here, there, everywhere—as deadly as wasps, and as hard to corner.

Again and again the column was halted, and faced about to meet our attack. But we presented no solid front to their fusillade.

Scarce a man could be found on whom to train their muskets. But from wall, fence, copse, and boulder our leaden messengers sang. And as the march would be resumed, we again flocked to the charge.

The British officers shrieked and cursed. But to no avail. Here was a lurking, deadly foe, such as no British force had encountered since the Braddock massacre a score of years earlier.

Human nature could not stand it. Mortal nerves could not endure that ceaseless volley which could not be effectively returned. The column, from a stately walk, broke into the "double quick."

But they could not shake us off. Across the fields we streamed, to confront them at each new turn of the road.

As snow melts and breaks up under the pelting of spring rain, so the British ranks dissolved beneath our hot rain of bullets. From steady, stately march to orderly quickstep; from quickstep to wild, terror-stricken run. From that to panic rout.

Soldiers hurled away muskets and haversacks and rushed in a mad pell-mell scamper for safety, like a huddle of stampeded sheep. Never before were Britain's proud infantry in such rout.

In vain did the officers seek to restore some semblance of order. In vain did they shout to rally their stricken men and try to beat them back into line with the flats of their swords.

The terrified redcoats ran over their own officers in the frantic attempt to escape the leaden death that everywhere clung about them.

Could this jostling, screaming horde of scrambling fugitives be the massive war-machine of an hour ago? Could the scared wretches that choked the lanes and roadways be the veterans who had guffawed aloud at sight of our puny force of Lexington Minute Men?

We discarded caution now and pressed in upon our fleeing foes, doing fearful execution.

Back through Lexington poured the stricken redcoat rabble. And at every step the panic grew more frantic!

Out through the streets, across the historic village green they fled. I verily believe, in another ten minutes the whole scourged, fear-crazed pack must have surrendered to us.

But just beyond the bridge were massed a strong regiment of British reenforcements, Lord Percy at their head. In hollow square they were formed, and at every side of the rectangle bristled level guns and bayonets. As well have charged the stone wall as that formidable defense!

We halted in surprise. For we had not thought of the reenforcements which Colonel Smith had earlier summoned out from Boston. Our chase seemed at an end.

Into the safe enclosure of the bayonet-edged hollow square staggered the exhausted redcoat fugitives, flinging themselves upon the ground from sheer fatigue.

There they lay in the dirt, panting like tired dogs, their tongues hanging out, their chests laboring heavily, their once-spruce uniforms torn and mud-caked.

Our pause of astonishment was brief. In renewed rage at seeing our prey escape, we hurled ourselves upon the hollow square. Yes, and we, the ill-armed farmers of Massachusetts, beat back that solid array of infantry; beat them back by sheer courage and ferocity, so that they turned in retreat toward Boston.

They were too strong, and we too weak, for us to demoralize them and drive them before us like sheep as we had done with the advance body of six hundred. Nevertheless, they could not hold their own against us.

We hung on their flanks and blazed away at them from behind every bit of cover. Under our galling fire (to which they responded fiercely, but with wofully poor effect), the whole British force retreated.

Keeping good order, but nevertheless in full flight, they made their way back to Boston.

On that first day of the Revolutionary War, the British lost full 273 men against our loss of 93.

I had taken scant account of my own actions. Firing with scarce a miss, halting to reload, then running on again to the chase, I had worked with a sort of mechanical, unconscious precision.

But now, I saw a homespun lad rise from behind a bush to fire. He caught his toe on a root, and fell prone. A half-dozen British skirmishers sprang from the ranks to seize him.

I was nearer to the boy. I sprang forward, jerked him to his feet and swung him back out of peril. As I did so, a redcoat clubbed his empty musket and struck for my head.

I ducked nimbly. But the blow still fell glancingly across my skull, half stunning me.

My hot musket dropped to earth and I reeled, for an instant, helpless. Before I could recover, a dozen hands had seized me. A rope pinioned my arms, and I was thrust forward between two files of grenadiers.

I was a prisoner. The first American prisoner in the Revolutionary War.

CHAPTER XI.
Near the Noose.

IN an anteroom of Government House I cooled my heels. With bound hands, I sat huddled on a hard bench. A sentinel paced up and down in front of me.

Truly, distinguished treatment for one farm-bred rebel! But, as I was the expedition's sole captive, I supposed they were seeking to make the most of me.

My recollections of the march—or retreat—or flight—back to Boston, were hazy. I recalled being hustled along between a couple of hurrying ranks, and menaced with bayonet-points when I tried to break free.

My head, at first, hummed and throbbed from the tap the grenadier's musket-butt had given it. Later, when my mind cleared enough to note things more calmly, we were beyond pursuit and were tramping into Boston.

Rumors of the day's events, in some garbled form, had reached the city ahead of us. For every street we passed was close-lined with wondering, eager people.

And as the populace saw the bedraggled, weary state of the troops, the wide gaps in the ranks and the hundreds of dead and wounded soldiers carried on stretchers, there arose from everywhere an indescribable murmur of exultation that would have been a cheer but for the menace of the regulars' muskets. It was a sound I can never forget.

In time we had come to the barracks, where the redcoats gave gruff, shamefaced replies to their comrades' wondering queries. And I was dragged on, by a captain's order, to Government House.

In the stuffy, twilit cubbyhole of an anteroom where I was placed, I could hear distinctly through the thin partition a furious conversation from the general's study beyond. The talk was apparently at full height as I arrived.

"Scrape me raw!" Gage was fuming, "but 'tis a black disgrace to England's arms! And I wonder at you, my lord, that you can stand there so dashed cool and tell me of it."

"Why not?" drawled a calm, pleasant voice that I recognized as Lord Percy's. "There is scant use in glossing over the truth when we chat among ourselves. Of course, when your excellency sends report to England, it can be put in whatever light you may choose."

"No light can glaze over the wretched truth," retorted Gage. "Is there no palliating circumstance, man, that will help us save our face? Try to think!"

"We were thrashed," replied Percy. "That is all. Thrashed by a swarm of shoddy backwoodsmen. My own command was but driven hither in good order by them. As to Pitcairn and Smith, their six hundred were forced to run a monstrous fast foot-race."

"Before a gang of provincial louts!" growled the general. "Oh, the shame of it! What will Howe say when he comes back next month? He and the coffee-house wits will gibe and lampoon us till we be sore to the bone. Have we *naught* to show for the affair? No list of their killed? No arms or luggage or prisoners?"

"Some of them were slain," assented Percy. "But scarce one to our three, I fear. As to arms and luggage, we captured none. Though we left plenty of our own along the route. Prisoners? I doubt if we took

any.

"Captain," he called to a man farther down the room, "does your report say aught of prisoners?"

"The full report is not yet in, my lord," answered the man addressed. "But I ordered that any captives who had been taken should be brought to Government House for disposal before they were sent to the cells."

"Have them in, then!" roared Gage. "Have them in, I say! As many of 'em as can be crowded into the room! I'll wait for no court martial, but hang the whole pack as felons, assassins, and traitors to the king's majesty."

"But, your excellency," protested Lord Percy, in a lower voice as the captain departed upon his errand, "surely, as prisoners of war, they—"

"Prisoners of war?" rasped Gage. "There *is* no war! These be traitors who took up arms against their king and who murdered our troops in cold blood. They shall hang, even though there be a full thousand of them."

I heard no more. The sentry before my door entered the anteroom, pulled me roughly to my feet and pushed me, bound and helpless, before him down the corridor to the general's study.

The sunset's rays lighted the long apartment. Save for a military secretary writing at a table near the farther window, Gage and Lord Percy were the only persons in it.

The general's eyes fell balefully upon me. I squared my shoulders and met his gaze firmly.

I had been brave enough that day. But now, the thought of the vile felon's death that awaited me turned me strangely sick. Yet, I made shift to appear indifferent as I faced the angry Englishman.

Gage's wrathful gaze shot past me through the door, then at the guard sergeant who stood on the threshold.

"Well! Well!" he snarled. "Where be all the rest? Bring 'em in! Am I to be kept waiting like—"

"May it please your excellency," faltered the sergeant. "There *are* no others."

"*What?*" bellowed Gage.

"Only one prisoner was taken to-day, your excellency," answered the sergeant. "There he is."

Gage went purple. He gasped like a new-caught fish. I half thought

he would fall into an apoplexy.

"His majesty's best regiments have been trounced by a parcel of yokels," he sputtered, whirling on Percy. "And all we have to show for it is—*this!*"

He pointed in dramatic contempt at me, as he gulped forth the words. Percy's handsome face grew red in an effort to choke back an unbidden smile.

"So it seems, your excellency," said he gravely.

The general pounded on the floor with his cane until the walls reechoed. And again he fought for speech.

"Oh, monstrous! *Monstrous!*" he managed to pant thickly at last.

His goggle-eyes roamed the room in frantic, helpless fury. At last they rested once more upon me.

"Take him away!" he roared to the sergeant. "Take him away and hang him! I'll send the warrant at once by an orderly. String up the murderous traitor. He—"

But Lord Percy, who had hitherto glanced but casually at me, looked again, as Gage spoke, and this time, of a sudden, more closely.

"Pardon, general!" he broke in now. "May I speak with the fellow?"

"If you care to soil your lips by speech with an arrant rebel," acquiesced Gage in sulky surprise. "But to what purpose?"

"Are you not the half-witted provincial who broke in upon his excellency's ball the night before last?" queried Percy.

Night before last! It seemed a century agone.

"I did so intrude," I made answer.

"Into the library where Mistress Winthrop and Major Pitcairn and I were talking?" he went on.

I nodded, perplexed.

"I never forget a face," he exclaimed in triumph, "I recall the whole thing now. Your excellency," leaning toward Gage, "I fear you must e'en forgo the tiny morsel of revenge you promised yourself. This is no rebel."

"How? What?" snapped Gage incredulously. "The deuce you say! But he was caught—"

"He is a nuisance, I am told, and I suppose he were better hanged," went on Percy. "But, for all that, I fear it would be impolitic to string him up."

"Why not? Who dare gainsay—"

"He is no rebel," pursued Lord Percy, "but a sun-crazed bump-kin whom old Simeon Winthrop supports. I doubt if he were within ten miles of to-day's brawling. He is daft on the theme of rebel plots and—"

"How know you all this?"

"From Mistress Marjory Winthrop's own lips," was the reply, "and no longer ago than night before last, at Government House ball. The fellow burst in upon us, in the library, full of some cock-and-bull tale of a rebel conspiracy. We were for throwing him out. But Mistress Marjory intervened. She told us he was her father's dependent and craved our mercy for him."

How clearly did I recall the lie whereby Marjory had explained my presence! And how I blessed, where once I had cursed, it! Gage looked puzzled.

"H'm!" he reflected, half under his breath. "Old Simeon Winthrop is the most important provincial and the stanchest Tory in all Boston. Just now—especially after to-day's reverse—we need all the Colonial sympathy and aid we can win. It would have angered the old Tory, I doubt not, had we strung up his servant. I thank you for reminding me, Percy. Let the crazy lout be lodged safely in the madhouse of the town, and—"

"If Winthrop wished him in a madhouse," suggested Lord Percy, "would he not have clapped him into one long since? I fear, your excel-lency, we would offend almost as much by locking the imbecile up as by stringing him up. Does it not appear so to you, general?"

"As you will!" grumbled Gage. "Cut the fool's tether, one of you, and turn him loose. But listen, sirrah!" he shouted, once more facing me, "if ever you are seen within the bounds of Government House again, you shall be flogged to the bone. 'Tis enough for me to be sur-rounded by fools in uniform without adding idiots in homespun to my list. Be off!"

The sergeant loosed the bonds on my wrists, wheeled me about and pointed to the broad stairway leading to the front doors. You may be well assured I needed no second hint. In a trice I was out in the hall and half-way down the steps.

But, as I crossed the threshold of the street entrance, a light touch

fell on my shoulder. I turned, startled. Lord Percy was at my side.

"My friend," he drawled, in that quiet, pleasant voice of his, "if you are of godly bent, you may say prayers of thanks this night.

"For your neck was parlous near to the noose, just now. 'Tis lucky I chanced to be there. You are no more crazed than am I. Nor are you a servant of Simeon Winthrop. But since 'twas Mistress Marjory's sweet whim to say so, why, who am I to gainsay her? I return you to her with my humblest respects. Tell her so, I pray you. And—you are a plucky fellow. You fought well this day. I saw you. Better luck attend you next time!"

On the last word he was gone; and I passed, marveling, into the street.

I had in a single half–hour witnessed all that was worst and all that was best in British military life of the day.

As I turned my face toward Paul Revere's shop, I suddenly realized that I ached in every bone, that I was utterly worn out, and that the long strain of excitement and hot action had left me strangely weak and unable to endure further hardship.

Also, I was of two minds as to what reception might await me at Revere's hands. When last he had seen me, I had been spurring after him at top speed, flourishing a horse-pistol and shouting to him to surrender or be shot. Scarce a prelude to hospitable welcome, now that I was returning to his house!

But as I came around the corner of Milk Street, I saw something that drove all other thoughts from my mind. Hastening toward me, very evidently on her way to Government House, was Marjory Winthrop.

She did not at first see me. Her glance was downcast and she was hurrying on, oblivious to everything around her and evidently much preoccupied.

Fast as she walked, I noted that her light step had lost the old buoyant gaiety that had carried her, lightly as a feather, over Boston's rough highways.

I also had space to observe that her flower face was robbed of its wonted flush and that there were dark circles under her big, brown eyes. She looked haggard, ill—indescribably miserable.

I halted at sight of her. Here—far more than with Revere—had I

good reason to doubt the nature of my receiving any rapturous welcome.

When last I had seen this dainty beauty I had scourged her with the lash of my brutal anger. I had left her crouching, heart-broken, alone, in a ghostly belfry, at dead of night and far from home; while I had hastened away, deaf to her sobbing appeals, to wreak mischief to the cause she loved.

Truly, I can scarce blame my own cowardice that I stood stock-still there, watching her come toward me in the dying sunset, and daring neither to accost her nor to slink away unobserved.

Then—a bare five yards distant—she raised her eyes. And she saw and knew me.

CHAPTER XII.
I Reap My Reward.

YES, she saw and knew me. Our eyes met, and for the briefest instant we stood facing each other, moveless, silent—she, tiny and infinitely graceful in her flowered dress, with that highbred, aristocratic air of hers; I, gigantic in my torn, blood-stained, muddy, blue suit.

Then, with a little cry, she sprang toward me; both her white hands were outstretched; her lovely face was aglow.

"You are free!" she exclaimed, her voice trembling. *"Free!"*

"You—you *care?*" I muttered, utterly dumfounded at the joy that transfigured her.

"They said you were captured," she hurried on, still unconsciously leaving her little hands close clasped in my great rough palms. "And General Gage swore he would hang every prisoner that was taken to-day. I—I—"

"You know, then?" I exclaimed. "You've heard—"

"Yes, I know everything. A hundred others know. And you have won the friendship of every patriot in all Boston. You have—"

"The 'friendship'?" I echoed. "I left here a rabid Tory. I galloped after Revere, to stop him at all hazards from bearing the warning to

Concord. I even drew pistol on him at—"

"And, single-handed, you sought to charge the British line at Lexington," she broke in exultantly. "Men say you fought like a demon, that you fired until your rifle was too hot to hold, and that every shot of yours brought down a redcoat. That it was in saving another from capture or death that you were—made prisoner. Oh, the story of your deeds has preceded you. We—"

"'Tis an exaggeration," I mumbled, horribly embarrassed at her eager praise and at the hero-worship that blazed in her big eyes. "They make too much of what a thousand others did far better. I—I myself scarce know how I chanced to turn, in a breath, from Tory to rebel. 'Twas laughable! I—"

"You did not turn so in a breath," she broke in. "You were ever a patriot at heart, though you knew it not. And ever you were but waiting the right hour to find it out. I knew it from the moment, a month ago, when you seized the soldier who stole my fan. So did Master Revere. We knew, and—we waited. Would I otherwise have so employed you to flash the signal from North Church belfry? Yet it pained me sore that in the instant you learned what you had done, your heart did not tell you on which side you belonged. But I knew full well that you must learn it this day when first the British should clash with the patriots. 'Twas for that reason I let you follow Revere."

"You *let* me follow him?" I repeated, half amused, half amazed. "Surely you did all in mortal power to hold me back!"

She smiled up at me through the bright tears that welled in her eyes—and it was a ghost of the gay imperious smile that I had known so well.

"Master Sessions," she said quietly, "in my cloak last night I bore two loaded and primed pistols. Pistol-shooting is not deemed fit pastime for a woman; yet such slight skill at it have I that at fifty paces I can bring down a flying swallow. Think you I need have let you escape to check Paul Revere, had I not wished to?"

"You would have killed me?" I cried, unbelieving.

"I *could* have killed you," she corrected. "But it would not have been needful, even had I wished to stop you. A single bullet through the foot would have done you no lasting harm. Yet it would have ended all chance of your riding last night. I let you go because—I

knew you would go the way of a brave man and a true American. As, forsooth, you did."

I eyed her in dumb bewilderment. When, I wonder, will the wisest man learn to understand the simplest woman? And what hope, this side of Judgment Day, had a thick-head like myself of coping with the witch brain of Marjory Winthrop?

She laughed at my discomfiture; then she grew grave.

"You have not yet told me how you got free," she said. "News came that you were a prisoner. I was hurrying with all speed to General Gage, to entreat your life—to use in your behalf what poor charm and eloquence I may possess. And now, it seems, you got scot-free through no help of mine."

"You are wrong," I answered. "It was *you,* and you alone, who set me free."

"You jest!" she exclaimed. "I did not—"

"You told certain officers, night before last, that I was a lunatic hanger-on of your family. And—"

"Ah, forgive me!" she pleaded. "'Tis ungenerous to remind me that—"

"And," I resumed, "when to-day's only prisoner turned out to be no rebel at all, but that selfsame lunatic in whose welfare your Tory family is so interested—why, his excellency very diplomatically strengthened his influence with your father by setting me at liberty."

She clapped her hands together like a delighted child, and broke into a silvery laugh of sheer joy.

"Oh, the simplicity of it!" she cried. "The clever, stupid *simplicity* of it! Tell me everything! 'Tis as rare a jest as any of playhouse making."

I told her my story. When I had finished Lord Percy's share in it, she said musingly:

"Yes, 'tis like Percy—or like Howe. Both are strange, whimsical men, who hide big hearts under cynical, dissolute exterior. Had either of them his own way, the fate of the patriots, I doubt not would be far different. But each must obey harsh, unjust orders. So, each obeys in the least brutal way he can. Would there were more like them!"

Down the winding street, from toward Government House, came the tramp of running feet.

Marjory paused to listen.

"These are soldiers," she said. "I know by their tread. Why can they be in such haste? One would think British troops had had enough running this glorious day to suffice them. They run as if they were in chase of some fugitive."

We glanced at each other; and the same thought came to us both.

"It is *you!*" she panted. "It is you they seek!"

I drew myself up.

"If it be so," I made reply, "I am too spent and too weary to fly. I must e'en make such defense as I can. For, if they have learned their error about me, then capture means hanging."

"Oh!" she cried in hot remorse. "And I have kept you standing here in peril! Quick!" her eyes sweeping our near vicinity for points of vantage. "Into the vestibule of this closed draper's shop!"

"To be caught like a rat in a drain?" I expostulated, eying the narrow passageway scarce three feet across and three deep.

"Quick!" she repeated in frenzied appeal.

And, as was ever my wont, I blindly obeyed her.

"Kneel down!" she ordered.

And again I obeyed. I looked up, to see her standing listlessly, her back to me, her furbelowed, caped dress and cloak quite filling the front of the short passage.

Oh, it was a ridiculous position for a grown man to be in—and it was a shameful thing to hide, literally, behind a woman's skirts!

Were our scare to be in vain—as seemed more than likely to me now on second thought—a pretty figure I should cut. She would always look on me as a coward, as a skulker who let a woman bear the brunt of danger for him.

At the thought I half rose from my crouching posture. But she heard me, and whispered imperiously:

"Back! They are rounding the corner just above. And I was right. They are soldiers—a provost marshal guard. Young Captain Waytt is leading them. They are searching every doorway and angle—for *something.*"

"Ten to one it is not for *me!*" I retorted, vexed at myself for so slavishly obeying her. "And I—"

"*Hush!*" she commanded in a tense whisper.

76

At almost the same instant the noise of approaching feet came directly to where Marjory stood. She was waiting, in the front of the shallow vestibule, as though she had just stepped back from the roadway to allow the hurrying file of redcoats to pass.

"Halt!" came the command in the high-pitched nasal tone affected by youthful officers of that period.

The shuffling footsteps ceased. Then the same high voice spoke again, this time in accents much modulated by respect, if not by admiration as well.

"I crave your pardon, Mistress Winthrop, for daring to trouble your ears with so vulgar a matter. But we be sent, hotfoot, in chase for a rebel who by mistake was but now set free at Government House. He was seen to pass into the street, walking slowly. He cannot have gone far."

"A rebel?" lisped Marjory in the silly "die-away" tones much cultivated then by women of fashion. "A rebel? Oh, la, sir! Is there but *one* of the pestilent breed left in Boston?"

"Prodigious witty!" applauded the officer. "No, the town swarms with the pests, and the whole countryside as well; but the special one we seek was a prisoner caught in to-day's riots at Lexington."

"Caught at Lexington?" lisped Marjory. "But, Captain Waytt, I sure heard tell that his excellency was to hang all prisoners taken in to-day's brawling. Why did he not hang this fellow while he had him? Why set him free?"

"'Twas a rare blunder," murmured the captain, sinking his voice so his men could not hear—"a rare blunder. Split me, else! The rogue claimed to be no rebel at all, but a peaceful servant of your father's. And—odd enough—Lord Percy backed the villain's words.

"Percy is near-sighted, and, I doubt not, mistook the man for another. His excellency turns the vile scoundrel loose, mind you, as a compliment to your worthy father. Not five minutes later your father chances to drop in for a dish of tea with Madam Gage. And the general tells of the good turn he has just done him by setting his 'servant' free. And your father declares, in a passion, that he has no such servant at all. So off we are sent to—"

"But while we prattle, he escapes," cut in Marjory, with the tone of one reluctant to bring so charming a narrative to a close.

"'Twas not for prattle that I halted, believe me," the captain protested. "Though Mistress Marjory Winthrop's face might well turn a whole regiment of dragoons from duty. I stopped to ask had you seen such an one fleeing—or loitering—along Milk Street?"

"What like was he?" she queried, all interest. "The street at this hour is so near deserted, and so slowly did I stroll in waiting for my coach to meet me, that I might well have seen him?"

"He is a giant of a fellow, with a shock of yellow hair, and clad in blue clothes of Colonial cut," began the captain; "and he—"

"A handsome, powerful man, of fine carriage?" Marjory caught him up. "I saw him not two minutes agone. And I noted his looks no less than his speed; for he was running like mad. Doubtless he walked slowly till out of sight of Government House, and then—"

"Which way went he?" broke in the captain in eager interest.

"Down to yonder alley. And then he whipped about the corner to the left toward the Common."

"March! *Double quick!*" came the high-pitched orders.

The sound of running martial feet again broke upon my ears and fast died away in the distance.

"Alas!" sighed Marjory in mingled relief and comic remorse. "What am I coming to? I was ever a truthful maid. I scorned a lie and I loathed a liar. Yet here, in three brief days, I have told two *amazing* lies. And both in *your* behalf. The first, I verily believe, that ever seared my lips. And yet—somehow I cannot feel for them the grief I should. There!" in a more businesslike tone. "The last of the searchers has turned the far corner. You are safe for the moment. But what next?"

"I owe you my life, my freedom!" I replied, rising and looking down at her with a gaze that somehow brought the red flush back to her pale cheeks. "I owe all to you. That is the sweetest part of my liberty—of my life itself—that I am in your dear debt for it, Marjory! I—"

She had heard me with glowing face and with parted lips. Her wondrous eyes I could not read. But they had never left mine.

Now, midway in my mad, impulsive speech, a look of utter terror flashed over her face and she screamed.

A hairy, brown hand had reached forward from amid the deepening shadows of the street beyond, and was dragging her bodily away from me.

CHAPTER XIII.
I Am Outlawed.

EXCEPT that she had turned to face me, Marjory had not hitherto moved from her position at the entrance to the short vestibule. Thus, to any one passing along the street, she was visible, while I was not.

Whoever it was that now silently gripped her shoulder and drew her out of the passageway had evidently not seen me.

It was uncanny enough—that huge, discolored paw reaching forward out of the street's twilit gloom, fastening itself on the shrinking girl and dragging her back from me.

For the moment, tired of body and heavy of wit that I was, I watched the odd action, numb with inertia.

Then, as she screamed, a rough English voice drawled:

"Whist! I'll choke that throat of yours if you try to cry out, my lady! You know me? Of course not! But it was through *you* that Sir William ordered me fifty lashes on the back and fifty days in the guard-house. For snatching your fan. Through Pitcairn I was let loose to-day. And now you'll pay for what you've caused me. Your purse! And those rings! *Quick!*"

I take shame that my weariness and crass amaze had thus long held me spellbound. But, as the fellow apparently snatched for the purse at her girdle, Marjory cried my name in appeal.

Then, all my fatigue gone, I was out of the vestibule at one bound.

Even by that waning light I recognized the fellow. I had bare time to recall him as the soldier whom I had turned over to Howe for stealing Marjory's fan from Paul Revere, before I was at his throat.

He knew me, too. For, as he released Marjory and whirled to meet my attack, he shouted my name.

Then we were at death-grips. Speechless, tense, ferocious, we fought. He was a powerful, wiry man. I was exhausted from the day's adventure. He seemed to feel his advantage, for he fought me like a wild beast. Strain my overwrought muscles as I might, I could scarce withstand the assault of the writhing, snarling creature whose grip was well-nigh to crack my ribs and whose sinewy fingers ever crept searchingly toward my throat.

How I yearned for the fresh, invincible strength that I had lavished during that long day of fighting, riding, and pursuit! But, be a man ever so strong, his muscles can endure only just so much without rest.

Yet I fought on with a fury that atoned in part for my ebbing power. This scoundrel had dared to lay rude hands upon the woman whom I now knew was all the world to me. He had insulted her, had sought to rob her, and he should be punished.

Yet it is one thing to vow vengeance against a powerful opponent, and quite another to put that vengeance into execution. And this I was rapidly learning.

Strive as I would, his fingers at last closed about my throat. I could not breathe. Nor could I shake off that strangling clutch. I felt the fight was well-nigh at an end. Breathless and choking, I could endure little longer.

And she—Marjory Winthrop—of all women would see me beaten, overcome, hurled helpless to earth, by this brute of a redcoat! I had sprung to her defense.

And now, having insulted her, the fellow would thrash me, her defender! Oh, it was too degrading to endure!

No man likes to appear badly in a woman's eyes. It is vanity's death-blow to allow the woman one loves to see one overthrown in fair fight. I could fancy the scorn in Marjory's proud little face when my foe should stand exultant over me.

And with that mental vision came madness. My strength, like Samson's of old, rushed back upon me for one fleeting instant, goaded into action by fear of a woman's scorn. And in that brief moment I had torn the soldier's grip from my throat, had caught him up in my arms, and flung him from me.

So great was this sudden access of false strength that he fell prone, half stunned, to the cobblestones. Then I reeled toward him.

My momentary access of power was gone, leaving me weaker than before. I could scarce keep my feet as, panting and gasping, I lurched forward.

Luckily, the fall had knocked out some of his wits, or he must have noted my helpless plight. As it was, seeing me bearing down upon him, he scrambled to his feet in a trice, whipped off his muddied coat,

hurled it full in my face to baffle my adventure, and took incontinently to his heels.

By the time my shaking fingers could tear away the enveloping garment, the soldier was a full fifty yards away, and running at top speed.

It was evident he had no taste for further grappling with a man who had so easily hurled him to the ground. Nor, in his flight, could he note how utterly spent was that same victorious antagonist.

Yet over his shoulder, as he ran, he shouted back in impotent rage:

"You are the rebel they seek! I was at the corner and heard her send Captain Wyatt and his squad on a false scent. I'll rouse the hue and cry for you at the barracks. Yes, and she shall lodge in jail, too, for aiding a felon and enemy of the king. *Yah!* 'Twill be short shrift for the pair of ye!"

He was gone, and I turned to look at Marjory. She was eying me with flushed, excited face.

Her hands were tight-clasped, and she leaned forward breathless, as though still seeing the combat.

"Oh, you were *splendid!*" she cried impulsively. "It seemed for the moment that he was overcoming you. But you shook him off, like a Hercules, and—"

"You heard what he said?" I broke in. "He will keep his word. The hue and cry will be quickly after me. Yes, and after *you*, too. Coming at the heels of your tale of my being a dependant of your father, the fact of your shielding me just now will work you ill. Gage has scant mercy for those who aid rebels."

"I fear you are right," she sighed. "Well, it had to come one day. And I have done my country some slight service ere they found me out. I am not unprepared—"

"But that the exposure should come through aiding *me!*" I exclaimed. "It is for *that* I cannot forgive myself."

"For whose sake could it have better come?" she asked gently. "And now take me to Master Revere's. He will know what to do. He made preparations months ago for this very event. As indeed he is ever prepared for all contingencies."

"To Master Revere?" I argued. "Why not to your father?"

Her bright eyes brimmed suddenly with tears.

"My father and I," she said sadly, "have ever been estranged. And since my mother's death he has scarce troubled to see me once a month. Now that he learns I am a patriot, he will cast me off as though I were a leper. No; it is to Master Revere I must go, as do all who are in trouble."

"Revere will expect you? You are *sure?*"

"Yes. Even now he himself is making ready, with his wife and children, to flee to-night. Boston is too hot to hold such a man after to-day's work. He has a cottage at Lexington. Thither his family are going. And they will take me."

I heard a high-pitched military order far down the street. Captain Wyatt and his posse were returning from their wild-goose chase.

I started up. With the hue and cry from Government House about to begin, and with this squad of Wyatt's in front of me, I should indeed be finely caught between two fires.

As always, it was Marjory whose quick wit intervened. She snatched up the soldier's discarded scarlet coat from the pavement. Beside it lay the sugar-loaf hat that had tumbled from his head at the first onset.

"Off with your coat!" she commanded. "And don *this.* Now for the hat. *So!* Bend your head!"

Dully, I did as she bade me. I could feel her soft hands running nimbly through my long, loose hair. The touch thrilled me.

In another instant my locks were roughly massed in a cue and bound, together at the nape of my neck with one of her own hair-ribbons.

She stood off and eyed me critically.

"The coat is a monstrous bad fit," she commented. "And the hair is ill-cued. Yet, at dusk, and topped by the hat, both will perchance pass muster. See, they are rounding the corner. Don't be seen talking to me. Make for Revere's shop. I'll join you there.

"*So!* Walk in the middle of the road. Swagger! Be not afraid of the redcoats. They will take you for a grenadier off duty. Go, now! And Heaven's own luck go with you! 'Tis but a chance. Yet—it is your *only* chance."

CHAPTER XIV.
When Love Was King.

GRAY dawn—or, rather, the slow paling of a black night.

And, under the faint gleam, a horde of two thousand five hundred swarming creatures, scarce human in their crouching attitudes, rushing here and there, and toiling like mad at some strange task.

The scene was the crest of one of two twin hills that reared their blunt heads above the lower ground of the Charlestown district.

The time was June 17, 1775.

The characters of the dawning drama were the self-styled Continental army.

The sun, whose approach now faintly whitened the east, was that day to look down on the most stirring, epoch-making scene in all American history—the battle of Bunker Hill; which, by the way, was not fought at Bunker Hill at all.

Will you bear with me while I sketch, in a mere mouthful of words, the events of the two months that had elapsed since the night when, disguised as a British grenadier, I had escaped from Boston with Marjory Winthrop and the Reveres?

The news of Concord and Lexington had spread like wildfire through the thirteen Colonies. And it was a wildfire that set ablaze the long-gathered fuel of hatred, vengeance, and yearning for liberty.

From Maine to Georgia, men rushed to arms. Every road to Massachusetts was choked with hurrying recruits. Massachusetts was the cradle of American liberty; and Boston was the center of the mighty movement.

Israel Putnam, grizzled Indian fighter and pioneer, had been plowing on his Connecticut farm when word of Lexington's fight had reached him.

He had cut the traces, sprung upon his unsaddled farm-horse, and galloped to the front.

Dr. Benedict Arnold, at the news, had shut his New Haven apothecary-shop, rallied every patriot within reach, seized the local British ammunitions, and marched to the aid of liberty.

Grim, savage old Ethan Allen had called his Green Mountain boys to arms.

Dr. Joseph Warren had cried aloud:

"God's sun hath risen on a glorious day! The British have *begun* the war. Any one could do that. But we alone can end it."

Boston was the central point of attack. The British garrison there, to its supreme disgust, found itself practically in a state of siege. The hills, the woods, the villages around the city were alive with Yankee militia; too weak to storm the town, but too strong to be driven away.

In May, Ethan Allen and Benedict Arnold had further raised the patriots' hopes by capturing the strong British fort at Ticonderoga, first calling on its defenders to surrender, "In the name of the Great Jehovah and the Continental Congress."

In May, too, Howe came rushing back to Boston, with Sir Henry Clinton and "Gentleman Johnny" Burgoyne, to try to stem the roaring tide of revolt.

Israel Putnam, with some 2,200 Minute Men and recruits, pressed as close upon the city as he dared, making Cambridge his headquarters. Once, near East Boston, he actually clashed, in skirmish, with the British.

The Tory press was wild with virtuous indignation at the uprising of the patriots. One "loyal" Boston paper denounced it thus:

"The annals of the world have not been deformed with a single instance of so unnatural, so causeless, so wicked a rebellion."

As the weeks wore on, the patriots grew impatient that no decisive blow was struck. Now that actual blood had been shed, they were no longer content to wait until they grew strong enough in numbers and money before pressing the war. The British, too, were furious at the continuance of the siege. From these two causes sprang the battle of Bunker Hill.

On the night of June 16 Putnam and Colonel Prescott secretly marched a body of 2,500 militia to Charlestown. Their orders were to take and fortify Bunker Hill, thus to have at least one stronghold that should overlook and menace Boston.

To this day no one knows exactly why the plan was altered at the last minute; so that not Bunker Hill, but the near-by Breed's Hill was chosen. Some say we mistook the one hill for the other in the black

darkness. Others claim that our leaders suddenly decided Breed's Hill was the easier to fortify.

The matter is a mystery. And neither Putnam nor Prescott, nor any of the rest, ever wholly explained it. Personally, I believe they blundered onto the wrong hill; and that, when the mistake was discovered, it was too late to change.

The conflict there will always be known as the battle of Bunker Hill. Yet, as every one should know, it was really the battle of Breed's Hill.

In any case, we worked like mad all night long to turn the hill into a fortress. Paltry enough were our means of defense. And few of us had ever been taught the art of breastwork building, or any other methods of fortifying a position.

Tacticians might well have laughed at our bungling, amateurish work of that night. But no living man, be he British or American, can laugh at our defense of our rude fortifications on the following day.

Here was the position: A hill, rising above the low ground that sloped to the water. On the opposite side of the river, Boston. To the right of our hill lay Charlestown. To attack us the British must cross the river and mount the hill.

So much for history. Now, back to my story:

I was no longer "Roger Sessions, country yokel." In reward for certain petty exploits of mine in the East Boston skirmish and for a rough knowledge of tactics that I had picked up while drilling with the Wilbraham train-band in the old days, I was now "Captain Sessions, of the Massachusetts Infantry Militia."

The pay was—nothing. The sword and uniform I myself had bought. My command consisted of seventy-two backwoodsmen and farmers clad in homespun and armed with old-fashioned muskets and fowling-pieces.

I had been kept busily at work during the past two months. Not once in all that time had I found enough leisure hours to ride to Lexington, where Marjory Winthrop still abode with the Revere family.

The Continental army's mail service was inefficient in those days. And, since leaving Marjory at the door of the Revere cottage, I had not heard from nor of her.

Yet, through all my military duties, I could never quite lose the memory of the girl. I loved her. I knew that now; but, as I thought it over in cold blood, and considered her position and the attentions that had ever been showered upon her by bearers of the proudest names in all the Colonies, I grew to understand that I could be nothing to her.

I was a rough son of the soil. She a dainty little aristocrat.

All that had ever really bound us together was our mutual patriotism. And, now that she was far away, she had doubtless forgotten my very existence.

As I moved to and fro among my busily toiling men, giving an order here, suggesting an improvement there, my mind kept wandering back to her with a persistency that half angered me.

Never in these two long months had the girl seemed so near to me, so vividly present, as at this hour when all my thoughts ought to have been concentrated upon my task.

A burly figure came toward me. In the growing half light I recognized the bald head and keen, heavy-browed eyes of General Putnam—"Old Put," as we affectionately called him.

"Captain Sessions," he called, as he caught sight of me, "a dozen new loads of hay have come. They are at the rear, beside the hospital-tent. Take thirty of your men, and have the hay brought forward to this redoubt. There is a gap here that a whole squadron could charge through."

I saluted, summoned a group of my militia from their labor of trench-digging, and started for the rear. Five minutes later the great hay-wains were being tugged by thirty brawny men toward Putnam's redoubt. I watched the starting of the last load, then followed.

As I passed the long, tattered awning, rigged upon hop-poles, and called, by courtesy, a hospital-tent, I glanced in. By the light of tallow-dips five or six women were busy arranging mattress cots, scraping lint, and kindling a fire whereby to heat water. In a far corner Dr. Joseph Warren and a young surgeon were looking over a case of surgical instruments.

Early in the morning as it was, the air was heavy and hot, presaging a scorching day.

The workers in the close tent must have felt the heat more than did we who were in the open. Indeed, as I was about to move away, one

of the women arose from her task of rolling bandages and came to the tent door for a breath of fresher air.

At sight of me she halted on the threshold; then came forward with outstretched hands. Her back was to the candle glow. It needed a second glance for me to recognize, by that half light, the figure in the shapeless brown linsey-woolsey frock and long apron.

"Marjory!" I cried, incredulous.

At sight of me, she halted on the threshold; then came forward with outstretched porcelain in a barn-yard. I peered eagerly down into the little upraised face. These two months had wrought a subtle change in her.

If the fiery, "spoiled–child" look had faded, its place was taken by a womanly sweetness and patience that transfigured her. Nor, now that I saw more clearly, did the homespun gown and apron detract from her loveliness. Rather did they give her slight form a certain dignity.

Yet her presence in camp here I could not understand. Still clasping both her hands, I exclaimed:

"Why are you here? When the British discover that we have occupied these heights, they are sure to attack us. There will be danger for you."

"Shall American women stay safe at home while American men are in peril?" she asked, with a flash of her old spirit. "There was a call for nurses. So I came."

We had stepped out from the tent. An odd sort of constraint seemed to grip us both. I could not understand—nor overcome—it.

Together, without speaking, we moved slowly across the broken ground toward the fortifications.

I had longed so to see her, to be with her. Yet now that she was at my side, I could find no words, not even commonplaces, to address to her. We paused on a little elevation, and stood looking down at the horde of fast-working militiamen.

"There, just beneath, are the breastworks," I said, in order to break the strained silence. "That longer line is the rail fence, with a huge barrier of hay stuffed about it to stop bullets. The big, bald man over there in the butternut shirt is General Putnam. The slenderer shorter man talking with him is Colonel Prescott. See," pointing across the river, "Boston is beginning to wake up. There are lights in the windows.

Yonder, behind the mist that covers the bay, are the British war-ships. We are within range of them. They will cause us trouble, I'm afraid."

"Tell me about yourself!" she demanded. "You are wearing a captain's uniform. I heard you had been promoted. I was so glad."

"I am a captain," I said. "The honor is slight, the pay nothing, the work hard. Yet I am not in need of any great honor and I do not fear hard work. As for pay, my father died a month agone. I suppose I am what most provincials would call rich."

"You speak as if that counted little," she commented.

"It does," I answered bitterly. "I would part with every shilling of it if I could get in exchange such manners and such birth and such personality as should make me the sort of man I want to be."

"The sort of man you *want* to be?" she echoed. "I don't understand."

"It is hard to explain. But here is an instance. Two months have passed since I saw you. Yet, when I meet you again, I am loutish and stupid. I can find naught to say, except to point out to you our troops' defenses. Were I such a man as Pitcairn or Howe or Percy, I should be able to tell you—to tell you—"

"Yes?" she whispered softly as I paused.

But the devil of awkwardness and timidity had again gripped my tongue.

"To tell you," I went on lamely, "how glad I am to see you."

Her face fell. I continued, the more boldly for her embarrassment:

"To tell you how your memory has been before me every minute since we parted. How it has ever come between me and my duties. To tell you how I dreamed of meeting you again and of all the graceful, clever speeches I planned to make when we should meet—and all of which I have now clean forgot. To tell you that though I know you look on me as a country boor, yet I—"

"Stop!" she cried. "You have no right to say such things. I—"

"I know full well I have not," I muttered, crushed by what I deemed her scorn at my presumption. "I forgot myself and the difference in our stations. I crave pardon for—"

"Why will you forever misunderstand me?" she broke in. "I meant nothing like that, and you should know it!"

"But you said—"

"But I said—or meant to say—that you have no right to assume that I look on you as a 'country boor.' You are a gallant man, a true patriot and a true friend."

"A 'friend'" I repeated, forgetting all my sanity and well-planned caution. "That is just it! Were I such a man as Howe or Percy—or even as Warren—I might hope to find means of making you regard me no longer as a friend."

"No longer as a friend!" she echoed. "You do not value my friendship?"

There was hurt surprise in her sweet voice. She drew a little away from me.

"No!" I retorted, carried away by the heart whose whisperings I had so long and so vainly sought to smother. "I am as bold—as hopelessly bold—as the beggar lad, in the fairy tale, who wooed the princess. Once I would have given my life to hear you deign to call me 'friend.' Now I know I was at heart a hypocrite when I longed for that. For, when a man loves—when he loves with all his heart and soul and mind—when love is his whole existence and when one woman fills his entire world and crowds out all else—then the offer of 'friendship' is as the gift of a heavy bar of gold to a drowning man."

She made no answer. And madly I plunged on:

"I love you, Marjory! Two months ago I did not know love existed. Since then I am as a man, born blind, who first sees God's sunlight. I love you with every atom of life and longing there is within me. And a hostler might adore a queen with as much hope of return. I have gone insane. I have spoken presumptuous words that will make you turn from me as from some over-impudent black slave. Never again now can I hope you will call me 'friend.' Yet you know the truth. And now you know, too, why I should blithely part with all my wealth if only I might become the sort of man you could learn to care for, and in time love."

Still she spoke no word. I dared not look at her, to see the silent outraged scorn I knew must blaze in her face. Indignant amazement had no doubt robbed her of words.

"After what I have said," I ended bitterly, "you will not want to see me again. And I will never have the courage to seek you out. Our paths henceforth lie in far different ways. But, when you have for-

gotten your resentment at my audacity, it may not anger you to know that I shall always be the better, the happier for this wondrous love of mine. You have been kind to me past all my deserts. And I have repaid you by thrusting my unwelcome love-tale upon you. In a few hours I shall be at death-grips with my country's enemies. I shall not regret losing a life that—"

"No! *No!*" she cried, brokenly. "You must not speak of that! And you must guard yourself to-day as never before. If you fall, I—"

"*Quarters!*" bellowed Putnam's voice from below.

And our bugles took up the command. From every side, officers and men were rushing pell-mell to the trenches. From one of the war-ships in the bay boomed a signal-gun. It was answered from Boston.

I turned for a last look at Marjory. Her great eyes were alight with a miraculous glow that fairly dazed me.

Then, with wildly pulsing heart and brain in a whirl, I dashed down the slope to my post of duty.

CHAPTER XV.
BEFORE THE STORM.

From such rascals as these may we fear a rebuff?
Let fly, grenadiers, with the hot, leaden stuff!

CLEARLY to us through the sultry, scorching noonday air came the words of the quaint old British grenadier song, that marching red-coat regiments had sung in every land from China to the colonies.

And, from a company of round-cheeked farm-boys behind a corner of the hay redoubt was roared in answer a fragment of our newest camp ditty:

For, oh, we're marching on Quebec!
The drums they are a beating;
Americay has won the day,
The British are retreating!

Yankee Doodle, keep it up! Yankee—

"Silence in the ranks!" bawled a red-haired colonel. "D'ye think this is a singing-school? Look to your primings, and rest your lazy bodies while you can!"

This was the spirit on both sides, at the opening of the battle of Bunker Hill. Song, laughter, irritable reproof. For, such things, in moments of stress, are quite as indicative of tremendous excitement as are blanched lips, drawn features, and trembling limbs. Apparent gaiety, at times of that sort, is a form of intoxication. Yet it serves to keep up men's hearts.

At early dawn the "watch" on the harbor war-ships had discovered our presence on Breed's Hill. Quickly the news had reached Boston. From sunrise and for hours thereafter sounded the roll of drums, the blare of trumpets, the faint thud of rhythmic marching feet.

Then the long line of red had flowed down the narrow river streets and to the water's edge, where barge after barge, loaded to the gunwale, plied across to the Charlestown shore, bearing the redcoats to our side of the stream.

Infantry, cavalry, artillery—men, horses, cannon—had all morning been ferried across in a ceaseless line. Hourly the British army on the plain below Breed's Hill had swelled in numbers, until some five thousand regulars were massed for the attack.

Through my field-glass I studied the serried ranks.

In the vanguard I could see Sir William Howe, dandified, bored, dressed as though for a ball. His scarlet, gold-laced coat, his feathered chapeau, his snowy-frilled shirt, white satin breeches, white silk stockings, and gold-buckled shoes—all bespoke a man of fashion on his way to a revel rather than a grim warrior facing possible death.

Pigott, too, I made out, and Lord Percy, and many another of the gallant fops who had worshiped at Marjory Winthrop's shrine.

On our side, our simple preparations were already complete. All that remained to us was to lie waiting behind our rude barriers. And this, you will believe me, is the hardest part of any battle—or of any other struggle in this mortal life of ours.

Our unkempt, half-uniformed, ill-armed rabble was a pitiful contrast to our spruce, well-drilled veteran foes on the plain below. From

the very first, the wiseacres had claimed that no undisciplined force of provincials could hope to hold their own against the flower of England's army. And now the croaking prophecy bade fair to become all too true.

We were barely twenty-five hundred men and boys, all told. The British were full double our number. They had boundless ammunition. Our supply of powder and ball was wofully inadequate. They were seasoned warriors. Three-fourths of us had never smelled powder in conflict.

These, then, were the odds against which we were to strive in this, the first battle the Revolution; a battle on whose outcome hung the fate of America.

The heat was terrific. The broiling June sun beat mercilessly down upon us as we lay there. One or two men keeled over with sunstroke and were carried to the rear. Women and little boys passed back and forth along the lines, bearing pails of "sugar water" and coconut-gourd cups.

Putnam and Warren and Prescott were everywhere; encouraging, counseling, inspecting. By their orders our guns were loaded, not only with full charge of powder and the customary single large bullet, but each was charged with from three to nine buckshot as well. A rough, odd load, but one that could scatter death at close range, with murderous efficiency.

All morning the British had been forming and reforming. Drop-shots from the warships had now and then reached us. But the red-hot sun had passed the meridian before the bugles sounded the signal for the actual attack.

Every hill and house-top for miles was black with spectators. At last came the order to charge.

The red lines moved forward with stately tread toward the hill-foot. Howe and Pigott led the columns in person.

I can speak of only my own view of the battle, from the hay-barrier fence—the point of attack by Sir William Howe's detachment. But that was typical of the whole fight.

At the hill's first rise, some two hundred yards below us, Howe halted his column. In the hush that ever precedes a storm, his clear-called words to his men reached us distinctly.

"Veterans of China and of the Continent wars!" he cried, pointing carelessly back over his shoulder at us, "unless we can drive those farmers from the hill, we can't stay longer in comfortable old Boston. It is going to be hot work. Worse than you think. But I ask no man to do more than follow where I lead."

The British cheered the simple speech till the air throbbed with their yells. Then facing about, with drawn sword, Howe shouted an order. The bugles caught it up. Like a vast scarlet wave, the regulars surged up the hill. Ten paces ahead of his men, his florid, tired face alight with excitement, ran Sir William Howe.

"Stand firm, boys!" rumbled "Old Put's" heavy voice along our waiting line. "Red clothes don't make great men. Hold our fire till you see the whites of their eyes. You sharpshooters, pick off the officers. You'll know 'em by the shoulder-straps. Hold hard, now! The man who pulls trigger, before the word comes, will be drummed out of camp for a coward and a traitor. Aim low! Aim *steady!* A walking regular ain't half so hard to hit as a running deer."

Up the hill moved the British. From the war-ships the fire grew heavier. At a distance of barely one hundred yards from our hay fence, Howe gave a quick, barking command.

Instantly his men deployed in as pretty a maneuver as any I ever saw on a field-day, and, with changed formation, came toward us in a series of long, wide-spread single files. Then they opened fire.

And still we made no move, gave no sign of resistance. Up to eighty yards—to seventy—to sixty—the British column advanced. The regulars' faces, sharply visible to us through niches in our barricades, had lost their exultant look. They were frowning and puzzled.

Even Howe's handsome brows were knit in perplexity. This was something wholly outside his military experience.

He had marched his men to within sixty yards of an entrenched foe. Yet not one shot had that foe fired. Not one cry of command had been heard. Not a single face had peeped from above the rough ramparts.

The British might as well be charging a body of invisible, soundless ghosts. It was a silence and suspense calculated to shake the strongest veteran's nerves. It was something unknown before in all the annals of warfare.

For what the British knew, we might long since have fled, leaving our entrenchments empty and desolate. They knew not whether they were marching upon a lurking foe or against vacant breastworks.

The ruse which we had employed merely in order to save our too scanty ammunition from waste, was now proving our best ally by sapping the courage of the host marching to our destruction.

It was one of those moments, tense as a drawn bowstring, that try one's nerves and endurance far more than could the most perilous crisis in active battle.

Howe shook off the momentary feeling of dread that had well-nigh mastered him.

"*Forward!*" he yelled to his men.

The red line—barely fifty yards away now—hurled itself bodily at our entrenchments.

A rasping shout of command from Putnam shattered our stillness. A hundred voices took up the cry.

Then pandemonium broke loose!

CHAPTER XVI.
The Battle of Bunker Hill.

FROM fence shelter, from earthworks, from behind every barrier, rose one solid mass of motley humanity. They sprang up, at the word of command, as a single man.

"*Fire!*" was our officers' cry.

And the line of ill-assorted muskets belched forth into a sheet of yellow flame.

At that ridiculously short range, a ten-year-old child could not have missed the broad, red-coated target that was pressing close toward us.

Not a man of us but was a far better shot than the average disciplined soldier. Not a man of us but knew just where to aim and when to draw trigger.

And from our rifle-muzzles whizzed that leaden torrent of mingled ball and buckshot, straight into the heart of the charging British

column.

I have sometimes wondered what our advancing foes must have thought when those seemingly deserted breastworks became all at once crowned with hundreds of sun-browned faces; and when, at the next instant, that death-blast of lead poured into their oncoming files.

Perhaps never before in warfare's annals had so small a body of men dealt such destruction at one volley. Whole ranks of redcoats were mowed down as if by some monstrous, invisible scythe. The ground was strewn waist-high with fallen men.

The British had begun to fire on us as they came within a hundred paces, and they had kept it up as they advanced. But, thanks to our "home-made" defenses, their shots had done little execution. Again there had been some sort of a fusillade as we appeared above our breastworks.

But that withering blast from our leveled guns had ripped and crumpled and utterly destroyed their prim, soldierly formation. It had stricken the survivors with abject terror.

At sight of their comrades falling by the score on every hand, the veteran regulars turned and rushed pell-mell, in crazy confusion, down the hill. Anywhere and everywhere they ran, to escape from that scathing rifle-fire of ours.

Here is where their brave officers should have stood ready to brace the demoralized men, to hold firm the shattered remnants of the line, and encourage the fugitives to press the attack.

But here, too, was the result of "Old Put's" shrewd orders to our sharpshooters. For fallen officers were sprawling everywhere. There were not enough left to rally the soldiers.

And that vainglorious advance of British regulars, marching confidently to the destruction of a farmer-foe, ended in a ridiculous, sheep-like scramble to safety.

Yes, and that first attack on the hill fortifications did far more than merely to end in the rout of our assailants. It proved, once and for all, that untrained farmers, who fought for liberty and country, could hold their own—and more than hold their own—against the once dreaded and seemingly invincible veteran soldiery of Great Britain.

Down the hill fled the troops, their few officers frantically screaming to them and beating them with the flat of their swords, to stay the

hopeless flight.

I could see Howe, in the very midst of his scurrying men; raging like a fiend from the pit; carried on, in spite of his struggles, by the avalanche of flying soldiers.

At the hill-foot the officers were finally able to stay the panic which had threatened to sweep its victims clear into the bay before it could be stopped.

Gesticulating, shrieking, jumping up and down with wild rage, the subalterns and captains set to work reforming their scared troops. Howe alone did not share in the general excitement. Now that the flight had stopped, his anger died.

He stood calmly to one side while his officers worked like mad among the men. He was gazing up toward us, with an air of wild wonder on his handsome, tired face. Yes, and it merged into a look of genuine admiration as he noted once more our meager defenses and the havoc he had wrought.

I doubt if the British were more surprised at their repulse than were we. We had just clashed with the foremost troops of Europe. The most sanguine among us had scarce expected to withstand their first onrush. That we should drive them helter-skelter before us seemed nothing less than miraculous.

And, in that moment, was born in men's hearts the calm belief that one day or another we should wholly conquer these red "bugaboos" that for so many years had been thrust before our eyes as a menace and a whip to cow us.

Putnam and Prescott were passing among us, calling loud encouragement and praise. The few who had fallen were carried to the rear. The rest of us crouched quietly, cleaning our guns, reloading them, and chatting in lowered voices.

Gone now were the false gaiety, the irritation, the tremulous excitement. We were for the most part as calm as if on a day's hunting jaunt.

Suddenly came a cry of anguish from a Charlestown man in the center of my own company. He was on his feet, pointing in dumb excitement to the far right.

We sprang up to look. Below us lay the defenseless village of Charlestown. From a dozen points the settlement was bursting into

red flame.

The British, in revenge for their disgrace, had fired Charlestown. A chivalric reprisal!

A murmur of fury, almost of despair, ran down our line. Many a Charlestown man was in the patriot army.

Dr. Joseph Warren left his work among the women and sprang upon a rampart; his stalwart, graceful body vibrant, his face alight.

"My brothers!" he cried, his voice carrying, trumpet-like, to the farthest confines of the fortifications, "my brothers, they have burned your homes behind you. Nothing left for you now but to go forward— ever *forward*—until victory crowns you! You have seized this ground. *Hold* it! You have beaten back the proud power of tyranny. Let it never again encroach upon you! Never rest until America is a freemen's land!"

The bugles of the British crashed in upon his ringing speech. "*Quarters!*" called our officers.

And once more, gun in hand, eye steady, we turned to the grim game of war.

CHAPTER XVII.
The Last Volley.

UP the slope the British were toiling. They were no cowards, these stiff, machine-like men in red. Because we had once taken them unawares and had smashed their routine of attack, that was no reason for them to shrink from another charge.

They were men of bulldog pluck, these English; men who never knew when they were beaten. Wherefore they had conquered half the world.

And it was only we Colonials—men of their own blood—who could ever make headway against them.

Up the hill they came, in solid phalanx. And, as they neared the strewn ranks of their fallen comrades, they did not flinch, but ever moved onward toward that fatal barrier.

Far from down in their throats they were growling fiercely that

same old marching song of the grenadiers:

From such rascals as these may we fear a rebuff?

Howe was still in the lead. How he had escaped death in so exposed a position, during that first disastrous charge, is a mystery.

At a hundred paces from the barrier the British halted, fired, marched on again; halting and firing at intervals as they came.

And once more we held our fire until they were within fifty yards of us. Then out crashed a terrific volley from behind our defenses.

The scarlet column halted—wavered. The officers were here, there, everywhere, urging on their men. Howe, his hat struck off by a ball, ran forward bare-headed, unscathed, amid the hail of bullets.

The red line straightened, stiffened, and moved—*forward!*

They had withstood our fire, and were returning it with galling effect.

"Aim for the belts and for the officers!" roared Old Put.

"My best horse to the sharpshooter who drops Sir William Howe!" bawled the red-haired militia colonel.

By this time the powder smoke hung so thick between the British and ourselves that our men aimed more by guesswork than by sight.

Up to thirty yards—less than one hundred feet of the barrier the regulars had come. The hay, in places, was ablaze from the burned powder and the smoldering loading-wads.

"Fire!" came the order.

And again we rose as one man and emptied the contents of our overloaded guns into the center of that smoke reek. From the dense powder-cloud burst a serried line of red flashes. The British were holding their ground and returning our fire.

At close quarters we discharged a second and a third fusillade. The smoke was strangling-thick and blinding. Yet our strained ears could detect no return of our volley.

We crouched and waited, breathless, expectant. Had they halted to reform their lines, or to fire, or were they already upon us and about to swarm over our barricades?

Slowly, majestically, the cloud lifted. And a hoarse cheer of tri-

umph rang along the whole line of our breastworks.

Down the hill they were stumbling, staggering, running; utterly beaten. As before, their officers were striving in vain to check the panic rout.

I caught one glimpse of Howe, amid the tossing, plunging forms. His white breeches and stockings were dyed as red as his scarlet coat by the tide of death through which he had waded, waist-deep.

The British slain lay in windrows as high as our own defenses.

At the hill's foot—less quickly, this time—the red ranks reformed.

I could see Pigott and other officers clustering about Howe, gesticulating, arguing, entreating. But he only shook his head to each plea and pointed upward toward us.

I learned later that they were imploring him to give up the attack and to return to Boston. And he stubbornly refused, vowing he would take the hill, if it cost the life of every man in his whole command.

Meantime, we were jubilant. Twice had we beaten back the enemy, with terrible loss. Our own list of dead and wounded was, thus far, ridiculously small in proportion to the ravages we had wrought.

One thing alone clouded our glee. Valiant Dr. Warren lay dead across the breastworks, his hero heart pierced by a British musket-ball. Rest his brave soul! Never has this world known a truer man, a purer patriot.

Putnam alone showed no exultation in our victory. From a quick talk with one of the powder-guards, he turned to me.

"What ammunition has your company, Captain Sessions?" he asked.

"Barely one round to the man," I sorrowfully replied. "I had already sent back for more, but—"

"But there is no more!" he snapped. "'Tis the same tale everywhere. Scarce a single round of powder and ball left to each gun. If they attack again, we must fall back."

"Fall back!" I echoed in dismay, forgetting even such slack military etiquette as we provincials were wont to maintain toward our superior officers. "Fall back, after twice beating them down the hill?"

"It is enough to make a man want to die!" he groaned. "With four more rounds of ammunition we could drive back a third charge as we did the other two. But with only one? And victory was in our grasp. A

victory that neither England nor America—no, not the whole world—would ever have forgot."

He strode away, his big head sunk on his chest. And as he went the British bugles from below sounded the charge.

For the third time, up the hill they came. Howe, in his blood-stained, torn finery, still limped along in front. They opened fire as before, and ever crept onward.

As we rose, at fifty yards, to send our last volley at them, a crash of musketry from the left swept our lines transversely. Howe had sent another column up the hill from that side, and had caught us in a murderous crossfire.

Our single round of ammunition was discharged in the faces of the oncoming British. As before, entire ranks of men fell. But, after only a moment's halt, on they came again.

Our men in helpless fury shook their empty guns in the faces of the oncoming foe. Some of the militia madly clawed up stones from the ground at our feet and hurled them at the advancing column.

Then the redcoats fired full at our defenseless ranks.

And we fell back.

Leaving the rough barriers we had so carefully built and so doggedly defended, we tumbled backward in retreat. We were as helpless now against our foes as any peaceful farmer might find himself against a fully-armed bandit.

Oh, it was a bitter, black moment!

Raked by that fearful cross-fire, charged by the British from in front, our men fell by the hundred. It was during that pitiful retreat that we sustained our chief losses of the entire day.

Over our breastworks swarmed the British. We were at their mercy.

Huddled together and unarmed as we were, impeded by our very numbers, in that slow retreat they could have fallen upon us and slaughtered us all like so many cattle in the shambles. And, knowing the nature of our foes, I think none of us expected anything less.

But it was a day of miracles. As the redcoats seized our defenses, Howe gave a sharp order. The bugles sounded a halt.

We could not believe our senses. Howe had us safe in his grip. He could have destroyed us utterly then and there, with scarce the loss of one of his own men.

Yet, he had ordered a halt, and was actually letting us get away unscathed!

An orderly galloped up the slope and drew rein beside him.

"General Clinton's compliments, Sir William!" loudly announced the rider. "And he wishes to know the meaning of this halt. He desires that you advance at once and—"

"I was ordered to take this hill," retorted Howe sternly. "I have taken it. There my duty ends. I shall not advance a step."

A strange man. A gallant man. I have heard him cursed as a tyrant and a butcher. Yet, in my heart—and in every American's—there should perchance be a soft spot for this same inveterate gambler and tricky, reckless warrior.

For, at that moment, he held nearly two thousand helpless foes in his power. And he let them go. He was able to crush us. His men longed to. And Clinton had commanded it.

Yet—whether from a mere whim or from some promptings of humanity or fair play or recognition of brave, unfortunate antagonists—General Sir William Howe spared us. Be that remembered to his credit when patriots revile his memory!

The battle was over. Yet, here and there, at isolated spots in the stricken field, little knots of men were still fighting hand to hand. Seeking to withdraw my own company with as slight loss as might be, I found myself cut off by two British troopers.

"Surrender, you rebel cur!" called a high-pitched voice in my ear.

I wheeled to confront Captain Waytt. His sneering words and his laugh of contempt were more than my overtaxed nerves could endure.

Sword in hand, I sprang at him. Caution and self-preservation were thrown to the winds.

I yearned only to kill ere I should be killed.

CHAPTER XVIII.
My Fate Is Sealed!

I LEAPED at Waytt, sword in hand. And our drawn blades clashed. I had but such passable knowledge of fencing as every fairly well-

born man in my young days was expected to possess. Yet I had the strength of a giant and a wrist of steel.

Also, I was desperate. And let me tell you, an antagonist who cares not whether he be killed or not, so long as he may first kill, is far more dangerous than a normal man of twice his prowess.

Such a man was I as I sprang forward to attack this foppish, supercilious British captain who had sneered at me and my cause.

Therefore, though he met me right valorously, and with an adroitness far greater than my own, I was strong enough—yes, and quick and vehement enough—to make him break ground.

I was after him on the instant, beating down his guard, sending in a lightning series of thrusts and lunges that took his every effort to parry and left him no scope for attack.

Dully I realized that if, for ever so brief a space, I should allow him to take the aggressive in the fight, his superior skill must at once enable him to pass my clumsy guard.

So I drove at him with all my power and speed. Our blades clashed and grated and whined, their sweeping parries making shining arcs of light about us.

Once my point reached his chest, and a stain of scarlet began to spread upon his ruffled shirt-bosom.

Then, as he sought to lunge, and as I smote down his blow with full force, the blade of his rapier snapped clean in twain. Its fragments tinkled to the ground.

Waytt stood, foolishly grasping his bladeless hilt. Barely soon enough, I jerked back my hand in time to save myself the shame of slashing a disarmed man.

Our whole duel, which I have described so awkwardly and in so many words, had really endured a bare thirty seconds at most. As I have said, I had been cut off from my men, finding two British regulars between me and them. Then Waytt had insolently called me a rebel cur, summoning me to surrender. We had fought. Now, as I drew back when his sword broke, something swished through the air just behind me.

I felt a staggering shock on the left shoulder that well-nigh crushed me to earth. Instinctively, my whole left side momentarily numb, I wheeled to meet this new assault.

I found myself face to face with the British soldier who had stolen Marjory Winthrop's fan, and whom I had later fought, there in the twilight of Milk Street.

He was one of the two redcoats who had cut me off. It was a blow from the butt of his clubbed musket, aimed at my head from behind, that had smitten my shoulder so sorely. Now, as I turned, reeling from the pain, he was swinging the clubbed gun aloft for a second, more accurate stroke.

"'Tis our third meeting, Master Rebel!" he yelled. "T'other two times you were the winner. Now that the vixenish rebel maiden is not with us, 'tis *my* day!"

Still with that wild Berserk rage upon me, I launched myself, sword in hand, at his throat. As I jumped, he struck.

Down, through the air whizzed the ironbound musket butt. I recked nothing in my blind rage of its crashing descent.

All my strength and fury were concentrated upon the effort to reach him with my out-thrust sword before the end should come.

Deep into his brawny throat—yes, and *through* it—bit the point of my blade. So much I saw. Then I noted a whole battery of flaming tongues—a carnival of whirling lights. The earth and sky danced dizzily about me, and night came.

After a million ages I slowly rose to the surface from a deep, deep plunge into unfathomable waters. The roaring of the depths were still in my ears. My head throbbed abominably. And I was very tired. Very sleepy.

There had once been a battle somewhere—on some hill—and I had seen it—or heard of it. People were still talking of it. I could hear them with increasing distinctness.

The talk did not interest me one atom. The sound of voices vaguely annoyed me. So I lay, with closed eyes, and hoped the speakers would go away. But they did not. The more fully my senses drifted back to me the more audibly each word became.

Some one, whose voice I knew for Howe's, asked a question. I could not catch its drift. But it was addressed to somebody whom he called "Major."

And the latter replied:

"Yes, sir. It is a rough estimate, but fairly exact, I think. I've just

gone over the first list handed me. Out of five thousand men, our loss is about one thousand and fifty-five. The rebels, I understand, mustered twenty-five hundred strong. In killed and wounded, they have lost a bare four hundred and fifty. Of course, later count may show—"

"May show that his majesty's best troops lost still more heavily in a battle with scarce half their number of raw provincials?" observed Howe. It is quite possible."

"No, no, sir!" protested the major. "I meant not that. And even if our loss be heavy, still 'twas a complete and glorious victory for his majesty's arms."

"Rarely 'complete and glorious,'" assented Howe dryly. "We charge twice. Our men are sent scrambling to safely like scared rabbits. Then, because their ammunition is exhausted, our rebel friends withdraw from the slaughter. Scrape me raw, but 'twas indeed a 'glorious victory!' And two more such 'victories' will drive clean out of America his majesty's forces and his majesty's sovereignty."

"We could have cut them down, at the last, like so many sheaves of wheat," grumbled the major. "And, if I may suggest, Sir William—"

"You may not!" retorted Howe in a voice like ice-chilled steel. "Take your report on to General Clinton."

I opened my eyes, and feebly looked around me. I lay where I had fallen. Not ten paces away, jauntily swinging one foot, Sir William Howe was seated on the disabled caisson of a cannon.

The level sunset light streamed over him. He was glancing at a sheaf of papers. Two or three members of his staff were grouped about him.

Evidently the general had paused on the hill-top and had chosen this spot whence to issue orders for the removal of the British dead, and where he might receive his first reports of the losses and other details of the battle.

His once brilliant, gold-laced scarlet coat was torn and soiled. Its gilded braid hung down in tatters. The snowy shirt-ruffles, breeches, and hose were caked with blood and dust.

His neatly powdered cue had come undone, and his long, dark hair hung unkempt over his brow and shoulders. From time to time he would pause in the reading and signing of papers to bury his face in a mighty pewter tankard that was set on the caisson beside him.

Such was the valiant conqueror of Bunker Hill in his hour of victory.

It was an effort to keep my eyes open even for that briefest of glimpses. So I closed them again.

And now that I was slowly coming back to my full senses, and the pain and the roaring grew less, I became aware of a soft sobbing from somewhere near by.

I knew the voice. It was Marjory Winthrop's. And I knew then that I was delirious.

For how should Marjory still be on that stricken field whence our people had fled? And, even were she there, why should she be sobbing over *me?*

Yet it was sweet, even in delirium, to fancy her near me.

And I lay very still and tried to breathe lightly, so that I might still hear her.

And now I became aware also that some one was bathing my throbbing head with some cool, infinitely refreshing liquid. And that my head was not upon the hard ground, but that it rested in somebody's lap.

Soft fingers were those that smoothed away the matted yellow locks from my forehead. Not the rough hands of my comrades. And their very touch gave me a sweet sense of utter happiness.

So content was I to lie thus, strength and life slowly flowing back to my battered self, that I resented it when Howe, who had evidently laid aside his papers for the moment, fell into talk with one of the officers in the personal staff around him.

"Account for it at headquarters?" he responded, in answer to some question. "I shall not try to. Since when have I deigned to 'account' to any one for anything? At worst—as I sent word to Clinton—my orders were to take the hill; and I took it. If he wanted the lads shot down in a battue, why did not he come and do it himself? If I was to be trusted with the peril of taking the hill, then they must trust my conduct after I got to the top. There will be enough Yankee women weeping this night without my swelling the death-roll."

"War is war," observed his aide philosophically.

"Ay," returned Howe, "and women are women. And war and women should be as far apart as heaven and earth. But fate is forever linking them together. Look yonder, for example! See that strapping,

yellow-haired dead rebel captain lying there? And that poor, weeping country wench in her hideous brown homespun and apron?

"See how tenderly she holds his head on her knees and how she sobs as she bathes the cut in his forehead. She has done King George no ill. Yet, because the king's bullets have slain her lover, her life is wrecked. Poor soul."

"She looks as though she might be pretty," commented the aide, somewhat bored by chief's preachment. "I would she would raise her head. That great mob cap hides her face. And, see! In spite of her rough, shapeless garb, her hands are white and small."

"Hush, man!" growled the general. "Hast no respect for sorrow, but you must intrude on it with talk of women's looks? But no matter! She hears us not. I doubt she would hear a cannon fired three feet from her ear. Love is all engrossing. Yet," he added thoughtfully, "this is no place for her.

"When night comes, this hill will be infested with the scum of Boston, searching the dead for gold."

I heard him move across the narrow strip of ground toward us. But his words had set me thinking. The sobs—the brown dress and apron—the white hands—

I opened my eyes wide, and half started up.

Above me looked down a face divine in its pity, haggard and tear-stained in its grief.

"Marjory!"

I spoke her name, my eyes holding hers as a dying man might cling to his fleeting breath.

And the quick color rushed to her face, the light of joy to her eyes.

"You live! You *live!*" she panted.

"My good woman," said Howe gently, as he came to a stop beside us, "you must not stay here. Is there aught I can do—?"

She looked up involuntarily as he touched her shoulder. The general recoiled a pace in crass amaze.

"Mistress Marjory Winthrop! By all that's wonderful!" he gasped.

"He is alive!" she cried, scarce recognizing him, but eager to tell her wondrous news to some one. "He is *alive!*"

"It—it was for love of this rebel," asked Howe, curious yet hesitating, "for love of this rebel that you left home and father and friends

and—and loyalty—and vanished from the sight of us who loved you, and whose stay in Boston your presence so brightened? For love of—*him*—you did all this?"

"For love of him I would go to the world's end—and beyond!" she answered simply; adding joyously once more: "And he *lives!*"

Long and silently Howe looked from one to the other of us. I had reached for one of Marjory's hands and I held it weakly, yet adoringly, in my own, and kissed it.

What mattered the loss of Bunker Hill? What mattered my wound? What mattered the presence of this cynical British chief?

"For love of him," she had said, "I would go to the world's end."

Yes, *she had said it!*

I was not delirious now. She loved me. What else in life could count for aught?

"Your name, Yankee?" Howe asked me.

"Roger Sessions," I made answer, "captain in the—"

"So!" he cried in genuine surprise, "I heard tell of you last week in Boston. You are the rich farmer who had not the sense to go home to his farm, but must run his neck into the noose! So be it! Since you have chosen the noose, the choice is your own. You are our prisoner!"

Marjory, with a little cry of frightened protest, caught my head to her breast.

"It is cruel!" she flashed. "It is brutal!"

"I am not to be moved by a woman's tongue," retorted Howe coldly. "He has incurred the noose. The noose it shall be."

He beckoned an aide and gave a hurried, whispered order. The aide saluted, sprang on a horse, and galloped off.

"Luckily," went on Howe, "a provost marshal's guard and an impromptu hangman are easily found at a time and place like this."

Marjory had left me. Now she flung herself on her knees before the general. But he caught her up, seizing both her hands, before she could voice her passionate appeal, and courteously raised her to her feet.

"It is not meet that you or any other woman should kneel before a man like me, Mistress Winthrop!" he said in quick reproof. "Nor would prayers move me. My duty is plain."

"No, no!" she cried. "I implore you—"

"Marjory," I panted, getting to my feet and lurching toward her, "you shall not humble your sweet self for my sake! I am a soldier, I took a soldier's chances. If Great Britain hangs prisoners of war, then I shall go to my Maker like a brave man and a true American. Oh, sweetheart, you must not weep so for me! Cannot you see that your love has made me too happy to flinch even at the noose?"

But she sobbed blindly, uncontrollably.

"Sir," I said, passing an arm about her shaken little body and turning to Howe, "this lady suffers on my account. As I take it, torture of women is not included even in a British execution. May I beg you to spare her by having me taken to my fate without further suspense or waiting?"

"Your 'fate,' young man," he said, smiling, "is being brought to you. Here!"

He broke off as a traveling-coach drawn by two stout horses lumbered up the slope and came to a halt in front of us. The aide rode beside it.

"You seem too weak as yet to walk far," said Howe. "So, for Mistress Winthrop's sake, I have strained a point and sent for a conveyance to carry you."

He strode to the coach-door and opened it.

"Deuce take it!" he exclaimed in loud astonishment, "the executioner himself is inside! No need to carry you to your doom. You can best meet it here and now. Stand up and face it like a man."

I drew myself to my full height, my arm still encircling Marjory's slender waist. Her head was buried on my breast.

Holding her hand, I turned to face my death. They should not call me a coward, these British officers who delighted in thus racking the sensibilities of heartbroken girls.

"Executioner!" ordered Howe to the dimly seen figure in the coach. "Stand forth! Make ready the noose!"

Out of the vehicle, on to the grass before us, stepped a tall man clad in black garments of semimilitary cut. In his hand he bore some small object. Marjory glanced at his approach. Howe, his staff behind him, stood like statues.

"To your fell work, Sir Executioner!" commanded the general firmly.

The man in black bowed slightly to Sir William. Then, turning again upon the trembling Marjory and myself, he spread wide the object he had hidden in his hand.

It was a book. Glancing at its pages, he intoned after the sonorous fashion of British army chaplains:

"Dearly beloved, we are gathered together here, in the sight of God and in the face of this company, to join together this man and this woman in holy matrimony."

So *this* was the "noose" whereof Howe had spoken?

Heaven and all the stars! 'Twas the *marriage* service the chaplain was reading!

And to Marjory Winthrop and me!

THE END

Appendix I

Original source publication

This novel was serialized in five issues of Argosy, from June through October of 1910.

It was not illustrated.

June 1910

Chapters I through IV

Front text:

Author of "The Spy of Valley Forge," "From Flag to Flag," "On Glory's Trail," etc.

A Story of Early Boston, Showing How a Famous Battle Came to BeKnown By the Name of the Hill Where It Wasn't Fought.

July 1910

Chapters V through VIII

Front text:

Author of "The Spy of Valley Forge," "From Flag to Flag," "On Glory's Trail," etc.

A Story of Early Boston, Showing How a Famous Battle Came to Be Known by the Name of the Hill Where It Wasn't Fought.

SYNOPSIS OF CHAPTERS PREVIOUSLY PUBLISHED.

THE story, told by Roger Sessions, opens in Boston in the early spring of 1775. Sessions, just turned twenty-one, son of a rich farmer in Wilbraham, has come to the city on a commission for his father and to see the town. Somewhat of a boor at the outset, he is taught a lesson in politeness by Mistress Marjory Winthrop, with whom he had by chance collided in the street. Later on he sees a redcoat of King George's army deliberately snatch a handsome fan from a man coming out of a goldsmith's-shop, makes after the fellow and, with his superior strength, drags him back to the scene of his crime, where he demands that somebody take the fellow to the lock-up. In the midst of the excitement Sir William Howe, of the British army appears, and calls Sessions a Yankee rebel for daring to lay hands on one of his maj-

esty's soldiers. But a different face is put on the matter when Mistress Marjory, who has been attracted to the spot, suddenly recognizes the fan as hers, and Howe orders fifty lashes for the trooper.

Sessions has received a slight wound in the arm in his tussle, so Paul Revere, the goldsmith, takes him into his shop and binds up the hurt. To him Sessions announces his intention of remaining in town, going to the barracks and enlisting as a recruit in his majesty's army, but on Revere's representing to him that his recent rough handling of the trooper would insure him a flogging if nothing worse, he decides to accept Revere's offer of a position with him.

A stanch Tory, only his gratitude for what the goldsmith has done for him prevents Sessions from going to the authorities with a report of what he considers certain treasonable utterances of Revere's. He is a night watchman at the goldsmith's shop, and one morning, just before turning in, he reads for pastime the sentences made by a series of flashes with a bit of mirror on a sign across the street. He makes out the announcement of a meeting to take place at eleven that night in the ruins of an old malt-house. Even the password is given, and with the impetuosity of youth, Sessions resolves to find out what it all means. He goes to the spot and seeks to raise the heavy slab giving entrance to the malt house cellar-way, but in vain. As he straightens himself from the task, he is suddenly gripped from behind, while the cold circle of a pistol-muzzle is clapped to his face.

* Began June ARGOSY. Single copies, 10 cents.

August 1910

Chapters IX through XII

Front text:

Author of "The Spy of Valley Forge," "From Flag to Flag," "On Glory's Trail," etc.

A Story of Early Boston, Showing How a Famous Battle Came To Be Known by the Name of the Hill Where It Wasn't Fought.

SYNOPSIS OF CHAPTERS PREVIOUSLY PUBLISHED.

THE story, told by Roger Sessions, opens in Boston in the early spring of 1775. Sessions, just turned twenty-one, son of a rich farmer

in Wilbraham, has come to the city on a commission for his father and to see the town. Somewhat of a boor at the outset, he is taught a lesson in politeness by Mistress Marjory Winthrop, with whom he had by chance collided in the street. Later on he sees a redcoat of King George's army deliberately snatch a handsome fan from a man coming out of a goldsmith's-shop, makes after the fellow and, with his superior strength, drags him back to the scene of his crime, where he demands that somebody take the fellow to the lock-up. In the midst of the excitement Sir William Howe of the British army appears, and calls Sessions a Yankee rebel for daring to lay hands on one of his majesty's soldiers. But a different face is put on the matter when Mistress Marjory, who has been attracted to the spot, suddenly recognizes the fan as hers, and Howe orders fifty lashes for the trooper.

Sessions has received a slight wound in the arm in his tussle, so Paul Revere, the goldsmith, takes him into his shop and binds up the hurt. To him Sessions announces his intention of remaining in town, going to the barracks and enlisting as a recruit in his majesty's army, but on Revere's representing to him that his recent rough handling of the trooper would insure him a flogging if nothing worse, he decides to accept Revere's offer of a position with him.

A stanch Tory, only his gratitude for what the goldsmith has done for him prevents Sessions from going to the authorities with a report of what he considers certain treasonable utterances of Revere's. By chance he stumbles on a meeting of Colonial conspirators and entrusts the report of it at Government House, to Marjory Winthrop, who later uses Roger as the man who unwittingly gives the signal to Paul Revere to start on his famous ride. Then, for the first time, Roger knows that she is not a Tory like her father, storms at her for having made of him a traitor to the king, and then recalling that Revere had ridden by the lower road, starts off with the intention of intercepting him by the upper one.

* *Began June* ARGOSY. *Single copies, 10 cents.*

The following line:
Could the scared wretches that choked the lanes and roadways be the veterans who had guffawed aloud at eight of our puny force of Lex-

ington Minute Men?

...was changed to:

Could the scared wretches that choked the lanes and roadways be the veterans who had guffawed aloud at sight of our puny force of Lexington Minute Men?

September 1910

Chapters XIII through XV

Front text:

Author of "The Spy of Valley Forge," "From Flag to Flag," "On Glory's Trail," etc.

A Story of Early Boston, Showing How a Famous Battle Came To Be Known by the Name of the Hill Where It Wasn't Fought.

SYNOPSIS OF CHAPTERS PREVIOUSLY PUBLISHED.

THE story, told by Roger Sessions, opens in Boston in the early spring of 1775. Sessions, just turned twenty-one, son of a rich farmer in Wilbraham, has come to the city on a commission for his father and to see the town. Somewhat of a boor at the outset, he is taught a lesson in politeness by Mistress Marjory Winthrop, with whom he had by chance collided in the street. Later on he sees a redcoat of King George's army deliberately snatch a handsome fan from a man coming out of a goldsmith's-shop, makes after the fellow and, with his superior strength, drags him back to the scene of his crime, where he demands that somebody take the fellow to the lockup. In the midst of the excitement Sir William Howe of the British army appears, and calls Sessions a Yankee rebel for daring to lay hands on one of his majesty's soldiers. But a different face is put on the matter when Mistress Marjory, who has been attracted to the spot, suddenly recognizes the fan as hers, and Howe orders fifty lashes for the trooper.

Sessions has received a slight wound in the arm in his tussle, so Paul Revere, the goldsmith, takes him into his shop and binds up the hurt. To him Sessions announces his intention of remaining in town, going to the barracks and enlisting as a recruit in his majesty's army, but on Revere's representing to him that his recent rough handling of the trooper would insure him a flogging if nothing worse, he decides

to accept Revere's offer of a position with him.

A stanch Tory, only his gratitude for what the goldsmith has done for him prevents Sessions from going to the authorities with a report of what he considers certain treasonable utterances of Revere's. He is a night watchman at the goldsmith's shop, and one morning, just before turning in, he reads for pastime the sentences made by a series of flashes with a bit of mirror on a sign across the street. He makes out the announcement of a meeting to take place at eleven that night in the ruins of an old malt-house. Even the password is given, and with the impetuosity of youth, Sessions resolves to find out what it all means. He goes to the spot and seeks to raise the heavy slab giving entrance to the malt-house cellar-way, but in vain. As he straightens himself from the task, he is suddenly gripped from behind, while the cold circle of a pistol-muzzle is clapped to his face.

By chance he stumbles on a meeting of Colonial conspirators, and entrusts the report of it at Government House to Marjory Winthrop, who later uses Roger as the man who unwittingly gives the signal to Paul Revere to start on his famous ride. Then for the first time Roger knows that she is not a Tory like her father, storms at her for having made of him a traitor to the king, and then recalling that Revere had ridden by the lower road, starts off with the intention of intercepting him by the upper one. Roger is not able to overtake Revere, however, and, on reaching Lexington, suddenly becomes an ardent patriot himself, on seeing the British regulars mow down the homespun-clad Colonials. Later on he is the only prisoner taken by the British, and narrowly escapes being shot. Set free through the good offices of Lord Percy, he encounters Marjory Winthrop in the street. She conceals him from a British captain set on his trail by General Gage, and he is thanking her when his speech is interrupted by the thrusting forward of a hairy, brown hand in the shadow of the approaching night, which drags her away from him.

* Began June ARGOSY. Single copies, 10 cents.

October 1910
Chapters XVI through XVIII

Front text:

Author of "The Spy of Valley Forge," "From Flag to Flag," "On Glory's Trail," etc.

A Story of Early Boston, Showing How a Famous Battle Came To Be Known by the Name of the Hill Where It Wasn't Fought.

* Began June ARGOSY. Single copies, 10 cents.

Appendix II

Paul Revere's Ride
by Henry Wadsworth Longfellow

Listen, my children, and you shall hear
Of the midnight ride of Paul Revere,
On the eighteenth of April, in Seventy-Five:
Hardly a man is now alive
Who remembers that famous day and year.

He said to his friend, "If the British march
By land or sea from the town to-night,
Hang a lantern aloft in the belfry-arch
Of the North-Church-tower, as a signal-light,—
One if by land, and two if by sea;
And I on the opposite shore will be,
Ready to ride and spread the alarm
Through every Middlesex village and farm,
For the country-folk to be up and to arm."

Then he said "Good night!" and with muffled oar
Silently rowed to the Charlestown shore,
Just as the moon rose over the bay,
Where swinging wide at her moorings lay
The Somerset, British man-of-war:
A phantom ship, with each mast and spar
Across the moon, like a prison-bar,
And a huge black hulk, that was magnified
By its own reflection in the tide.

Meanwhile, his friend, through alley and street
Wanders and watches with eager ears,
Till in the silence around him he hears
The muster of men at the barrack door,
The sound of arms, and the tramp of feet,
And the measured tread of the grenadiers

Marching down to their boats on the shore.

Then he climbed to the tower of the church,
Up the wooden stairs, with stealthy tread,
To the belfry-chamber overhead,
And startled the pigeons from their perch
On the sombre rafters, that round him made
Masses and moving shapes of shade,—
By the trembling ladder, steep and tall,
To the highest window in the wall,
Where he paused to listen and look down
A moment on the roofs of the town,
And the moonlight flowing over all.

Beneath, in the churchyard, lay the dead,
In their night-encampment on the hill,
Wrapped in silence so deep and still
That he could hear, like a sentinel's tread,
The watchful night-wind, as it went
Creeping along from tent to tent,
And seeming to whisper, "All is well!"
A moment only he feels the spell
Of the place and the hour, and the secret dread
Of the lonely belfry and the dead;
For suddenly all his thoughts are bent
On a shadowy something far away,
Where the river widens to meet the bay,—
A line of black, that bends and floats
On the rising tide, like a bridge of boats.

Meanwhile, impatient to mount and ride,
Booted and spurred, with a heavy stride,
On the opposite shore walked Paul Revere.
Now he patted his horse's side,
Now gazed on the landscape far and near,
Then impetuous stamped the earth,
And turned and tightened his saddle-girth;
But mostly he watched with eager search
The belfry-tower of the old North Church,
As it rose above the graves on the hill,

When Liberty Was Born

Lonely and spectral and sombre and still.
And lo! as he looks, on the belfry's height,
A glimmer, and then a gleam of light!
He springs to the saddle, the bridle he turns,
But lingers and gazes, till full on his sight
A second lamp in the belfry burns!

A hurry of hoofs in a village-street,
A shape in the moonlight, a bulk in the dark,
And beneath from the pebbles, in passing, a spark
Struck out by a steed that flies fearless and fleet:
That was all! And yet, through the gloom and the light,
The fate of a nation was riding that night;
And the spark struck out by that steed, in his flight,
Kindled the land into flame with its heat.

He has left the village and mounted the steep,
And beneath him, tranquil and broad and deep,
Is the Mystic, meeting the ocean tides;
And under the alders, that skirt its edge,
Now soft on the sand, now loud on the ledge,
Is heard the tramp of his steed as he rides.

It was twelve by the village clock
When he crossed the bridge into Medford town.
He heard the crowing of the cock,
And the barking of the farmer's dog,
And felt the damp of the river-fog,
That rises when the sun goes down.

It was one by the village clock,
When he galloped into Lexington.
He saw the gilded weathercock
Swim in the moonlight as he passed,
And the meeting-house windows, blank and bare,
Gaze at him with a spectral glare,
As if they already stood aghast
At the bloody work they would look upon.

It was two by the village clock,

When he came to the bridge in Concord town.
He heard the bleating of the flock,
And the twitter of birds among the trees,
And felt the breath of the morning breeze
Blowing over the meadows brown.
And one was safe and asleep in his bed
Who at the bridge would be first to fall,
Who that day would be lying dead,
Pierced by a British musket-ball.

You know the rest. In the books you have read,
How the British Regulars fired and fled,—
How the farmers gave them ball for ball,
From behind each fence and farmyard-wall,
Chasing the red-coats down the lane,
Then crossing the fields to emerge again
Under the trees at the turn of the road,
And only pausing to fire and load.

So through the night rode Paul Revere;
And so through the night went his cry of alarm
To every Middlesex village and farm,—
A cry of defiance, and not of fear,
A voice in the darkness, a knock at the door,
And a word that shall echo forevermore!
For, borne on the night-wind of the Past,
Through all our history, to the last,
In the hour of darkness and peril and need,
The people will waken and listen to hear
The hurrying hoof-beats of that steed,
And the midnight message of Paul Revere.

**Turn this book over for another complete novel
by Albert Payson Terhune!**